JENNIFER BROWN

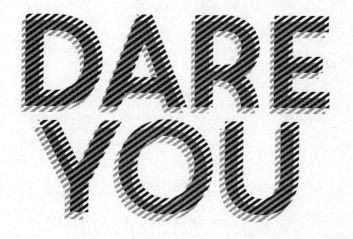

DARE YOU

A SHADE ME NOVEL

KATHERINE TEGEN BOOKS
An Imprint of HarperCollins Publishers

Katherine Tegen Books is an imprint of HarperCollins Publishers.

Dare You
Copyright © 2017 by HarperCollins Publishers
All rights reserved. Printed in the United States of America.

Library of Congress Control Number: 2016949688
ISBN 978-0-06-232446-7

Typography by Carla Weiss
17 18 19 20 21   PC/LSCH   10 9 8 7 6 5 4 3 2 1
❖
First Edition

FOR SCOTT, WHO MAKES MY
WORLD MAGENTA

PROLOGUE

THE FIRST THING she needed was a shower. A hot one.
So hot the mirrors would become fogged and the towels would feel dewy and opening the bathroom door would . be like stepping into a refrigerator. Her feet would be bare. And she would walk from the steaming water to the sink without wrapping a towel around herself like armor. She'd dreamed of that shower—literally dreamed of it—last night. Like her brain just couldn't wait to wake up and make it a reality. The shower. Right away. First thing.

She'd been sitting on the edge of her bed for hours now. Motionless. Muscles frozen. She didn't even twitch when a determined fly landed on the top of her ear and crawled around with its prickly little feet, only to pop up in a dizzy swoop and light on her again, this time on her cheek. Her knees and ankles were clamped together. Her spine was straight. Her hands rested flat, palms down, on the cover of a journal. Leather-bound, each page meticulously kept, in neat, all-caps handwriting.

8:10 A.M. AWAKE

8:22 A.M. SHOWER, DOOR CLOSED

9:10 A.M. BREAKFAST, CEREAL, DRY, COFFEE, CREAM, SUGAR, DIDN'T FINISH

9:30 A.M. STUDYING, OPEN TEXTBOOK, GEOGRAPHY

9:56 A.M. CIGARETTE BREAK 1, COMPLETE TO FILTER, NO BRAND CHANGE, DISCARDED BUTT SAVED, RETRIEVED, AND LOGGED

Pages upon pages of tedium. Six months of it. Boring as hell. Thank God she wasn't the one in charge of writing it all down.

She allowed herself to blink, but was otherwise absolutely still on the edge of her bed. Still as a statue. Still as a corpse. Heartbeat slow, rhythmic. *Ka-thud. Ka-thud. Ka-thud.* She could feel her blood swooshing around inside of her like an out-of-control river, carrying her life force through her organs, souring and poisoning all the tissue, the gristle, the fat.

As if she had fat. Please.

She imagined the inside of herself as boneless, muscle-free, an inky-black and never-ending cavern, the bottom filled with tarlike sludge. To her, the popularized portrayal of a red devil was far from the truth. He wasn't red. No. He was midnight. He was what you couldn't see until he surprised you from the depths within yourself. He could only be found by those truly looking for him. By those who'd already died inside. Those who were walking rot.

She was walking rot.

Gorgeous, rich, popular walking rot.

The best kind, really. Life was so easy when you were gorgeous, rich, popular walking rot. Before, when she cared about *making impressions,* when she tried to *do it all the right way,* her life was anything but easy. She was left to subsist in ordinariness while those others—those imposters—were living her rightful life. She had to fight tooth and nail to get to the pot of gold at the end of that luscious rainbow.

Ha. Rainbow.

She'd stopped caring. She'd gone still and let the rot take hold and make everything easy.

Well. Mostly easy. Until that bitch came along and screwed it up for everybody. Screwed it up for her.

10:24 A.M. EMAIL CHECK, DELETE

10:37 A.M. GEOGRAPHY, BOOK OPEN, MOVED FROM DESK TO BED

10:37 A.M.–11:02 A.M. SOCIAL MEDIA. NO ENGAGEMENT, JUST SCROLLING

"You ready?"

She raised her head, slowly, evenly, as if on a tight hinge. Dolores. Young. Half-afraid. Pretty. Liked to tell kindergarten knock-knock jokes, as if they were all there because they just didn't know any better. Dolores didn't mind when the TV stayed on too long. Didn't even seem to notice the journal. Dolores was easy. Maybe Dolores was rotting, too. Maybe she knew all about that devil sliding around inside of herself.

Dolores leaned forward, her hands tucked into her guard uniform pockets. "You ready?" she repeated.

Finally, as if shocked into life, the heartbeat sped. Ready? So ready she could taste it. So ready she could feel that shower streaming down her back. So fucking ready she had to grip the journal tightly between her hands to keep from shoving her thumbs right through good old shy Dolores's eyes. *Knock-knock, Dolores, who's there? Death, that's who.*

Her entire body clenched. Her shoulders pressed up so tightly against her ears, they ached. Her fingers were white around the leather journal cover. Her feet felt numb, like she was floating. Every open door was a birth as she passed through.

He was waiting in the vestibule, all dimples and teeth and *yes, ma'am* and *no, sir.* He understood the importance of what he was embarking on. He understood the *gravity of the situation.* Whatever it took, he was prepared. He would make sure neither of them messed this up.

Have a great life, Dolores, you dingbat, she thought as she walked through that final open door, squinting against the sunlight all the way across the parking lot.

"Have you heard anything?" he asked, opening the car door for her. She slid into the hot vinyl interior, grimacing. He paused, looking down at her, waiting for her to respond, and then shut the door. She waited until he came around the car and got in behind the steering wheel. "Well?" he said, fumbling the key into the ignition slot.

"Of course not. Information comes when it comes. You think I'm just going to be having casual conversations about it over my tapioca? What, are you fucking stupid?"

He laughed, rocking back against his seat. She couldn't even look at him—his hair so white it practically glowed in that impossible sun.

"Only stupid enough," he said. "And that?" He gestured at the journal.

Her fingers gripped it tighter. "What about it? Jesus, turn the car on. It's hot. I don't want to die in this parking lot." They connected eyes, considering, with dirty grins, the irony of that statement. She chuckled. "You didn't bring a cane, did you?"

He sobered. "Still looking for it."

She rolled her eyes. "That was a joke, moron."

He twisted the key in the ignition; the air blew into her face full blast. The car had been parked too long and the air, too, was hot, like standing too close to an open oven door. She squinted against it and started to tilt the vents away, but then imagined the heat curdling the internal rot and decided she liked it that way. *Rot away, sludge.*

"Has it been helpful?" he asked, gesturing toward the book in her lap.

"I need a shower," she said.

"I asked you a question."

She leveled her eyes at him, taking him in fully for the first time. He disgusted her. He was such a chameleon, it was almost impossible to tell who she was dealing with at any given moment. But he would do anything for the love of his life. He'd said so himself. He'd come clean when the shit hit the fan.

And besides, he was all she had right now, so she was just going to have to deal.

He was the only person who could stand between her and what she'd been waiting for, planning, for six months.

Only he could keep her from Nikki Kill.

"Yeah," she said, hugging the journal to her chest, finally allowing herself to relax into the seat. "Very helpful, actually."

M Y HANDS SHOOK as I struggled with them behind my head.

I wasn't exactly a jewelry kind of girl to begin with, and my chewed-to-the-quick thumbnails weren't made for tiny metal necklace clasps. Then again, I was hardly a Flower Pink lipstick kind of girl, either, but damned if that wasn't smeared all over my lips, too. Sweet makeup, hair brushed to a gloss, jewelry, heels. I felt like a parallel universe version of myself: *Plastic Doll Nikki, for your special-occasion needs!* Special occasions like high school graduations that nobody expected you to actually achieve. *Graduate Nikki, now with stunned eyebrows!*

I finally got the clasp and let the topaz teardrop dangle,

touching it lightly with my fingertips as I stared into the mirror. Sunlight streamed in through my bedroom window—God, what I wouldn't have given for a quick smoke before heading off to be Barely Achieving Student on Parade—and reflected off the facets of the gem and onto my face. Faint blue starbursts caressed the scar on my cheek, moving when I moved, swirling and blending with brown and peach, the colors that reminded me of heavy hearts and nostalgia. The same colors I always saw when I looked too closely at my scars. Colors that made me think of Dru.

Would Dru have come today to see me graduate? Doubtful. He wasn't the type to sit in a crowded auditorium with a bouquet of roses in his lap. He was more of the type to meet you in the basket of a hot-air balloon with a bouquet of roses and tickets to a Vegas show. I guessed. The truth was I didn't know exactly what type of boyfriend Dru was, because he and I had never exactly gotten to that stage.

And now it was too late. A putrid brown-and-peach swirl splatted against my forehead and dripped away into nothingness.

Hell, who was I kidding? Dru and I would have never gotten to that stage, no matter how long we'd had together. Because I didn't do that stage. Ever. And he probably didn't, either. Which would have been one of the things that attracted me to him in the first place. How screwed up was that?

"You look just like her," I heard behind me. I whirled around, the remaining brown-and-pink swirl shooting up into surprised gold fireworks. My hand slapped over my heart.

I let out a heavy breath. "You scared me, Dad."

"Sorry. I forgot the rule."

The rule was no sneaking up on me, ever. Not unless you wanted to eat a few knuckles or perhaps get a really close look at the ball of my foot as it slammed into your face. Not to mention unless you wanted to give me a heart attack. Ever since that night at Hollis Mansion seven months ago, I'd been fighting a pervasive jumpiness, as if bad guys were waiting around every corner to attack me.

Last I heard, the bad guys were gone. Bill and Vanessa Hollis were hiding in Dubai, and Luna was locked up for killing Dru. But I'd spent so much time looking over my shoulder, it was pretty much habit now to assume that any-one coming up behind me was one of them, trying to kill me.

I picked up my mortarboard to distract myself from those memories and placed it on my head, reminding myself that they were in Dubai and juvie for good reason, and nobody had heard from them in months. Hell, nobody had heard from anyone in months. It was like nothing had ever happened. The entire world—minus yours truly—had forgotten all about it. I wished I could forget about it.

The mortarboard scrunched down over my hair, flattening it even further. I fumbled with a bobby pin, and Dad stepped up behind me.

"Here, let me."

I handed him the pin. He slipped it up into the bottom of my cap, scraping it along my scalp, and held out his hand for another. I winced as I passed it to him. Dad doing my hair was nothing unusual—he'd been doing it since my mom died when I was eight. He'd had to be both Mom and Dad, which was too bad, because he wasn't particularly great at being either one.

"You do, you know," he said softly. "Look like her. Especially wearing her necklace."

I tried not to react. Tried not to even hear his words. I'd spent a lifetime working on forgetting my mother—forgetting how it felt to lose her, forgetting the nightmares and the crimson, crimson, crimson of death that had followed me everywhere after she'd been murdered. It took ten years of effort, but I'd finally managed to be able to think about Mom without being overwhelmed by images of wet brown paper sacks and rushing muddy rivers of sadness. I'd even sometimes begun to be reminded of magenta and pink—the colors I associated with love and happiness—when I allowed myself to pull up memories of her.

But not anymore. Not after what happened with Peyton Hollis. Not after the letter she left for me—*I've known you were my sister for a while now. . . . Your mother, Carrie, was my mother, too. I know this because I've followed a very long trail of deceit.* Now every time I thought about my mother, my colors went crazy. They all pushed in on one another— anger, betrayal, danger, death, suspicion, fear. Sickly yellows and grays and browns and seething, pulsing midnight—a monster's galaxy.

"I think it's good," I said, tugging on the mortarboard, choosing to ignore the big dead mother elephant in the room. "Thanks."

He put his hands on my shoulders and gazed at our reflection in the mirror. "She would have been so proud of you today."

I gave him a thin smile, concentrating on the blue of the mortarboard and hoping it wouldn't be drowned out by the bad colors. Or by the ocean of turquoise that so closely resembled what I had come to think of as cheater blue— that ocean being an endless sea of guilt that I, no matter how hard I tried, could not find the shore of.

Basically, I was a synesthetic time bomb, held down by a very flimsy lid. And I'd spent the last seven months trying not to let too much steam escape.

"She's probably pretty surprised right about now," I said. "I know everyone else is. The earrings? Or is that too much?"

It felt like too much, as I held one of the smaller teardrops up against my earlobes.

"Too much," he said, echoing my thoughts. I dropped it back into my drawer, noticing that its match was missing anyway. I rooted through my jewelry with my finger, but it didn't turn up. Weird. This was the second time something had gone missing on me this week. A few days ago, I had turned my room upside down looking for a half-empty pack of cigarettes and my favorite lighter—a vintage Zippo that I'd swiped out of the ISS teacher's desk drawer in seventh grade and carved my initials into. I loved that lighter and couldn't believe I'd misplaced it.

"And, for the record," Dad continued, "I'm not surprised. I knew you would graduate."

I raised my eyebrows at him.

"Okay, I'm a little surprised. But I had faith in you. And when I think about all that you've been through . . ." He shook his head, as though he felt sorry for me, and once again I had to concentrate on other things. My fingers itched to hold a cigarette. He took a breath. "Anyway. Your grandparents are going to meet us there. I thought maybe we would have dinner afterward? Someplace nice. You're dressed for it. Grandma and Grandpa would like that."

I sighed. My dad's parents lived in Flagstaff and didn't come around very often. I wasn't sure how much they knew about what had happened with the Hollises, but I was guessing not much. Dad was a pretty private person, and I was even more private than he. I still had never told him everything about that night—had shared only enough to satisfy him and make him stop hammering me with questions. Sometimes I felt guilty about it, like if anyone should know that Mom wasn't who she pretended to be, it should be him. The only explanation I had for keeping things from him was that I was afraid of hurting him, afraid of hurting us, our family, even if that "family" was only a memory. He'd never gotten over Mom's death. To find out that he'd spent a decade mourning a woman who'd cheated on him—with Bill Hollis, no less—would be devastation.

Or worse. I would tell him, only to find out that he already knew. That they'd both kept it from me. That they'd kept my sister from me. And then what? I would feel betrayed and I wouldn't be able to trust him again, and my dad was really the only person I had in this world. I was great at destruction—destroying people, destroying things, destroying hearts. The last thing I needed was to destroy my relationship with my dad.

So I'd told him only the basics. That I'd gotten in too deep with the Hollises. That I'd started dating Dru—even though that was hardly what we were really doing—and that his sister, Luna, had taken offense at me being so close to the family when they were grieving. I'd told him about how Luna had gone crazy, had drugged me, had held a gun on me, had shot Dru by accident instead. It was all a tragic mishap.

But that was where I'd stopped telling the truth. I didn't want Dad getting all up in my business, asking questions and demanding answers and locking me down, a prisoner in my own bedroom. Not that he wasn't already trying his hardest to do that. He'd felt so guilty about me getting wrapped up in a huge mess without him even knowing, he was constantly questioning me, and constantly searching for news on Luna's trial. He'd even written a letter to the juvenile judge, railing about how Luna had attacked me for no reason, and asking to be kept in the loop if anything should happen with her case.

But there never was any news. There was no loop. At least not a loop that I was part of. Which is not to say my classmates weren't talking about it; I just wasn't part of the discussion. If I was a nobody before Peyton's death, I was less than a nobody now. I finished out my senior year with home study, visiting campus only when I absolutely had to. I hardly ever went anywhere. And when I did, I avoided going any place where I might run into one of Peyton's or Luna's friends.

At least I no longer had police protection. When all the shit with Luna was going down, Detective Chris Martinez had followed me everywhere, and it drove me crazy. It was police protection that I didn't ask for and definitely didn't want.

So how come thinking about Detective Martinez caused violet bubbles to burst in my periphery? How come I could taste grapes and smell periwinkle just thinking of his name?

And how come someone who was stuck so tight to me I couldn't shake him no matter how hard I tried hadn't come around in seven months? Not even to see how I was doing.

"Hello?" Dad said, snapping his fingers in front of my face. "Earth to Nikki. What do you think? About dinner?"

I smiled. It felt thin. "That's fine," I said. "But I think I might have a party to go to later, if that's okay."

Dad rocked back a little. "A party? You?"

I rolled my eyes. "I'm not a total loser, you know." I bent to pick up my gown, still warm from the iron.

"Of course you're not a loser. You just never go to parties."

"First time for everything, I guess. If you don't want me to go . . ." I shrugged into the gown, watching myself in the mirror, pretending to be nonchalant, like this was a conversation we had every day.

"No, no, that's fine. It's great, actually. I'll tell your grandparents that dinner will have to be short."

I zipped myself into the gown. It felt billowy, like a tent. Definitely not the type of attire I was used to at all. But at least it covered the ridiculous dress I had on underneath. I was only wearing it because Dad insisted that jeans with frayed bottoms and scuffed-up Chucks was not appropriate graduation attire. I'd walked into the mall and pulled the first thing I found off the rack. I figured most of the girls in my class would be looking like supermodels in painted-on designer clothes, so what did it matter what I wore? Besides, I had this bright-blue tent to cover it anyway.

"So who will be there? At the party?" he asked, moving out of my way so I could sit on my bed and cram my feet into uncomfortable shoes. This whole pomp and circumstance nonsense was so stupid.

I shrugged. "Everyone. I don't know." But I did know. There would probably be a zillion people at the party tonight, and for a change it wouldn't be at Hollis Mansion. And everyone would be aware of that.

"And you'll be safe?"

I pushed my foot into a pump and smoothed the gown over my lap. Dad had stopped asking me if I was safe every ten seconds, but I could see the lines etched across his forehead that hadn't been there before the Hollis incident. There were so many things hidden between the two of us. It seemed like a chasm that could never be crossed.

I stood, faced him, and used my thumbs to smooth away the lines on his forehead. "I promise," I said. "Luna is in juvie. Her parents are in Dubai. Dru . . ." *Doesn't exist anymore.* The words caught in my throat, a brown-and-blue lump that pulsed in my mind. And something else. Something that made me think of endless loneliness.

I'd seen colors with emotions my entire life. Also with

numbers and letters. Three was always purple to me. Four, silver. Five, white. The letter *M* was zebra ice cream swirl. The letter *O* was wet black like a ripe olive. My name was mostly orange, and the word *echo* was mustard yellow. The feeling of love was magenta and the feeling of fear was bumpy gray and black, and sometimes—okay, most of the time—I saw the colors before I even realized I was feeling the emotion to go along with them.

When other people suspected someone was lying to them, they might get a strange feeling in their gut. But for me, that strange gut feeling rolled in on a cloud of mint-green mist.

It was almost impossible to explain, and it took a lot of doctors to figure out that I had synesthesia. Which basically meant that my senses combined, and I had a pretty good memory because of it. It also gave me—and I didn't actually know this until Peyton Hollis was brutally attacked in the parking lot of an abandoned building—great instincts. Only about 4 percent of the population has synesthesia, so nobody I knew understood what it was.

Well, almost nobody. Peyton understood.

My colors had been the same since day one. They didn't change. They didn't morph. And they didn't go away.

But when I thought about Dru, I discovered a new one. That endless lonely feeling. That midnight color. A lost-in-space color. A black-hole hue. After being rocked by it for so many nights in a row, I was finally able to identify it: regret. Not skipped-school-and-now-I'll-get-yelled-at regret. Not ate-too-much-cake regret.

The kind of regret that will never go away.

The kind of regret that leaves your heart wondering what the hell happened.

The kind of regret that has you sitting alone on your windowsill, a cigarette burning, untouched, all the way to the filter between your fingers, and swearing that you will never have that feeling again. That feeling came close to attachment. Intimacy. Maybe even a little too close to love. Maybe the kind of love that got people killed. Every. Single. Time.

I brushed away the midnight and kissed Dad's cheek. "It's just an after-grad party. It'll be fun to say good-bye to everyone."

Translation: it will be fun to get completely wasted and make the aching midnight go away.

"Just don't drink and drive," Dad said, pointing at me sternly. Which almost made me laugh. We both knew he was anything but stern.

"I promise. No drama, Dad. You know me."

He studied me, and for a second, I thought he was going to get all mushy-parent-of-the-grad on me. But instead, he jumped, checked his watch. "We should go. You're going to be late as it is. You wouldn't want to miss the whole thing."

I laughed. "It would be kind of perfect if I did, though. Since I missed most of my senior year."

Dad chuckled, but on the inside, I knew he didn't find it funny. On the inside, I knew he didn't believe that I would be safe.

On the inside, he would worry that I would end up just as dead as my mother.

2

SOMETIMES I WONDERED how different I would be if Mom hadn't been murdered. Would I have been one of the giggling idiots sitting two rows behind me, using my cell phone camera to check my makeup every five seconds? Would I have been the dorky super-prep valedictorian, sitting on the stage, my palms sweating around a rolled-up speech? Would I have wanted to be at the podium, instead of swiping at the beads of sweat rolling out from under my tilted cap and wishing the guy at the podium would just stop talking?

Or would I still be the girl swimming in a sea of beige, beige, beige boredom? Bottom-of-the-ocean boredom. Suburban-cookie-cutter-house boredom. Dull-skin boredom. My legs itched.

I looked over to my left. Someone had propped a framed photo in the seat of the first chair of the very front row. I couldn't see the photo very well from where I was, but I knew who was in it. Peyton Hollis. The girl in first place, always. The girl who was All Things High School. The girl who was Head of Everything. The girl who probably would have been voted Most Likely to Take Over the Whole Fucking World.

The girl who gave it all up in the end. And the only people who knew why were all dead, in jail, on the run . . . or me.

Before the ceremony began, my classmates had gathered around the photo, crying into one another's shoulders, leaving flowers and teddy bears and little gifts. Someone had draped a poster for Viral Fanfare, Peyton's underground band, over the back of the chair. There was a mountain of sadness around that chair, and all of it felt like lies to me. I could barely see the chair for the dirty gray fog that hovered over it.

Even Jones had been in the crying crowd. Jones, who had admitted that he only went to Hollis Mansion for the parties, and who seemed to think the family was as royally screwed up as I did. After all, he had repeatedly warned me off Dru. But maybe that was just his hearts-and-flowers magenta talking. Maybe he liked Peyton a hell of a lot more than he liked the thought of me hanging out with Peyton's brother.

"God, can you believe it?" the girl next to me whispered, following my gaze toward the chair. "I mean, I knew she was gone, but it just seems so much more real now that she's not here. It's so sad." She used a manicured finger to wipe the completely dry corner of her eye. Fake.

"I didn't really know her," I said. But of course everyone in the school was suspicious about what my connection with Peyton had really been. They'd all been very well aware of the vigil I'd kept by Peyton's hospital bedside. They'd all been very well aware of the showdown at Hollis Mansion, even if nobody knew exactly what had happened there. Not knowing never stopped anyone from talking about it, like they'd had front-row seats.

"She was amazing," the girl said. "She should have been here. Her sister should be the one in the cemetery, after what she did."

I blinked. Not that I didn't agree, and not that I hadn't said those same words many times already, but it was harsh to hear it come out of someone else's mouth. I caught Dad's eye, up in the third row of bleachers. My grandparents waved at me. Proud. I waved back. "At least she's in jail," I said.

The girl excitedly clutched my wrist. "You didn't hear? Oh, hang on." The principal started giving instructions on how we would come up to get our diplomas, his voice booming compared to the tentative voice of the valedictorian.

"No, what?" I whispered, but she pretended she didn't

hear me. She wiped her eyes again and sat forward expectantly in her seat as the first row of students got up and made their way to the stage. "What?"

"We've got to go," she whispered.

Eventually, our row stood up, and I took my diploma in a haze of spearmint curiosity so strong I felt I was chewing gum. I barely heard Dad's and my grandparents' cheers when I shook hands with the principal. I couldn't smile or feel grateful. I could only move mechanically, wondering what the girl next to me had been talking about, what gossip I hadn't heard. We somehow managed to get scrambled on the way back to our seats, and when we sat down, the girl was four people away. My chance was gone.

"You did it!" Dad exclaimed, weaving his way toward me through the crowd when the ceremony was over. He hugged me so hard he knocked my mortarboard off. Which was no big deal, since I was pretty much the only one who hadn't thrown it into the air; the floor was carpeted with discarded hats. "I'm so proud of you, Nikki. So proud." When he pulled away, I could see that his eyes were bloodshot and puffy. It had been a long road for both of us, and no matter what he said out loud, I knew neither of us ever thought we would get here.

"Good job, honey," my grandmother said, shoving in for a hug.

"Yes, yes," my grandfather added. "What's next for you,

Graduate? Where are you going to college?"

I smiled thinly at him. Obviously, my dad hadn't clued them in about anything at all. They still thought college was something I might do. They probably thought I was a great student. Boy, wouldn't they be surprised?

"What's next is cake," Dad said. "And a big plate of pasta to go with it. What do you say, Nik? Ready to celebrate?"

"Sounds perfect," I said, my voice edging away some of the spearmint. Whatever the unheard gossip about Luna was, I needed to let it go. I needed to take my life back, stop letting the Hollises have it. "I just want to say good-bye to someone." I pointed over my shoulder toward the giant mass of people who milled about with cameras and gifts.

"Sure, sure," Dad said. "We'll go get the car and meet you out front."

They disappeared, but instead of diving into the crowd, I headed back for the now-empty rows of folding chairs on the other side of the stage, where we had only moments ago been sitting, still high school seniors. Peyton's chair, which looked so full and loved before the ceremony, just looked abandoned and isolated now, a puddle of wrinkled programs dropped next to it. We had officially all left her behind.

The photo was of Peyton in her heyday. Before the ragged haircut and the neck tattoo. Before her break from her family. She was leaning against a wooden column in a sundress, smiling, her buttery hair snaking down her shoulders in purposeful "messy" waves. I recognized the beam as part of the gazebo in the backyard of Hollis Mansion. I hadn't been in that backyard since Detective Martinez literally carried me out of it.

Dru had died only a few yards away from where Peyton stood in the photo. The grass around her feet began to seep crimson.

I closed my eyes. I hated crimson.

"It's weird, her not being here, isn't it?" I heard. My eyes flew open.

Vee, whose real name—Vera Reed—I'd just heard for the first time, when the principal called her up to the stage to get her diploma, was standing next to me. She'd combed out her dreads and looked about as uncomfortable in her spring makeup palette and cork wedges as I felt in my grad getup. In some ways, Vee and I were probably a lot more alike than either one of us wanted to admit. Vee had been the bassist in Viral Fanfare, and, despite a falling-out at the very end, had been Peyton's friend. Maybe her only real friend.

"Seems like she should be," I said.

Vee nodded, both of us staring at Peyton's picture. I forgot to blink and my eyes filled with tears, so that Peyton almost seemed to move against the column. "Like she's going to burst in any moment, cussing and laughing about her alarm not going off and making us start the whole thing over."

"My housemaid forgot to wake me with my peaches and cream," I said in a lofty voice. "Off with her head!"

Vee said, "You know she wasn't like that, right?"

"I know. Neither was Dru."

"But Luna."

"Yeah. Luna."

Vee shifted, tossed a guitar pick onto the chair. It landed on top of a rose and bounced a little, settled at an angle against the stem. "You think she sees this?" She shrugged, embarrassed, then gestured around the room. "I mean, from like, heaven or whatever? I don't know if Peyton believed in heaven or not. I don't know if I do or not, either. It's weird to think about her looking down at us or something. But at the same time, it's kind of comforting. I don't know. I'm sure I sound stupid."

"No, you don't," I said. "I've wondered the same thing." I had, and I hadn't. I'd thought about and wondered about and talked to Peyton before she died. Practically begged her for answers, sure she could hear me and somehow "see" what I was doing. I'd felt such a connection to her, sitting by her side in the hospital. But after she died, it was like that connection just snapped. She felt like a misty piece of the past. Like a memory of a dream. Something that never actually happened. Sort of the same way Mom felt to me. A pleasant invention in my mind.

But Dru, on the other hand, seemed just as alive to me

as he had when he was stroking my side under the sheets in Peyton's apartment. I had to force myself to ignore the feeling that he was watching me, always. That he was blaming me for his death.

Vee chuckled. "She would have had the most monstrous party tonight. We talked about it so many times. Viral Fanfare was going to tear it up. She bought her bikini months ago. She wrote three new songs to debut at the party. It was going to be our big announcement about the record deal she was sure we were going to get."

"With Leo Powers," I said.

"Yeah. The guy her dad got us in with." She unzipped her gown and pulled it off, revealing a grungy pair of cutoff camouflage shorts and a ripped tee beneath. She wadded up the gown and dropped it on the chair next to Peyton's, then wound her hair up into a messy ball. "Graduation was really important to her. And then she just stopped talking about it. It was like she knew, somehow, that she wasn't going to make it to today. Do you think she knew?"

"Definitely." The word popped out before I could even think it over. Because I didn't need to. Peyton definitely knew that something was going to happen to her. She knew that her time was limited. She communicated that much to me without ever speaking, once. "But it's over now," I said. I cleared my throat and said it louder. "It's over. And it's time to move on. Half the people who put flowers here didn't even know her at all. They just wanted to know her, because knowing Peyton Hollis was practically a competitive sport. It's ridiculous, and I'm glad to be done with it. Did anyone ever actually know her?"

"I did," Vee said. "And I think on some level you probably did too."

"I don't know anything," I said. I never did, and I didn't think I ever truly would. My life would be all about unanswered questions, from start to end. I turned to Vee. "Hey, listen. About the stuff with the band. Before."

She waved me off. "I get it. You thought Gib was behind what happened to her. And I would do the same as you, you know. If I knew who did it, I would rip them up."

"I'm still sorry."

She smiled. It was weird to see Vee with a real smile, rather than one of her sardonic half grins. "It's okay. We're still together. We got a new lead singer. Do you know Shelby Gray?" I shook my head. The name sounded vaguely familiar, but I was hardly connected to the heartbeat of our school. Shelby Gray could have been any face in the building as far as I was concerned. "Technically, she's a sophomore. Well, going to be a junior now. So she's kind of young, but she can sing. And, more importantly, she can write. We can cover a lot of singing problems with the instruments, but we have to have songs to play, and none of the rest of us are any good at writing. Plus, she knew Peyton. Hung out over there pretty often, actually."

Suddenly, the name clicked to a memory. Luna Fairchild, sauntering into the school, part of a snickering trio of besties, while I waited for her outside the sophomore entrance. The trio was made up of Luna, a girl named Eve, and Shelby Gray. Shelby knew Peyton, but I highly doubted she was one of Peyton's friends. If she was at Hollis Mansion often, it was to hang with Luna.

"You should come listen to us," Vee said. "You know, just sometime. We might be getting a show at Teragram this summer."

"Wow, that's really cool. But what about Gib? I wouldn't blame him for not wanting me there."

She waved me off again. "Gibson will be just fine. He's a lot more bark than bite. Especially if I put a muzzle on him." She laughed. "No, really, he'll be chill, I promise. It would be good for you to come. I can't explain why, but having you there would feel a little bit like having Peyton there. Weird, huh?"

Not really. But of course Vee didn't know that. Nobody outside of the Hollises, except for Detective Martinez and me, would understand why Peyton and I seemed so linked.

"I'll come to a show," I said. "It'll be fun."

Vee beamed. Something I'd never seen before and thought I would never see. But there was petal-pink happiness bursting from that smile—the kind of pink that looked like babies and smelled like daisies. Nothing fake here that I could sense. Vee truly liked the idea of me coming to one of her shows.

Someone called her name and she took off, kicking her shoes under a chair and running away barefoot, leaving me alone with Peyton's photo and all the flowers. I didn't have anything to add to the shrine, which kind of made me feel like an asshole. Hell, even tough-as-nails Vee left the pick. But on the other hand, where were all these people when Peyton needed them most? They weren't crying by her hospital bed—they were making a guessing game out of what might have happened to her. They were accusing her of all kinds of things. They were saying she had a freak-out. They were reveling in her downfall.

Fake bastards.

"So you would have hated it anyway," I said quietly to Peyton's photo. "All blue. Everywhere you look, blue. Can't tell anyone apart because we're all blue. Plus whatever color you associate with boredom. If you do that. Do you do that? Or is it just letters for you? Or maybe something else. It is pencil beige in here. That's my boredom color. It's so bad, I can actually smell pencil shavings if I close my eyes and concentrate. I hate that. I bet you did too. Or maybe you still do, if Vee's right." I sighed. "I wish you could have told me what your boredom color is. It would have been nice to have one person in this world who understood. Just one." I felt a tear prickle the corner of my eye and angrily blinked it away.

I had willed myself not to cry again since that night at Hollis Mansion. I'd cried myself inside out while curled up on the pool deck next to Detective Martinez, and promised myself that it was over. The crying was over. But I hadn't thought about things like pencil shavings at graduation. I wondered how many other things I had yet to think of. "So congratulations, Peyton," I said. I placed my mortarboard on her chair and moved the tassel from right to left. A teardrop landed on top of it, spreading out a darker blue blotch on top of the lighter blue. "Let's party, huh?"

Dad was probably in a near panic by the curb, thinking I'd been kidnapped and left for dead by now. Somehow I was going to have to get control of him. He'd always been so easy before—barely even noticing when I was home and when I wasn't. I was almost nineteen, I had graduated, and it was time for me to live my own life. Whatever that life was.

I straightened, unzipping my gown as I did, and that's when it caught my eye. A movement, quick, so unnoticeable I wondered if I'd really seen it at all. A shadow over by the bleachers, sliding left into the crowd.

Dark buzzed hair over ears that stuck out just slightly, and a tanned neck, carefully groomed. Erect posture and muscular arms stuffed into a polo shirt that was tucked fastidiously into khaki pants.

And a badge stuck to the waistband.

A badge that glowed yellow. Serve-and-protect yellow.

"Was that . . . ?" I said to myself, and then started forward. "Detective?" I picked up my pace, trying not to turn my ankle in my ridiculous shoes, wishing I'd abandoned them like Vee had abandoned hers. "Hey, Martinez!"

But when I burst into the crowd, it gave way, dissolving into a semicircle of graduates and their families, all hastening toward the doors. I looked right and left, even stepping backward and peering behind the bleachers. Nothing.

I darted to the side door and shoved it open, nearly hitting a girl who was coming back inside. Ignoring her indignant sigh, I pushed past her and scanned the parking lot.

Where I saw a familiar car. A very familiar detective behind the wheel. A very familiar detective who hadn't said so much as boo to me for seven months.

I didn't wave. Just watched him go.

It was like he'd never actually been there.

But I still felt the yellow sunbeams that told me he had.

THERE WAS A tiny part of me that thought Peyton must have been spinning circles in her grave as I walked up the long driveway to whoever's beach house this was. A *beach party?* I could imagine her saying, her eyes rolling upward. *In this tiny place? Cliché much? How lame.*

It was a house I'd never been to before, and I wasn't exactly invited to the party, but who was invited to these kinds of things? It was an after-grad gathering. Even if I managed to piss off everyone there—which could definitely happen—they would all forget me in a week, anyway.

Tall and skinny, the house had the appearance of being crammed in between two other houses. It seemed to spring up to the sky, as abrupt as the cliffs just a few yards down

Santa Monica beach. It was nighttime, but there were enough lights blazing for me to see that it was painted a cheerful yellow, a color that reminded me again of Chris Martinez. Had he really been at my graduation ceremony? After seven months of not talking at all? Why?

There were so many cars, I had to park forever away, but the thumping music and the sounds of people partying led me all the way from my car to the front door. I could hear splashing in a swimming pool, along with the muffled whumps of balls being hit or kicked or who knew what on the beach. People seemed to be everywhere, and not all of them seniors. Not all of them students at our high school at all. There was something comforting about that.

The front door was open, but the mob inside was so dense I couldn't see much past the door. Suddenly I felt very exposed. I wasn't ever named in any of the news coverage of the Hollis story (something I can only attribute to Protection, Courtesy Detective Martinez, the Great and Mighty Defender), but everyone knew the third person in the backyard of the mansion that night was me. Everyone saw my bandages and my scars. Everyone talked, even if they didn't have the first clue what they were saying. But I had promised myself that I was done letting situations like this intimidate me. I held my breath and squeezed through the door.

Inside was a writhing mass of salt and sand and sticky skin. The music was so loud I could feel the bass in my chest, making my heart feel like it was racing to catch up to the beat. The furniture had all been pushed to the outer edges of the rooms and was draped with people. The hardwood floor was covered in grit, and there were Solo cups on every conceivable surface. It was still pretty early in the night—there was no way that this house wasn't going to be completely trashed by morning.

Not my problem.

I wouldn't be stupid enough to invite the entire graduating class and half of California to my house for a good time. Or any kind of time.

Besides, I wasn't here to worry about that kind of thing. I was here to forget, and I intended to forget.

I snaked my way into the kitchen, which looked like a liquor store. I grabbed a bottle at random and dumped its contents into a cup until the cup was half-full. I filled the rest of it with half a can of soda. Not wanting to be wasteful, I grabbed a second cup and mixed another drink. Leaning against the counter, I took three long swallows of the concoction, then coughed and gagged as the alcohol battered the back of my throat.

"Easy there," a guy wearing only a pair of board shorts said as he filled a cup from a keg in the corner. "We don't need any pukers. Party just got started."

I wiped my watering eyes. "I won't puke," I said. "Puking's for freshmen."

He laughed, held up his cup toast-style. "Damn straight. I stand corrected. Drink up, then."

I held my cup up in the same cheers gesture and took another drink. I coughed again, but less this time, and my eyes squinted of their own accord but didn't water.

The guy pointed at me with his cup. "Didn't you used to date the dude with all the . . ." He mimed flexing his muscles.

I nodded. "Jones. Yeah. For a while."

"He's here," he said. "Just saw him. Out on the front porch. He was looking pretty lonely, if you know what I mean." He gave a dude chuckle—the kind that always made my skin crawl—and winked at me.

"Thanks for the report." I drained the rest of my first cup without coughing at all, crushed the plastic, and tossed it into the corner with about a thousand other cups that were overflowing a small stainless-steel trash container. It was a swamp of foul-smelling alcohol.

"Two points," the guy said. "She shoots, she scores." He paused to drink and went back to pouring.

I curtsied, then grabbed another random bottle by the neck and carried it in my free hand on the way out.

I decided to head down to the beach, where I could blend in and decide if maybe a grad party wasn't exactly my thing after all. What was I expecting to find here? Acceptance? Forgiveness? Some sort of proof that I could have been Peyton's sister in more than just blood? Or maybe just a chance to celebrate like a normal person?

I found a spot, unlaced my shoes, and kicked them off, and sat with my toes dug into the warm sand, my arms around my knees. For the longest time, I listened to the ocean—a sound that always brought shimmery iridescent salmon to mind, the pink of happiness combined with the opalescence of opulence. *Ocean* was one of the few water words that wasn't a shade of blue to me. I sipped from the bottle and closed my eyes and floated up and down the color, fading away, blissed out.

Until I was smacked on the cheek with a ball. My eyes flew open as I rocked back into the sand.

"What the—?" I said, pushing myself upright with my elbows. My cheek stung, and the bottle had knocked over, spilling brown booze onto my leg.

There was laughter, and out of the darkness two images came into view. "Oh, sorry," a set of very white teeth said. "We didn't mean to."

But the giggling coming from behind her said they weren't exactly trying not to, either.

The girls stepped into a beam of light coming from the house then, and I could see who they were—two seniors who'd been in my government class this year. Tanned and endowed God's-gift-to-the-world types who spent far more time whispering about other people than they ever spent actually studying American government. Not that girls who looked like that needed to be rocket scientists to get ahead in this world, anyway.

"Whatever," I said, throwing the ball to the one in front. A little too hard, maybe, because she shook her hand after catching it.

They started to leave, whispered again, then turned back. "Hey, so we like, heard about what happened to Dru Hollis," the one with the gleaming teeth said.

"Only you and the whole rest of the world." Incessantly. For as long as the media could bleed the story dry. "Your point?" I rubbed my aching cheek. Even through the fog of alcohol, the skin felt warm.

The one in back glared at me, but Teeth simply patted the ball with one manicured hand and continued. "So it sounded really awful. Was it?"

I pulled myself to standing, brushing the sand off the seat of my jeans and where it had stuck to the alcohol on my leg. There was stupid, and there was really stupid . . . and then there was this girl. "What kind of asinine question is that? No, it was the best night of my life."

She glanced over her shoulder nervously and turned back again. "We just wanted to say we're like, sorry or whatever. You and Dru were a thing, right?"

Sorry or whatever.

Or whatever.

God, was there not one genuine feeling in all of this ridiculous town?

"No," I said. "We weren't *a thing*. Not that it's anyone's business, but we were trying to figure out who hurt Peyton."

"You mean who killed her," the girl in back said.

I leveled my nastiest gaze at her. *"Or whatever."*

The girls exchanged looks again, and then the one with the ball turned back toward me. "I don't know why you have such an attitude about it. We were trying to be consoling."

I bent and picked up the half-empty bottle. "Oh, is that what this is? You're consoling me? So if I'd told you all the dirty details of what happened, you weren't going to run right over there and tell your little friends all about it?" I gestured toward the loose crowd of people standing near a cooler, most of them staring at us.

She shook her head. "No, I—"

"Spare me. You want to get the dirt. And I don't have any to give you. They're dead. Both of them. Maybe you should let them rest in peace."

I stormed away, realizing with shock that my chest felt heavy and my throat full, as if I were going to cry. I churned my feet extra hard through the sand, hoping to grind away the emotion before it blew up into color. So, so sick of emotions and colors. I took a giant gulp from the bottle and then chucked the whole thing into the sand behind me.

"You've got an attitude problem, Nikki Kill," I heard one

of the girls shout behind me.

I turned, walking backward, and flipped them a double bird. "So I've heard! Well, up yours with my attitude problem, how about that?" Without missing a beat, I turned facing forward and continued marching toward the house, keeping my middle fingers extended high over my head. They wanted to talk? Might as well give them something to talk about.

The alcohol had begun to hit me, making me feel fuzzy and warm. I didn't notice the bodies I bumped into as much as I worked my way back through the house. I felt contained, in my own zone. I knew I was still the gossip everyone passed around, but with the buzz in the back of my brain, I no longer cared. Why would I give a shit what fake ditzes like those girls thought about anything? *It sounded really awful. Was it?*

As a general rule, I didn't drink a lot. Gunner, my *kyo sah nim* at LightningKick, would kill me if he knew I even thought about drinking. Drinking made you slow and lazy and took you off your guard. A *drunk can't defend herself, Nikki,* I could almost hear him saying. Gunner was always treating me like a little sister he had to protect, and I can only imagine the Big Brothering he would be doing since the mess I'd got into with the Hollises. Not that I'd let him. The *dojang* was a part of my life I hadn't gotten back to yet. I'd cracked one of my metatarsals on the back of Luna's head, but even after it healed, and my excuse to avoid my workout disappeared, I still couldn't work up the courage. Pummeling people just wasn't as enticing to me as it used to be.

But, Gunner's feelings about alcohol aside, I didn't like to drink because drinking made my synesthesia lie to me. My colors went haywire. I interpreted things wrong, and that usually ended up with fights.

I was never more aware of the way I relied on my synesthesia to help me take the temperature of a room, of a situation, than I was when I was drinking.

Unless, of course, I drank so much the colors just went away.

The thought made me go back into the kitchen and pull a beer out of an ice bucket. I plowed back through the crowd, daring someone to fuck with me, pausing here and there to guzzle from the can.

It seemed I took the longest way ever, and maybe even got lost once or twice, but finally I found myself stumbling out onto the front porch without really remembering much about how I got there.

I sipped my beer, realizing with confusion that I wasn't holding my shoes. I stared at my hands for a beat and then let the ragemonster overtake me. Those shoes had stood on Dru's blood. I couldn't lose them. I couldn't.

I swung around, trying to take inventory. Faces, faces, faces, all of them painting over with crimson. With ragemonster. With crimson. Back and forth.

"I lost my shoes," I said to nobody in particular. Was I even talking out loud? I wasn't sure. I took a deep breath and tried again, shouting, "Has anyone seen my shoes?"

My legs felt weak, and all of a sudden I was really tired. People were laughing. I was pretty sure they were laughing at me. But I no longer cared. I only wanted to find my shoes and go lie down somewhere. Or go home. Or both.

I sank to the porch floor and let gravity take over, lying back and blinking hard, trying to clear my vision. Or my mind. Or something. I wasn't quite sure what anymore. I only cared that the porch boards felt cool against my back, and steady, like they were the only things in this world anchored down.

Blink. Ceiling. Warped ceiling that swooped like a sheet in a breeze.

Blink. Brick wall. Curved wall that made me feel like I was in a fishbowl.

Blink. Someone's feet. Super loud on the wood floor.

Blink. A face.

I squinted, trying to recognize it. *Blink.* And I did.

Like magic, Jones was there, bending over me, his chest bare, his board shorts low on his hips, highlighting most of the V of his abdomen. I squeezed my eyes shut again, but he was still there when I opened them. I felt so much relief, seeing him there. I actually surprised myself with all that relief. Maybe it was true what they said about absence making the heart grow fonder.

"Come on," he said, and though he seemed a little wobbly on his feet as well, I took his hands and let him pull me back to standing.

"I lost my shoes," I said.

"I've got them," he said, holding up one hand, my shoes dangling from two of his fingers.

"You're the best," I said, throwing my arms around his neck and lunging into him so hard we both almost fell over.

"Let's get you some space right now. Here, give me that." He plucked the beer can from my hand and handed it to a guy standing behind him.

"I was drinking that," I said, shoving into his shoulder with my fists playfully. He barely moved.

Jones smiled, his chin dimple joined by the two adorable dimples in his cheeks. I'd forgotten how adorable those dimples were. "Yes, you definitely were," he said. "And I'm trying to keep you from getting sick. Or worse. Come on."

He led me off the porch and around the house, back toward the beach.

"I don't want to go down there," I said sourly, trying to wrench my hand free, but I had no muscle behind it.

I hated feeling weak and was grateful that this was Jones leading me away. Jones was safe. He would never hurt me. Which was one of the things I liked most about him. And I didn't understand that. When had I started cataloguing the good things about Jones? "There's bitches down there. They're so sorry about Dru and *like whatever*." I said the last in a sarcastic mimic of the whitened-teeth girl.

"We'll stay away from them." Jones kept walking, yanking me along behind him. "We're just getting air."

We went a long way down the beach—almost to the spot where the cliffs met the sand—until we were far enough away from the house to no longer be able to make out words. We could still hear the beat of the music, but it was mostly drowned out by the waves and sounded way farther off than it actually was. The fresh air was clearing my head a little. Or maybe it was making it even more muddled, because I suddenly didn't mind being with Jones. In fact, I kind of liked it. A lot.

Jones stopped, turned, and pulled me up close. "Feeling better? I can take you home if you want." He smelled so good, like chlorine and sunscreen and sweat. I splayed my hands across his chest.

"I've missed this," I said, unsure whether I said it out loud or just thought it.

But I must have said it out loud, because Jones tipped his head back and laughed, the sound coming through his chest in a deep rumble that I could feel under my fingertips. "You are so drunk, Nikki Kill."

I pressed my forehead into his chest, inhaled, stepped even closer so that our hips were touching too.

"I missed you. I missed us." I trailed my finger lightly down one bicep. "Why did I let you go?"

"You're drunk," he repeated.

"I'm not that drunk. I'll feel the same way tomorrow."

"The only thing you'll feel tomorrow is a headache."

I bit my lip, keeping my face completely serious. "Take me home and try me."

We must have stood there for a full minute staring at each other, neither of us moving, neither of us breathing; the only sound registering was the waves crashing onto the shore. The moon, which I could see over Jones's shoulder, was bright white, and I wasn't sure what that meant for me. My colors were suddenly missing, which was exactly what I'd been hoping for, but now that they were gone, I desperately wanted them back.

But *everything* was suddenly gone. Peyton was gone. Dru was gone. Luna, Vanessa, Bill, all gone. Those stupid girls were gone. The things that had made my life scary and miserable were gone. Thank God. It was just me and Jones, our warm skin radiating off each other.

"Nikki. I don't want to do anything you don't—"

"God, shut up. I know what I'm doing. Even stubborn Nikki Kill can change her mind sometimes, you know."

He grinned. "Well, I can honestly say I've never seen that happen."

I grinned back. "There's a first time for everything."

And then one of us moved. I didn't know if it was him or me, but it didn't matter. All that mattered was that suddenly he was kissing me, we were pressing up against each other, and my mind was exploding with violet. The right color. The only color that mattered.

We kissed on the beach until our mouths were sore and our bodies were covered with sand. Jones refused to do any more than kiss—"I don't want you to wake up sober and regretful," he'd said—but it still felt good. It felt right, being with Jones again. It felt safe.

Finally, we decided we would go to his house to shower off the sand, and for me to sleep off the alcohol. I texted Dad, letting him know that I was going to stay at a friend's house, and he texted back that he would be gone early, taking the grandparents back to the airport, and that he would see me when I got home. And to stay safe. Always stay safe. If you get into any trouble, call me ASAP, he texted. Keep your eyes open.

I slipped into my shoes and held Jones's hand as we walked back up the beach, our hips bumping every few steps. Before we got back to the house, he turned and pulled me close again.

"So does this mean what I think it means?" he asked.

"What do you think it means?"

He pressed his forehead to mine and kissed my nose. So

sweet, so Jones. I didn't deserve someone like him. But I was too selfish to care. "Are we back together?"

I closed my eyes so I wouldn't have to see if he was beaming magenta at me, or if I was beaming cheater blue to everyone else. Right now, all I wanted was to bathe in the sexy violet. "Why not?" I asked. "We were pretty good together before."

Even though I had a million reasons *Why not*, and if I was sober, I might have let some of them sway me, I left it at simply *Why not*, and at the goofy smile on Jones's face. I was lonely and Jones was familiar and maybe it was about time to start living my life again. Dru wasn't coming back. Time to stop acting like he was.

He kissed me again, long and deep. "Come on, let's get you into a cold shower."

We had only taken two or three steps before we saw the lights of a police cruiser bouncing off the sand, turning it blue and white . . . and crimson.

I was instantly transported to that night at Hollis Mansion, transported further to the day I found my mother dead. To the beeping machines in Peyton's hospital room. The lights, the crimson. The crimson. Jesus, that relentless crimson. I staggered. Jones's arm tightened around me.

Someone turned off the music, and people started rushing down the length of the beach, ditching cans and cups and bottles as they went. People, still dripping with pool water, were spilling out the back door as shouting voices trailed behind them.

"Come on," Jones said, hurrying me away from the house. "My car is this way."

We walked past several houses and started around a sprawling white house, the owner of which was standing in a window, watching everyone run. "Hey!" he called through the open window as we hurried past. "You two!" But we ignored him and kept moving.

"I'm right over here," Jones said, pulling me toward his car, which was parked right across the street from mine. Did we get to the party at the same time? Weird that I hadn't seen him. Maybe Dad had a point, telling me to keep my eyes open.

Right away, I could see that an officer was peering into my car, a flashlight pointed at the driver's side window.

"What the hell?"

"Stop right there," the officer said, and Jones and I froze. My heart sank. Great. I almost never drank, and when I finally decided to cut loose, I was going to get busted. Forget what Gunner thought about alcohol—Dad was going to have a fit.

The officer said something into his radio, then started toward us. A few seconds later, another cruiser pulled up behind us. The officer inside was big and angular and very serious looking. Slowly, he got out.

"Get an ID?" he asked.

"Not yet." The first officer turned to me. "You have ID on you?"

I pointed. "It's in my car."

The first officer stepped to the side, aiming his flashlight at my car. "That car right there? That's yours?"

"Yeah."

He made eye contact with Officer Serious and flicked his head toward the window. The serious officer started toward it, clicking on his flashlight as he went.

The first officer turned back to us. "You mind letting us have a look inside?"

"What? Why?" I started toward my car, but the officer stepped in my way. I could hear police radio chatter coming from down the street. The music had turned off. Everyone had gone quiet. Party over.

"Miss, we got a call from a concerned neighbor."

I thought about the guy watching from his window in the white house. *Way to ruin a good time, Neighbor of the Year.* "It's not my party," I said. "I was just leaving."

The first officer's eyes bored into me. "The neighbor alleges he saw some kids dealing drugs from this car right here."

My mind swam. "What? Drugs? No. I don't deal dr— I was on the beach. Jones, tell him we were on the beach." But

Jones stood still as a statue, dumbstruck.

The serious officer was pointing his flashlight through my window, just as the first one had been doing when we arrived. "So you're saying that bag in there doesn't belong to you," he said.

"What bag?" I maneuvered around the first officer and peered in where the light was illuminating.

There was a plastic bag on the front seat.

It was full of pills.

Pills I recognized. Buddhas, crowns, Pac-Man, ghosts.

The same kind of Molly that Luna had been holding in a photo I'd stolen from Peyton's apartment months ago.

HAD I NOT been drinking, maybe I would have cooperated, tried to calmly explain things. Or maybe not picked a fight with two armed police officers, at the very least. Probably not. Cooperation and calm explanation weren't really in my repertoire. And I didn't have the best history with police officers, either.

Jones stood by, immobile and silent, as I went rigid. "Are you fucking kidding me?" Luna's pills. How had they gotten onto my front seat? "I have no idea where that came from."

"This will go easier if you just let us into the car," the serious officer with the flashlight said.

"Just to clear things up," the first officer said, obviously trying to look like the nice, friendly one. "Get to the bottom of things."

I went back to Jones's side, both officers following me close. I had no idea what was going on, but I knew enough to know that letting those cops into my car was not going to end well for me. "No way. Not until you get a warrant. Or whatever it is you have to get. Those pills aren't mine." I tried to hook my arm through Jones's but felt him stiffen. I forgot that Jones probably wasn't really well versed in police run-ins.

"We don't need a warrant. We have probable cause. Why don't you go ahead and step to the back of the vehicle." The serious officer reached toward me and I jerked, smacking his hand down before I could even think about what I was doing.

"No need to get out of hand here," the friendly officer said. "You're just going to make it harder on everyone if you get crazy."

The serious officer reached for my arm again and I snatched it away, dropping into a fighting stance. Guess maybe Gunner was wrong. I could defend myself with a gut full of vodka. Or whiskey. Or whatever it was I'd been drinking. Besides, with all the adrenaline rushing through me, I suddenly felt much more sober. But this was bad. Fighting two cops was a terrible idea. I knew it even as I was doing it.

"Okay," he said. "You're coming with us."

"I haven't done anything wrong. Aren't you listening? They aren't mine."

He took another step toward me, his face getting a bored I-have-to-do-this-shit-way-too-often look. "That no longer matters. You're going to come with us one way or another."

"On what charges?" I asked angrily. "Someone put those there. I'm being set up!"

"Well, now, drunk and disorderly, if nothing else," he said. "Minor in possession. Striking an officer. Possession of narcotics. Possibly dealing. You're just digging yourself in deeper every second."

"This is bullshit and I'm not going anywhere." I started toward Jones's car, like I was going to get into it, even though Jones didn't follow me at all. But I'd gotten only a half-dozen steps before the officers were on me.

M Y MUG SHOT was a disaster. By the time the two
officers wrestled me into the car, I was scraped and
scuffed on my elbows and knees, my face smeared with mascara. Jones stood by, eyes huge and frightened, as they took
me away. I screamed to him to find Detective Martinez.

"Get answers, Jones! Find out what's going on!"

Whether or not he would was a bit up in the air.

Jones had just come back into my life and already there
were problems. He knew there were no promises when it
came to me. He could walk away, save himself the trouble.
Hell, he *should* walk away and save himself the trouble. He
would be crazy not to bug out now. Even I wouldn't blame
him.

The police station was so much grimier than I remembered it from the last time I was there. There was something about coming in through the front door with all the cards on your side that made a place seem friendlier than when you were walking in handcuffed and confused and fighting for your life.

They added resisting arrest to my list of charges.

I waived my right to call Dad. He would never understand. He would be so embarrassed, especially with my grandparents there. He would be worried about me. He would have to be a last resort.

I would wait the night out and let Jones save me in the morning. I didn't like the idea, but I could handle it. I'd handled much worse.

I DIDN'T SLEEP. But I also didn't puke, so the guy at the keg was wrong about me. Morning took forever to come, especially since Jones didn't show up right away. I'd begun to think maybe he really had bugged out.

When the scowling guard came to get me for a visitor after lunch, my heart leaped and then sank again, as the person sitting in the tiny interrogation room wasn't Jones, but was a pretty redhead in a sharp navy suit.

"Nikki Kill, yes?" she asked, standing and holding her hand out to shake mine.

I nodded, surly, ignoring her hand. "And you are?"

"Blake Willis." She let her hand drop and settled back into her chair, then flashed me a smile. "Assistant DA. I need to ask you a few questions. About the murder of Peyton Hollis."

"Oh, hell, no." I backed toward the door. "Take me back, please," I said to the officer who'd brought me in. "This isn't a visitor. I don't want to talk to her."

Blake remained perfectly calm, her hands folded on the table in front of her, as if she did this every day. Which maybe she did. How would I know? "I'm your best bet in avoiding a murder charge, Nikki, so I would suggest you close your mouth and open your ears. Up to you, of course." She gestured toward the chair across from her. "Have a seat."

"Close my mouth? You're kidding, right? Isn't it all kinds of illegal for you to be here?" I asked. "I haven't even seen a lawyer yet. I'm not talking to you."

"You might want to rethink that," she said, unfolding her hands and sifting through paperwork. "Given the position you're in."

"Position? What position? I had nothing to do with Peyton's murder. I'm not in any sort of position, *prosecutor*." I said the last with a sneer. "So you might as well look for someone else to lock up, because it's not me."

She stopped sifting, momentarily, and glanced up at me, again with the smile. "Nikki," she said quietly, "I don't want to lock you up. Yes, it's unusual for me to be here, and you're right, I shouldn't be. And nobody but you, me, and a few select officers know I'm here. But I'm trying to get to the bottom of Peyton Hollis's case. Of course, the search for answers naturally led me to you. And when I heard you'd been arrested, I decided it would be a good opportunity for us to talk." She lowered her voice to a whisper. "The police are looking seriously at you. But that doesn't mean the search for Peyton's attacker has stopped. Not for me. Don't you want to help us find her murderer and bring him or her to justice?" She held my gaze for a long moment before straightening up again and going back to her papers. "That is, of course, unless we can't find anyone but you. There's new evidence that you are that person." She gestured to the chair again.

When I looked down, the seat of the chair went from beat-up jail gray to mint green, the edges feathering into sage. In the center were drops of yellow, the same kind of yellow that I'd seen on Detective Martinez. Detective Martinez. Where the hell was he in all of this? Was he the one also *looking seriously at* me?

Reluctantly, I sat. But I kept my weight thrusted forward, just in case I should decide to get the hell out of there, and fast.

"So it looks like you put up a real fight last night." She glanced at me but didn't wait for me to respond. "Not the best idea in the world, but not a huge deal. This, though."

She ran a finger down a paper. "A little more problematic. You want to tell me what your relationship was with Peyton Hollis?"

"We didn't have one," I said. We both knew I was lying, but I meant it when I said I wasn't going to give her anything. She may have wanted my trust, but she didn't know who she was dealing with. Trust was so rare for me, I wasn't even sure I would recognize it when I felt it.

She pursed her glossed lips and then let out a gust of air, ignoring my denial. "And it says here that they recently found her car. Cherry-red Mustang convertible, license plate FNFAIR. You know it?"

I remained motionless. I had told Martinez about the car months ago. Why were they only finding it now?

My head had begun pounding, and I wished more than anything that I could rewind the clock to just before I decided to start slamming booze last night. Or maybe before I went to the party at all. Or maybe, while I was rewinding, I could go all the way back to when I was eight. Get a do-over. Warn Mom that something horrible was about to happen and change my entire life forever. "Everyone knows that car."

She nodded. "Well, it looks here like they found it in a wooded area behind an abandoned grocery store."

Exactly where I had told Martinez to look for it. This made no sense. "So? What does that have to do with me?"

"So. What that has to do with you is that your

fingerprints were all over it. And there was a half-empty pack of cigarettes inside, along with a lighter." She turned a paper so I could see a photo that was printed on it. "You smoke, correct?"

"A lot of people smoke. This is hardly earth-shattering."

"True. But aren't those your initials on the lighter?" She tapped the picture. "I mean, they could probably lift your prints off it if they want to, but why bother to deny it and make it come to that, right? I'm sure there are plenty of people who've seen you with that lighter, starting with that boy. You call him Jones, am I correct?"

But I couldn't speak. Could barely even breathe. The cigarettes and lighter. The ones I thought I'd lost. They hadn't been lost at all.

Someone had lifted them and had planted them in Peyton's car. From my room, my car, I didn't know. All I knew was that meant someone had gotten close to me again, without me even knowing it.

"You recognize them," she said. A statement, not a question. I didn't budge. I couldn't look away from the photo. I couldn't take in all that it could mean. She took a deep breath and went back to her file. "So I'm guessing you'll probably recognize this, too." She reached into a bag on the floor next to her feet and pulled out a plastic bag with bundled black cloth inside. She tossed it on the table.

I knew what it was before I touched it. "My jacket?" The

words popped out before I could even think them. I picked it up and gazed at it, dumbfounded.

She pulled the jacket away from me. "So you recognize that as well. Any idea why it was in Peyton Hollis's trunk?" She produced another photo—a close-up of Peyton's open trunk, my jacket wadded among the contents.

My mind reeled. I knew I was staring at my jacket, but it didn't make any sense to me. I had worn that jacket for months after Peyton's death, before I had anything to do with her family, her house, or her car. I hadn't worn it since it got hot outside, but I was sure—a thousand percent sure—it had been hanging in my closet. "No," I said.

"So you didn't let her borrow it, maybe?"

"No."

"And you didn't have a relationship with her."

"No."

"Never hung out with her?"

I shook my head. I was in an impossible place. There was no right answer.

"But your jacket was in her car."

I shrugged, helpless.

She reached for another plastic bag. "Do you often carry a knife, Nikki?" I didn't even need to look to know that my penknife was in that bag. It only made sense, right? Well, in the context of nothing making a fucking bit of sense whatsoever, it made sense.

"It's not mine," I said, my lips numb.

She nodded, took the bag back. "Here's the thing. We've had a new witness come forward, as well."

I jolted. "What? Who? Witness to what?"

She shook her head. "I'm not sure about the details, because I wasn't there when the statement was made. My boss handled it. But apparently whoever it was, they reported that you and Peyton were fighting. Something about Peyton not wanting you to date her brother. Apparently you were overheard telling Peyton that she would regret it if she tried to keep you two apart. That you were trained and not afraid to kill someone if you had to. Were you and Dru Hollis . . ." She flipped through some pages. "A thing? Your statement a few months ago claimed that he had admitted to being present during Peyton's attack. Were you there with him?"

"We weren't a thing," I said. "We were . . ." But I found I couldn't really explain what exactly we were, because even to my own ears, it sounded like a story. *We were grieving. We were searching for her attacker. We were . . . consoling each other.* "Whoever this witness is, they're lying. I didn't say any of those things. I didn't fight with Peyton. Ever. I didn't even know—" I stopped myself, clamping my mouth shut, remembering that even if Blake Willis was here "helping me out," her job was to find Peyton's killer, even if that meant putting me away. I shouldn't have said a word. "I want a lawyer."

Blake switched into full DA mode and continued on as if she hadn't heard me.

"Well, you definitely broke into and entered Peyton's apartment—fingerprints there, too, and a positive ID from an officer who has made a statement that you were there when he arrested Dru Hollis. And you also broke into her parents' house. You admitted that in your statement. You can imagine how it looks that you've broken into two of Peyton's residences, and your cigarettes and lighter, and your jacket, with a knife in the pocket, was found in Peyton's car, along with a school file with your name on it, after you allegedly threatened her."

Damn. The file. I had left it there for Martinez to find out about my synesthesia. It was still there. The car was still there. But Martinez was not. What the hell had happened?

"I didn't threaten her. I didn't leave my jacket there. None of this is true."

She continued. "Luna . . . Fairchild, is it? Yes, Luna Fairchild has given a statement that you stole something from Peyton's bedroom, and that you assaulted her and her parents when they tried to stop you. And that you'd come back to the Hollis house on some sort of vengeful mission, and she was only protecting herself when Dru got in the way." A flash of Dru's body crumpling to the ground streaked through my mind, painful crimson. I stared at my hands and willed myself not to say anything. "What did you steal,

Nikki?" I said nothing. She leaned in. "This is where you can help me help you. Denying things will get you nowhere. You have to give me something to work with."

My mind reeled, trying to make sense of all I was hearing. Luna was spinning this onto me? And they were believing her? Had she taken my cigarettes? How was that even possible? How did someone steal from juvie? Whose help did Luna have?

"Okay, we don't need to know right now. But again I need to ask you, did you have anything to do with Peyton Hollis's murder?" Blake Willis asked. She leaned forward and dropped her voice again. "I have theories, Nikki. Theories that I can take to the DA if you just help me out a little. Luna is—"

"Luna's a liar," I said. "A liar and a killer. You're never going to get actual facts from her."

"She's also free and you're in jail," Blake said.

A wall of shock smashed into me—confetti and dots. My heart skipped about a thousand beats. I felt like the wind had been knocked out of me. My lungs didn't want to expand.

This must have been what the girl at graduation was trying to tell me. Luna was out of juvie. The crazy, dead-eyed girl who wanted me obliterated more than anything in the world was no longer locked up. Oh, God, I'd been going on about my life, thinking I was safe, letting my guard down, reassuring Dad, berating myself for still being paranoid, while she was combing through my things, setting me up. She had gotten into my car before, so I knew she could do it. Suddenly I felt incredibly naked and vulnerable. My neck stiffened at the thought of stepping outside this building. *Boo! Found you!* I heard her say, remembering the terrifying image of her face popping up over the trash can I was hiding behind next to her pool house. *Boo! Boo, Nikki! Boo!*

"So, when you're ready to talk, and to give me something to work with, I can—"

"She's out?" I barked, my voice gruff, low.

Blake Willis looked up from her paperwork. "What?"

"You said Luna is free. When did that happen?"

She nodded. "About a month ago. She has been released into . . ." She checked the paperwork again and nodded. "Yep, her father's custody. She pled manslaughter, self-defense in which her brother accidentally got in the way, and was given probation. I'm guessing her family has some pull somewhere."

You think? I wanted to shout. *You think they might have some pull somewhere?* The Great Bill Hollis, who had gotten away with murder, literally, and was living it up on some beach in beautiful Dubai while I was stuck in a filthy jail cell and his own children were stuck in the ground, might have some pull? Maybe just a little, Blake Willis. Maybe just the teeniest tiniest bit.

But I couldn't speak those words because even thinking

them chilled me. Bill Hollis was powerful. Anyone with a brain could see that. But I was starting to get a sense of just how powerful he was. Above-the-law powerful. Influence-from-the-other-side-of-the-world powerful. Which made Luna powerful too. And I would be lying if I said I wasn't at least a little bit afraid of her, especially knowing that she was out of juvie now.

"Okay," Blake Willis said, shoving the papers back into a file folder, sliding a blank yellow legal pad toward me, and giving me a smile. She leaned over the table and whispered. "Like I said, the only reason I'm even here talking to you is because there's something about this case that just doesn't add up. But it's up to you to save yourself, Nikki. So you start thinking about details of what happened that night at the Hollis home, and write them down. Anything at all to do with Peyton, with her family, anything about the Hollis house. You never know what minutiae might turn out to be important."

Minutiae. Ha. I specialized in minutiae.

"You'd be surprised," I mumbled, but I was still speaking through numb lips. My arms and legs felt bumpy gray and black, like cold, rough asphalt. Nobody knew better than a synesthete how true it was that missed details could contain the clue to everything. I leveled my eyes at her. "I didn't do anything. I was trying to help Peyton. Luna is the one you should be locking up."

Blake Willis stood, adjusted her suit jacket. "You can't worry about Luna. You have to worry about you now."

"One and the same," I said. "As long as she's out there, I have to worry about both of us."

"Whatever you're thinking right now," she said, pointing to the pad of paper, "you need to write down. If there's something you know about Luna that could help this case, we need to know it. Otherwise, you could find yourself arrested for something much bigger than drunk and disorderly."

I stared at the pad. It trembled, the yellow popping into bumpy gray and black burnt popcorn. *Fear, fear, fear,* those bumps said as they undulated across the page. Blake Willis didn't understand how hopeless this was. "Okay," I said. She produced a leather satchel out of nowhere and stuffed the folder into it. "Hey, if you could get in big trouble for even being here, how did you get in to see me in the first place?"

"Time's up, counselor," a voice said behind me. "All charges dropped."

It was a voice that I recognized.

Blake Willis held back a smile. "Someone did me a favor. And did one for you, too."

"I brought you a coffee," Detective Martinez said, holding a cup toward me. "Don't worry, it's not French vanilla."

I DIDN'T NEED your help in there, you know," I said, following Detective Martinez to his car, the tantalizing coffee steam wafting up into my face. I totally did need his help—and we both knew it—but I generally wasn't great at playing damsel in distress. We both knew that, too.

"I could see you had it all under control. Care to tell me why you didn't call your dad? Or a lawyer, maybe?"

"Care to tell me why I was arrested in the first place?"

"The way I understand it, you were arrested for doing what you do—jumping in with both feet before thinking. Resisting arrest, drunk and disorderly—sounds like the Nikki I know. But drugs? Now, that doesn't seem like you. Something is definitely wrong with that one. You could have cooperated, you know. Gone in, answered some questions, been back on the beach by sunrise. Doing whatever it was that you were doing." He glanced at me over the top of his sunglasses, a violet feeling that stroked a blush from my cheeks.

Okay, even I would admit, Detective Martinez always looked amazing in the morning. Fresh and groomed, his short black hair gleaming in the sunlight, his clothes still pressed and crisp. I sipped on the coffee as a distraction.

"Still. Way to warn me," I said. "But you would have to actually talk to me to warn me, right?"

"You stopped taking my calls," he said.

"I stopped taking everyone's calls. You're not special." Truth, plus I was a little bit more than freaked out that I'd let him in as much as I had. And not in the same way that I'd let Dru in. It wasn't about sex; it was about intimacy. Detective Martinez knew more about me than most everyone else. More about me than I wanted him to. And there was the little matter of how his color had changed from yellow to grapey purple last time I saw him. He confused me. He scared me. If anyone was special, it was him. And I hated him for it. Special never led to anywhere good. "Besides, you stopped calling."

He opened his door and propped one foot on the floorboard. My hand was still hovering near the handle on the passenger side. "There was nothing to call about."

I laughed out loud, pulled open the door, and plunked myself inside the car. When he got in, I said, "Oh, I don't know. How about, 'Hey, Nikki, the girl who almost murdered you twice is out of juvie now.' That might have been something worth calling about, don't you think? A good opener, at least."

"I didn't know."

"How could you not know? It's your case. You were there that night. You were the first officer on the scene, in fact. You followed me everywhere to solve it. I told you where Peyton's car was. You were supposed to finish Luna. You said you were going to. And instead, you're turning the case onto me? You're deciding that some bullshit witness and a half-empty pack of cigarettes mean I was the one who murdered her? I let you in and you completely sold me out. And now you show up, months later, with coffee—" I crammed my cup into his console, a drop sloshing out of the lid and landing on the edge of his seat. "And get me out of jail that you're trying to put me into? You make zero sense."

"I'm not trying to put you in here. I have nothing to do with it," he said, taking off his sunglasses and tossing them onto the dash. His dark eyes searched mine. "You're your own worst enemy, Nikki."

"What do you mean?"

He sighed, and I could feel something heavy on the sigh, but it wasn't clear enough to come with a color. Reading

Detective Martinez was different from reading Jones or half the other people in my life. Chris Martinez had secrets, and he was very good at hiding them. "I pulled myself off the case," he said. "I never even looked at the car because you'd told me your fingerprints were inside it, and I didn't want to be in a position of having to incriminate you. Because for some insane reason, I actually believe that you're innocent. I've been purposely ignoring evidence all these months to keep you out of trouble, and I got to the place where I couldn't feel right about it. I was just . . . too close . . . to the whole situation. I turned everything over to another detective a few weeks ago and let him find the car. I had to distance myself."

So he hadn't seen my school file in the trunk after all. Which meant he still didn't know about my synesthesia. I didn't know how that made me feel. Mostly relieved. But it also made me feel cheated in some small, unexplainable way.

"So you took yourself off the case because you believed in me but gave it to someone else to prove you wrong? It's still not adding up, Detective."

He sighed again, pinched the bridge of his nose. "There was another reason I took myself off the case." He peeked at me, but I only shook my head at him uncomprehendingly. "I've been dating Blake Willis."

I blinked, incredulous. It took a moment for me to absorb

the information. A long, deep indigo moment of betrayal—a color I'd never seen, and never thought I'd see, with Detective Martinez.

"The DA? You've got to be kidding me. Right? It's a joke. This is why you so graciously gave her a favor?"

He shook his head. "I didn't know she was involved in the case until we were already . . . together."

"You didn't know. How convenient for you. How the hell could you be dating her and not know? It was your case."

"*Was* my case, Nikki. Was. And when we started dating, they weren't even talking about you as a suspect. She knew I'd recused myself, but she didn't know why. As far as anyone knew, you were just an unfortunate victim who fell in love with the wrong guy and ended up in the middle of an ugly family fight. The end."

"I was not in love with him!" I shouted, realizing that this wasn't what really had me angry, but unable to stop myself. "Everyone needs to quit saying that. He was a good time, period. He was a complication, and I wish I had never met him."

He held his hands out like I might float out of my seat and he would need to push me back down in it. "Okay, okay, bad choice of words. You need to calm down. You—"

"No," I said, reaching for the door handle. "I won't calm down. Your girlfriend is going to have me arrested and Luna is free, and this is all just crazy. I'm leaving. I'll walk home."

"Nikki, stop."

"And, for the record, I didn't tell you where the car was to help you build a case. I told you where it was to—" I stopped. I didn't want to tell him the truth—that I'd done it in hopes that he would find my school files that Peyton had stolen. I'd done it to open up to him about myself. I felt like a fool now.

"Calm down."

"And I don't need you coming back all of a sudden to bail me out and . . . and to what? Follow me again? Protect me? Beat up the bad guys? Well, in case you've forgotten, I beat up the bad guys all by myself last time, thank you very much, with no help from you. In fact, if you remember, when I sparred with you at the *dojang*, I actually—"

"Enough!"

I stopped, startled. I'd never heard Detective Martinez raise his voice, not even when he was really, really angry with me. My hand fell away from the door handle.

"I want to help you, and if you'd shut up for five seconds, you would already know that."

I swallowed. "I don't need your help."

"But you will. I know the case they're building against you, and you will. There's evidence. And a witness." He turned slightly so he was facing me and reached out to grab my hands. I started to resist, but found myself unable to. His grasp was strong, but warm at the same time. "I've seen your jacket. I know it's yours."

"I don't know how it got there."

"I know. The Hollises are behind it. I believe that. And I think Blake believes that, too. She hasn't said as much, but I know her and I think that's what she suspects."

"So what am I supposed to do—hop a plane to Dubai and make them fess up? Ask them how they magically teleported my shit into Peyton's car? Ask them how Luna got into my closet? Because we all know that's who did it."

He shook his head. "Not necessarily. Remember, there's another player in this game."

I breathed. Yes, of course there was another player. Luna didn't kill Peyton herself. She and her parents—*And don't forget Dru*, I reminded myself. *He may have had a change of heart, but he was in on it, too*—hired someone else to do the dirty work.

"Arrigo Basile," I said.

"Yes. Rigo is the one who swung the weapon that killed Peyton. I would bet my life on it. We just can't prove it. We have no video, no murder weapon, no Rigo. He would have every reason to plant evidence to make sure you went down for the crime. And I think if we find him, we can begin to get to the bottom of this. We can clear you. Until then, there is nothing tying Rigo to the crime other than a friendship with the Hollises. Which isn't enough."

I would bet my life on it, he'd said. I didn't want anyone betting their lives on anything anymore. I wanted this to be over. I wanted to forget I ever heard the names Peyton Hollis or Luna Fairchild or Arrigo Basile. "But you're not on the case anymore."

"I've already worked it out. As of this morning, I'm back on it," he said. "Not as the lead, just backing up. This is wrong and we can prove it. You and me, together."

I didn't say anything. What could I say? This was something I'd spent the past seven months trying to put behind me. Trying to forget about it, trying to outlive the shock and fear. It took forever for me to convince myself that they were all actually gone. I wanted to close my eyes and hide, which was so totally unlike me, it hurt.

Detective Martinez reached up and grabbed his sunglasses from the dash, put them on, and turned on the car. "Okay," he said. "Come with me."

Before I could protest, or even get my hand wrapped on the door handle again, he backed out of the parking space and squealed out of the lot.

7

A S SOON AS I saw the cemetery, I knew what his
plan was. The asphalt under our tires shot up panicky
metallic fireworks as we approached the open gate.

"No," I said. "Let me out."

"I think you should see this," he said, turning on his
blinker and waiting for oncoming traffic to pass so he could
pull in.

"I don't want to see it. I'll jump out."

He didn't take his eyes off the traffic. "Suit yourself. But
you know I'm your best chance of fixing this problem that
you're in. You jump out and you're on your own. You stay
here, listen to me, and we can work together to keep you
from celebrating your sixtieth birthday in prison."

I let out a shaky breath, fearfully casting my eyes over the graves as we drove by. None of them looked fresh. There'd been enough time for the grass to grow back over Peyton's and Dru's. Their graves were no different from anyone else's. If Luna'd had her way that night, it would have been my grave here instead.

Detective Martinez turned into the driveway and maneuvered through the cemetery, finally pulling over and putting the car into park. Neither of us spoke as we got out.

I followed him to a headstone, lonely and set apart from all the others. A cluster of colorful plastic flowers were poked into the soft earth in front of it. I couldn't help thinking that Peyton would have loved the color but would have wanted to die over the tackiness of plastic flowers. A note, faded and wind-beaten, was wrapped around one of the stems. I bent and read it.

GONE 2 SOON.
B

The 2 flashed out at me—pink, and so did the *B*—primary blue, tickling what felt like a memory in the back of my mind. Why did I feel I had seen this note before?

"Do you understand now why I brought you here?"

I shook my head. "Because you're an asshole with serious control issues? And let's not even talk about your superiority complex. Do they have shrinks in cop school? Because you need one."

He grinned, ducked his head. "Well, I'm glad to hear you're being yourself. I thought maybe you'd be mad at me."

I moved past him and headed back toward the car. "This was a waste of your time. I'm not interested in graveside sobfests." I knotted my fingers together to keep them from shaking. Surely Dru was planted somewhere nearby. And on the other side of the cemetery was the grave I had been neglecting for ten years. Mom. I hated this place.

He followed me to the car, turned me around just as I reached the door. "But do you see it? I mean, really see it?"

"See what?"

"Look harder."

I gestured futilely. "It's a headstone in the middle of a field of headstones. No different. So what? It's depressing as hell and it has nothing to do with m—"

But then I did see it. *It was a headstone in the middle of a field of headstones.* But also set apart from them. On its own. Dried grass clippings strewn over Peyton's name. An odd bunch of plastic flowers from some mysterious "B" the only adornment.

I looked around. Most of the other graves had clusters of flowers. Some had them in vases and in the ground. Some of them had wreaths and other decorations. They'd been brushed off, tended to.

Peyton's seat at graduation had been overflowing with so many gifts we had to walk wide around the chair.

Yet nobody had been to her grave. Nobody except for this B had dropped by with flowers.

Why?

Because, truly, Peyton had nobody. It was something we had in common that I'd never considered before. I never pretended to have anyone more than Dad; she had the appearance of friendship and family. But in the end, it was just appearance. People only loved Peyton when the spotlight was shining. In a way, we were both alone in this world. Had she lived, we might have clung to each other.

"You see it now, don't you?" Detective Martinez asked quietly. "You get why I brought you here."

A wind had kicked up from nowhere, pushing my hair across my face. I didn't bother to shake it off. "She looked like she had everything in the world," I said. "But she was missing so much. It's sad."

The detective leaned against his car, pushing his hands into his pockets. I lifted my face to catch the breeze and cool my forehead. "When I last saw you, I gave you a letter from Peyton. Do you remember?" I didn't respond, but he pressed on anyway. "In it she talked about a woman who could answer all your questions. Did you ever get in touch with that woman?"

I shook my head. "I couldn't find her."

Not exactly true. I couldn't find the mysterious Brandi Courteur, who Peyton referred to in her letter, because I hadn't bothered to look. At first I'd been certain that I could locate her, and that I could solve the mystery—how my mom ended up being Peyton's mom, and how Peyton ended up a Hollis. I'd been determined. I would finish the job that Peyton had started.

And then the reality of everything that had happened, and all the implications that could come from knowing, set in, and I was paralyzed with fear. I wanted only to concentrate on graduating like my dad wanted me to do, and then to get the hell out of Brentwood. Where I would go, I had no idea. My life had been one big, ugly question mark since the whole disaster went down. That letter was still tucked inside a binder in the bottom drawer of my desk at home. Let old ghosts stay dead.

"Nikki, Peyton left you that information for a reason. She wanted you to know the truth. Look at her grave—you were all she had. That's what I wanted you to see here."

"Where's Dru's grave?" I asked, my words being whipped away on a sudden gust of wind. My hair blew across my mouth, as if to silence it, and I brushed it away.

"Cremation," Detective Martinez said. "Apparently he'd told a cousin or grandparent or someone that he wanted it that way. They cremated him and scattered him in the ocean."

The ocean. Free and unpredictable, at times violent, cold, at other times, warm and consoling. A mystery. A force. Uncontainable and unknowable. Just like Dru. I could think of nothing more perfect.

"Can we go now?" I tried to sound bored, put-out, but my words came out whiny instead. I didn't care. I just wanted to go home.

"Sure." He pushed away from the car and opened the door. I noticed a bead of sweat rolling down the side of his neck and into the collar of his polo, which was finally starting to lose some of that maddening morning freshness. I slipped into the car, welcoming the coolness of the interior and how it made me feel sealed away from Peyton's grave. From the crimson that was always so present at cemeteries.

He got in and turned on the ignition, adjusting the vents so the air-conditioning blew right on me. I shivered. He put the car into gear but, before taking off, said, "I can help you get to the truth. I can help you find Rigo."

I glanced out the window. I could see the note on the flowers flutter with the breeze. Pink, primary blue. Something so familiar about them . . .

"What do you think?" Detective Martinez asked, interrupting my thought. Despite the cool air blowing in my face, I still had a ring of sweat across my hairline. "It's the best option you have right now."

Actually, at the moment it appeared to be the only

option. I was hardly swamped with offers of help. And I was at a total loss for ideas how to save myself.

Finding Rigo might solve a hell of a lot of problems with the Hollises and with Luna and with my current predicament. And if I needed Detective Martinez's help to find him, I would just have to live with it. I could live with it. I could. Couldn't I?

Just to be safe, I would make sure I took point on this. That way this would be more of a partnership than a rescue. Blake Willis had said it was on me to save myself. So, fine, I would save myself. Or at least go down trying.

"Okay," I said. "We'll find Rigo and go from there."

He looked relieved. "Actually, there's someplace else I'd like to start."

'D NEVER BEEN in an evidence locker before. Not that it was particularly sexy or exciting, but I suppose I did in some way expect more. Basically it was a little hole of a lobby dominated by a beat-up counter, behind which sat a completely bored-looking woman. She was reading a paperback.

Behind her was what looked like a warehouse filled with random crap. There were boxes, envelopes, tubs, and bags lining shelf after shelf after shelf. There was an entire shelf filled with guns. Another one lined with computers.

"Hey, Martinez, what're you up to?" the woman said when we walked in. She set the paperback down. I could see a very steamy-looking cover on it. Imagine, reading romances while being the person to guard all those guns.

"Just doing my job," he said. "Nabbing bad guys and saving the city. The usual."

The woman laughed and swatted the air. "Listen to you, thinking you're a superhero. Where's your cape, baby boy?"

He ducked his head, shy. Was he blushing? This was a new demeanor on him, and it made him look younger. "I left it in the car," he finally said. "I hate to show off. Got to protect my secret identity."

There was more laughter, and then the woman finally sized me up, tilting her head so she could capture me through her glasses. She sobered a bit, but still smiled pleasantly. I wondered how often she got company in here. I guessed not often. It would be hard to maintain a pleasant personality in a place this lonely. Hell, it was hard for me to maintain a pleasant personality anywhere.

Either way, it was pretty easy to tell she had a crush on Detective Martinez. She probably wanted him to be on the cover of that book with her.

"What brings you into my little cave?" she asked, talking to Martinez, but still looking at me.

He pulled a paper out of his back pocket and smoothed it out on the counter. "Got a property release form." He slid the paper at her. She pushed her glasses up on her nose and studied it.

"Hollis case?" she asked. "You kidding?"

"Willis signed off on that property last night."

The woman frowned. "On an open case?"

"It's just property they've already cleared. Sitting around waiting for auction anyway."

"And it belongs to you, I assume?" she said, leaning so she could see me behind him. I started. I had no idea why we'd even come here. This was as much news to me as it was to her.

"Yep," he answered for me. Thank God.

She studied the paper again and then shrugged and pushed her chair back. "Just give me a few," she said.

She disappeared into the maze of shelves, shuffling slowly on sensible shoes. She had a bit of a limp, and I wondered if maybe this place was where they sent officers who were no longer able to do their duty on the streets. Or maybe she just liked it here; who knew?

Detective Martinez leaned on his elbows against the counter, casually watching her disappear. He turned to me and I gave him a questioning look.

"It's just a few things we took from the Hollis place and both apartments. It's been cleared as evidence and now is just sitting around waiting to be claimed. But we both know it isn't going to be claimed."

"What about Luna? Can she claim it?"

He shrugged. "She probably doesn't even know what we have and what we don't have."

"She's smarter than you think," I said. "No other family?"

"Not any that wants to get in the middle of a murder investigation."

"I guess that makes sense, but it's an awful lot of money to stay away from," I said. I heard the shushing of the woman's shoes coming back. She was pushing a cart with four boxes stacked on top of it.

"That's it?" Martinez asked. "You sure?"

"Everything else is evidence, honey. Beggars can't be choosers." She tapped a combination into a keypad and pulled open the door that separated us from the evidence. Detective Martinez held it while she pulled the cart out. "You need me to help you get it into your car?"

"We'll manage," he said. "But thank you for everything. I still owe you that lunch, don't I?"

She smiled wide, her hand fluttering around the buttons on her shirt. "I'm not holding my breath. Can't trust you superheroes, you know. Always having to fly off in the middle of the salad course."

"I'll make you eat those words," he said, grabbing the cart handle and pushing us toward the door.

"I'll believe it when I see it, sugar," she called back. The door shut behind us, cutting her off.

Martinez pushed the button for the elevator, and the silence stretched between us, a noticeable hum.

"What?" he said, when he caught me watching him.

"'Baby boy'? 'Honey'? 'Sugar'?" I mimicked the woman's voice.

He shook his head and rolled his eyes up to the ceiling, his hands pressed low on his hips. "She calls everyone those things. Nothing special about it."

"Whatever," I said. "She totally wants you."

"Would you lower your voice, please? I work here."

"Or what? You'll zap me with your superpowers, baby boy? Wrap me up in your cape?"

The elevator chimed and he pushed the cart in, barely leaving enough room for the two of us. "She's twice my age," he muttered, reaching across me to push the lobby-level button.

"Which is what, exactly?" I asked. He didn't answer. "I mean, I've always wondered. I saw you blushing in there. You seem kind of young to be a detective, is all. Isn't there some kind of, like, age requirement?"

He continued to stare daggers at me, until I was uncomfortable enough to let it go. "Whatever," I said again, under my breath. "Excuse me for thinking you're a regular human."

The elevator opened and we stepped out. Detective Martinez pushed the cart around to a remote hallway, and we went out a door that dropped us into the side parking lot. Our car was the only one in the lot. Detective Martinez pushed the cart to the car and started unloading the boxes, setting them on the sidewalk. My stomach tightened as I saw flashes of familiar color—the word *Hollis*, their address, Peyton's name, Luna's.

"You want to go through them now?" he asked.

"Right here?"

He looked around. "Why not? Nobody out here. I'm not saying we pull everything out. Just maybe give it a quick once-over, see what we see."

I lowered myself to the sidewalk and sat on my knees, running my hands across the top of a box. "Did Blake really sign off on these?"

He crouched next to me, never fully lowering himself onto the pavement. "She wasn't thrilled with the idea, but yes."

"Why?"

"Because I asked her to."

I cocked my head to the side. "Really."

"Yeah, Nikki. Because she knew it had already been dismissed as evidence. And because I asked her to. I know this is a foreign concept to you, but sometimes people are reasonable with each other. Makes the world run a lot more smoothly."

"Not my world," I said, although to be fair, it had been a long time since I was last reasonable. With anyone. Reasonable wasn't my style. Reasonable was dangerous. You start being reasonable and people will start walking all over you. That's just the way it is.

He pulled a knife out of his pocket and sliced through the tape. My palms got sweaty as he yanked open the box flaps. Was I ready for this? I wasn't sure.

Inside the box was a mishmash of clutter. Paperwork—letters and numbers jumping out at me in crazy colors—and tools and things I remembered from the pool house. Nothing useful, nothing that had anything at all to do with that night. Detective Martinez reached in and sifted through the paperwork.

"Bank statements," he said. "Bills, credit card statements. Personal accounting stuff. Looks like Dru's."

"What's that going to tell us—that he was behind on his cable bill when he died?"

Detective Martinez dug out another handful and flipped through those, too, ignoring me.

I reached over and yanked open a second box, ripping right through the tape without the knife. When I opened the flaps, my breath caught.

Mementos from Dru's apartment. A sparkling geode, a foot-tall tiki with a fearsome face, a piece of coral—from New Caledonia, he'd told me. I turned the coral in my hands, remembering the feel of Dru's touch, the smell of his skin. Detective Martinez wasn't looking, so I stuffed it in my pocket. It had been released to me, after all. It was mine, and I couldn't explain why, but I wanted a keepsake of Dru.

I reached into the box and scrambled things around

a little. I saw a Post-it pad, *You have an interview Monday. GO TO IT!*—V written on the top note. I'd seen that note before, in Dru's office. I blinked away the putrid brown that had dripped over the words like muddy rain. I was looking for evidence; I didn't have time to be sad.

I continued pawing through Dru's things, and a flash of maroon and black seared me back into a memory. Dru, standing in his apartment doorway, dropping something into his pocket. Something I'd found and he'd taken from me. Me, nauseated and short of breath, getting into an elevator. Me, certain for the first time that he was somehow involved in Peyton's attack. I knew exactly what that flash of maroon and black was. A camera card.

Frantically, I dug through the box until I saw it again, then picked it up and held it in the light. Was it the same one? Had he died for whatever was on this card?

"Find something?" Detective Martinez asked.

"I don't know. Probably not," I said. A gust of hot wind fluttered the pages in his hand. I lifted the hair off the back of my neck. "Can we do this another time? It's hot out here, and I would love to go home and take a shower."

He stood, stretching his quads. "Yeah. Good idea. I'll load the boxes if you want to take the cart back." He handed me his key card.

"Sure," I said, taking the card hesitantly. Not many people trusted me. It was hard to trust someone who kept herself as emotionally locked away as I did. In general, I didn't mind—after all, I didn't trust anyone else, either. But there was a feeling I couldn't describe when he handed me that card. Something between pride and incredulity. And a feeling that I wanted to do things right, even if I knew, in the back of my mind, that I would screw it up somehow anyway. I tucked the card, and the camera card I'd found, into my back pocket, and started to push the empty cart down the sidewalk.

"Twenty-four," he said to my back.

I turned, swiping at the chunk of hair that the wind was blowing across my face. "Huh?"

"I'm twenty-four," he said.

"That's it? I thought detectives were, like, old."

"I'm the youngest detective here. I worked hard and I'm good at it. Got where I am fast. It's not a big secret or a big mystery."

"Okay," I said, because I didn't know what else to say.

He picked up a box and carried it to the open car door. "Just thought you'd like to know I'm a regular human."

"Noted." I grinned. "I thought your superhero cape was in the car."

He paused. "I left it at home today."

"Nice to know, Twenty-Four." I turned and pushed the cart toward the door.

B Y THE TIME I got home, Dad had already returned
from the airport and was sitting in his office sipping
coffee and going over a spread of his latest shoot. He'd found
a new model—Marisol, her name was—and had taken her
down to El Matador to get some full-length shots for her
portfolio. They were stunning.

I was glad to see him doing something other than stress-
ing out about my life. No way could I ever tell him about the
predicament I was in. About the police *looking seriously at*
me. He was so worried about losing me the same way he'd
lost Mom, so worried that Luna Fairchild would somehow
come back and finish what she'd started that night in her
backyard, he would never live his own life. He would never

let me live mine. Which meant I would never find Rigo and clear myself. If Dad got involved, I might as well tell Blake Willis to put the handcuffs on me herself.

"Wow," I said, walking up behind him and picking up a photo of Marisol, covered in fine white sand, disappearing into the shadows of a keyhole. "These are amazing, Dad."

He turned, startled, nearly knocking over his coffee. "Hey, you're home."

"Grandparents gone already?"

"Winging their way to Arizona as we speak." He examined a photo. "I think I went too dark on some of these. What do you think?"

I picked up another. Marisol, back turned, a demure silken dress blowing across her body, like a princess being lured into a dark, evil cave. "No way, they're perfect. How old is she?"

He gave me a look. "I know what you're thinking, and too young."

I'd been bugging Dad to start seeing someone for years now. Not to replace Mom, but to fill some of the loneliness in his life. Until he moved on, I felt like I never would be able to; at least not guilt free. I would always have that feeling of having abandoned him. It wasn't fair. Plus, he was good-looking and bored and hanging out on a beach in Southern California with a beautiful model. There was no reason for him to be alone. And the more I could get him involved with someone else, the less time he would have for worrying about me.

I dropped the photos back on the table and held my palms up, innocent. "I wasn't thinking anything. Just . . . she looks a little older than your usual models, is all. Maybe early thirties, even."

He gathered the photos into a stack. "Well, she's not." He set them aside and gave me an appraising look. "You look terrible. But maybe not quite as hungover as I thought you might be."

I smacked him on the shoulder. "Thanks? I think?"

"So clearly you didn't get into too much trouble last night, then. No phone calls from the hospital or the police."

He was joking, but the laughter dried up in my throat. No phone calls from the police, because I didn't want him called. Because Detective Martinez bailed me out . . . once again.

Looking at his expectant face, his searching eyes behind the totally out-of-date glasses he wore when he wasn't wearing his contacts, I decided my first instinct was right. I couldn't tell him about last night. About Luna. About Peyton and Mom. About anything. He'd been so freaked out about everything that had happened with the Hollises, and how that had brought up all kinds of old fears that had to do with Mom, and he'd been so happy about my graduation— at dinner cracking jokes and bragging to everyone that I was now a graduate—there was no way I could break his heart with the truth. As far as he knew, Mom was devoted to him only. Why mess with that now?

I hated having so many secrets from him, but that was the way it had to be. For now. I would find a way to make it up to him later.

Besides, if Detective Martinez's plan worked out, we could find Rigo and clear my name before any formal charges were ever made. Before I went in front of a judge—or, dear God, a jury—to decide if I should live free or be locked up for what "I" did to Peyton Hollis.

God, would the tabloids get hold of this?

"So were the parties epic, dude?" he asked in his goofy "teen voice."

I laughed, wandered over to the other side of his office, where his old portfolios were stored. When I was a kid, I used to pull them out and leaf through the pages—choosing favorites, making up stories for the models. I hadn't looked through them in a long time, and they'd multiplied. It had happened so gradually. I hadn't really noticed, but Dad had thrown himself into his work since Mom died. I pulled a book off the shelf and opened it. It was from the late 1990s, maybe early 2000s—I could tell by the outfits on the models.

"I only went to one," I said, trying to sound distracted. Trying not to give away any of what had actually happened last night. "Mostly just people saying good-bye. You remember Jones?"

Dad made a smoochie face. "How could I forget? He's so dreamy."

"Stop." I flipped the page and looked at some more photos, then shut the book and slid it back onto the shelf.

Dad straightened up, trying—and failing—to look serious. "Sorry. Yes. I remember Mr. Muscles."

"Well, he was there last night. We kind of . . . got back together. Sort of."

Dad nodded appreciatively. "Kind of and sort of. Sounds like true love."

"Hardly." I pulled open a file cabinet, ancient film canisters rolling around inside, bumping up against random pens and pencils, old rolls of gaffer tape, battery grips and a gutted flash meter. The parts and pieces of Dad's job that I'd always found fascinating when I was a kid but had lost their luster as I'd gotten older. I rifled through it to make myself look busy. "More like just a way to pass the time."

"Until?"

I knew he was looking at me. I knew he was waiting for me to give him some kind of answer, a hint at what I planned to do now that I was out of high school. But I still didn't have one. Sometimes it felt like I never would. And especially not now, given what had happened. How could I plan a future with possible prison time looming in front of me? I kept my eyes firmly planted in the drawer, picking up and dropping erasers and paper clips and long-forgotten filters. I shrugged.

"Until summer's over, I guess. He'll probably go away to college or something anyway."

I slid the drawer shut and opened another. Just stacks of unusable photos. Nothing to fidget with there. I quickly flipped through them and placed them back in, then pulled open an overhead cabinet.

"You really need to clean out your office," I said, running my fingers along the spines of photography books.

"Ah. So this is where I'm supposed to let the subject be," he said. I could hear him unzip his camera bag, so I knew his eyes were no longer driving into my back.

"Yep."

"And when do you think we can have the 'what's next for Nikki' discussion?" he asked.

I closed the cabinet and opened the one next to it. "I don't know. Never?"

He chuckled. "That's my little go-getter." I heard another zipper loosen. "Listen, I know you don't want to think about your future. And there's a part of me that can't really blame you. You've been through a lot. I get it. School hasn't been easy for you, and maybe you want a little break, and that's fine. And there was the stuff with—"

He continued talking, but I tuned him out, my attention grabbed instead by a box tucked away behind *Irving Penn: Platinum Prints*. It was a white box, what looked like a large dress box or maybe a coat box. Old. Yellowed on one corner, like it had sat in a spill of some sort. The words *Carrie's Films* were scrawled on the side, my mom's name coming across, as it always did, in lavender. I touched her name and my fingers came away dusted with rusty peach and spearmint. A sherbet of nostalgia and curiosity. Why had I never noticed this box before?

"What is this?" I asked, interrupting him.

"Huh? Oh, that. Just some old films your mom made back when she was working at Angry Elephant. She was trying to learn. Wanted to work her way up, produce something of her own someday, I think. Mostly they're experiments. I haven't watched them all."

"Can I?" I started to pull the box down from the cabinet. It was heavier than I expected, and I almost dropped it. "I've never seen any of her work."

Dad rushed over and helped me push it back up onto the shelf. "Maybe when I clean out my office, we'll pop some popcorn and see what's there," he said. "It'll be good motivation to spruce up the place, don't you think? I'd . . . like to watch them with you, if that's okay."

There was something about the way he was looking at me—helpless and hopeful and so trusting, despite everything that had happened, holding Mom between us in that box. I was more certain than ever before that I couldn't tell him about Peyton's letter and my involvement in her case. Even if that felt like a huge lie and I knew he'd be so disappointed to find out that I'd hidden it from him, I just couldn't do it.

Which meant I *had* to make the problem go away.

Which meant I *had* to find Arrigo Basile and get proof that the Hollises were behind Peyton's death.

Dad had turned back to his photos of Marisol, and I headed upstairs to shower the beach party and jail cell grime off myself. Afterward, I slipped into some comfortable shorts and an old Go Sailor tee. I hadn't thought about it until after Peyton had been attacked and I'd watched all those videos of her band, trying to find dirt on Gibson Talley, but something about Viral Fanfare reminded me of Go Sailor's sound, and I spent a solid two months aching that I hadn't gone to see any of Peyton's shows. Maybe I would take Vee up on her invitation. It would be hard to listen to one of Luna's ridiculous cronies singing in Peyton's place, but it would still somehow make me feel closer to Peyton if I went. Maybe Future Nikki was a different Nikki. One who got out there and did things, who had a life that didn't revolve around anyone else's death. Maybe Future Nikki was a devoted sister.

I was tired—so tired—but also restless. I had told Detective Martinez I would wait to hear from him before doing anything, but that didn't mean I had to actually do it. He knew me—surely he didn't expect me to just sit back and let him take the lead. I sat at my desk and pulled up my laptop.

I had promised not to approach Rigo without him, but I could definitely look for dirt about him online.

The top five entries for "Arrigo Basile" were all about a major bust in the Basile family five years before. From the looks of things, some of Rigo's brothers, Lucca and Abramo, were imprisoned for running an illegal offshore gambling ring, along with a range of other Basile family members— Edmondo "Eddie Mon," Savio, Gulio "Jewels," and Sal. Why, I wondered, had Rigo been spared their fate? Or had he already been to prison and back out again? Had the Hollises helped him stay out or get out of trouble? It seemed likely, given what I now knew about their reach.

I found a smallish article buried amid all the scandalous ones. It was on a local blog called KnowLA. It featured various small businesses and local hangouts throughout the city. Their April 2010 feature was a downtown antique art store called Tesori Antico. It happened to be owned by one Zanobi Basile, the patriarch of the Basile family.

I knew the area. I closed my eyes and concentrated until I could "see" the store in my mind. When I opened them again, Tesori Antico jumped off my computer screen in dancing green—the color all foreign language words came to me. I had definitely seen this store before. I could picture the white, melon, and black adhered to the wall under the awning. 570. An address. And I knew exactly where it was.

I T TOOK A lot less time to find Tesori Antico than I'd thought it might. My instinct took me down only two wrong streets before my color memory brought me to it. As soon as I pulled up to the curb, the dancing green and the white, melon, black address clicked home just like I thought they would. I parked the car and looked around. The only other car was a van, parked in the tiny lot alongside the shop.

Inside, Tesori Antico was crammed with a captivating mixture of art, antiques, knickknacks, and plain old junk: menacing statues and old chairs, paintings of saints coming to their untimely, gruesome ends, gold filigree everything, and half-cracked vases that looked like they might hold the remains of distant kings. Rusty peach, tainted by putrid brown, hovered over me—a heavy blanket of color that threatened to steal my breath away.

I could see a glass case with a cash register on top of it, and hear the voice of a woman behind it, but there were about a zillion depressing and dusty and horror-filled things between me and her. Depressing and horror-filled things that I had to at least act like I was interested in owning.

I wove through the crammed aisles, afraid to touch anything, sure that my elbow would snag a grimacing gargoyle and the whole place would domino into a pile of broken shards. Still, at the same time, I was fascinated by the treasures, which seemed to have been artfully stuffed into every nook and cranny. Not artfully in a carefully considered way, but artfully in a carefully balanced way. Overhead, a violin-and-accordion instrumental softly whined, giving the whole place the feel of having stepped back into an old world. My footsteps felt loud in the empty store.

Empty store.

Rich L.A. women loved antique shit—why weren't there any of them shopping here? It was an unsettling emptiness, and I had to swallow against a lump in my throat, suddenly wishing I'd waited and come here with Detective Martinez instead of just by myself.

As I plowed through the store, the woman's voice became clearer—obviously the one-sidedness of a phone conversation.

"And they'll have it?" she said. A pause. "You've made sure?" Another pause. "No, no, as long as it's been found, we can take care of it. Okay, we will send someone." Pause. "One of the boys, yes, yes. Maybe I will go myself, just to make sure it doesn't get lost again. No, I'm writing it down now. Thank you for letting me know." She said her good-byes and set the phone on the counter.

I tore my attention away from the snarling lion statue at my knee. *One of the boys.* Was Rigo *one of the boys*? The woman looked up at me and I quickly turned my attention back to the shelf, picking up a glass paperweight that was filled with a mesmerizing pattern of shapes and colors.

"It's from the Rubloff collection," the woman said, making me jump. She did not smile or even try to look friendly. Her demeanor was more watchdog than salesman. "Very rare. A good price for a good find."

I nodded and turned over the paperweight. The sticker on the bottom read *Baccarat 1848 $3,000.* I nearly dropped the weight. Three thousand dollars? For a paperweight? Did people even use paperweights anymore? I set it back on the shelf. Even if I had three grand to blow on a ball of glass, I wouldn't have. And I didn't anyway, so it was a moot point.

I browsed some more, stopping to fiddle with a folding bellows camera.

"In working condition," the woman called.

Dad would have loved to own something like that, but

a quick glance at the price tag—*Early 1900s $800*—told me it, too, was out of my price range.

"You looking for something particular?" she asked when I stepped away from the camera.

I gave her a bored hand wave, trying to convey a wealth I most definitely did not have. "Just browsing," I said.

I picked up a few more things before finally landing on a figurine. An elephant made of blue glass. The tag on the bottom read *slag glass*, and I had no idea what that meant, but it was only twenty-five dollars, and I did have that much on me. Buying the elephant would give me a chance to talk to the woman, even if only for a second. Plus, it was kind of cute.

I took the elephant to the case and handed it over. The case was covered by porcelain tea sets and crystal lampshades. Inside, the shelves held trays overflowing with glittering costume jewelry set in tarnished mountings. They came at me in a multifaceted silvery glow. The cash register, sitting on top of the case, was simple and old-fashioned. A dusty credit card machine was pushed against it. The woman behind it was tiny and had full, graying frizzy hair and olive skin. Only when I was up close did I realize she was quite a bit older than I'd originally thought. Was this the matriarch of the Basile family? Zanobi's wife? Had she seen her sons go to prison? Did she know that one of them murdered a teenager? Maybe she was just as far in it as the rest of them.

"Trunk is up. That's good luck," the woman said as she hopped off the stool she'd been sitting on and took the elephant from me. She tapped the elephant's trunk, then immediately and expertly began wrapping it in paper.

"I need all the good luck I can get," I said, scanning the register area furtively, trying to block out the bric-a-brac and find something useful to go on. Loose papers, a spray can of furniture polish with a rag draped over the top of it, a silver bowl filled with peppermint candies—all normal business things. I tried to eye the little pad of paper that she had been writing on when I came in, but all I could see from my angle was a mishmash of colors—a couple of A's, the number 2, nothing really identifiable. To put the colors together into something that would make sense would mean I would need to lean over the counter, which I obviously couldn't do with the Basile matriarch standing two feet in front of me, talking about elephant trunks.

"Yes, we all could use more luck, I think," she answered, pulling out a receipt book. She scribbled something—I recognized the word *slag*—and totaled up the purchase with a quick stroke of her pen on the receipt—*pink-white-black*—then pushed a few buttons on the register and opened the cash drawer.

"Twenty-six eighty-seven," she said. I handed her two twenties and she made quick change.

Wait.

Pink-white-black.

Pink-white-black was not twenty-five. Pink-white-black was two hundred fifty.

Maybe I had seen it wrong? I squinted toward the receipt book. Pink-white-black clearly came back at me.

"Can I have a receipt, please?" I pointed at the ledger.

"Yes, of course," she said. But when she went to rip off the carbon, it wasn't there. "*Uffa!* Those boys, they never prepare the book correctly." She flipped the book open and pulled out the pristine carbon paper, which had been blocked from its partner by the cardboard separator that was meant to protect all the receipt carbons from picking up the writing on one receipt. "Here, let me write a new one." She bent over the carbon and wrote directly on it. $26.87—pink and green like Easter grass—just as she'd charged me. Definitely not pink-white-black.

She tore off the receipt. "There you go. Good as new." She attempted a smile, finally, but it only came across as an uneasy grimace. One that said, *Now, get out* much more than *Thank you, come again.*

As I studied the receipt in my hand, trying to brain out how I could have possibly mistaken the Easter colors in my hand to be pink-white-black—it was possible—she began rooting around beneath the counter.

She huffed. "They also never restock the bags. You want something done, you do it yourself, yes? I will get you one. Just a moment."

I nodded, distant, still studying the receipt. Had the carbons been mistakenly left under the cardboard, or had it been purposeful? And, if purposeful, why?

The woman scurried through a darkened doorway that was separated from the rest of the shop by a bamboo beaded curtain. It rattled when she pushed through, and I couldn't explain why, but the sound reminded me of something skeletal. Rusty peach and putrid brown enveloped each bead. Beneath the scent of lemon furniture polish lingered the must of antiques, which only served to further the creepy feel.

The deadly feel.

My heart started racing as crimson threatened to push in on me. I felt twitchy—as if Luna would suddenly appear from behind the bamboo, the skeletal rattle actually the crocodile sound of her cold eyes sizing me up.

Boo! Found you!

I glanced around. A phrenology head on the shelf to my left was smeared with a single drip of crimson. A centaur relief on the wall behind me floated in a crimson bath. Everything darkened, pushed out the peach and brown, bubbled up in gray and black.

I had to get out of there.

Now.

But I couldn't just go empty-handed. If I was going to come here—and most likely get my ass chewed by the detective for doing so—I had to come away with something to show for it. I snatched the woman's phone off the counter and thumbed it on. Fortunately, there was no password protection. I went to recent calls and mentally logged the colors of the last call received. White, white, white, sea green, bronze, white, purple. I repeated the colors to myself, then replaced the phone.

"Now where would you put the darned bags, Zanobi?" I heard the woman mumble from behind the curtain, punctuated by the industrious sound of drawers opening and closing. "I'll be right back with you," she called.

My eyes landed on a pad of paper. Whoever she'd been talking to when I'd walked in, she'd told them she was writing down whatever they were saying. Where she was sending *one of the boys*. Sure enough, the top sheet was a pulse of colors.

"Aha!" the woman said. "Found it!"

Boo! Found you!

Without thinking, I lunged across the counter, my shirt rising so that my belly pressed against the cold glass, and ripped the top sheet off the pad. Crumpling it in my fist, I crammed it into my front pocket. Stretched across the counter like that, my nose was practically in the receipt book. And

I had been right—pink-white-black. I didn't know what that meant, but I thought maybe it could mean something—if not to me, then maybe to Detective Martinez. I pulled out my phone, leaned over the counter, and snapped a photo of the receipt, then started to run. Two steps from the counter, I turned back and grabbed the wrapped elephant. I really did need all the luck I could get.

Crimson pushing at my feet, I raced out the door, nearly toppling over a mannequin head that was modeling a crusty feathered hat, and practically fell into my car. I dropped the keys on the floorboard and had to spend a terrifying minute searching for them.

I squealed away from the curb just in time to see the woman come to the front door. She gazed after my car, holding a stack of plastic bags. I'd seen crazy. Luna had come at me with fully loaded crazy. But somehow this calm detachment seemed to scare me a little bit more.

AFTER I GOT on the highway and had time to calm down, I told my Bluetooth to call Detective Martinez.

"I'm kind of in the middle of something here," he said by way of answering.

I ignored him. "Tesori Antico," I said. "Ring a bell?"

There was a pause, during which I swore I could hear him mumble an *excuse me*. "What about it?" he asked, his voice low and urgent. "Don't tell me you went there."

"Don't tell me you knew I would be walking into a mob house if I did."

"Don't tell me you didn't know that before going. Damn it, Nikki, I told you we would do this together."

"You move too slow," I said.

"Yeah, it's been a whopping few hours. You must be so frustrated that I haven't solved the case yet."

"Every hour counts," I said. "This is my life we're talking about here."

I heard a door close, and Detective Martinez's voice got louder. "That's right," he growled. "This is your life, Nikki. Not a game. You can't just go rushing into things all by yourself and expect everything to come out fine."

"But everything did," I said. "For all they know, I was just a random shopper." I tried not to think about the interested way the woman had watched my car pull away.

He sighed, the sound roaring through the phone into my ear. "So what did you find?"

"I have a phone number for you. Got a pen?"

"Go."

White, white, white, sea green, bronze, white, purple. "Five, five, five. Six, nine, five, three."

I could hear him mumble the numbers as he wrote them down. "And this number is?"

"Not sure. I only know that it's somehow related to this. Hang on." I edged to the side of the highway, turned on my flashers, and pulled the crumpled paper out of my pocket. I smoothed it on my leg. "You still there?"

"Where am I going to go?"

"Just checking. Jeez. Here." I read the blocky handwriting scrawled across the paper. Powdery tan, the color of moth wings, blinked out at me. The word *auction*. "There's an auction. Looks like it's Thursday night. Says Tesla here. What does that mean?"

"Tesla," he repeated. "As in Randall Tesla?"

"Who?"

"Randall Tesla. Serious wealth. Did he die recently?"

"How the hell would I know?"

"More importantly, what does this have to do with finding Rigo Basile?" Detective Martinez asked.

"I'm not sure," I said. "She said she was going to send one of the boys. Maybe we should be there."

"Maybe," he said.

A toilet flushed in the background.

"Wait. Are you in the bathroom?"

"Don't worry about where I am. I'm more worried about where you are."

I smiled, the nerves fading away a little. "Well, I'm not sitting on a toilet. Classy, Detective. Hopefully it's at least a halfway decent bathroom. You're not talking to me from a gas station urinal, are you?"

"If you must know, Nikki, I'm at dinner. With Blake. I

excused myself from the table when my phone rang."

"Ooh, romantic times, a date," I teased. "You know, you really shouldn't be answering other girls' calls when you're out with your girlfriend. It's kind of skeevy."

"Listen, Nikki. I want you to go home and . . . do something normal. Take a nap or watch TV or read a book or something. Forget about—"

"My potential murder charge? Oh, sure, okay, I'll just let that one go for now while I watch some romantic comedies. Maybe I'll make some cookies too, and then everything will really be okay."

"That's not what I mean."

"Well, come on, how do you expect me to just relax and pop in a movie? I could go to prison for life, Detective, as you have been so very eager to point out to me. And while you might be able to scarf down some cheese dip and margaritas with your squeeze, I can't do that."

He got quiet. "I know," he said.

"Luna is out there. So is Rigo."

"I know," he said again.

I drove for a good stretch, unsure how to force words past the lump in my throat. "I'm scared."

"I know."

I swallowed back the lump and rolled the window down to get some fresh air on my face. "But I'll go home so you can finish your dinner or . . . planning my case together or . . . whatever it is you and Blake are doing."

"That's not what we're doing," he said. "You know that."

I was reminded of lemonade and butter every time I thought of Detective Martinez. He was that trustworthy-yellow, inside and out. But something still felt wrong about knowing that he was sexing up the woman whose job was to put me away. Even if she claimed she didn't want to.

"Go enjoy your dinner, Detective. Let me know what you come up with on that number."

There was another hesitation, and then, "And you're going to stay safe and wait for me?"

"Sure," I said.

"You're going to stay away from the Basiles?"

"Yep."

As I pressed the button on my steering wheel to hang up, I turned my car in the exact opposite direction from my house. I was going to stay away from the Basiles, but I had no intention of going home.

I pressed the Bluetooth button again and said, "Call Jones."

11

"OH, JESUS," JONES said, lurching out onto his front stoop the moment he saw me. He wrapped me into a hug, a magenta blast. I couldn't breathe.

"Whoa, dude, okay," I said, pushing him away. "Let me live." I chuckled uncertainly as he stepped back and closed his front door. I could feel him trying to hold back his magenta so I wouldn't see it. He knew how that crap freaked me out.

"I didn't know if you got released or what," he said. He sounded out of breath, upset. "I was going to call your dad if I didn't hear from you by tonight."

Shit. This was the danger of letting Jones in. He was way too goody-goody, by the rules, Mr. I Genuinely Care About You. Of course he would call for backup. "No. Jones. Do not call my dad. For any reason. He doesn't know. And I don't want him to."

Jones searched my face uncomprehendingly. "He doesn't know what?"

"Anything. He doesn't know about any of it. I was supposed to be spending the night at a friend's house, so I just played it off like I had."

"Then how did you get out?"

I thought about Detective Martinez showing up at the jail, holding two coffees, and ushering me out to his car. For some reason—a reason I couldn't even explain to myself—this seemed like information Jones did not want to hear. "They let me go. Charges dropped."

"Charges dropped. Just like that." He grabbed my hand and guided me to the porch swing, just like we were in a dorky romance movie. Everything about Jones was a dorky romance movie. I wouldn't have been surprised if his mom came out with two iced lemonades on a tray for us. I sat, relieved to have somewhere safe to rest. My legs had never lost their noodly feeling from my shopping foray at Tesori Antico.

"I talked to the assistant DA about Peyton Hollis. The police think I murdered her." He jerked, surprised, his mouth dropping open. "I know this sounds totally cliché, Jones, but I'm innocent. I didn't have anything to do with Peyton's murder. Those drugs weren't mine, and I have no idea how

they got into my car. I think someone's trying to frame me."
I leaned into his chest. "You believe me, don't you?"

I could feel it through his skin—he would have believed anything I had to say. "Of course." He kissed me lightly. "You want to take a walk? Maybe shake some of the nerves off?"

I didn't. Walking in the open still made me feel a little too vulnerable. But he was right—I was pumped full of the jitters, and maybe a little fresh air would help calm me. "Sure."

Twenty minutes later, we were side by side on the bike trail behind Jones's house, our feet scuffing the dirt and gravel with each step. I hadn't worked out in months, and it felt good to get air pumping through my lungs again, even if it was just walking air. The old Nikki would have scoffed at calling a walk a workout. I felt a far-off itch to jam my elbow or fist into a sparring dummy. The feeling took me by surprise. I swept it away. Walking was one thing, but I wasn't ready for fighting yet. I strolled in silence, listening to Jones ramble on about everything that flitted through his mind.

"So my mom is starting to freak out about me going to college," Jones said. "She can't let go. Says I'll never come home again. It's just New Mexico, you know? But she's acting like it's the other end of the earth. She didn't bust her guts when my sister moved out. I don't get it. You'd think she'd be used to it. My sister says it's because I'm the favorite, but as you already know, my sister's a bitter person. But it's hard to argue, when our mom is acting like this. I swear if I told her I'd changed my mind about going to college, she would be thrilled. It's messed up. Isn't she supposed to want her kids to move out and have lives?"

"I think secretly my dad would be thrilled if I were going away, because it would mean I was doing something. Maybe we should get them together." I was only half joking. Jones's mom and my dad would make a good pair. If Jones's mom wasn't already married. And if my dad wasn't so dedicated to his loneliness.

"Have you figured it out yet? What you're going to do?"

We walked a few feet, a squirrel racing across our path. "Next subject," I said.

He paused. "Okay, how about the stuff that went down at the Hollises' that night? You've never told me about it."

"Not that subject."

"Come on, Nikki. Don't you think it's time? Especially now, if they're saying it was you."

"What is there to tell? You saw it all on the news, I'm sure."

"Yeah, but have you ever actually talked about it? To anyone? Luna Fairchild tried to kill you. She shot a guy right in front of you. And you're okay with that?"

"Of course I'm not okay with it. Christ, Jones, you know me. You know what happened to my mom. This whole thing scared the shit out of me. And now that it's over, I just kind of want to let it go. I need to get my life back."

"You're right, I do know you. And you're not working out. You're not doing tae kwon do. You're getting wasted at a beach party. Which tells me you haven't exactly let it go."

"I'll get back to my old self. Give me some time. I'm not a robot."

He slowed both of us to a stop and reached for my hands, but I pulled them away, aggravated. My chest felt full—full of fear and confusion and irritation and determination to chase those things away, even if I didn't exactly know how. Jones reached for my hands again and corralled them. He peered deep into my eyes.

"Can I help you, Nikki?" I started to protest, but he shook his head to interrupt. "No, I mean can I help you get past it? You want to let it go, let me help."

Jones was sweet. Too sweet. It irritated me. Which made me a bitch—I was well aware of that. But this was all getting too touchy-feely for me. All these men offering to help me. Didn't they understand that I didn't need any help? Even if it looked like I did.

"Walking helps me," I said, wrenching my hands free of him. I turned and started walking again, recognizing that my pace was too fast, nearly a jog, but too determined to get away from that sappy magenta puddle on the trail to notice.

Jones waited only a beat before hurrying to catch up

with me. "Okay, then we keep walking," he said. "If that's what it takes."

"In silence," I corrected.

"Sounds like fun." He was being sarcastic, but at least he stopped talking.

The trail curved into a wooded area and we curved with it, leaving behind runners and cyclists who took the short loop back around to avoid the woods. A veil of slate uneasiness dropped over the trees, making the whole world—the trees, the path, the foliage on the ground—feel like it was made of shale. Like I could go off the path and my footsteps would still sing out, I would still feel the impact of rock under them. The path was safe—I knew it was—but there was something about being secluded that bothered me.

She's also free and you're in jail. Blake Willis, in my head. I blinked hard, twice. I couldn't think about Luna right now, not when I was heading into the shadows of woods where the only person to hear me scream was Jones. He was strong and quick, but could he protect me from a bullet?

Dru did. And Jones probably would, too, if need be.

No. I refused to think about that.

"You okay?" Jones asked. "You slowed down."

"Just walk," I said.

Every step that hit the ground came with an image. Luna, standing over me in Peyton's closet. Luna, repeatedly slapping me in her parents' office. Luna, pointing a gun at my chest. Luna, springing out from behind a trash can. Luna, Luna, Luna, everywhere I looked. I stopped walking. Jones stopped with me.

"She's out," I said, my voice ragged. "She's everywhere." I tapped my temple. "At least she is in here."

"Who?"

"Luna Fairchild. She got out, and I see her everywhere. I feel like she's always right there, watching me. I can't explain it. I feel . . . stalked."

Jones stopped, looked around the woods, as if he could find her by looking hard enough. "Then the best thing you can do is this, right?" he said. "Live your life. No fear. And go back to the dojo."

"*Dojang*," I corrected.

"Do-whatever. Go back. I'll go with you."

"Okay," I said, after a pause. "I will. But just me. I don't want company."

We walked the rest of the way out of the woods, both of us sneaking glances behind every tree, while trying to pretend that we weren't. Jones went back to yammering on about his life, and I thought about what it would be like to get back to sparring. I was going to get my ass handed to me, but Jones was probably right. Especially with Vanessa and Bill and now Luna still out there. I needed to get back to who I was.

We finished the trail and walked back to Jones's house. I

let him wrap me up on his porch, leaning into his scent and his muscles. Jones could be very annoying, but he wasn't all bad. He was safe, at least.

"I've got this taken care of, and you don't have to worry. I'm not going to prison." I reached up and stroked his cheek with my hand, violet arcs raining down on me.

"Of course you're not," he said. He leaned in to kiss me, and a few minutes later, when he led me upstairs, motioning for me to be quiet because his parents were home, I went willingly, happily.

Jones loved me.

If it were possible for me to love, he would have been the perfect person to fall for.

If it were possible.

LUNA WAS LIVING at her father's house. Peter Fairchild—a car salesman with a tidy turquoise house in Mar Vista. A total unknown. Didn't even have a Facebook page. According to Vanessa Hollis's Wikipedia page, Peter had been married to her for a whopping sixteen months before she decided to leave him and Luna behind for bigger and better things in Brentwood. My guess, the bigger and better thing was a certain john she'd met at her escort service, Hollywood Dreams. A very rich, very powerful movie-mogul john named Bill Hollis.

Luna didn't burst onto the Hollis scene until she was twelve, which told me she'd most likely lived in said ordinary turquoise house for the first twelve years of her life before something must have happened to make Peter give her up. Maybe they'd had a fight. Maybe Vanessa had decided she wanted to parent her own daughter after all. Maybe Luna just insisted. Everyone knew Luna got exactly what she wanted, exactly when she wanted it, even if that meant she had to hurt people to get it.

So now Luna was back in her boring, ordinary, non-Hollywood life, with her boring, unknown, non-Hollywood father, which couldn't have been working out for her at all. Maybe it made her so miserable she was willing to plant evidence in her sister's car.

Not maybe. Likely. But how?

My phone buzzed. A text from Detective Martinez. His date with Blake must be over.

Matt Macy

I frowned, trying to figure out what he meant.

Come again?

The phone number you gave me. Belongs to someone named Matt Macy. No known connections to Rigo as far as I can tell. Ring any bells?

It did, actually. I just couldn't place it. Matt Macy—soft red-orange and ringed with maroon, kind of like a sunset. Where had I seen that before? I closed my eyes and tried to envision the color combination, tried to associate it with an anchor. Something, anything.

It came to me—pink-white-black.

I scrolled over to my camera roll and pulled up the photo I'd taken of the receipt book at Tesori Antico. Next to it, half under it in a scatter of papers, was red-orange ringed with maroon. Of course, the maroon. Maroon meant technology.

He's a photographer, I texted.

Photog? Make sense to you?

Commercial photographer. Idk.

Maybe it means nothing. Dead end.

Yeah.

But I couldn't help thinking that almost nothing meant nothing when it came to the Hollises. Everything was connected; I could just never see exactly how. I tossed my phone on my desk with a frustrated grunt and rolled away from it. I'd told myself that after I was done reading what I could about Peter Fairchild, I would go to the *dojang*. But now that I was done, all I could do was stare at my gym bag, feeling helpless. I hated this.

I couldn't just keep going like I was going. Afraid to move, afraid of everything and everyone. It wasn't like me. At all. I had to start doing something before I lost Nikki Kill completely.

For the first time in months, I pulled open my bottom desk drawer. The black binder I'd slipped Peyton's letter inside was still there. I stared at it. I'd tucked the letter away when the nightmares had kept me up one night too many. When I'd realized that I wasn't going to just go on about my life, searching for answers the way I thought I would. The letter had sat folded up on my desk, practically glowing at me, getting bigger and bigger, scarier and scarier every time I looked at it. One night, feverish and shaking from a nightmare—or a memory; sometimes it was hard to tell which was which—I'd gotten up and buried it in the binder. Out of sight, out of mind.

But of course I knew it was always there, waiting for me to come back. It would never be out of my mind.

Because eventually I would have to go back to it, right? I couldn't hide from myself, my past, forever. Eventually, I had to help Peyton on Peyton's terms instead of just my own.

I pulled out the binder and set it on my lap. I ran my

hand over the cool cover, feeling for heat or vibration or some sense that the letter was in there. That the colors were still beating inside, even if I couldn't see them. Of course I felt nothing but vinyl. I opened the binder and pulled out the letter, nearly gasping at the rainbow that leaped out at me, even though I knew it would be there.

Nikki,

    I'm putting a ton of faith in your synesthesia right now, but if I'm right about what you can do, you're reading this letter.

    So basically this is one of those if-you're-reading-this-I'm-probably-dead letters. I've known you were my sister for a while now. I even watched you a little at your house, at school, stole your records from the guidance office, that kind of thing, trying to decide how, and when, to tell you. But I started discovering other things, too. Things about my family. I was afraid of putting you in danger. I finally decided I would write this letter and leave you clues, and would only bring you into this if things had gone really wrong and my life was on the line. So you'd think I'd be really scared writing this letter, but I'm kind of not. I've been scared for a long time. Scared of where my life was going, thanks to the people who raised me. Scared of who, or what, I will become. Writing this letter is actually a relief.

Everything about the Hollis family is a lie. We are not who the world thinks we are. We have secrets, Nikki, and they're bad. And when I say "we" I actually mean we. Including you, Nikki. Maybe you've figured this part out already, but if you haven't, I'll tell you now. Your mother, Carrie, was my mother, too. I know this because I've followed a very long trail of deceit. But I've included in this letter a lock of my hair, just in case you want to have it tested for DNA to be sure. I don't need to see a DNA test. I already know.

It all started when a woman named Brandi Courteur came to one of Viral Fanfare's shows in Long Beach. I can't tell you anything more about Brandi because it will be very dangerous to her if this letter should fall into the wrong hands. I know that sounds very mysterious, but if you're reading this, you obviously can do mysterious. Let me just say that what Brandi told me after that show changed my whole life. My entire life was a lie. Fake. A show. Everything started to make so much more sense. And I learned things about my father, about Vanessa, that could ruin them.

Find Brandi, Nikki. When you do, you will understand everything.

Also, take care of Dru. I've told him about his own mother, but he's still in denial. He's still trying to please dear old Daddy. He doesn't know what he's doing, but he's good on the inside. I know this because we've lived the same lie.

Peyton

Brandi Courteur. According to Peyton, Brandi Courteur, whoever she was, had answers. I wasn't sure if I wanted them yet. Or ever. But part of me felt obligated to try. Peyton had died getting these secrets to me. The least I could do was try to find the woman who started it all.

I pulled up my laptop again and entered Brandi Courteur's name.

As before, nothing came up. How was that possible? It seemed like by now, everyone in the world should have some sort of online trail, even if it was small and insignificant. It was as if the woman didn't exist. Even more unknown than poor old Peter Fairchild.

I tried Brandie Courteur. Nothing.

I searched Facebook and Twitter and every possible social media site I could think of. Brandy Courteur, Brandie Courteur, Brandi Corter. Nothing, nothing, nothing. I tried the white pages. I tried the yellow pages. I tried birth parent search sites. I tried personal ads. No Brandi Courteur. Not anywhere.

She wanted to be hidden, and hidden well. So why she reached out to Peyton—why she insinuated herself into the Hollises' lives—made no sense whatsoever.

After an hour, or longer, my eyes felt dry and tired. My head felt heavy, my brain exhausted from trying to block out letter and number colors so I could concentrate. I put the letter back inside the binder and stored it back where it had been before, in the bottom desk drawer. I closed my laptop and walked over to my bed, flopping backward on it, letting my arms fall over my face. I didn't intend to, but I slept the whole night that way.

DETECTIVE MARTINEZ CALLED bright and early the next morning, waking me up.

"Don't you know what summer break means?" I asked thickly, my eyes closed, refusing to welcome the world. I fumbled in my nightstand drawer for a cigarette. Sometimes I felt more awake just holding one, even if I was too lazy to get up and light it.

"Summer break is for people who aren't looking at murder trials," he said. "Get up."

I groaned and sat up, glanced at the time on my phone. "Jesus, it's five thirty. What is your deal?"

"We need to talk."

"Why?"

"Get up and I'll tell you."

"It's five thirty. I'm not getting up unless you know something." I tucked the unlit cigarette into my mouth.

"Would I be calling you if I didn't?"

"Well, you can't come over here. Not this early. My dad isn't the most observant person in the world, but he would definitely notice a cop showing up at the table for coffee and toast."

"I wasn't going to come over there."

"What, then? Breakfast? I don't generally eat before the sun is up. It's bad for digestion."

"Stop being such a drama queen. The sun is up. It's not that early. I had something a little more active in mind."

DETECTIVE MARTINEZ'S "GYM" was a glorified hole in the wall. Buff-looking gorilla types sauntered in and out, their arms so built up they couldn't press them flat against their sides. I sat in my car, imagining the smell inside that place. It had to be rank with testosterone and sweat. And ego. Smelly man-ego.

Why on earth had I agreed to meet him here? If I was smart, I would turn my car back on and leave. He didn't have any control over me. He didn't get to say when and how and where I got back to working out or getting on with my life. It wasn't up to Jones, it wasn't up to my dad, and it sure as shit wasn't up to him.

I was so lost in my own thoughts, I didn't even see him pull up. Didn't realize he was there until he knocked on my window, jarring me. I rolled it down.

"You getting out anytime soon?"

"Why wouldn't I?"

He shrugged; his T-shirt stretched across his shoulders and pecs. The sleeve inched upward, showing the bottom inch of a tattoo on one bicep. "I don't know. Scared, maybe?"

I made a *pssh* sound. "Scared of you? In your dreams, Detective." I let myself out, forcing him to back up a few steps. His legs were tan and scarred, not too hairy, tight with muscles, poking out from under his shorts. "Unless you meant scared of making you look bad. Again."

He grinned, the tops of his cheeks nudging his sunglasses upward. "That's exactly what I meant. You keep telling yourself that." He gestured toward the door with his gym bag. "After you."

"First, what is it you have to tell me that's so important?"

He ducked his head. "Nothing. I just told you that to get you out of bed. I knew you would never come with me if I didn't dangle a carrot in front of your nose."

"Nice," I said. "Really freaking nice. I could be sleeping right now." He tried to cover up his laughter, but failed. "You're a real asshole, you know that? Psychopath."

I pushed past him, letting my shoulder bump into his, and strutted into the gym like I owned the place.

There were a few weight benches off to one side with racks of free weights nearby, a couple of treadmills, and one stair climber. But mostly the room was dominated by heavy bags. Row after row of them, like we were in a damn Sylvester

Stallone movie or something. A few speed bags hung like teardrops along one wall, and back in the corner there was a boxing ring, inside of which two huge men were currently beating the crap out of each other, a couple of trainers yelling instructions at them from the perimeter.

"This?" I asked. "This is where you work out?"

"Every day," he said.

"No wonder you're no good at sparring," I mumbled. "This is shit."

"This *shit*, as you call it, kept me out of a lot of trouble over the years. Been coming here since I was a kid. It was a good way to burn off some steam without ending up in jail." He pulled off his sunglasses and slid them into his duffel, then gestured with his head for me to follow him to a nearby bench. "Come here, I'll set you up."

"What makes you think I need to be 'set up'?"

"Okay," he said, handing a rolled-up strip of cloth to me. "Wrap yourself." When I didn't move, he grinned and took it back. "That's what I thought. Hold your hand out like this." He spread his fingers wide, palm up. I mimicked him and he began winding the cloth around my hand, between my fingers and over my palm. The cloth was beige. But it turned violet with every loop around my hand. I watched the guys in the ring to distract myself.

"We going to do that?" I asked. "Because if I'm being honest, I don't think you're really up to it."

"Oh, I'm more than up to it," he said. "Get more up to it every time you open your big mouth. But I thought we'd start a little slower." He nodded toward the heavy bags. "Get you back on the horse and all that. Give me your other hand."

I squeezed my wrapped hand into a fist, liking the way it felt—tight and tough. He held up a second wrap and I took it from him. "I watched you. I've got this."

"That's the Nikki I know."

"Miss Kill to you," I reminded him, for old times' sake.

He nodded to himself, pulled another wrap out of his bag, and began winding it around his own hand. "I stand corrected."

TWO HOURS LATER, Detective Martinez and I sat on the bench, unwinding the wraps from our hands. My arms were jelly and my hair was soaked with sweat, but I felt good. I wasn't used to hitting the way he showed me to hit the heavy bag, and the gloves felt hefty and clunky on my hands, but there was something satisfying about letting loose a blizzard of punches without scraping up my knuckles.

"So what's the plan?" he asked. He picked up the wadded wrap mess I'd let drop at my feet and began patiently rolling it.

"What plan?"

"Don't play with me. I know you. There's always a plan. So what is it?"

"Maybe you're wrong this time."

He finished rolling the wrap and dropped it into his bag with the other wraps, then leaned down and picked up the second one, which I'd dropped in exactly the same place. I snatched it from him. "Here. Let me."

"I'm not wrong. And you'll save us both a lot of hassle if you will just tell me what you're going to do next so I can tell you you're crazy and try to talk you out of it and you can ignore me and do it anyway, and I can plan my evening around sitting in a parking lot, wishing you weren't so hard-headed."

I snorted. "Pretty accurate, Detective."

"I know. So what is it?"

"Well." I paused while I finished rolling the wrap, then handed it to him. "I hadn't really solidified it into an actual plan yet, but I was sort of thinking our business has some photography needs."

His hand froze over mine. "What?"

I shrugged. "We should probably get an appointment with Matt Macy, commercial photographer, to help us market our business."

"We don't have a business."

"You're terrible at imagination, did you know that?"

"Doesn't it make more sense to just go question him on record?"

I rolled my eyes. "Because he's just going to tell you

exactly how he's involved with a murderous couple of families. And even if he's not, he at least talks to the Basiles. I would guess he would be super excited to share with them that the cops questioned him. Have you learned nothing yet? Besides, the Hollises are ghosts. Nobody ever knows anything about them. Everyone covers for them."

"He's just a photographer. He really may know nothing."

"Which we won't know until we go look around the place a little bit. As budding entrepreneurs. Of . . . artisan soaps."

He squinted at me. "Soaps."

"Or pot holders or pillows. I don't know. I don't even care. We aren't actually going into business. We're just going into his business."

He looked at the ceiling, his jaw working. "And this doesn't seem the least bit deceitful or potentially dangerous to you? Because it feels like that to me."

"Which was why I wasn't going to tell you about it. Now you see." I tapped my temple. "Not hardheaded, just practical." I picked up my gloves and handed them over. He tucked them into his duffel.

"And a little bit stupid, you know that, right?"

I placed my hand over my heart. "That would hurt. If I cared what you thought."

"And if I say no to this idea?"

I shrugged. "I'll go without you."

"If I let you."

We went out into the parking lot. It was true that I hadn't solidified the plan. I hadn't even really considered it an actual plan until I was saying it out loud. But after seeing his reaction, hearing his doubt and his name-calling and his Neanderthal notion that he could stop me from doing something I wanted to do, I decided it was something that had to happen as soon as humanly possible.

"I'd like to see you try to stop me," I said.

Truth was, he could probably keep me from doing anything he wanted to keep me from doing. He had boxed circles around me, hitting the heavy bag so hard the chain holding it to the ceiling rattled, then pummeling the speed bag in a steady rhythm that forced me to stop and watch, his biceps curled into themselves, sweat soaking into his shirt, the tattoo more visible, yet still too blurred to make out. There was no way I could outbox him, and it made me wonder how much he'd held back when we were sparring, but it felt like enough of a personal victory to just get out there and hit something again, without seeing Luna's crazy face or hearing Dru's dying breath. It felt like a win to dare someone to slow me down.

He said nothing.

"Good," I said. "I'll call and make an appointment."

13

EVEN THOUGH IT was only June, it was already hot outside. Fire was the only color I could think of when I thought of heat—not a color, but a mix of ever-changing colors that were sizzling on my cheeks and the tops of my ears. I didn't even want to smoke when it was this hot. I could feel the backs of my legs sweat against the leather seats in my car. I pumped the air conditioner up to full blast, aiming it right at my face. I also pumped up the music to help me think. Sometimes, the buzz of a guitar could distract me from my synesthesia long enough for me to have a coherent thought. If my teachers had let me listen to music in class, I might have been a better student.

I thumbed on my Bluetooth while navigating to the

pharmacy and cranked up the volume so I could hear over the air-conditioning. I dialed in Matt Macy's number, and while I waited for the line to connect, my heart raced with fear that somehow he would know I was being dishonest. That I would show up at his studio only to find Luna there, ready to finish what she'd started in her backyard. But I figured I'd been required to do much more complicated things on the fly and had done just fine. Apparently, I was a hell of a liar.

The phone rang four times before anyone picked up, and when it finally clicked alive, the voice on the other end was polished, businesslike.

"Macy Photo."

A shot of silver squiggles coursed through me. My voice threatened to stay locked inside me. I cleared my throat. "Hi, my name is Ava Glass. I understand you can help me with my marketing campaign. . . ."

STEPPING OUT OF the cool car into the heat felt like a furnace blast to the face, and I hurried across the parking lot into the refrigerator-like atmosphere of the pharmacy. I couldn't remember the last time it had gotten this hot in Brentwood.

I found a photo kiosk and slid the camera card I'd taken from the evidence box into the slot. It may have been a dead-end clue—probably was—and I hadn't even bothered to tell Martinez that I was pursuing it, but I'd been wondering exactly what Dru was hiding when he stuffed this card into his pocket the night Luna poisoned me. It was a little like picking a scab; I had to know.

It only took a few taps on the screen to pull up the photos. I leaned in and squinted, even though the colors jumping out on them told me what they were right away.

Black and white, Peyton knee-deep in water, a life preserver looped over one arm. *SOS*. I knew this photo almost as well as I knew my own face. I'd studied it and studied it while Peyton was still fighting for her life. A few photos later, a family picture, standing on a pier. After that, Peyton at a bus stop, *Fountain View* peeking out from behind her head in the same blue I associated with all water words.

This was definitely the card from Peyton's camera.

And there were more photos on it. A lot more. Photos that must not have made the cut in Peyton's clue-dropping. Still, I'd brought them here; I might as well look at them. I scrolled all the way to the bottom and decided to work my way up.

Most of them were from school—Peyton posing with friends, smiling wide, her arms around some lucky admirer's shoulders. Whoever she had deigned to pay attention to that day looked as if they'd won the lottery. All of them. I could feel the admiration oozing out of the kiosk screen— not quite grapey; more like mulberry, a dizzy wine.

There were some photos of Viral Fanfare. Everyone looked happy. Everything looked fine. Peyton's hair was long, her neck bare, her clothes designer grunge. Marc Jacobs skirt. Alexander McQueen shirt. Rips and frays strategically placed. This was clearly before her infamous freak-out.

But as the time stamp on the bottom right-hand corner of the photos got later in date, they began to change. They got darker, more abstract. No more were photos from parties and Homecoming and lazy days at the beach. Now there were close-ups of cigarettes in wrinkled mouths, a man's belt curled up on nubby carpet next to a high school sweatshirt. The front of what I now knew to be Hollywood Dreams, Vanessa Hollis's secret little family escort service, with the bottom of Bill Hollis's shoe poking out through the front door. Dumpsters and broken glass and a briefcase full of pills. Me, leaving my locker, my face pointed to the ground. A tattoo chair with ink spilled on the seat. Someone—Peyton, perhaps—had written the word RUN in the ink with her finger. The ink was black, but the word RUN was airy blue and white, almost like a cloudy sky. I didn't like the way the juxtaposition made my head feel, so I quickly scrolled up to bury it at the bottom of the screen.

There were several photos of a building—a warehouse with graffiti on the side. An amazing portrait of Jimi Hendrix. I chuckled. Some people postulated that Jimi Hendrix had been a synesthete. In case I hadn't picked up all her other clues, Peyton had left me this glaring synesthetic message. The graffiti artist had scrawled the words *PURPLE HAZE* next to Jimi's head—one of the few phrases in my mind that actually looked exactly like what it said it was. Peyton had known what she was doing. This was practically a billboard: *Hey, dummy! I'm a synesthete, too!* I supposed if I'd taken longer to figure it out, this was meant to be my final clue. The load of bricks over my head.

There were a few more shots of the building, from different angles. In each of them Jimi stared out at me. A bird sat on a window in two of them and was midflight in the third. A van had pulled in front of Jimi on the last one, blocking out the bottom half of his face. The changes in the photos gave the scene a feeling of movement, like I was watching a video rather than looking at still shots. If she was trying to show me something more than the synesthesia link between us, I couldn't see it.

I scrolled up until I was back to the photos Peyton had begun sharing on her aesthetishare.com account. The photos I knew so well.

These were Peyton's pictures. She had been trying to make a case with them. A case that only I would understand.

"Can I help you?" I turned and a smocked employee was standing behind me, smiling pleasantly. I jumped, almost feeling like I needed to cover the screen—to shield her from seeing the evidence Peyton had left behind. But there was no evidence here, was there? To this woman, these would look like any other amateur photographer's photos of city life.

The thought flitted through my mind that maybe that was what they were, and I'd only gotten lucky in following them to answers before.

No. Dru stole these photos. There was something to them, and he knew it.

"Do you need help?" the clerk repeated, pointing at the kiosk.

"No," I said, popping the card out of the machine. I held it up. "Brought the wrong card. I've already had these put on a CD. Duh." I tried to let out a goofy-me laugh, but it only came out sounding more like a croak. "I'll come back."

"Sure," the clerk said. "We have a sale on candy bars, if you're interested."

"No. Thanks, though." I shoved the card back in my pocket and started toward the door, but then turned back. "Actually, I'm not sure where that CD is. Maybe I ought to have these printed. Can you do that?" I handed her the memory card, not wanting to let it out of my hands again, but for some reason certain that I would someday need these photos.

It was a hunch. I could almost hear Detective Martinez say it: *You and your hunches.*

14

"ARE YOU SURE you're up for this?" Jones asked as he turned off Brentwood Boulevard toward Lone Tree Way.

I rolled my eyes. "For the thousandth time, yes." I flipped down the visor and studied my face in the mirror. There were dark circles under my eyes; I pressed my fingers into them. When did I get so rough-looking? Probably when I stopped sleeping. Again. "What I'm not up for is another nine hours of sitting in your bedroom with you looking at me like I'm already on death row."

Which was exactly what we'd been doing since I got to his house after leaving the pharmacy—lying on his bed, his chest deliciously bare and warm, but ruined by the magenta that pressed into my brain, swirled with slate wisps of worry. Every so often he would click his tongue and shake his head ruefully, or run his finger down my arm like he was afraid I would slip away at any moment.

And the questions. He would not stop with the questions. *What are you going to do, Nikki? Aren't you afraid of prison? What if they really put you away? Is that detective helping you at all? What's the point of having him around if he's not even helping you? Are you scared? Do you need to cry?*

I wanted to pummel the questions out of his face. Instead, I pulled up Viral Fanfare's Facebook page on Jones's computer to see when their next gig was. They were doing an open show tonight at a bonfire party. Thank God. Something to do to take my mind off Luna and Rigo and Peyton and Dru and the weird connection with Brandi Courteur. It seemed like I almost couldn't remember a time before the Hollis mess was all I thought about.

As soon as the sun fell, I'd pressed Jones into taking me. And being Jones, who would do anything I asked, he got dressed and out to the car in record time.

"Fair enough," he said, lifting his hands off the steering wheel momentarily, and then putting them back on. He turned down a gravel road. "But if it gets to be too much for you and you need to leave . . ."

"I'll be fine," I snapped. "Stop treating me like an invalid. It's really annoying, Jones."

He looked like he wanted to say something but instead bit his lip. He probably wanted to forgive me for lashing out at him. In which case it was a good thing that he changed his mind. I was constantly reminded of why we'd broken up in the first place. It was so hard to hang on to the fun violet sensations when he was so very needy. I didn't want him to need forgiveness. I wanted him to throw things back in my face. To challenge me. To call me on my bullshit. To be like . . . like Dru.

Not for nothing, Nikki, but also like Detective Martinez.

We bumped along the road, peering into the night, little pieces of gravel dinging the sides of his car. It was dark here. Country. The houses were spread apart, sprawling, hidden behind groves of fir and cedar and pine trees. Each house butted up to undeveloped land—lots of it—which was undoubtedly why Viral Fanfare chose to play there.

"I haven't seen the band since Peyton . . . ," Jones started, and then, realizing his mistake, trailed off.

"It's okay, you can say it," I said. "I haven't seen them since Peyton died, either." In all honesty, I hadn't seen them play live, ever. I wasn't high enough on the popularity list to be seen at a VF concert. I didn't live in a mansion and my daddy didn't drive a Lambo. I was too combat-boots-and-thrift-store for the lip-gloss-and-boutique crowd.

But something had happened when Peyton died. I'd told myself that I was every bit good enough to go wherever

I damn well pleased, even if it meant I didn't exactly fit in with the it crowd. Because, as Peyton showed me, you never know what the it crowd is struggling with at any given moment. The it crowd could be completely miserable.

Or in trouble.

Big, deadly trouble.

Besides, Vee had invited me. And being here made me feel close to Peyton. And it was a free fucking country.

"Truthfully, I think there's no way they can be as good without her," Jones said. "She was a snotty girl, but she knew how to sing."

"I'm sure they wouldn't replace her with someone who can't sing," I said. I pointed toward a house hidden behind some trees. "It's up here."

Jones parked along the side of the road, with about fifty other cars. It was like graduation night all over again—everyone in Brentwood at the same party, the music a buzz that could be felt through the car seats—and I shivered a little, remembering the feeling of the handcuffs around my wrists, the red of police cherries bouncing off my skin.

This wasn't going to be like that. I was determined.

The minute we stepped out of the car, we could feel the music. It was a thrashing, speeding, heavy sound, like chain saws and jackhammers being thrown down a well. Behind it all, I could hear a high voice, strangely melodic, ethereal, out of place. It made ragemonster red wobble in my temples. I pressed my fingers against them to stop it.

So Viral Fanfare had changed their sound. I'd never seen them live, but I'd watched enough YouTube videos to know that Peyton's voice was sharper, more assured, the heavy punk downbeat the star, not the guitar. I supposed Gibson decided to finally take over the band in her absence—of course he'd make the guitar the star.

The house was lit up, but there was nobody inside. I had no idea whose house it was, or if it even belonged to anyone I knew. It didn't matter. We were all here now. It was ours. For a few hours, at least.

We walked around to the back, and then to the back-back, behind the trees, following the glow and smoke of a bonfire. Beyond the fire were dozens and dozens of coolers lined up, dozens and dozens of people surrounding them. And about forty paces away was a short, portable riser with a river of extension cords flowing to it, Viral Fanfare furiously scrubbing out a song, and even more people dancing in front of the stage. Or more like jumping and thrashing to the beat.

Jones peeled off toward the kegs, while I tried to shake the melted cherry Popsicle tension from myself as I walked closer to the stage. My teeth practically vibrated the closer I got, and I stayed off to the side, to avoid getting whipped by someone's hair or getting an elbow to the eye.

The music was good. Not as good as when Peyton was

singing it, but it was still good. Edgy. Tight. I could see them getting a record deal any day now, which I knew was huge to them.

The song worked its way up to a feverish instrumental showcase, and I watched as Seth pounded away on the drums, sweat flying off him, his bare chest so slick it shone. He volleyed over to Gibson, who wore only a Speedo and a pair of cowboy boots, his green Mohawk so stiff it could've been a weapon. He drained chords out of his guitar like a plug being pulled from a bathtub, and then it was Vee's turn. Bass solos were usually pretty short, and Vee was no exception. She stared straight down at her hands as she plucked the strings. When she was done, she flipped her hair off her forehead and stared into the crowd, immediately locking eyes with me. She smiled and tipped her head, and then was thrust back into the music as the song crescendoed its way to the end. I found myself loosening up, bouncing a little to the beat.

Suddenly, I was gripped with a feeling of being watched. The hairs on the back of my neck stood up and my mood washed over with a mint-green hue. Slowly, I turned circles, studying each body, each face, as well as I could. But it was hard work, locking in on individual features in the rotating colored lights and the wildly dancing people. Nothing. There was nothing. I was being paranoid. Letting the whole Luna's-out-of-juvie thing get to me.

But I couldn't shake the feeling, and soon my colors were confusing me—was I seeing crimson in my mind, or was that just one of the stage lights? I squinted, moved through the crowd, feeling pulled and strangely numb. Gold fireworks popped in my head, and that time I knew the culprit was my own adrenaline. I needed to get control of myself. I couldn't keep jumping every time my synesthesia dumped a little mistaken green on me. After what had happened at Hollis Mansion seven months ago, it would be normal for my colors to be off. With some dedicated work, I could make it better. At least that was according to the shrink Dad made me see. For exactly three sessions before I knocked his bullshit textbooks off the coffee table and told him to peddle his happy crappy to someone else. I was too angry for therapy. And he was too right.

Just to be sure, though, I plowed through the crowd, getting bumped, taking shots to the ribs, the back, not feeling any of it. I focused in on every blond, and suddenly it seemed like every girl around me was fair-haired.

Luna.

She was in my head. I couldn't get her out. I just wanted her out.

The song finished and the crowd stopped moving, erupting into cheers that made me wince. I kept walking, focused, taking in faces, as the singer talked, her mouth too close to the microphone. Every so often someone would whoop nearby and I would swing around, my heart in my throat, my hands balled into fists, only to find a surprised face—not Luna's face, not Luna's—peering back at me.

I was just coming out on the other side of the throng when I felt a hand clamp down on my shoulder. Without even thinking, I dropped low and spun, my fists out in front of me to protect my face.

"Whoa! Easy there, slugger! Let me live!" Vee, laughing, held up her hands to ward me off. "Jumpy much?"

I let my hands fall to my sides and shook out my fingers, trying to get feeling back in them. The fireworks pop-pop-popped into a fizzle. I tried to let out a laugh, but it only came out in a couple of short, sharp breaths. "Hey."

"So?" Vee asked, her eyebrows going up.

"So . . . ?" I flicked a quick glance over my shoulder. I couldn't help it—the feeling was still there.

"So what did you think?"

"Oh. The band. It's different. But a good different."

"But you liked it?"

I nodded. "Yeah. Of course. It was good. You done already?"

She gestured back toward the stage, where Gibson was bent over his guitar, fiddling with the tuning pegs—turning them and then strumming, his ear cocked over the strings, then turning them some more. "Taking a break. Seth wants a beer. Whatever. I can't play if I'm all fucked up, but he says he plays better." She laughed again. "He probably does, now that I think about it." I glanced across the yard again and she leaned close. "Everything okay? You seem kinda skeezed out or something."

"I'm fine," I said. "I just . . . thought I saw someone."

"There you are," I heard behind me, and I had to force myself to turn slowly, not jump like I did at Vee, but my fists were still balled up by my sides. My throat felt dry; Seth wasn't the only one who needed a drink. "Gib wants to start up again soon." Shelby Gray was twisting through the crowd toward us, her skin dewy and the ends of her hair damp.

Shelby Gray was the yang to Luna's yin. Where Luna's white-blond hair cascaded down her back like a Barbie doll, Shelby's was short, jet black, and kind of spiky. Luna was pale while Shelby was olive toned. Luna was soft, almost ghostly. Shelby was tough, muscular, loud. Most of all, she didn't share Luna's serpent eyes. But hers were almost worse—so dark they looked flat black, like something you'd find under the grim reaper's hood.

The only quality they shared—other than bitchiness, of course—was affluence. Had you not known that Shelby was a designer's closet waiting to happen every second of every day, you might have thought the so-called punk girl was wearing her Valentino ironically. Rich little punk girl. Too bad Peyton did it first. Shelby was just a follower. But something told me she would not like to hear that.

"Oh, hey, Nikki, you know Shelby, right?" Vee said.

Shelby smirked at me in a way that told me she knew everything that had gone down between Luna and me, down to the very last detail, and that she didn't like me any more than her friend did. Her eyes narrowed daringly.

I refused to break eye contact. "Yeah, we've crossed paths," I said. I offered Shelby a similar smirk. "How's Luna?" My heart skipped a beat at the mention of her name.

Shelby's smile deepened. "I wouldn't know."

"Yeah. Of course not," I said.

Ka-pow! An orange burst into pieces in my mind, the entrails turning bumpy gray and black like asphalt as they rolled away.

"So Gib doesn't want to take too long," Shelby said to Vee. "He's convinced people will start leaving the minute the music ends because this party is so lame." She rolled her eyes and gestured toward the drinkers. "I mean, it's coolers in a field."

"I don't know," Vee said, scanning the crowd. "Seems pretty amped to me. I'm not worried."

Shelby shrugged and walked back toward the stage. "Just the messenger," she said.

She started to turn, but for some reason I couldn't let her go. Something about her. She knew more than she was ever going to let on. "You don't know anything about how my stuff keeps ending up in weird places, do you?" I asked, though I could barely feel my mouth moving at all.

Instead of turning toward the stage, she turned to me. The smile came back. A drop of sweat rolled down the front of her neck. "I have absolutely no idea what you're talking about."

"What's up?" Vee asked, her voice sounding funny, curious, her signature flintiness gone.

I didn't answer. I closed the space between us, so close I could almost feel the dampness radiating off Shelby's skin. "Listen, I could go to prison for the rest of my life if Luna's successful in framing me. You and Luna are friends. If you know something, I'd suggest you tell me now. Because I won't let it go. And I won't leave you alone. I will follow you so hard you'll start to think I'm part of your wardrobe."

Another place where Shelby and Luna differed—in indifference. Luna wouldn't have batted an eye in the face of my threats. Her blood would have cooled and slowed until she was almost cadaver-like. Shelby tried to be that person, but I could see her top lip tense, even though she made a valiant effort to maintain her shitty smile. She swallowed, licked her lips. "All I know is that last time she called me from juvie, she told me you were going to be out of her hair forever soon, and that she had some guy making sure that happened."

"Guy? What guy?"

She gave an annoyed head shake. "I don't know. Does it matter?"

"Yes, it fucking matters!"

Vee stepped between us. "Come on, you guys," she said, her hand on each of our shoulders. "Let's not do anything stupid, okay? This is a good gig and I don't want to get invited to leave. You get me?"

"Why didn't you say anything?" I was too focused on Shelby to heed Vee.

"Okay, let's go," Vee said, placing her hand on my chest and walking me backward away from Shelby. "Time to cool off." She whispered, "You can't kill my lead singer. We just got her."

Shelby's black eyes bored into me as I backed away from her. "You and I are hardly besties, Nikki Kill. I wasn't there. I don't know who did what. Besides, I don't care if you go to jail or not."

"You have to tell someone!" I shouted. People were starting to stare now.

Shelby pursed her lips and furrowed her eyebrows, as if she were thinking it over. "No, I really don't. How am I supposed to know who's telling the truth? I just want to stay out of it."

The only thing I was aware of in that moment was the rusty starbursts that flickered in the back of my mind, flint striking stone. *Ragemonster, rust, ragemonster, rust,* like a flashing neon sign.

Vee continued pushing me away from Shelby. "Come on," she said. "I see Jones."

Vee shoved me toward Jones, who was two-fisting beers already. He slung an arm around my shoulder, finally relaxed—just when I was kaleidoscoping my way into full-on panicky rage.

People began cheering, jabbing the air with their fists, ready to dance some more. Slate and mint green muted the orange, all of it pulsating in my mind, making me want to run away or drink or do . . . something.

"Come on, Jones, I don't feel well," I said, ducking his arm. I tugged on his shirt.

"Not yet, baby. Let's hang out for a while. Have you met my new friend Doug?" He pointed, but "Doug" had taken off as the band warmed up again, leaving Jones pointing to empty space. He cracked up. "I swear he was just there." He tried for my shoulder again, and I moved away from him.

The band cranked up a few disjointed notes, and Shelby screamed into the microphone, "You guys ready to blow this shit out or what?" The crowd cheered in response. Jones cheered next to me, slopping his beer down my arm. Neon green started to mute the other colors, and I pressed my fingers against the bridge of my nose.

"Jones, I really have a headache now. Can we go?"

He looked irritated but finally nodded. "Let me finish my beer first?"

I sighed. "Okay, whatever."

I shoved my hands into my back pockets and tried to relax.

Something was missing.

The camera card. Shit. I had put it in my back pocket after my photos were printed at the pharmacy. I felt my back and front pockets. Empty. I turned a circle, scanning the ground for it, hoping that maybe I'd somehow dropped it right at my feet. But it wasn't there. Shit, shit, shit. I gazed into the crowd. I must have lost it in there. And if that was the case, I was never going to get it back, because the last thing I wanted to do was plunge back into that pulsing crowd.

Well, at least I'd had the photos developed. Not that they'd done me any good anyway.

But still. Losing that card was making this shitty party even shittier. My head felt like it was going to explode into colorful confetti.

I focused on Vee, who was fiddling with her bass the same way Gibson had been during the break. Her hair, stringy without her signature dreads, fell over her face, completely obstructing it. Gibson gazed out into the crowd, pausing for a moment when he saw me, his jaw squaring. He strummed one downstroke on his guitar loudly. "Okay,"

Vee said, coming back to the microphone. "Let's start this half with an oldie but goodie." She pressed her lips into the microphone. The crowd hooted and cheered. "It's a little song called 'Black Daisy.'"

Seth clicked his sticks together and they took off.

I froze, my heart sinking.

"Black Daisy" was an old Viral Fanfare song.

One that Peyton had written.

Luna might be everywhere.

But so was Peyton.

So was my sister.

JONES WAS PLANNING to spend the next day dorm shopping with his mom—a totally Jones thing to do, and another piece of evidence that we were the wrong two people to be together. Ever.

But the way he'd held me last night after leaving the party. The way he'd murmured in my ear that he could feel me shaking. The way he'd assured me he would protect me. I hadn't believed any of it—for all his muscles on top of muscles, Jones was just too nice to fight his way out of a paper bag—but it was sweet.

Sweet pissed me off. Sweet was Tootsie Rolls dropped in a puddle of blood. Sweet was the way my dad pined after my mom, forever empty.

Sweet was vulnerable.

In my world, vulnerable people got dead.

Pink, primary blue.

I sat up in bed. Dead was crimson. Why was I suddenly thinking pink and primary blue?

I'd seen them, that was why. At the cemetery. *Gone 2 soon. B.* Pink, primary blue.

But I'd also seen those colors before that.

Suddenly I was struck with a memory. Far, far back, so far I wasn't sure if it was real.

I was eight, wandering through the jungle of plants and flowers at the front of the funeral parlor. Running my fingers along petals and leaves, toeing terra-cotta pots and plastic buckets and pedestals, leaning in to sniff a carnation or rose here and there, reading tags filled with names that were meaningless to me.

God bless you, Milo, and little Nikki, too. The Simons

Praying for your healing. Marge and Tony Elgin

May you be comforted in your time of need. Selma

I didn't care about those flowers, or the people who'd sent them. But spending time focusing on them meant I wasn't spending that time focused on Mom, waxy and pale and slack-faced, looking nothing like Mom, five feet away. Or Dad, who looked like he had the flu, unshaven and uncomfortable in his navy suit, standing right next to Mom's casket, his hands folded in front of him as people came to hug him and tell him how sorry they were.

I'd said good-bye to Mom, in my mind. I'd cried a million tears. I'd had nightmares about what I'd walked in on the day she was murdered. I couldn't close my eyes without jerking upright with a shriek. She was gone. I'd seen it with my own eyes. I could never unsee it for as long as I lived.

But if I approached that casket, if I said good-bye to her there—it would mean she was really dead, and I wasn't ready to face that yet.

In some ways, I still wasn't ready to face that, even though she'd been gone for ten years. In some ways, I was still shrieking my way out of sleep.

Please call if you need anything. Sam and Peter B.

She will be greatly missed.—The Entire Team at Angry Elephant Productions

A pale-green ceramic vase filled with crème de la crème roses and white lilies. Rest in peace—Dorothy Frank.

A tall blue glass vase filled with pink azaleas and African violets. God bless. Becca, John, and Lilly Marks.

Pots full of leafy plants that I knew to be peace lilies from when Mom's mom died. Gus Bernard. Sara & Liam. The Cork Family. Your friends at Flight Fitness.

And behind them all, tucked almost into a corner, lonely and unadorned, a basket filled with a collection of crayon-colored flowers. Roses, lilies, asters, chrysanthemums. Wrapped around the stems, a note.

GONE 2 SOON.
B

Pink 2. Primary blue *B*. At the time, I hadn't even wondered who "B" was. I had simply noted that it was the only arrangement that didn't include a full name. But it was no more familiar to me than any of those other names. "B" could have stood for Brenda or Betty or Belinda or Barbara or Bettina.

Or Brandi.

Brandi Courteur.

God. Her again. I glanced at my desk, at the bottom drawer where Peyton's letter waited for me.

"I can't find her, okay?" I said aloud, as if Peyton could hear me. As if saying *I can't* made it truer than *I don't know if I want to.*

* * *

DAD WAS IN his office, cropping photos on his computer. This time his model was an absolutely gorgeous guy with dark hair and sparkling green eyes.

"Wow, who is this?" I asked, leaning over Dad's shoulder.

"Jace," he said. "Trying to break into the soap opera business, of all things. I thought that business was dead."

I imagined the guy making out with some busty temptress, lit candles and a bubble bath in the background. "I can totally see it," I said.

Dad saved the photo and pulled up another one, equally as perfect. "So what are you up to today?" he asked, sounding distracted.

"I thought I'd hang out with you for a while, then go work out." I sat on the edge of his worktable and picked up an eraser.

He scrolled down, expertly trimming the photo. "I'm afraid I won't be much company. I promised Jace I'd have these to him tomorrow."

"Can I deliver them?" I teased. "Just to be helpful, of course. I'll try my hardest to keep him from falling in love with me and swearing off all other women and ruining his soap career. Pinkie swear."

Dad barely glanced at me. "Very funny."

"I can at least help you clean up a little, like I promised," I said, sliding off the table and going to the other side of the room, where his disastrous desk sat. I began picking up papers and sorting them—bills, invoices, printed emails, shit so old nobody would even know what it was. If he'd had a wife, this mess probably would have been cleaned up long ago.

Truth was, I was looking for anything to do that would take my mind off the Hollis mess. While I worked, I idly talked to Dad about Jace, about photography, about anything other than Luna Fairchild or anything Hollis.

I worked until I saw a desk under the clutter, and then moved on to the drawers, bundling up pencils and pens, winding rubber bands into a ball, dropping paper clips back into their smashed boxes. If it was broken, I threw it away. If it was so old it was yellowed, I threw it away. If it belonged to a camera he didn't own anymore, I threw it away. Soon I had most of a trash bag full of junk.

"You're going to be so happy to get all this crap out of here," I said. "See? It's a good thing I'm not going to college—who else would do this for you?"

"Uh-huh," Dad said. He'd gotten to the so-distracted-he-wasn't-even-hearing-me-anymore stage.

I pulled open the bottom drawer. It was full of old photo envelopes. God only knew what they were—pictures of me in a preschool music program or in the bathtub or something equally as mortifying. I opened the first envelope.

And sat down hard under the wave of crimson.

There she was, smiling at the camera, all teeth and cheekbones and hippie hair. I touched her face, ran my finger down the length of her body, my breath taken away by the flood of brown and cyan and crimson so thick it felt like blood on the back of my tongue. I flipped through the stack, faster and faster, some of the photos dropping onto the floor between my legs.

Mom smiling under the sun. *Mom lying in a pool of her own blood.* Mom posing on a park bench. *Mom stretching her hand out toward me, telling me to run.* Mom sitting on a fire escape. *Mom breathing that last guttural breath.*

How could it be the same Mom? I didn't remember her like this at all. I only ever remembered her last terrible moments.

"Did you take these?" I asked, my voice croaky and bent. Dad didn't answer. "Dad? Did you take these pictures of Mom?"

"Huh?" He barely glanced over. "Yeah, probably. She was my first model."

"Was I born yet?"

"Depends on the picture. Some, yes. Some, no."

I opened another envelope of photos. There were more of Mom, this time holding my tiny hand. Dad with us, a huge hat dwarfing his face. Another one of her stretched back against a bar. Leaning heavily at an awkward angle. Her smile was only on her lips, and it looked tired and sick.

And in that picture, I could see it—a tiny baby bump. Nothing that I would've noticed if I hadn't been looking for it. I pressed my finger onto her stomach. Was that bump me? Or was it Peyton? Did Dad know about the baby when he was taking this picture?

The next photo was one of Mom at a bus station, holding two suitcases, looking frazzled and nervous. A giant white wool coat engulfed her, making her look tiny beneath it. Behind her, ancient boards told the arrivals and departures of the buses in blues and greens and grays. Salinas, Modesto, Bakersfield—bubble blue, muted gray, spongy tawny. Colors you'd see on a forest floor. I could smell moss.

"Where were you going in this one?" I asked, holding the photo out for Dad to see.

He flicked a look, then studied it. "Oh. Not we. Just her. She had an assignment. Somewhere. I can't remember now. We lived apart for a while, just you and me rattling around the old house without her." He grinned sadly. "Who'd have known it would end up being a permanent rattle someday, huh?"

I studied the photo again. It was impossible to tell what was under that coat. "How long was she gone?" I asked.

"Hmm." His hand paused on the mouse. "I guess about five months or so. Too long."

Five months or so. Long enough to have a baby?

"What was the assignment?" I asked in mint-green

puffs, a spearmint cold front.

He shrugged. "I don't remember. The project fizzled. Never got produced. Something about the funding being pulled. She was pretty torn up when she got back."

Oh, Mom.

"I think she was pretty disappointed about it," Dad said. "She went through quite a bit of depression for a few months. It was a tough time for her, even though we were certainly glad to have her back."

I forced myself to put away the picture of Mom at the bus station and opened the last envelope. It was a movie set, that much was for sure. I didn't see Mom anywhere. Just props and random cast members and scenery that I didn't recognize.

And then a photo of a dinner. Dad in the foreground, his arm wrapped around a tall man whose skin was so tan and hair was so white, it looked like he'd been living on the surface of the sun. The white-haired man wore a huge belt buckle, the letters VP—candy cane and mustard—pressed into it. I wondered if VP meant vice president, and what he might have been vice president of.

Both of them had their heads thrown back in laughter. I started to ask Dad who the guy was when something caught my eye. Papers scattered on each of the tables in the background, along with confetti and champagne glasses. Flyers, their tiny print coming at me in glittery lilac.

A glittery, shimmery lilac I'd seen before.

A lilac that made me feel stuck in gray-and-black quicksand.

The papers were flyers for Hollywood Dreams.

One of the photos slipped out of my hands and fluttered to the floor, swept under the desk on an air current.

Licking my lips, which had suddenly gone very dry, and trying to look nonchalant, I slid off the chair and knelt to pick it up.

Something pushed far back under the desk caught my eye. A black box. Metal. About the size of a shoe box. Closed, with a combination lock. A thick layer of dust—mint-green dust—coated the top of it. How long had it been there? And why had I never seen it before?

Because I never really hung out in Dad's office, that was why. It was boring. Plus, it was his space. He was territorial about it. Always worried that I would "lose something" or "ruin his work" or "leave a mess."

Or maybe he was worried about what I might find in here. So far, I'd found far more than I'd ever expected. Dad knew about Hollywood Dreams? He had to have known. No way could he have missed all those flyers at that party.

And now, this.

"I think she really had her hopes set on that project being her big break," Dad said, still unaware that I was on the floor.

"Yeah, probably," I answered. I reached out and spun

the combination dial with my fingers. Of course, it was still locked.

I needed to find that combination.

I needed to find out what exactly Dad was hiding from me. And why it was so important he had to lock it in a box.

I had no idea what the combination might be. And I could hardly hang out on the floor trying to figure it out, with him right in the same room. I had to act like there was nothing amiss. Like I hadn't seen anything, not even in the pictures I'd found.

I pulled myself off the office floor, straightened the photos with shaking hands, and crammed them into their envelope, which I dropped back into its spot in the bottom drawer. I would leave them there for later, when Dad wasn't around. When I could sit in here and try to figure out just what it was I was missing.

I NEEDED TO think, and I always did my best thinking while smoking. Or at least that was what I liked to tell myself. So the first thing I did when I got back to my room was light a cigarette. I pulled open my window and sat with my legs hanging out, tapping my bare heels against the side of the house. I blew out a stream of smoke and took a deep breath. Already it was hot, and I wasn't even out of my pajamas yet. If this heat kept up, it was seriously going to cut into my smoking time. Which, if you asked Detective Martinez, would probably be a good thing.

I mentally catalogued every number that might be important in Dad's life. His birthday. Mine. Mom's. Our house number. Our phone number. Any combination of any of those numbers could open that box. Or numbers I hadn't even thought of yet. Was it possible that I would ever figure it out? Probably not.

I tossed my unfinished cigarette to the ground and swiveled back into the air-conditioning, lifting my hair off the back of my neck, which was already getting sweaty.

My phone buzzed. Jones.

Coming over today?

I chewed the side of my nail. I really wasn't in the mood for more babysitting, courtesy of the most caring boyfriend on earth.

Can't. Staying in.

He must have been waiting for me to respond, because I'd barely pressed send before it buzzed again.

Want me to come over?

A memory of Jones's bare chest, his powerful hands on me. A flash of violet that made my legs feel weak. But . . .

No. Hanging with Dad.

Later?

May be going to dojang later. I'll call.

That was the second time this morning I'd mentioned going to the *dojang*. It wasn't until I pressed send again that I realized that I did actually feel like going to Lightning-Kick. It was the only place I felt like going to. I couldn't walk around in fear all the time. And the more I kicked the shit out of a plastic dummy torso, the less fearful I would be. I took a quick shower, let my hair hang loose and wavy down my back, and climbed into a pair of yoga pants and a T-shirt. When I got out, I noticed that I had another alert on my phone.

"Damn, Jones, give it a rest," I said aloud, folding my legs underneath myself as I sat on my bed. But it hadn't been Jones. It had been Detective Martinez.

I hit call.

"Nikki," he said, picking up after the first ring.

"Miss Kill," I reminded him for the thousandth time.

I could hear an exasperated puff of air into the phone, but I knew that if I were with him, that puff of air would be accompanied by the slightest grin, leaving me wondering what his eyes looked like behind his sunglasses, and guessing they would be smiling. "What's up?"

"You didn't listen to my message?"

"Nope. Didn't even notice that you left me one. What's the deal?"

He sighed, sounded impatient. "I need to see you."

Ordinarily, this would leave me annoyed. He was always needing to see me—almost as bad as Jones. Seven months ago, he was constantly following me in the name of "protection." It annoyed the shit out of me. But right now, even if I didn't want to admit it to myself, much less out loud, I sort of didn't mind the protection. Plus, I had gotten kind of used to him. In a passion-fruit kind of way. Even thinking the word *passion* while on the phone with him made me blush. *God, Nikki, get your shit together. He has a girlfriend. And the last thing you need is a crush on a cop.*

Cops were definitely not my favorite people in the world. Cops had screwed up my mom's investigation and eventually just shelved it altogether. Cops had put me and Dad off for months, maybe years, before we finally gave up. Cops couldn't help Peyton. Cops couldn't save Dru. Cops couldn't put the Hollises away. Not even Luna, who they had right in their hands.

"Negative," I said. "I'm staying home today."

"It's not a request," he said. I heard a door open and close. "It's an order."

I laughed out loud. "I take orders from you now? In that case, I really don't think so. I'm staying home."

A woman's voice in the background. *See you tonight.* The sound of a kiss close by, like someone had just pecked him on the cheek. I rolled my eyes. I knew in theory Blake Willis was supposed to be helping me out. But I also knew that if we couldn't find Rigo and prove my innocence, she would be right there in the courtroom taking me down. It was her job.

"There've been some developments that you should know about," Martinez said.

"What developments?"

"I really feel like we need to discuss these things in person."

I leaned back against my headboard, pulling a string on the seam of my yoga pants. "Okay," I said. "I'm going to LightningKick. You up for a little sparring?"

"You just can't get enough, can you?" I could hear the smile in his voice again. I could almost taste passion fruit on my lips.

"Y OU HEADING OUT?" Dad asked, still absorbed by the photo spread on his computer as I walked by.

I jumped. "Huh? Oh. Yeah. Off to the *dojang*."

He swiveled to face me, pushing his glasses up on his nose to study me. "It's been a while," he said. "You're up to it?"

I nodded. "I guess I'm about to find out."

I expected those words—the prospect of fighting again—to make me nervous, but found that they didn't.

The last thing I'd kicked was the back of Luna's head.

I needed to kick something again.

* * *

TECHNICALLY, IT WAS time for the four-year-old class. Mommies led impossibly little boys and girls, swimming in crisp *doboks*, by the hand through the front doors. Every time someone pulled a door open, I could see my instructor, *Kyo Sah Nim* Gunner, standing at the front desk, ready to check everyone in. I could tell he saw me, too, but was waiting to see what I would do.

Even I wasn't exactly sure what I was going to do.

You're going to get out of your car, Nikki, and you're going to go in there. And you're going to kick the hell out of the sparring dummy and prove to yourself that you can do it.

I wasn't sure. I was a good liar, after all, even to myself. But I knew I would never forgive myself if I didn't at least try.

Gunner was leading the kids in a stretch, but he got up when I walked in. "Keep stretching, guys, I'll be right back." He jogged over to greet me.

"I thought that was you," he said. "I was starting to worry that you wouldn't be coming back at all."

"Just needed a break," I said. "I was kind of burnt out. Busy with schoolwork. Getting ready for graduation, that type of thing." Lies, lies, lies. But the kind of lies I needed to tell, if I was going to do this.

He nodded, looking skeptical. He knew what had happened with Luna and the Hollises. He knew I'd beaten them using my skills. And he probably knew that was what had scared me from coming back. He gestured toward the mat. "I've got the tigers class, so I can't really talk."

"That's okay," I said. "I was just hoping I could hit the dummy a few times? I know it isn't open gym, but . . ."

He looked uncertain, which surprised me a little. Usually Gunner treated his black belts like part owners, giving us unending trust and our run of the *dojang* pretty much anytime we wanted it. "Yeah, okay," he finally said. "Just try to keep it down. I've got some easily distracted ones over there."

"No problem."

I turned toward the locker room to put on my *dobok*, but Gunner touched my shoulder, stopping me.

"Hey, listen. I haven't had a chance yet to tell you I'm sorry about what happened to you a few months ago. Had I known the situation was so dangerous . . ."

I smiled. "Don't worry about it, Gunner. You were there, even though you weren't technically there." I tapped my forehead. This seemed to please him. I gestured downward. "I broke my foot, though."

He grinned. "Sounds like you gave it your all, then."

"Have you ever known me to give it anything less?"

"Not once." One of the moms jumped up from her chair, leaned over the half wall that separated the viewing area from the floor, and yelled at her kid to stop messing around. "I should get back before I lose them," Gunner said. "Whose idea was it to start a four-year-old group?"

"Well, you know you're all about the money, money, money, Mr. Greed."

He laughed out loud. "Yeah, that's it." Then, just before he bowed at the edge of the mat, he turned again. "It's great to have you back, Nikki." He ticked his head toward the sparring dummy, looking pasty and suffering on his base. "Go easy on him."

"Now why on earth would I do that?"

I WAS ALREADY twenty horse kicks and half a dozen four-knuckle strikes into the sparring dummy by the time Detective Martinez arrived at the *dojang*. Sweat poured down my forehead, and my *dobok* stuck to my chest and lower back.

Every strike, every kick, was accompanied by the same thought, over and over: *Dad is hiding something. Dad is hiding something. Dad is hiding something.*

But was he really? Lots of people kept important papers in locked boxes, right? Things like mortgages and marriage licenses. *And death certificates.*

No. I knew where Dad kept those things—in a short file cabinet in the basement.

And then there was the photo of him, all those Hollywood Dreams flyers on the tables surrounding him.

Why would he have a secret box under his desk? Did he know who owned Hollywood Dreams? And what else did he know that he wasn't telling me? Did he know about the affair? Did he know about Peyton?

God, how mixed up was my family in all of this?

Just thinking about it made me nauseated.

"Save some energy for me," Detective Martinez said, shuffling out onto the mat. He was in a pair of skintight gray sweats and a police T-shirt that stretched across his pecs. I could almost see the six-pack beneath, lit up in violet lines. I shook my head. I didn't have time for violet, not now.

I turned and bowed to him. "I've got plenty to go around, Detective. Glad you came to get your share." I dropped back into my fighting stance.

Detective Martinez liked to fight close. He relied on the grab, on the takedown. I was a distance fighter, using my feet as my weapons. I knew if I let him close the space between us, I would lose. I hated to lose.

"So what is this about?" I warmed up with a few front snap kicks to his midsection. After the first one, he blocked them all, batting them away without even looking.

"Mostly it's about checking to make sure you're okay." He jabbed, but it was listless, tentative. He knew that going easy on me would piss me off and I would do something rash, giving him plenty of opportunity to take me down. I was not going to bite. *Go ahead and throw your wimpy swats, Detective. I've got all day.*

"Oh, so we're back on that, are we? Will you listen to

me if I tell you I'm fine and you don't need to bother, or am I just wasting my breath?" We danced a little, feinting and pulling back.

"Probably a little bit of both." I went in for a forefist jab—not my strongest move, and almost a total mistake. He blocked my jab and rushed toward me with a quick right-left block-strike that knocked me off balance. Instead of taking me down, though, he simply pushed me away and grinned. "For what it's worth, I don't think Luna will mess with you."

I let out a laugh, regained my balance, danced a little. Threw a light hook that he batted away. "What on earth would make you think that? Luna lives to mess with me. And if she can prove that I was the one who attacked Peyton—something she's already done a pretty good job of proving, by the way—things will get much easier for her. All she has to do is say I was there to finish her off, and Dru got caught in the crossfire of self-defense. Done. Nikki goes to prison and Luna continues her life as a drug dealer, high-dollar hooker, and general pain in the ass."

I threw another hook. He blocked. "True. But if she messes with you, she runs the risk of being caught. And the last thing she wants is the authorities getting hold of her now. She could say good-bye to any sort of probation."

"Well, you'll forgive me for being cynical. Or paranoid. Or whatever it is. But I've seen the way Luna operates, and she is pretty good at not getting caught." I flashed back on the way she'd mimicked Peyton's voice, Peyton's manner-isms, Peyton's life. She got away with it for so long. "So what is this about, then, if it's not about her?" I decided to go for a big move. I faked low and when he slipped back to avoid it, I popped high, hitting him right in the chin. I held back, so I wouldn't break his teeth, and he knew it. I saw irritation cross his face. This time he was the one off balance. Mentally. Just as easy to defeat as an opponent who is physically off balance. Maybe easier.

I faked low again and then tried to sweep his ankle, but this time he saw it coming and dodged, moving toward me rather than away. Instinctively, I threw a punch, but he was too close. He smacked it down with an inside block, closed the gap between us, grabbed the back collar of my *dobok*, and pulled me low so that my back was arched, using his right hand to block my free hand, my other hand trapped by the arm that was wrapped around me. Our faces were inches apart.

"Surveillance," he whispered. "I've got a friend who can get me surveillance tapes from the parking garage across the street from that escort service."

"Hollywood Dreams?" I asked, the shimmery lilac words scratching my throat on the way out. The flyers flashed in my mind again.

He nodded. "Hollis's place. I can get recordings. A bunch of them. It'll take a while to watch, but it's worth a shot.

Maybe we can get a license plate or something to help us track down Rigo. You should come over to help me go through them."

"What would Blake have to say about me coming over?" I went for the obvious—knee to the groin—but he was too quick. He tucked, blocking my knee with his, and then yanked the back of my *dobok*. We both went down, him on top of me, balled up like a bug. An impossible-to-penetrate bug.

"She knows."

"She knows."

"Yes, she knows, and she's okay with it. As long as she's not there when we're watching them. She has to kind of turn a blind eye. You really should trust her, Nikki."

My mind raced for ways out of his lock. All I could think of was to use my legs. I wrapped them around his waist, feeling him press into me. Probably more of a distraction than a benefit, a string of violet running between us as he pressed in closer. "You'll forgive me if I'm the tiniest bit skeptical about trusting my future to the assistant DA."

"So trust yourself. And me."

Before I could answer, I caught movement out of the corner of my eye, just over his shoulder. Jumpy as I was, instant gold fireworks popped me into motion. I jammed my forearm into his throat and pushed upward, just in time to see Jones pull away from the half wall, a look of disgust on his face.

"Jones?" But before I could even get off the mat, he was already storming out the front door. "Shit."

I had no idea why, but I chased after him. I, Nikki Kill, destroyer of all things romantic, decrier of love, champion of the forever-single, was chasing after a boy just like some empty-headed girl in a schmaltzy chick flick. I hated myself for it, even while I was doing it, but the thing was, he had misunderstood what he saw. There was nothing going on between the detective and me.

He was a cop, for God's sake. An annoying pain in my ass. He was so yellow I practically had to wear sunglasses to be around him. People that yellow didn't belong around screwed-up people like me. He was a necessity in my life; Jones was my luxury. My safe luxury.

My safe luxury who was already in his car and backing out of the parking lot by the time I got through the front door.

"Come on! Jones! Don't be like that! It wasn't what you think!" I yelled, but he only briefly glanced at me, his brow furrowed angrily above his sunglasses, and sped out, his back tires kicking up rocks in their wake. "Damn it!" I took a step forward and immediately stepped on a rock. "Son of a bitch!" I yelled, hopping on one bare foot. I plopped down on the curb between Detective Martinez's car and mine to massage my injured foot.

"You should have shoes on," Detective Martinez said,

sitting beside me. Calmly, as if nothing had happened at all. As if Jones hadn't just stormed out of my life. I hadn't even heard him come outside.

"Thanks for the tip," I said, giving him a sarcastic glare.

"He seemed pretty pissed."

"You think? You know, I don't know what you're doing, helping me. I don't even know if you're helping, or if you're messing up my already messed-up life." The photo I'd found in Dad's office nagged at me. "But Jones was the one thing in my life that wasn't complicated. One thing. And now even that's messed up."

"He'll be back."

"He's leaving for college in two months."

"He'll still be back."

"How do you know? You know literally nothing about Jones. Sometimes I'm not even sure how much I know about him. I'm not great at paying attention to other people's lives."

"I know he'll come back," he said, scratching his bicep, which was still shiny with sweat, his tattoo peeking out, "because guys like Jones always come back to uncomplicated relationships with someone like you. If you can even do uncomplicated. Which I highly doubt."

We locked eyes for a moment, and I swore I felt grape wine course through my veins. I cleared my throat to break the tension. "That sounds like the voice of experience," I said.

He scratched an eyebrow, seemed to think it over. Finally, he looked up at me. "You remember that story I told you? About my brother?"

"The one in the gang," I said. "Yeah. José or something."

"Javi," he corrected. "And remember me telling you about his rival? Leon?"

I nodded. "The guy who shot up the car and killed your sister."

"Leon had a sister, too." He stopped. I gave him a *go-on* look. He mirrored the look back to me.

"And?"

He shrugged. "And . . . it was complicated."

"Oh," I said, finally getting it. "Ouch. With the dude's sister? When you do complicated, you really do it up right."

"I told you I wasn't always the person I am today."

"I guess not." I was unsure what to say to all of this. Detective Martinez messing around with some *gang rival's* sister was something I almost couldn't imagine. "Well," I said, to break the awkward silence. "If it makes you feel any better, there really is no such thing as uncomplicated with a person like me."

He chuckled. "Boy, ain't that the truth!" He grabbed onto his knees and rocked backward, laughing.

I couldn't help it, the laugh was contagious. I felt the corners of my mouth curl up just the slightest. "Shut up," I said, playfully punching his shoulder. "Nobody asked you."

His laughter died down. "So you in?" I stared at him blankly. "For the surveillance videos?"

"Sure, but not today."

He raised his eyebrows.

"We have a business meeting this afternoon," I said. "With our photographer. You probably should shower."

He shook his head slowly. "You're impossible, Nikki." He stood, turned, and reached a hand out to help me up. I grabbed it and let him pull.

"You don't know the half of it."

As I leaned forward toward the front panel of his car, I noticed three holes poked through the metal. "What is this?" I asked, letting go of his hand and touching one of the holes. "Are these bullet holes? They look like bullet holes."

"They're nothing."

"Bullet holes are not nothing."

He frowned, stepping up onto the curb and heading back toward the *dojang*. "I'm a cop, Nikki. Cops have guns. Guns have bullets."

I refused to budge, still running my fingers over the holes. "Yeah, but cops don't generally shoot those bullets into their own cars."

He turned, hand still on the door, a flash of annoyance on his face. And something else too. That familiar gray that had every now and then tinged my consciousness when I was around him. That gray feathering around the edges of his yellow. That feeling that told me he was hiding something from me. "I wasn't in the car when it happened, if that makes you feel better. I got vandalized. Let it go," he said. "It's not your business."

So I did.

But even as I went inside and headed for the locker room, I couldn't help thinking that maybe I wasn't the only complicated one. And I wasn't the only one hiding things.

Y OU WOULD THINK that being the daughter of a photographer, and having been around cameras my whole
life, I would be really comfortable in front of a lens. But
that couldn't be further from the truth. In pictures, I always
ended up looking half-terrified and half like I wanted to rip
your gall bladder right out through your belly button, which
probably wasn't altogether inaccurate. I had hidden from
Dad's photo-snapping finger so many times he eventually
gave up on me.

My nervousness as I got ready for our meeting with Matt
Macy was only made worse by the knowledge that I would
not only be in front of a camera, but I would be in front of a
camera as a sporty model with Detective Martinez watching

me. I hated the idea, but "boxing gym" was the first thing that had popped into my mind when I was making the appointment, so "boxing gym" owners we would be.

I still had a pair of shorts and a crop tank from a running phase I went through my sophomore year. It was a short phase, and the clothes were like new. They were also super bright—the shorts vibrant red and the tank covered with a giant sugar skull—and I practically had to squint as I put them on. They were also super short and super tight. I couldn't remember bright and sexy ever being my style. I was pretty sure I had lost my mind for a while there in tenth grade.

But for a sporty photo shoot, they were perfect.

I felt self-conscious as hell, but I looked pretty good. Turning in front of the mirror, I idly wondered what Detective Martinez was going to think when he saw this getup. Or what Jones would think.

Shit. Jones. How was I going to handle Jones?

I'd tried to call him. Over and over again. He wasn't answering. He wasn't texting. He was pissed, there were no two ways about it. The question was . . . did I care? I would miss the way he held me, but otherwise, probably not. It was probably for the best for me to let him go.

Even if I didn't really want to.

Matt Macy's studio was spacious, with red leather couches and globe lights and brick walls. It felt cozy—in some places dominated by photos that dazzled, and in other places muted with red wallpaper that would have looked more at home in Tesori Antico. I let my eyes adjust and scanned the room, feeling very unsteady in my outfit, even though I'd thrown a T-shirt and a roomy pair of sweats over it.

"Would you calm down already?" Detective Martinez said from the couch on the other side of the room.

"What?"

"You're acting so nervous. Cut it out. Be cool. You're just here to market your boxing business, remember? You should be excited. Or at least professional." I started to explain to him why it was completely impossible for me to be excited about getting in front of a camera in basically no clothes, but was interrupted by a smallish man with receding brown curly hair, who came around the corner from a back area. He carried a camera in his hand—one that made my dad's cameras look like toys. He looked a little surprised to see me at first, but then seemed to remember our appointment.

"You're . . . ?" he said, coming at me with his hand outstretched.

"Ava Glass." I took his hand. "We talked on the phone?"

"Ava," he said, staring into my eyes so deeply I felt uncomfortable. He pumped my arm up and down for a beat too long. I tried to will away the goose bumps that threatened to crawl up my bare arms. "Yes, of course." Finally, he looked over my shoulder. "And is this your partner?" he asked.

He'd pointed with his chin to Detective Martinez, who slouched, his hands dangling in his crotch, loosely clutching the handle of his duffel bag. As usual, the complete opposite of me—appearing totally comfortable. Relaxed, even. In loose gray boxing shorts, a too-small black tee, and a whole lot of exposed muscle, he looked ridiculous. And hot as hell. He kept his sunglasses on, even though we were inside, and methodically chewed a wad of gum. When we both looked over at him, he gave a lazy salute, a cocky lip-pooch screwing up his face.

It took all I had not to laugh.

Maybe this would be easier than I thought.

"This is Thorn Orion," I said, a smile flicking at the corner of my mouth at the memory of how hard I'd laughed in the car when he'd told me the name he'd chosen. *What, was Axel Armstrong taken?* I'd asked between giggles. "He's my partner, and hopefully co-model." I shot him an *I won, now you have to model too* smile.

Matt Macy gave one more glance at Detective Martinez, and then looked each of us up and down. "So you want to do a shoot?" he asked. "Did you have something in mind?"

I nodded, gesturing for Detective Martinez to open the duffel. "We brought our gloves. I guess I was thinking we could take some photos of us with the gloves on? That's really all I've got. I'm not super creative." True, but it was also true that putting myself and Martinez in the photo meant I gained access to Matt Macy's studio, rather than just the reception area.

"You're kind of short," he said. He looked Martinez up and down. "And you're going to have to look friendlier. Normally we would hire professional models for something like this. But I guess we can give it a try."

I beamed. "We won't let you down." *And I'm not too short to jack you right in the face with my knee if I have to,* I added in my head.

He fidgeted with his camera as he studied me. "I'm hoping you weren't planning to model in that outfit."

I lifted up my shirt just enough to expose the bottom edge of my tank. I could hear the creak of couch leather as Detective Martinez leaned forward, too. I dropped my shirt, my face burning.

"Okay," Matt Macy said. "That should work fine. Let's get you out of some of those clothes and into the spotlight."

Oranges and yellows rolled like fire in my head, exploding into starbursts and squiggles and fierce royal blue. I took a deep breath to steady myself. Was I ready for this?

I cast one last glance over my shoulder at Detective Martinez as I let Matt Macy lead me around the same corner he'd come around. The detective peeked up over his sunglasses and gave me the slightest nod. I heard couch leather groan again as he got up to follow us.

Code word. God, why hadn't we thought about a code word? This guy was connected to the Basiles, after all. What if it wasn't just a business connection? What if it was a *connection* connection? What if he knew Rigo and knew Luna and knew who I really was? What if he planned to finish off the job that Luna had started? *Rainbow. Prism. Rigo. Dojang.* The code-word possibilities were endless. We were stupid for not considering one.

The other side of the brick wall opened up into a sweeping studio area, one end draped with plain white paper and bathed in stand lights. Fans, props, tripods were everywhere. A hairdresser's chair sat in front of a mirror, near a bin full of props and costumes—sequined things, silky things, a fluffy bathrobe with makeup stains around the collar. My dad would have loved to have a place like this. A place where he could take his models for more controlled shoots. No worries about weather or birds or tourists who thought photobombing was the most hilarious thing in the world. Just photographer, model, and camera.

Or models, as the case may be this time.

I shook the thought away. I couldn't think about my dad right now. Thoughts about my dad inevitably led to thoughts about lies. I needed to concentrate on this moment, not worry about what he was hiding.

"You ever done anything like this before?" Matt Macy

asked, screwing his camera onto a tripod. I shook my head.

"Okay, well, go ahead and take off your . . ." He motioned toward my clothes and swallowed. "And then we'll see what we've got to work with. You staying in that, I assume?" he said to Detective Martinez.

"Got some gloves here," Martinez said, and I couldn't help noticing even his voice had taken on a simple, tough tone. He was totally in character. I pulled my shirt up over my head to hide another laugh.

"No logo shirts or uniforms?" Matt Macy asked skeptically.

Shit. I hadn't even thought of those things. "We're really grassroots," I said. "Trying to save money wherever we can."

"Plus, we want to look like regular people," Martinez added.

"Gotta start somewhere." I shrugged.

"Okay," Matt Macy said, but he looked unconvinced.

I busied myself with taking off my sweats. As soon as they were off, I felt very, very naked. I glanced over my shoulder. Martinez was looking at me. I gave him a *what the fuck are you looking at* glare and he averted his eyes, pointing them toward his shoes. But I could still see him smiling, almost laughing. I wanted to roundhouse the smirk right off his face. Throw him over my hip and see who was laughing then.

* * *

MATT MACY HAD gone over to the tripod and was waving for me to follow. "Why don't we take a few test shots to see how the lighting is working for you? Stand over there." He pointed to the white sheet. "We don't need you just yet, Thorn, so you can relax for a minute."

Relax to a detective was pretty much *You're free to start searching for stuff now.* Which was exactly what Martinez did the second Matt Macy turned his back. I watched as Martinez sauntered over toward a room that I immediately recognized as an old-fashioned darkroom. He poked his head inside, casual, uninterested, though I knew what he was doing. Looking for clues. Anything that might lead us to Rigo.

"Ava?" I jumped. Matt Macy was still pointing toward the white sheet.

"Sorry," I mumbled. "Nervous, I guess. I've never done anything like this before."

As soon as I got in front of the camera, he flicked the lights on, practically blinding me. Immediately, I could feel sweat bead up in the small of my back. How could I feel so exposed and be sweating at the same time?

He leaned over his camera and squinted into the lens. "Go ahead and pose," he said.

I didn't move. More like I didn't know how to move.

It never occurred to me that I would have to actually look like a model. In my mind, all I had to do was look tough and sporty. There were many things that I was not, but elegant and inviting had to be at the top of the list. My hips were for thrusting opponents to the floor, not thrusting forward for maximum sex appeal. My face had two settings: scowl and scowl harder. And flaunting was something I absolutely never, ever did.

I was going to have to fake it like never before.

He popped up over his camera. "Pose?" he repeated.

"Sure," I said. I bent my body into awkward shapes, trying to come up with a close approximation of the slightly broken look most models had, while also closing my hands into menacing fists. "So what kinds of businesses do you normally shoot?" I asked.

"Chin up," he answered, not bothering to respond to my question. I lifted my chin and let him take another couple of shots.

"I'll bet you get all kinds. Anyone famous?"

No response. The camera clicked a few more times.

"Elbow out," he said.

I moved my elbow. "I bet you have some pretty great stories."

Detective Martinez had disappeared into the darkroom but had popped out again, moving on to a cabinet across the room. I watched as he opened and closed drawers, so silently even I couldn't hear them, and I knew he was doing it.

Matt Macy snapped a few photos, stepped back to gaze

into the camera screen, and snapped a few more. He looked completely put out.

Well, you're not the only one, dude.

"Look," he said. "I wish I had time to chitchat, but I really have a lot of work to do." He shook his head and muttered, "You weren't kidding when you said you'd never done this before. Try turning your shoulder just a little bit toward me. Okay, more. More. Keep going."

I looked up in time to see Detective Martinez put his hands on his hips and stick his butt out, jutting his shoulder forward. He blinked rapidly, flirtatiously. I narrowed my eyes at him, feeling my lips pull into a tight line.

"Relax your mouth," Matt Macy said. Martinez doubled over with silent laughter.

Just get on with your investigation, Mr. Comedian, I thought. As if he could hear me, he ambled over to a worktable and set his duffel on it. He leaned back against it, like he was just propping himself up, bored, but I could see his eyes wandering as he pretended to stretch back.

Matt Macy peered into the viewfinder and sighed, straightening. "Tell you what," he said. "Let's get Thorn in here and see if that helps you relax a little."

Martinez lunged for his bag and unzipped it, pretending to dig around inside.

"Thorn?" Matt Macy called. Martinez turned as if startled. "Let's get you in here with her."

"These help?" Martinez asked, holding up two pairs of boxing gloves.

"Yeah. Yeah, definitely," Matt Macy said.

Martinez loped toward me, and next thing I knew, he was standing next to me, holding out a pair of gloves. I took them and shoved my hand in one.

"How about this," Matt Macy said, coming toward us with hands outstretched. He took Martinez's gloves and tied them together, then draped them over Martinez's neck. "You go ahead and put yours on," he said to me. He took a step back and assessed Martinez, his finger resting on his chin, then removed the gloves. "Let's try . . . could you maybe . . . ?" He mimed taking off his shirt.

Martinez hesitated, glancing at me. I raised my eyebrows at him. *Not so funny when it's you, now, is it?* my face said. Martinez matched my raised eyebrows and yanked his shirt over his head, exposing a chiseled brown chest with a fine dusting of hair that got thicker as it trailed down the midline of his six-pack. I turned my face, feeling myself blush.

"Great," Matt Macy said. "Now we're onto something." He hustled over to the prop area and came back with a stool, which he placed at our feet. "You sit," he said to Martinez. Martinez sat, and Matt Macy draped the gloves around his neck again so that they rested against his chest. He stepped back, studied the scene, then clutched my arms, guiding me backward a few steps. "You come back here. Gloves on.

Right, like that. Now hold this arm up like you're showing off your muscle." I did. "Good, good. And drape your other arm over his shoulder. Bend your elbow just a little bit. Get a little closer. Like you're claiming him." Swallowing, I pressed myself against Detective Martinez, feeling the heat of his back against the bare skin of my belly.

Concentrate on the shot, Nikki, I told myself over and over again. *You don't feel anything. You especially don't feel anything violet.*

Matt Macy clapped his hands—liking what he was seeing—and went back to his camera.

He shot about a zillion photos, making us move the slightest bit to the left or right: *Your arm is sagging, sit up straighter, don't smile, look tough. Good, good, so good.*

After a while he had us switch, taking out the stool so that I was standing in front of Martinez, my gloved hands on my hips. Instead of draping his arm over my shoulder, he snaked it around my waist, pulling me in against him. I could hear the blood rushing in my ears. I wasn't even aware of the camera anymore.

"I found something."

I was so in my own world, trying to concentrate on just breathing, I wasn't sure I heard Martinez whisper.

"Lower your hands to your sides, Nikki, only strong, like you could take him if you wanted to."

What do you mean could? *How about* can? But the

thought was rushed out when I felt Martinez's breath on my cheek, raising goose bumps all along my left side.

"Over on the worktable. I found something."

God, right. We were here to find something that would lead us to Rigo. I'd almost forgotten. I felt a bead of sweat roll down my spine.

"Why don't you two face each other? Hold up your gloves like you're going to fight. Good." *Click, click, click.* "Less mean, Ava. More playful. Let's have a smile." We smiled, our eyes locked, having entire conversations without speaking. He had found something. We needed to get it. We needed to do something.

"Press your foreheads together. It's a grudge match. Excellent." More clicking, and Martinez's shaky breath pillowing my lips.

"I've got it covered," I whispered, and I could feel his forehead press a little harder into mine—a nod.

"Okay, that should do it," Matt Macy said. "I think we've got some really good shots. Unless you have other ideas?"

I pulled off my gloves. "I was sort of thinking we'd get some close-ups of just the gloves?"

He took them, studied them, nodded. "Yeah. Okay. Just let me set up the shot real quick. You guys can get dressed." But Martinez was already half a step ahead of him, pulling his T-shirt back down over his belly before the sentence was even out of Matt Macy's mouth. He took his gloves to his duffel, giving me a barely perceptible nod.

Matt Macy hustled to the prop area and came back with a small folding table. He placed it in the middle of the set and then disappeared toward props again, muttering something about a sheet.

Martinez was hovering around the worktable, watching me like a hawk. Waiting for me to do something. I'd said I had it covered, but the truth was I had no idea what to do.

Short of causing a disturbance.

Distracting Matt Macy so that he completely forgot we were there.

While he was sidetracked, we could grab whatever it was Martinez had found and take off. *Cause a disturbance. Create a scene. Distract him.*

Distract him.

I knew how to distract him.

I wasn't exactly a photography wizard, but I'd messed with enough of Dad's cameras to know what I was doing. Quickly, without even thinking about what could happen if he turned around and caught me, I hit the lens release button and turned the camera lens counterclockwise. I rotated it until it released, and then pushed it back on, but barely. Just enough for it to hold, unless it was jiggled.

Thankfully, Matt Macy's tripod was identical to my dad's. I released the top clamps, holding the camera in place until it felt balanced, working as slowly and softly as I dared so I didn't bump into anything. When it looked semi-stable, I rushed over to my clothes, which I'd left in a pile, and began putting them on, being careful to meet Martinez's eyes again and to convey that imperceptible nod.

Matt Macy came back with a white sheet, which he draped over the table. Then he spent an extraordinarily long time arranging the gloves just so on top of it, occasionally glancing over his shoulder to make sure they lined up with his camera. I held my breath, hoping the tripod would stay stable until he got to it and that he wouldn't notice anything was amiss.

Finally, he was finished arranging, and he went over to the camera and bent behind it. Again, Detective Martinez and I locked eyes. I licked my lips. Matt Macy put his hand on the camera and the clamps I'd loosened flopped forward, taking the camera with it, the lens that I'd left barely attached flying off and landing with a crunch on the concrete. Broken plastic and glass hopped across the floor.

"What the fuck?" he said, peering down in confusion. But then he saw the broken glass and really started freaking out, in curse-filled half sentences. "How in the hell? Son of a bitch! Goddamn thing! Two thousand dollars! Holy shit!"

He came around the tripod and bent to pick up the ruined lens. His shoulders slumped briefly, and then he went back to cursing, turning the lens in his hands as if maybe it would repair itself if he just looked at it long enough.

There was a tiny part of me—the photographer's daughter part of me—that felt a little bit bad about destroying his camera. But then I reminded myself that I was doing this to prove my innocence, and my freedom was more precious than a thousand cameras put together. Matt Macy seemed like he probably wasn't a bad guy, but when you're fighting for your life, there is no room for guilt over things like smashed cameras.

He continued to carry on, forgetting that I was even in the room, which was, of course, what I'd been hoping would happen. He stomped off toward what looked like a storage room, kicking the prop box on the way. He wasn't even completely out of the room before Martinez and I leaped into motion, Martinez scrambling behind the worktable and grabbing a poster, which he quickly rolled and crammed into his duffel.

"Let's go," he said, and we started to run.

"Wait," I said, doubling back toward the set. I almost wiped out, slipping and catching myself with one hand on the ground. I lunged forward and grabbed the gloves. When I turned back, Martinez was looking at me with wide, impatient eyes.

"What?" I whispered. "I have to have something to spar with." I reached out with one hand and pushed the small of his back, propelling us both into motion, across the lobby, through the door, and out onto the sidewalk, then veering toward his car, which he'd parked a couple of blocks away. He was already rummaging his keys out of his pocket and had the door unlocked before we got there. We both slid in, him tossing the duffel into my lap. He careened around a corner and into a parking lot the next street over before I even had the door all the way shut. We were both breathing heavily.

"Whatever you found," I said between breaths, "it better have been good."

"You're going to look a gift horse in the mouth?"

"I broke the dude's camera!"

He leaned against the headrest, trying to catch his breath. "He has more."

"That's not the point."

"Would you rather I found nothing and we would still be in there modeling for your fake business?" I said nothing. He grabbed for the duffel handle. "I can take it back if you don't want it."

I grabbed the handle, too, before he could make off with it. "No. Of course I want it." He tilted his head, cupping one hand around his ear. "What? I said I wanted it."

"Does that mean you're going to say thank you? Do your lips form those words?"

I yanked the duffel handle out of his hand and unzipped it. "I'll say it after I see what it is."

I stuffed my hand into the duffel and pulled out the

rolled-up paper. I let the duffel fall between my legs and onto the floorboard as I unrolled it.

"It's a mock-up, I think," Detective Martinez said. "An advertisement poster. Do you see what I see?"

It only took about two seconds for me to see it. An advertisement for the Tesla estate auction. A collection of art and household items. An antique sewing machine, a painting of a boat in a storm, some dishes, a few scary-looking dolls, a familiar-looking statue, and an even more familiar-looking tribal mask.

And a cane.

A wooden cane with a silver ball handle.

My hand flew to my mouth, the breath sucked out of me.

"You think it's Rigo's?"

He took the poster from me and studied it carefully. "It almost has to be. Why else would the Basile woman be planning to send someone to this auction? You said she was after something in particular. Something that had been found. It's too much of a coincidence for there to be a ball cane at the same auction and not be his."

"They're going to the auction to get Rigo's cane back," I said. "The cane that he used to . . ." I couldn't finish the sentence.

"What I can't figure out is why the cane would be at that auction in the first place. What connection does Rigo have with the Teslas?"

I shook my head, tracing the tribal mask with my fingers. The peachy brown that stained the paper under my touch told me exactly why it had looked so familiar. And why the statue had as well. "These things don't belong to the Teslas," I said. "They belong to the Hollises."

Martinez let his hands, and the poster, rest in his lap. "So now we know why the Basiles have to be at that auction," he said.

I took the poster from his lap and rerolled it. I couldn't look at Dru's tribal mask anymore. I stuffed it back into the duffel.

"And why we have to be there, too," I said.

18

THE AUCTION WAS being held at the Tesla estate. We drove under what seemed like an endless canopy of jacaranda trees, their purple flowers gone for the season. They opened up onto an oasis of yellow light and shiny automobiles.

"Whoa," I said, leaning forward to peer through the windshield. Suddenly, being in Detective Martinez's ordinary car—with bullet holes in the front fender, no less—felt a little conspicuous. "You probably should have gone through a car wash."

"You're just seeing the important people. There are others like you and me." He steered his car away from the valets and bumped over the yard to a small parking area where there were more ordinary cars.

"If you say so."

"I do. Come on."

We got out, and I took a minute to hitch up the bodice of my dress, wishing I'd gone with the strappy thing instead of the strapless thing. Shopping for a formal dress was definitely something I didn't have a whole lot of experience with. Or patience for. What started out with me curiously cramming my boobs into a blue velvet monstrosity, pulling at the back of a pink baby-doll nightmare, and feeling like a leftover prom queen in a poofy green lace horror, eventually turned into me angrily chucking a black strapless chiffon cloud at the cashier without even trying it on. I almost choked when I saw the price tag, and then realized that Peyton would have choked that I was wearing something off the rack. How different our lives were.

I should have tried it on. The bodice was too big. Which only made me feel more uncomfortable. But I did like the way the fabric swirled around my legs.

"You clean up pretty good," Detective Martinez said when I joined him on the Tesla walkway.

"Back atcha," I said, taking in his tux. Truth, he more than cleaned up. He looked amazing, with his dark hair freshly gelled and his tan skin glowing against the white shirt. Everything fit him perfectly. He looked totally comfortable, like he belonged in a tux, like he was James Bond or something. I tugged at my bodice again, feeling like my clothes were wearing me instead of the other way around.

He crooked his elbow and faced the front of the house. I stared at his arm.

"What?" he asked.

"Are you trying to escort me?"

He crooked his arm more vigorously. "Yes."

"Like a granny at a church funeral."

"Like a date at a formal event," he said. "Just grab my arm and pretend you're easy to get along with for a few seconds."

I glared at him. "I'm not that good of an actress. Put your arm away. I'm not holding it." I clacked down the walkway. "And don't kid yourself—I can still kick your ass in chiffon."

"That's not what the heavy bag says." He caught up to me, jogging easily in his tux. It was unfair how he was so much more graceful than I was. He pretended to punch with a wimpy "girl punch."

"Join me on the mat again and we'll see what you have to say about it then."

"You should try to be a little less surly, you know."

"Why?"

"Because," he said, "we don't want to attract attention to ourselves, just in case."

I stopped. "Just in case what?"

"I don't know. In case someone here would recognize us."

I felt my toes go cold. "You mean a Hollis."

"I mean Arrigo Basile. In theory, he could be here with his family, right? That's why we're here, isn't it? Just . . . be cool, okay?"

I let out an exasperated breath. "Fine." I grabbed his elbow and flashed the biggest, fakest smile I could muster. "Better?" I asked through my teeth.

"Definitely scarier."

"Good. That's what I was going for."

INSIDE, THE TESLA estate was more like a museum than a house. Everything was marble and crystal and gold plated and soft leather and braided rugs. And old. We grabbed two numbered paddles out of a basket at the front door and mixed into the crowd, trying to blend in the best that we could. Which wasn't easy. Everyone else looked like they'd gotten lost on their way to the Oscars.

"Who are the Teslas anyway?" I asked. "And what on earth did they do for a living?" I watched a crystal teardrop shiver from the bottom of a chandelier above. I noticed soft classical music and peered into the room behind me, where a string quartet earnestly played.

He shrugged. "Not much, actually. Old money." He leaned to one side to let a waiter with a tray of canapés pass.

"Really old money. I know who they are because about three times a month some idiot or another tries to rob the place. Security everywhere. Why they think they won't get caught is beyond me."

"Well, at least the idiots are giving you job security."

"Point taken."

I rubbed my hand up my bare arm, feeling chilled. "This feels more like a cocktail party than an estate sale. Or like . . . a cotillion."

He grabbed a crab puff off a passing tray and popped it into his mouth. "There are appearances to keep up. Don't want the world thinking you need to sell off Mumsy and Puppaw's art to keep the family afloat after they're gone."

"You really think they died?"

He shrugged. "Well, not together. But this isn't exactly a garage sale. People this rich generally don't auction off their own things. They contact private buyers. If they're auctioning off everything, someone important kicked the bucket."

"How sensitive of you."

He waved his paddle in front of his face. "It's not really all that sensitive to be here bidding on their furniture, either, though, is it?"

I thought about it for a few minutes, listening as the quartet changed songs. There was a bar in the corner and suddenly I was dying of thirst and needing a cigarette and really, really wanting to get out of the incredibly uncomfortable sandals I was wearing. "It seems so morbid to be snapping up their whole lives like a bargain-basement sale." I picked up a statuette of a shepherd. His nose was chipped. "What if these things really meant something to them?"

He took the shepherd out of my hand and placed it back on the table. "If it makes you feel better, my guess is the family is keeping the really good stuff and selling off the rest here."

I trailed my finger along the intricately carved table. "If this is the rest, I would love to see the good stuff."

We milled around in the crowd, trying to stay in the background while looking for familiar faces. There were a lot of old people there. Like, a lot. Detective Martinez didn't want us to stand out, but we had to just by age alone. Probably everyone there was wondering how such a young couple could afford to step inside the Tesla estate, much less buy something there.

Detective Martinez scored us a couple of sodas at the bar. I'd found an empty chair near the front door and was scowling in it, wishing the straps of my shoes weren't so damn tight and the top of my dress wasn't so damn loose and I had a damn plan for being here in the first damn place. He held a fizzing cup out to me.

"Root beer?"

"Fancy," I said. "Who needs all that expensive champagne that looks so delicious and classy, anyway?"

"For all we know, this is imported from France."

I made a face. "French root beer?"

"Drink it or don't."

I took it and drank. He sat next to me. His leg rested against mine, and I didn't like that I noticed it right away, but I noticed it right away.

"So you see anyone you recognize?" he asked.

"No. You?" We peered into the crowd, which had gotten bigger. The quartet had begun to play louder to compensate.

"Not yet."

"Wait." I noticed a woman wearing a prim peach dress with delicate blue flowers and standing near a fountain in the center of the foyer. Her silvery hair fluffed and frizzed around her shoulders, which were slightly stooped. Something about her looked familiar. I leaned forward, willing her to turn around. Eventually she did. "That's the woman from the store."

I remembered the phone call she'd been making when I'd walked in. She'd been telling whoever was on the other end that she would be here, and that she would *send one of the boys* to take care of something that had been lost. I stood and craned my neck. We'd already guessed the lost something was Rigo's cane. *Please, God. Please let Rigo be the boy.*

There was a ringing noise, and slowly everyone quieted. All you could hear was the quartet, which had softened its music to exactly match the tone of the crowd. Impressive. A man in a shiny blue suit stood two steps up the central spiral staircase, holding a bell.

"Ladies and gentlemen," he said. He had a slight accent that I couldn't quite peg. Posh New England, maybe? Was it possible for Ivy League to be its own dialect? "Thank you for coming tonight. My father would be proud. As promised, all the money collected tonight will be sent to children's charities, as was his dying wish." There was a smattering of applause and some murmurs of appreciation, and Detective Martinez raised his eyebrows at me as if to say, *See? I told you he kicked the bucket.* The man rang the bell again and held up his other palm to quiet the room. "In order to maximize our donation, we have brought in a few items from some other local estates, so you're in for a real treat. We have some very sought-after pieces from some very well-known estates." More light applause. "In just a few moments, we will begin the auction. If you'll join us upstairs, you will find plenty of seating for all of you." He ducked his head, muttered another quick thanks, and began climbing the stairs, a tail of wine-carrying guests following him, excitedly chattering, their paddles tucked into their handbags or clasped under their arms.

I looked back where the Basile woman had been but could no longer see her. I stood and scanned the crowd, my fancy "French" soft drink forgotten on a coaster on what was probably a zillion-dollar end table. "Damn it. She's gone."

"She'll be up there," Detective Martinez said. He stood and placed his hand on the small of my back. I noticed that, too. "Shall we, Muriel?"

"Muriel?"

He shrugged. "Seemed like an appropriate name for tonight."

"Oh, okay . . ." I thought about it. "Chauncey."

"Chauncey? Do I seriously look like a Chauncey to you?"

"And I look like a Muriel? Chauncey is a family name. You were lucky you didn't get Kensington or Palmer."

We joined the crowd, allowing ourselves to be swept up the stairs. When we got to the top, and the crowd mobbed itself in the doorway of a cavernous room, he leaned so his breath was tickling my ear.

"Well, if I have to be Chauncey, then forget Muriel. You're officially Seraphina."

I thought it over. "Actually, I kind of like it."

THE TESLAS HAD a bona-fide ballroom right there in their house. A ballroom. I'd never known anyone who had a ballroom in their house. Not even the Hollises had a ballroom. I didn't know what young Mr. Tesla was planning to do with the house after the estate was all sold off, but if he was smart, he would never let this house go. A fucking ballroom!

Every inch of the ballroom was wood, polished so hard it looked like ice. I wanted to kick off my sandals, put on a pair of socks, and skate from one end of the room to the other.

A humongous chandelier that made the ones downstairs look like night-lights dominated the center of the room. The central air kicked on, and the crystals swayed and tinkled in the current. At one end of the room, someone had set up a short riser with a podium. Behind it were carts and boxes, which I assumed were filled with the items for sale. At the other end of the room was a table with a cash box. There must have been a hundred folding chairs lined up facing the riser, and Detective Martinez and I parked ourselves at the end of a row near the back. He fanned himself with his paddle and peered around as silently as I had been. I was guessing he didn't see a lot of ballrooms in his circle of friends, either.

"We'll have to bid on some things or we'll look really suspicious," I said.

"We can't afford anything here, I guarantee it," he whispered back.

"But why would we come just to sit here? We'll bid early and get out before it looks like it will even be close to final."

"You're paying for it if we end up accidentally buying some gold-plated toilet roll cover or something."

"Whatever."

The chairs around us filled in and eventually everyone got settled. I thought I caught a glimpse of the woman in the peach dress but lost her again, and before I could nonchalantly stand up to stretch or use the restroom or anything that might get me a better view, young Mr. Tesla stepped onto the riser and rang the bell again.

"We'll get started right away," he said. He bowed his head to a sweaty, red-faced man, who took his place behind the podium and introduced the first item.

I had never been to an auction before, so I had no idea what to expect. But generally speaking, it was mind-numbingly boring. Piece after piece of ugly, overrated art was brought to the forefront of the riser, and paddles sprang up while the man behind the podium rattled off numbers so fast it made my head spin, like someone had whirled a color wheel in front of me.

I bid on a painting of some geishas sitting by a river, a mantel clock with a couple of fat cherubs lounging across the top of it, and a silver candelabra that shone like the sun under the chandelier.

"Silver?" Detective Martinez whispered, elbowing me in the side. "Are you nuts?"

I held up my paddle a second time. "That way if I accidentally win, I can bludgeon myself and put me out of my misery."

He pushed the paddle down, against his leg. "Stop. I will bludgeon you for free if it means that much to you."

I pried the paddle loose and held it up one more time, just to spite him. "I think I might actually prefer life in prison to this," I hissed. Two women sitting next to us shot us angry *shut up* looks. I let the paddle rest on my lap, satisfied, and another bidder won.

There were two matching vases and a tapestry and more paintings, and I got so bored I stopped bidding, leaving Detective Martinez to do it for me, stress-sweat running down his temples and into the collar of his shirt. After each sale, an assistant carried the won item to the sale table and the bidder got up to pay for it. The crowd began to thin as winners left with what they'd come for.

"Our next item," the man behind the podium said, "is a mother-and-child statue. Solid brass, circa 1920s. I'll begin the bidding at—"

But I heard nothing else he said; my brain flooded with bumpy gray and black, with fireworks of pain and confetti surprise. The colors were framed by fuzzy gray, a memory.

My fingers went up to the side of my head, felt the scar there.

Vanessa Hollis had come at me with a statue. A brass statue of a mother and child. She'd tried to hit me with it, and when she'd failed, she'd thrown it at me. *You nosy bitch!*

I'd seen it on the poster, of course. But there was something about being in the same room with it that made the whole room dip and sway. I elbowed Detective Martinez.

"We're up," I breathed.

"What?" Detective Martinez was right at my ear.

"That statue is from you-know-where."

"What?" he said again, but he sat up straight, his attention drilled directly into the auctioneer's voice.

The statue sold fast, to a pudgy woman two rows ahead of me, who'd won the vast majority of the items, her jewelry clicking approvingly every time she raised her paddle. I melted into my chair, feeling numb and dizzy and scared all over again. Wanting nothing but to get the cane and get out of there.

The auctioneer banged his gavel, and his assistant approached with the next item.

"This Maori Koruru mask is hand carved out of wood, its eyes inlaid with paua shell . . ."

Dru.

Oh God, Dru.

I remembered barging into Dru's apartment, drugged and beat up and terrified. Luna had brought me to Hollis Mansion and I had escaped and gone straight to his apartment. That was the day he'd taken the camera card from me. It was the first time I'd seen his apartment in the light. And the first thing I noticed was the tribal mask that hung on the wall next to his kayak.

The same tribal mask the auctioneer's assistant was holding up in the air right now.

"Hey." Detective Martinez shook my shoulder. "What's up? You look pale. You okay?"

I didn't even feel my mouth open, but the words some-how came out anyway. "That was Dru's. I'm okay. I'll be okay." It seemed to take forever for the mask to sell. It was, after all, really ugly. But my hands twitched around my pad-dle, longing to buy it just to keep one last connection with Dru. Could I do it? Could I wake up every morning looking at that mask? Could I spend each day with a reminder of what had happened in that backyard literally staring at me? I thought about it too long. The gavel sounded, and I watched as a man in a gray suit made his way to his newly acquired prize. I instantly felt regret.

And then I felt a nudge on my knee. Martinez was nod-ding toward the stage, where the assistant was holding up the next item for bid.

". . . genuine silver ball handle . . . ," the auctioneer was saying. ". . . missing gemstone . . . quite the find . . . discov-ered wrapped in a blanket tucked in a corner in an attic . . ."

Detective Martinez and I exchanged looks. Rigo's cane. We didn't know how it had ended up here. Why hadn't Rigo taken it with him? Why hadn't the Hollises destroyed it? How was it that someone had found it, thought it was sell-able junk, and sent it off to an estate auction? None of that mattered at the moment. All that mattered was that we get our hands on it now.

My paddle flew up without my even realizing it, but I was quickly outbid by a couple in the front row and someone else a few rows behind that one. I held up my paddle again. And again. And again. And again, until Detective Martinez finally pushed my arm down gently. I didn't have the money to pay for this. And I knew what he was thinking—let someone else have it, and I would just have to figure out a way to get it from them.

The gavel sounded and a man stood to claim his prize. He was tall, lanky, had a head full of thick, dark hair, and had a perma-frown on his face. He came back to his seat and the auctioneer moved on to the next item. Was he *one of the boys?*

Shit. Now what?

Suddenly the air got very heavy, and I was sure I was being watched. I could feel it—the Hollis threat, the Hollis presence—hovering around me, pressing on my lungs. They were in Dubai, but the memory of everything that happened that night would never leave. "Can we go?" I whispered.

"They're not done yet." He gestured toward the stage with his paddle. The auctioneer mistook the motion for a bid. Detective Martinez winced and clasped the paddle in his lap again.

I grabbed his sleeve and pulled. "I really want to go."

"Just a few more minutes, Nikki. We've got to be patient. We want to keep that cane in our sight."

"This is stupid," I whispered, getting angry now. "There's a difference between being patient and wasting your time.

We lost. Let's go so we can figure out what to do."

The two women shushed us again. I slumped back in my chair, knowing that I was sitting in my chiffon dress like it was a pair of sweatpants, and not caring at all.

"The next item," the auctioneer said. And then *blah, blah, blah*, a bunch of stuff I didn't hear. And then a word. The one word that would grasp my attention every time. "Rainbow."

I jolted upright. He was holding the painting I'd seen in the poster. A melancholy painting of a bunch of men in a rowboat on a raging sea; the shadow of their ship going down in the background.

"What did he say?" I hissed at Detective Martinez. He was scrolling through text messages on his phone.

"What?"

I pointed toward the auctioneer. "What did he say about that?"

He shrugged. "I wasn't listening."

I shoved his shoulder with a frustrated grunt and leaned forward, poking my head next to the lady in front of me. "Excuse me," I said. She shot me an annoyed look. "What did he say about that painting? Something about a rainbow?"

She gave me a *You classless rabble* look and then whispered haughtily. "It's a reproduction of Ivan Aivazovsky's *The Rainbow*, of course. Mint condition, but just a print."

The Rainbow.

Rainbow.

Peyton's escort name. Peyton's tattoo, which instructed me to *Live in Color*. The decoration on the box in her bedroom where I'd found her old cell phone. Rainbow.

Everywhere that there was a rainbow, there was a clue. A clue from Peyton, left specifically for me.

I grabbed the paddle off Martinez's lap and raised it in the air.

He gave me a confused look. "What are you doing?"

"I need that painting."

"Why?"

"Just trust me on this."

Fortunately, I was the only one who bid, so the auction was over quickly and cheaply. I practically sprinted to collect my painting. I could almost feel it vibrating in my hands. I didn't know how I knew, but this piece of art was a message from Peyton. It had to be.

Just as I reached my seat—a very curious-looking Martinez staring at me with all kinds of questions in his eyes—the man with the perma-frown stood, holding the arm of the woman in the peach dress, who carried the cane protectively.

And they'll have it? You've made sure? she'd been asking when I'd walked into her shop.

They'd gotten what they'd come for, and they were leaving with it.

If they made that cane disappear, would there be any evidence against Rigo?

They slunk out through a side door, and I felt my dress begin to roll and boil, the black morphing into fiery golds and oranges, rippling, rippling, until I couldn't take it anymore.

"Come on," I said, pulling Detective Martinez's sleeve. "Let's go after them."

But he was already halfway out of the room before I finished my sentence.

We hustled down the stairs, my gown billowing behind me. My hair, which I'd pinned up for the occasion, had begun to pull loose from its bobby pins, and big hunks of it bounced against my bare shoulders. The bodice of my dress inched lower and lower with every step, and I clutched the painting by my side so hard my fingers cramped. But I didn't care. I couldn't care.

We raced through the foyer, followed by the surprised faces of waiters who were taking advantage of the lull to catch up on gossip, and plowed through the front door.

"Is everything all—" I heard at my back, but I didn't bother to turn around to see who'd said it.

I was only steps behind Detective Martinez when we hit the walkway, and had completely caught up with him by the time we got to the little parking area in the grass.

An SUV was pulling out of the parking lot when we

got there, its headlights blinding us both. It turned on the blacktop and roared through the tunnel of jacarandas until darkness and distance gobbled up its taillights.

"Son of a bitch!" I shouted, my free hand on my hip while I tried to slow my breath. "We missed them."

Detective Martinez's breath was coming as hard and fast as mine. "We'll just have to come up with another plan," he said.

"Right," I said, tugging up the front of my dress. "Just another plan. No problem. Any brilliant ideas on what this plan looks like? Because I'm out."

"We keep looking," he said, leading the way across the lot while digging his keys out of his pocket. So much for that whole elbow-escort chivalry thing.

"We've been everywhere," I said.

"Then we go back to everywhere." He took a few more steps, his keys jingling in his palm. "Nikki, sometimes finding the answers means you have to keep asking the same questions over and over again. Clues don't just fall into your lap."

Yes, they do, I thought. *At least they do for me. They fall into my lap with a tsunami splash of color.* But of course he didn't know that.

"Speaking of clues," he said, checking his watch. I had caught up to him at the car. "It's still early. Why don't you come by and we'll watch some of those surveillance videos?"

"Fine," I said, crestfallen that he could just shift his focus from the cane that quickly and easily. It was our one possible piece of physical evidence, and it would surely be gone forever now. The Basiles had let it get lost once; they weren't likely to do it again. "But I want to change. And take this home." I raised the boat picture.

"What's with the painting, anyway?" he asked, irritated. "You planning to tell me why you had to have it?"

"No."

He raised his palms. "Of course not. You just suddenly felt a need to redecorate?"

"No."

"So what then?"

"It's a clue," I said, and for the briefest second I considered letting him in on my synesthesia and how I'd been using it to follow Peyton's trail. But my synesthesia was so personal, and so difficult to explain without sounding like a crazy person. I was so guarded about it, I didn't know how to let that guard down. I didn't know how to let him in. And I was afraid to try. "I can't tell you how I know. I just do."

"A hunch," he said, his tone biting.

I nodded. "I know you hate it when I say that."

"No, I hate it when you say *only* that." I shrugged, the words not coming. He sighed, resigned, and took the painting from me. "We had something similar hanging in our bathroom when I was a kid," he said. "A boat out in a storm.

I didn't like it. It scared me a litt— Watch out!"

Before I could even react, Detective Martinez grabbed me around the waist and pulled me aside so fast our legs tangled together and we both fell against his bumper. The painting clattered on the ground and slid under the car. Out of nowhere, headlights appeared, coming from the lot where the SUV had been parked. Detective Martinez and I rolled between cars as a white van veered toward us, nearly running us over. It barely missed us, its rear tires so close I could have reached out and touched one. It screeched out onto the driveway and took off, leaving a trail of gold fireworks.

"You okay?" Martinez asked after it had roared away. We were both breathing heavily, checking our elbows and knees, brushing off our clothes.

I nodded.

"Who the hell was that?" He gazed in the direction the van had gone.

Luna. She's finally come out to play. "I don't know," I said.

"Did you catch the writing on the side?"

I closed my eyes, reached back until the colors flashed out at me. It was so quick, and I'd only seen it as it whizzed by. "I think it was some sort of distribution company?" I said, shaking my head. I didn't have a color association for those words, but the blur of individual colors that streaked past seemed to light up my mind with *distribution*. "But I can't be sure. The top word was short." I concentrated. Not a word. An acronym, maybe? Or a name. A three-letter name. Scarlet, avocado, maroon. "Dom?" I asked.

Detective Martinez opened the door to let me in, but he was still staring down the driveway. "Dom Distribution," he said. "Why does that sound familiar?"

I didn't know, but it tickled my memory too.

DETECTIVE MARTINEZ'S APARTMENT was one of those kind you have to be buzzed into. But instead of buzzing me in, he came down the stairs and opened the door for me himself. He'd swapped his tux for a pair of jeans and a plain white tee, his feet bare, his hair wet-looking, as if he'd just gotten out of the shower.

"Come on," he said, grabbing my wrist and pulling me inside. He made sure the door shut behind me, and even gave a quick scan outside, as if he expected someone to be there.

"I wasn't followed by the ghost of Peyton," I joked. But the joke felt too raw. I pressed my lips together and then tried again. "You're the only person who follows me, Detective."

Also not funny. I needed to stop talking.

"Just being safe," he mumbled, and then led me up a couple of flights of stairs and into a quiet, carpeted hallway. It felt much more like a hotel than an apartment building—sterile and contained. I wondered if Detective Martinez liked things so . . . bland. Something about him definitely did not fit with bland.

We stopped at a plain gray door and he pulled out a key, then stood back as the door swung open onto a surprisingly beautiful apartment. All hardwood and white walls. A stereo was playing soft music in the background. I kicked off my shoes, dropped my car keys inside one of them, and sniffed the air.

"I made some pasta," he said, almost embarrassedly, as he shut the door and passed me. "Just in case we get hungry. It's going to be a long night, I'm guessing. Have you eaten?"

I hadn't, but at the moment I was too distracted by a peacefulness that settled over me, silky and pink as strawberry mousse, like lying on the velvet inside of a jewelry box. "I'm good," I said.

He scratched the back of his neck, his tee riding up and revealing his tanned, taut belly, a thin line of hair disappearing into his waistband. I felt myself blush—swollen grapes, bruises, faceted amethysts—and looked away.

"So the TV's over here." He gestured toward a black leather couch and headed that way. "I got the videos downloaded onto DVDs so we can watch them on the big screen. Maybe pick up on something easier that way." He settled on the couch and grabbed the remote.

"So how legal is it for you to have these DVDs? And for you to be showing them to me?" He cleared his throat uncomfortably. I mock-gasped. "Are you breaking laws for me, Detective? Have I officially lured you over to the dark side? I thought it would never happen."

"Are you done?" he asked.

I joined him on the couch, plopping down like I owned the place. "Probably not, but it'll do for now. I'm ready, Detective Martinez. Let's do some recon."

He grinned. "Totally the wrong word, but okay."

"Whatever. I'm not a cop."

"Thank God for small favors," he murmured. "The thought of you running around with a gun . . ."

I propped my feet on the coffee table. "Very funny. I bet you'd be surprised how good I could be with a badge."

He smiled wide. His teeth were so white. Did he have them bleached, or did they come that way naturally? They seemed impossibly white for natural teeth. Maybe they were fake. *Maybe you're thinking just a little too much about how perfect his teeth are, Nik.* "You're right, I would be very surprised. Like, alternate reality surprised. And for your information, it's not exactly illegal for me to have these DVDs."

"Not exactly illegal is not the same thing as legal."

"Well, if you want me to give them back while we wait for red tape . . ."

I yanked the remote out of his hand. "Let's just do this. I don't have all night."

Actually, not true. Dad was up in Chico, working on some still shots for a movie promotion. He wouldn't be back for a few days, like always. Usually I would hate it that he was gone. Would feel like I was living with someone who only pretended to be a dad. Would wish that he'd find someone to settle down with in Chico. But right now, I didn't know what to think about Dad.

It was jarring to find out that the only person in this world that you definitely thought you could count on had been hiding things from you.

I pressed play and the TV blinked to life. Detective Martinez and I settled in, silent, both of our brows furrowed as we watched the comings and goings of Hollywood Dreams. Which was really super boring.

After about an hour of nothing, silence, a few fast-forwards, pauses, and rewinds here and there, Martinez finally paused the video. He rubbed his eyes with one hand. I fought the urge to do the same.

He stood, stretched, and yawned loudly. "I need food or I'm going to fall asleep."

"It's amazing how much nothing can happen on one

street, right?" I asked, turning so that I was kneeling, looking over the back of the couch while he puttered in the kitchen, which was separated from the living room by a breakfast bar.

"Generally speaking, I like streets with nothing happening on them," he said. He got two plates—trendy, black—out of the cabinet and lifted the lid on a pot on the stove. Steam billowed out.

"Well," I said, plopping back down on the couch. "I don't. Not this street, anyway. How far have we gotten?"

He came around the bar and into the living room, a plate of pasta in each hand. It smelled amazing. My stomach growled. "Not far enough," he answered. He sat next to me and dug into his food. "About three weeks," he said around a mouthful.

"And how much footage do you have here?"

"Three months." Another mouthful.

I groaned. "In that case, I hope you made enough for seconds."

NEXT THING I knew I was being shaken. Luna had gotten to me—had poisoned me and was shaking me so hard my teeth rattled. I tried to fight, but I couldn't. My arms and legs were heavy, slow. They didn't work right. My vision was starting to fade. My breathing was labored. This was it. She'd finally won.

"Nikki," I heard. Not Luna's voice; a man's. "Nikki, wake up."

I opened my eyes. It wasn't Luna shaking me; it was Detective Martinez, and I was curled up next to him on a black leather couch. I sat up, blinking, as reality slowly came back to me. The last thing I remembered was texting Jones five times, getting frustrated that he wasn't responding, stretching back on the couch, and saying I was going to take a catnap and to wake me if anything got interesting.

The clock on the DVD player read 1:55.

Shit.

"I fell asleep," I said, my voice thick. I checked my phone. Still nothing from Jones.

He chuckled. "No kidding. You've been out for a while."

I looked down and saw that I was covered with a soft, colorful crocheted blanket. It looked handmade. I gazed at the TV, which was paused on a still shot of the front of Hollywood Dreams. "You've been working all this time?"

"I'm used to long nights. Plus, I don't get a lot of sleep these days."

"Why not?" I yawned and pulled myself to sitting.

"You're not my only case," he said. "Never mind. Not important."

"Uh-huh," I said. I was no detective, but I was willing to bet his lack of sleep had something to do with those bullet holes on the front of his car.

He ignored me. Which, of course, only made me want to know the story all the more. But I knew when Martinez could and couldn't be pushed, and this was a *don't push* moment if I ever saw one. "Just . . . you need to look at this." He aimed the remote at the TV and pressed play. At first, nothing happened. More of the same empty doorway on the same empty sidewalk.

I yawned again. "Seriously, if it's someone's job to sit and watch this security feed live, it's the worst job ever."

"Just wait for it," he said.

Soon, someone appeared in the shot. A woman wearing a poured-on pair of pants and thigh-high boots, her hair wisped around her head like fresh cotton candy. Vanessa Hollis. She expertly pulled a key out of her purse and whisked inside the building—so quickly it was like she'd never been there.

"So?" I said. I rubbed my eyes. They felt dry, and all I really wanted to do was go home so I could sleep for real. "It's not news that Vanessa Hollis owned the place."

"Watch," Detective Martinez said. He hit fast-forward, and the screen of nothingness jerked and blipped in front of us until something whizzed past.

"Wait." I pointed to the screen. "What was that?"

He backed up a bit and then let the recording play again. This time a man—short, balding, wearing a black leather jacket and a pair of crisp jeans—came to the door and walked in. There was something strange, though, about his walk.

"Go back," I said.

"Hang on, there's more," Detective Martinez said. He sped the recording forward until the door opened once again. Out popped Vanessa Hollis, and, right behind her, the same man. She turned to lock the door, he turned with her, and . . .

"Stop!" I cried. "A cane. He's got a cane."

Suddenly I was full of silver and gold like piles of jingling, restless coins. Detective Martinez stopped the recording and we both leaned forward, craning our necks to take in the screen.

"That's Arrigo Basile," Martinez said, confirming what I already knew.

I leaned back against the couch, resting my hand on my forehead. I smelled sweaty and a little bit garlicky from the pasta, and probably couldn't have looked all that great, either, but at the moment I just didn't care. "So all this does is give us evidence that the Hollises had ties with Rigo Basile. Which you already knew, long before Peyton was attacked. It doesn't really prove anything."

He stood, his shirt sticking to his back, showing a thin swatch of brown skin, so warm-looking I wanted to press my cheek against it. I looked away, swallowing the colors before they could even register in my sleepy mind. Right now was not the time.

"But it does more than that," he said. "He's got a cane. *The* cane, presumably." He reached for the coffee table, which had the poster, its edges still curled, spread out on it. He held it up, pointing at the photo. "The cane that was somehow mixed in with the Hollises' things, given to the Tesla estate, and bought at auction by the Basiles."

"Or a similar cane. Coincidental," I said. "For all a jury knows. There are probably a thousand canes just like that one floating around out there. A million. Besides, there is no way the Basiles haven't already destroyed it."

He frowned. "But this gives enough reasonable doubt to get you off the hook. Right? I'll have Blake take it to her boss."

I peeled the blanket off my legs and stood, too. "And they'll say I stole it from Rigo to frame him. Or that Dru gave it to me. Or that I just found it and figured it would be a convenient tool to kill Peyton. Or God knows what else."

He raked his hands through his hair, looking from me to the TV and back again. "We finally have something. And you're arguing. If I didn't know better, I would think you don't want to clear your name."

"No, I'm just being realistic. This isn't enough. I've been through this before, Detective. I saw how they escaped justice with Peyton." *And I saw how my mom's murderer escaped justice, too,* I thought. "What would make me think that I'm going to be any different? Peyton had far more power than I have."

"I don't know. The truth, maybe? The power of the truth?"

We locked eyes. The room began to burn yellow around the periphery of my mind, but in that yellow I also felt gray. "The truth," I scoffed. "Does anyone in my life even know anything about the truth?"

I started toward the kitchen. I desperately needed a glass of water. My mouth felt fuzzy from sleep. Detective Martinez followed me.

"What is that supposed to mean?"

"Nothing. Forget it." I searched cabinets until I found a glass and went to the sink.

"No," he said. "If we're working together on this, Nikki, we need to communicate. You can't shut down on me now."

I set the glass on the counter with a loud *thop*. "Okay, fine, let's communicate then. Why are there bullet holes in your car? Why were you looking around downstairs like you're expecting someone to jump out at you? Communication is a two-way street, Detective. So spill."

"We're not talking about that," he said. "It has nothing to do with this case."

"Of course not. When it comes to the truth, I'm the only one expected to live by any sort of standard. Everyone else gets to hide whatever the hell they feel like hiding, and it's all okay. We're not talking about the holes in your car, we're not talking about whatever else it is that's bugging you, my dad's not talking about shit, where does it fucking end?"

He shook his head as if to process something. "Your dad? What does he have to do with this?"

I'd said too much. If I told him about the photos I'd found, it would lead to conversations that I didn't want to get into. Conversations about my mom, about Brandi, about the metal box under my dad's desk. We had enough going on without adding ancient family drama to the list. Plus, I still wasn't sure how hard I was actually looking for Brandi, and I didn't want to be forced to look harder. "Nothing. I'm just . . . I'm tired." I took a sip of water, stretching it out to stall.

He squinted, as if he didn't believe a word I'd said, and then decided to let it go. Maybe he figured if he expected me to accept his secrets, he had to accept mine. We stood there awkwardly, me pretending to take the longest drink in the universe, and my eyes roved over to the TV.

Stupid Rigo Basile. Guilty as hell, but unless we figured out something, I was going to go down for his crime. Surely someone out there knew where he was. Someone out there knew something.

Silver-brown-purple.

I squinted harder at the TV.

Silver-brown-purple.

It hadn't jumped out at me before, because it was so quick, and the colors so muted by the things I'd associated with Vanessa—fear, danger, death. From the couch, it might have looked like a glare on the TV screen, maybe from the overhead light in the kitchen, but from this angle it was definitely . . .

"That address," I said, my voice echoing in my glass. I set it down, distracted. "I know that address."

"What?" Detective Martinez followed my gaze.

I skirted the bar and hurried across to the TV, where I knelt with my face just inches from the screen. Now the numbers glowed, screaming out at me from Rigo's hand. He had taken something from Vanessa, the move so subtle we had both missed it. But now I could see it, her fingertips still pressing the paper into his palm. I touched it. "That's the address of the parking lot." I tapped the screen and looked back at Detective Martinez, who had followed me and was bent over, so close to my shoulder I almost bumped noses with him. "The parking lot, Detective." He still looked uncomprehending. "The one where Peyton was attacked."

I stood and paced back to the couch, thoughts flipping and fluttering through my head so fast I could barely hold on to them. I was wide awake now. "Of course. She's giving him the address of where the attack is supposed to go down. We've got him. We've got him receiving the address from

Vanessa Hollis while holding the cane in his hand. Maybe you're right. Maybe this will be enough for them to at least consider Rigo another possible suspect."

"How could you possibly know that?" Detective Martinez asked.

"What do you mean? I just told you. The address and the cane and—"

"No, not that." He narrowed his eyes at the screen and then looked at me with curiosity. "The address. I can't even see it, and you're claiming that you can see it and not only that, but you remember it from seven months ago?"

"I had to type it into my GPS," I said. "And maybe my eyesight is better than yours."

He shook his head, rejecting that theory. "Who does that? Who memorizes addresses that they've punched into their GPS one time? And my eyesight is perfect."

I could feel unease well up inside of me. This again. Detective Martinez getting too close to the truth, looking for answers that I didn't know how to open up and give. But, like it or not, I would have to. He probably wouldn't believe me, just like the counselor at the high school.

I took a deep breath. "It's . . ."

"A hunch," he said with a sarcastic nod.

"Well, you don't have to say it like that."

I let out a frustrated breath, feeling totally crestfallen. *Crestfallen*: an ugly peppered word, something like a cross between sadness brown and ragemonster red with flecks of black.

"Well, how am I supposed to say it, Nikki? You have these weird hunches—something isn't right with them, and you know it—but every time I ask you about them, you clam up and guard yourself. You shouldn't shut people out like that. I—"

"Yes, yes, I know. You're just trying to keep me out of prison and I really should be more cooperative and let you in and *blah, blah, blah.*" I searched for my shoes by the couch, and then remembered that I had taken them off at the door. I breezed past Martinez.

He grabbed my elbow. "It's more than that, Nikki."

Something passed between us. Something that I could only describe as a feeling of being washed over in a rainbow, and sliding down, down, down, the violet stripe. I had no idea what it was, but something in the core of me felt shaky from it. I yanked away from him.

"It isn't that easy for me, okay?" I said. I hurried down the hall and stuffed my feet into my shoes, palmed my keys, and opened the apartment door. Somehow he was right behind me again. How did he keep doing that? "It's not like you tell me everything about yourself, either."

He placed his hands on his hips and tipped his face to the ceiling, letting out a sigh. "Fine. You win. I have a case that I'm working on," he said. "Some gang stuff. It's kind of a personal thing, and I'm just being extra careful right now. Vigilant. It's not a huge deal that you need to know about."

I didn't know what to say. I hadn't been expecting him to actually come clean. Clean*ish*, anyway. It felt too intimate. Too real. If he was expecting me to open up and start spilling my guts everywhere, he was crazy. I just needed to get home. Get alone and clear my mind. "Well, my hunches aren't a huge deal that you need to know about," I said.

He looked disappointed, but he didn't press. "Let me walk you down."

I stepped through the threshold of the door, glad to be standing in the fluorescent-lit hallway, where I could see again, where I could think straight without all that crazy color tossing me around. I turned to face him. "How many times do I have to tell you, Detective? I can take care of myself."

I WAS STILL fuming when I got home. There were a hell of a lot of things I didn't like, but being doubted was definitely one of them. I'd seen that address, and did it really matter how? Why couldn't he have just taken my word for it and moved on?

But was he really doubting you? my mind tried to ask. *Or was he trying to understand you?*

What was the difference?

I went straight to my room, kicking off my shoes and

tossing my keys onto the desk. They slid across and rattled against the side of the painting I'd bought at the auction. Another one of my hunches. As exhausted as I was just an hour ago, I was completely amped now.

I picked up the painting, studied it, and then took it to my bed, scooting backward until I was leaning against the headboard and holding it in my lap.

Detective Martinez had said a similar painting in his bathroom had scared him as a child. I could see it. The grays and blues and the white mist. The shouting men, the listing ship in the background. Not a vivid ship but the ghost of one. It looked like mayhem. Like it would be a miracle for any of those men to make it to shore without drowning.

Which was sort of how I felt sometimes. Through all of this Peyton nonsense, the ocean of lies and mist obscuring the truth. Most of the time I was certain I was swimming against the tide, and if I ever made it to dry land, I might not recognize it anymore.

It occurred to me that maybe this was how Peyton had begun to feel. I remembered the SOS photo—Peyton standing in water, a life preserver looped over one arm. She'd been asking for help in the one way she knew how: through art.

It seemed impossible that she hadn't left this painting—a similar theme with the word *Rainbow* in the title—just for me. But did she leave it for me to help me find answers, or did she just leave it for me because she thought I'd like it?

There was only one way to find out. I turned the painting over and over in my hands, studying it so closely I could
see the individual fibers of the canvas. I held it at an angle
to let the light reflect off it. I felt my way around the frame,
I studied the back side, rubbing my hands over it. Nothing.

I pried open the clasps and pulled the cardboard backing
off the frame. A folded-up piece of paper fell out and landed
in my lap. I set the painting down and picked up the paper,
unfolded it.

It was a poem.

The Seeker
Peyton Hollis
If we meet in the willow wood
The air thick as sweet Brandi
And we talk to the night
Our ruby hearts beating
Will you give me the answers that I seek?
Will I find myself in your eyes?
Will you take me home?

My fingers tingled and my eyes burned as I read the
poem again and again, the words jumping out at me in
golds and greens and reds and pinks and leathery browns, all
tricks, since the poem was written in pencil.

Except when I cleared my mind and ignored the colors, I

realized that not all of it was written in charcoal pencil.

Nine words were drawn in with colored pencil, the letters in a repeated rainbow pattern, making them stand out to me in bold.

The Seeker
Peyton Hollis
If we meet in the WILLOW WOOD
The air thick as sweet BRANDI
And we TALK TO the night
Our RUBY hearts beating
Will you give me the ANSWERS that I seek?
Will I FIND myself in your eyes?
Will you take me HOME?

Rainbow colors. Rainbow. Had to be for a reason. I was more certain than ever that Peyton was helping me, using her rainbow to lead me where I needed to go.

I read the poem again. And again. Trying to make sense of what she was hoping to say. *Brandi*, misspelled. That one was easy. If I was right, the poem was intended to lead me to Brandi. Great. If only she'd known how much I'd been avoiding finding Brandi, she might not have wasted her time.

But what if Brandi was somehow linked to the reason why Peyton was attacked? What if that was what she'd been trying to tell me all along?

I grabbed my laptop and slid back in bed, bringing it with me. I Googled "Willow Wood." Ohio, South Dakota, Fort Lauderdale. Apartments, medical supplies, assisted living, music stores. There were tons of places called Willow Wood, but none of them made sense. I scrolled and scrolled, waiting for something to jump out at me. Something to shoot fireworks into my brain.

But I had nothing.

I decided to concentrate on *ruby* instead. A gemstone. Why? Why would Peyton be talking about gemstones? Was I supposed to be finding jewelry? God, was this just a random poem not meant for me at all? Peyton was artistic. She wrote the lyrics to all of Viral Fanfare's songs. Maybe this was just another song. It was melancholy. Viral Fanfare liked melancholy.

But why would she hide it in a painting called The Rainbow *if it was just song lyrics, Nikki?*

It didn't make sense. I did more Googling—looking for anything to do with rubies that might fit. I came up with nothing.

Frustrated, I tossed my laptop and Peyton's poem to the side and flopped down on the bed. What was I missing? I closed my eyes to concentrate.

Fear Is Golden. Peyton had led me to answers with that phrase before. Did that somehow come into play now? Not that I could see. *Live in Color?* No. The word *ruby* was red to me, but how was I supposed to know what color the word *ruby* was to Peyton? It seemed unlikely that she would have expected me to know, but even if her synesthesia told her it was red like mine, what did red have to do with Brandi? And what did either of those have to do with Willow Wood, whatever Willow Wood was?

Ruby. Precious gems. Jewels. Woods. Brandi. Home. *Talk to.*

My eyes flew open. I grabbed the poem and studied it, blocking out everything except the rainbow words.

Willow Wood
Brandi
Talk to
Ruby
Answers
Find
Home

Shit. As usual, I had been letting my synesthesia make things way too complicated. Ruby was more than a gemstone and more than a color. Ruby was also a name. The Ruby in the poem must have been a person—a person who had answers about Brandi. Peyton was trying to lead me to her, telling me to find her home. It was all so incredibly obvious once I let Peyton talk to me in the language we both understood—the language of color.

I stood and paced, then picked up the laptop and brought it back to my desk. I plugged in *Willow Wood California*. It had to be a place, and it had to be nearby. How else would Peyton expect me to find Ruby? I got a hit. Sure enough, there was a market cafe called Willow Wood up in Graton. Graton wasn't that far away, but it was a tiny town—the kind of town where a Hollis would definitely stand out. That couldn't be it. Frustrated, I smacked my hand down on the keyboard, making the screen jump to the next page.

It was late and I was exhausted. Between the auction and the surveillance videos and the poem, I'd had enough mystery for one night. My eyes were tired and heavy.

I was just about to shut the laptop and give up—*you overestimated my abilities, Peyton*—when I saw a link for an apartment complex called Willow Wood.

It was fifteen miles away in Los Angeles.

20

JONES WOKE ME with the doorbell.

He'd been ringing it repeatedly for what felt like half an hour, commingling with my dream, just as my dream had absorbed Detective Martinez's shake the night before.

I sat up in bed, blinking away the ten minutes of sleep I'd gotten. My laptop was still open, the battery dead, and the poem was still lying half-folded next to it. The painting had fallen to the floor. I stumbled into the bathroom, grabbing my phone off my desk on the way and texting Jones to hang on. Mercifully, the doorbell stopped.

I was still in my clothes from the night before, my mascara smeared into raccoon rings under my eyes. My hair was a knotted mess. My chest felt tight and my throat scratchy. I studied myself in the mirror and then leaned away. I looked as bad as I felt. I splashed some water over my face and ran a brush through my hair. There wasn't enough time to do anything about my clothes, but at least I looked halfway human again. Hopefully I smelled at least halfway human, too. I sniffed my shirt—sweat and garlic and a hint of something distinctly Martinez-y. I spritzed perfume over it.

When I opened the front door, Jones was there, head bowed, hands on hips.

"Can we talk?" he asked.

"Of course. Come in." I backed up to make room, and shut the door after him. We went straight to the living room, Jones easing himself onto the very edge of Dad's recliner. I sank into the couch, yawning, trying not to give in to the pull of sleep. "I've been trying to talk to you, but you haven't been answering my texts. You totally misinterpreted everything," I said, but he held up a hand to stop me.

"I have some things I came here to say," he said. "So I would appreciate it if you'd just let me say them." I nodded. He took a deep breath and began talking, mostly to his feet. "I don't know what exactly is going on between you and that cop."

"Sparring, Jones. That's all that was going on between me and *that cop*," I interrupted, and again he held his hand out to stop me.

I'm not one who likes to be shushed, and it must have

shown on my face, because he followed it with, "Please? Nikki?" I glared but kept my mouth shut, and he began again. "I don't know what's going on between you and that cop, but you're more than just working partners or whatever you're trying to tell me." I squirmed, a flash of last night going through my head—that weird floaty rainbow sensation that I'd had when he looked in my eyes. I willed it away before it freaked me out again. Jones was wrong. Martinez and I were working partners, and that was it, violet rainbow stripe or no violet rainbow stripe. "But I've decided that I don't care."

He finally met my eyes. "I mean, I care. I don't really want you sleeping with him. Or anyone else, actually. But you're not my girlfriend and I don't have any right to tell you who to be with. If I don't like it, nothing's keeping me here. I think I finally got the message."

Something whooshed around inside me—both sadness and relief that Jones didn't consider me his girlfriend, and a sense that it was pretty unfair of me to be sad about that when I definitely didn't consider him my boyfriend. Did I? I had an uncomfortable feeling that maybe I had begun to think of him that way. "I'm going to be leaving for New Mexico soon, and I don't want to spend these last few weeks together fighting. And I don't want to spend them apart, either. I don't love you. . . ." He dipped his face to the floor again when he said this, his cheeks brightening and his hands picking at each other. He was lying. He did love me. But he knew that telling me that would be the best way to get me to leave him. He finally looked up. "I don't love you. But I care about you. And I have fun with you. And I want to keep doing that."

For a few seconds we just sat there in awkward silence. I was trying to let everything he'd said sink in, without me feeling like a total asshole. This was the relationship I'd always wanted with Jones—attachment free. So why did it feel so crappy when I finally got it?

"That's all," he said. "You can talk now."

Unsure what to do, I got up and walked over to him. I put my hands on his shoulders and he let his forehead rest against me. "Jones," I said, and then realized I didn't know what else to say. I ran my fingers over his scalp and down through his hair. He wrapped his arms around me and pulled me closer, burying his face into my stomach. I reached down and tugged on his chin so that he was looking up at me. "Detective Martinez is . . . a necessary evil. Just for right now. But I can promise you it doesn't go any further than that. And it won't. As soon as we clear me, he's gone." Now the gray that seeped into the room was settling around me. I leaned down and kissed Jones's forehead to drive it away. "He has a girlfriend. And I have . . . you. We may not be boyfriend-girlfriend, but we are something. And I want to enjoy the rest of our time together too."

He breathed, relief spreading across his face. "I was hoping you'd say that." He tugged my waist and I fell into his lap, facing him, my legs wrapping around his middle. Dad's recliner creaked with the added weight, but I ignored it. The truth was Dad would so rather find out I'd made out with Jones in his recliner today than find out where I'd been last night.

I bent and kissed him, feeling the violet rush through me, roller coaster fast, my fingers lost in his hair, my body pressed up against his. His hands crawled up the back of my shirt, his skin warm against mine. He kissed me forever, and then worked his way up my neck and jawline to my ear.

"Can I have you for the whole day?" he whispered.

Yes. Yes, I wanted to be with him for the whole day. I wanted to stay lost in his kisses, in his skin. But there was Rigo to find. And, more pressing, there was someone named Ruby to find.

"Let's just worry about right now," I said, and kissed him again.

He stood, sweeping me off my feet and into his arms. "I'll take what I can get," he said, and carried me up to my room.

Later, the shades drawn and my room dusky, I slipped into a nap, the feeling of Jones's knuckle tracing my bicep the only thing keeping me in the present. He stayed quiet for a long time. And then, so softly I could have been convinced that I had only imagined it, he whispered, "Why can't you just love me, Nikki?"

I fell into a nightmarish sleep where Mom, bloody, was begging me to help her, where Dad was a ghost that haunted me at night, and where the hand in the dark that I reached for—the one stroking my bicep—was brown and calloused and glowing bright yellow.

21

I T WAS EVENING before Jones finally left, summoned by his mom, who needed him to come home and fill out college paperwork. Our lives had never seemed further apart—Jones worrying about financial aid and sports physicals while I was worried about staying out of prison and not getting killed by a runaway van in a dead wealthy person's parking lot.

That van . . .

Dom . . . Dom . . . Dom . . . I wasn't sure about the *Distribution* part. But I was certain about the scarlet-avocado-maroon. I was sure about Dom. I just couldn't figure out where it fit.

With Jones gone, I needed a new distraction.

For old times' sake, I pulled open my window and

grabbed a cigarette, but I was too restless to enjoy the smoke. Funny to think that just a few months ago, the only thing on my mind while sitting in my window had been a stupid chem quiz. But now I sat in my window thinking life-and-death thoughts. Thinking secrets and lies and how my entire world seemed to be made of them. But, God, it had always been made of them; I just hadn't known it until now.

I thought about those photos of Mom. Of her baby bump and the bus station—Salinas, Modesto, Bakersfield—bubble blue, muted gray, spongy tawny—and Dad saying she went on a long business trip. Several months long. I tried to remember that time spent without her and came up blank. It was as if that portion of my life didn't even exist. That could only mean one thing—that I had to have been really young when it happened, because I had spent the last ten years of my life carefully cataloguing every single memory I had of my mom. Baking Christmas cookies, her hand guiding mine with the sprinkle jar. Swimming at the beach, the way her hair got ropy and sand-caked and how I liked to sit behind her and run my fingers through the ropes to break them up. Ordinary days spent watching TV, our sock feet tangled up together on the couch. Those things had all happened after her business trip—I was sure of it. Which meant that baby bump was about my age. It could have been Peyton. It almost had to be.

There was only one way to find out. Find Brandi

Courteur. Whether I wanted to or not.

I gazed at my desk drawer, the one with the black binder inside. My stomach knotted at the thought of holding Peyton's letter again.

Yes, I needed to find Brandi Courteur.

I needed to start by finding a certain gemstone in the Willow Wood.

THE WILLOW WOOD apartments were made up of several blocks of depressing brick buildings on a stark street near Skid Row. It was hard to imagine Peyton having anything to do with an area like this one—yet more evidence that I truly didn't have a clue who Peyton really was—and for a moment I wondered if I'd gotten the clue wrong. If it was even a clue at all.

It was, Nikki. Trust your synesthesia.

Uh, yeah. A lot easier said than done.

I found parking and headed out with pretty much no plan. A part of me had thought I would never find the place, or that I would get there and Ruby would be obvious, standing on a corner with a flashing neon sign around her neck. Instead, I stood next to my car and peered at what seemed like an impossible number of generic-looking apartments. How would I ever find someone here?

Well, one thing was clear. I would never find anything if I didn't start looking. I picked a building and found some teenagers sitting out on a stoop.

"You guys know anyone named Ruby?" I asked. They stared at me, wordless. "Someone who might live in this building?" More stares. "You ever see a girl named Peyton? Blonde? Pretty?" One of them lit up a cigarette, but still no one talked. "Thanks for the information," I muttered, moving on to the next building. And the next. And the next. Nobody knew anyone named Ruby. Nobody knew Peyton. Nobody knew anything.

After a couple hours of dead ends, I got in my car and drove around to the other side of the complex. It was getting dark now—and I started to feel uneasy as I traipsed through another courtyard, asking a couple of boys playing basketball, a woman pushing a baby in a stroller, and two men sitting on a bench sharing a bottle. Nobody knew anything; or at least nobody was talking if they did.

I was just about to give up, nervous about the dark. I couldn't deny that knowing that Luna was out of jail and existing in this same dark put me on edge. The last thing I wanted was to be caught out here, fighting off that bag of crazy in this unfamiliar place filled with uncooperative people.

One more try, I told myself, as I entered a crumbling brick building and climbed the steps. Nobody was outside anymore, so I would just have to start knocking on doors. If I got nothing, I would come back tomorrow and try again.

The first door opened a crack, and one eyeball appeared

in the space. A female eyeball wearing tons of makeup and fake lashes so long they almost poked through the door frame.

"Hello?" I asked when she said nothing. I could see a splash of blue above the eye—blue hair, maybe? I cleared my throat. "I'm looking for someone? Her name's Ruby?"

Still not a word from the girl, but the door edged a little farther open, and I was surprised to see that she looked about my age. She was wearing a tight black corset and a short pink skirt, showing tons of leg and boob. She pointed toward the stairs with one black-painted fingernail.

"Upstairs?" I asked, and the eye moved up and down; a nod. "Thank you so much."

Finally, I had something. Ruby was an actual person. In an apartment complex called Willow Wood. Somehow, our synesthesia had worked. My heart leaped as I took the stairs two at a time, trying to ignore the smells of fried grease and pot smoke. Trying not to think about Luna hiding in the shadows, maybe under the stairs, waiting for me when I got back.

There were two doors at the top of the stairs. One had a tattered welcome mat out front that said *Next Time Bring a Warrant*. I knocked.

At first there was nothing, and my heart sank. I pondered whether I should sit on the steps and wait for her to come back, or maybe even break in—the lock didn't look that difficult, and I had learned a thing or two about breaking and entering over the past few months. But what would I really expect to find here? Would Ruby be displaying anything that might incriminate the Hollises? Would Luna be behind this door? Would Brandi?

But just as I was about to turn away and give up until tomorrow, the door squeaked open. Unlike the door downstairs, this one opened fully, and right away I knew I had the right place.

"Hi," said the woman on the other side. She was huge. Tall, muscular, huge breasts, curvy hips. Her red hair was so tall it looked like it might scrape the ceiling. Actually, red couldn't even begin to describe the color of her hair. It was so red I expected it to hum. "Can I help you?" she asked. "You lost?"

Hearing her voice, which was soft and inviting, knocked me out of my stupor. "Yeah, are you—" I said, but it came out in a whisper, so I tried again. "Are you Ruby?"

She smiled, her fire-red lipstick smeared across her front teeth. "You're not lost. And you are?"

"I'm Nikki Kill," I said. "I'm looking for somebody. I was hoping you could help me."

Just like that, her smile fell.

"Oh my God," she said, her voice dropping about seven octaves. "It can't be. I think I know why you're here."

R UBY'S APARTMENT WAS as big and outrageous as she
was—filled with half-pornographic knickknacks and
full-on pornographic posters. Everything was red, red, red,
which was kind of good, because the overwhelming color
helped keep my own colors at bay. Or maybe that was a bad
thing. I sort of needed them to help me see when I needed
to be ready to run. Or fight. Or did I really? How much of my
instincts was color-coded and how much was real?

Either way, I hoped it didn't come down to running or
fighting.

Ruby puttered through the living room, pulling dirty
laundry and magazines off the couch and dropping them in
a laundry basket that was parked in the hallway. "Come in,

sit down. Sorry it's such a mess. I don't have a lot of visitors. And the ones I get aren't really interested in watching TV, if you know what I mean." She glanced at me worriedly, shielding her mouth with her hand. "Oh, I'm sorry. I shouldn't talk like that around you. You're a nice girl. Carrie would be unimpressed by my language. Come in, sit down. It's okay, I don't bite. Can I get you a drink? A nonalcoholic one, of course?"

My mind was spinning, but everything had screeched to a halt. She'd said *Carrie* would be unimpressed by her language. Surely she didn't mean . . .

"No, thanks," I said, trying to keep up with her one-sided conversation. I sat on the couch. A shoe poked me in the backside and I pulled it out and dropped it on the floor. "I'm sorry, did you just say Carrie?"

Ruby stopped fussing and stood awkwardly in front of me. "Well, yes. Isn't that why you're here? To talk about your mother?"

Forget the red. The floodgates were now open. Confusion, surprise, fear. Puffs of mint with jagged edges, surrounded by golden starbursts, all of it splatting on a field of gray and black so strong I hadn't seen it since Peyton died. I had a hard time catching my breath. My mother. How on earth did Ruby know my mother?

Ruby rushed to my side, sat on the couch next to me. She laid her hands over mine. They felt calloused and rough, which helped bring me back into the present. "Oh, my! I've upset you," she said. "What is it, honey? What can I do? Do you need a hospital? A real drink?"

I felt myself shaking my head. No, I didn't need a hospital. I didn't need a real drink. I needed answers. But I was afraid of those answers. I wasn't expecting them here.

She leaned in closer. "You're not here about your mother?" Confusion rippled her forehead. "Why are you here, then?"

"Brandi," I said. Hearing my own voice helped bring reality back. "I'm looking for Brandi."

Ruby sat back and smoothed her skirt. "I don't know anyone named Brandi, honey, I'm sorry," she said.

"But you know Peyton?"

She looked blank.

"Rainbow?" I asked. "Maybe you knew her as Rainbow?" Recognition settled over her face, and Ruby got up and brushed ashes off a coffee table into her cupped hand, then dropped them on the floor. "She's the one who led me to you. She wanted me to talk to you." Ruby moved to a stack of newspapers, which she fastidiously straightened. "Look, I'm in real trouble. They think I killed Peyton, but someone—I think Luna Fairchild—is framing me. And Peyton left me a bunch of clues, and I can figure them out most of the time, but I never have any idea how they all fit together. You've got to help me."

Ruby stopped tidying and touched my wrist. "Listen, honey. It's terrible what happened to Rainbow, but I'm afraid I don't have anything to offer you. The business has been shut down. I've been scrambling for work like a back-alley whore. I like my life. And I can't screw it up."

I felt weak with disappointment. All this work for nothing. I'd found the person who was supposed to help me, and she wouldn't do it. I got up and started for the door. "Okay," I said. "Can you at least tell me how you knew my mother?"

Ruby wrung her hands together and came to me. She guided me back to the couch. For a few minutes we just sat there, as I watched her try to work up the courage to talk. "Oh, what the hell," she said finally. "I owe her this much at least." She took a breath. "Carrie was an angel on earth. She really was. Didn't deserve the life she was dealt."

"How did you know her?" I repeated, while at the same time feeling myself go cold. I wasn't sure I was up for the answers to any of my questions about my mother. The more I knew, the more confusing my life got. The more confusing my family got. The more alone I felt.

Ruby's face scrunched up in a sympathetic look. "Honey, we worked together way back before you were born."

"At—"

Ruby nodded, cutting me off before I could even so much as say the glittery lilac words. "Only for a short while," she said hurriedly. "I was new, and she showed me the ropes.

I got up and running, and next thing I knew she met a mystery man and was gone."

"Bill Hollis," I said bitterly. "Not much of a mystery." So it was true. On some level, I hadn't wanted to admit it, even to myself. But I couldn't ignore what the facts were telling me. As much as I hated the very idea of my mom having anything to do with Bill Hollis, she did. And it was all starting to fall into place now. Horribly, horribly into place.

I supposed I had suspected it ever since I discovered that Peyton was my sister. But now it was more than suspicion; it was true.

Slick, inky outrage. My mom had been an escort for Hollywood Dreams. She met Bill Hollis. Got pregnant. Disappeared. What I didn't know was how. Or why. How was it possible that the soft, beautiful woman who raised me was working as an escort? And what led her there? Why did she do it? There was no possible way she was wooed by Bill Hollis. Was I just that wrong about her? Were my sketchy memories of her so off? Maybe she was swept away by his power. Or his money. Or, for all I knew, his drugs. Maybe she thought getting in with Bill Hollis meant she could get in with Hollywood itself—become the famous director she'd always wanted to be. Maybe she didn't know what she was getting into, and by the time she figured it out, it was too late to get out.

Maybe it was all totally out of her control. I had to believe that. I had to. Because believing she was in it just because she wanted to would be so unlike the woman I remembered, it would be like losing her all over again.

And my dad.

My dad was in the photo with the flyers on the tables. So he must have known about Hollywood Dreams. Did that mean he knew what his wife was doing with her time? Did he know about Peyton all along?

If so, everything he'd said to me while Peyton was in the hospital—and since!—was a lie.

More lies and more lies. Like they would never end.

I imagined them piled on top of me, an avalanche of gray.

My hands clenched into fists.

"I never met her guy," Ruby said. "But, no, I'm pretty sure it wasn't him. I think I heard that Carrie married her mystery man. We all thought it was pretty romantic, her meeting someone who got her out of the business. Just like in the movies."

I blinked. Dad? Mom had left Hollywood Dreams for Dad? Did that mean maybe he didn't know about it after all? Or did it mean she met him there?

Ruby continued. "I heard that she came back to the business for a short while, but before we could reunite, she headed off to someplace I'd never heard of. Oil Well . . . Oil Slick . . ." She waved her hand dismissively. "Oil something.

North of here." She thought for a second, then shook her head. "It'll come to me. Anyway, after that, we just sort of lost touch. I heard she had gotten into movie production, and I was still . . ." She placed her hand on my knee. It felt oddly comforting. "I always knew she was too good for this job, anyway. I was happy for her."

"How did you know me, though?" I asked. "If you lost touch before I was born."

Ruby shrugged. "I only found out about you when she . . . well, when she passed."

"She was murdered," I said coldly. And the list of possible suspects wasn't getting any shorter. The more I learned about her, the longer and more complicated the list seemed to get.

Ruby nodded. "Yes, that. I came to the funeral. Hid in the back." She chuckled. "I just remember feeling so sorry for you, up there crying your little heart out." She looked at me warmly. "You haven't changed much. And you look so much like her."

I squeezed my eyes shut. A memory I'd been happy to forget. Or maybe had been too willing to forget. Sitting in that front pew, seeing the profile of my mother's face—but she was not my mother anymore. She looked like a stranger. She was covered head to toe in crimson. I thought I would break in half with grief.

Ruby patted my knee, mercifully dragging me out of

that room and back into this one. "I was afraid that someday you might find out about her working for . . . the service . . ."

"Hollywood Dreams," I supplied. "You can say the name. It's not like if you say it three times in a dark room, Bill Hollis will appear with a machete."

Ruby winced, then plowed on. "I was worried that someday you might find out what she did for a living all those years ago and might come around looking for answers. I was right. But I was wrong about the answers you were looking for, apparently."

"Apparently," I repeated.

"Honey," she said, leaning toward me again. "Your mother was a truly good soul. What happened to her was a tragedy. She was gone too soon."

Pink 2, primary blue *B. GONE 2 SOON. B.*

Something clicked. "And you're sure you don't know someone named Brandi?" I asked. "Brandi Courteur?"

"Courteur," she repeated softly. "Courteur." She thought for a few moments and then brightened. "Yes. Come to think of it, the name does sound kind of familiar. I think maybe she worked with your mom before I got there. Carrie was quite fond of her. But she had moved on by the time I came around. But I want to say her name was something more common."

"Moved on. Do you know where?"

She shrugged. "Could be anywhere, really. Prison, for all

I know. Or maybe she went to work for them at their other place."

"Who? The Hollises? They have more than one business?"

Ruby looked incensed. She sighed. "Well, not anymore. Dreams is gone. All that's left is the other place."

"What other place?"

She shook her head. "That, I truly don't know. All I know is the . . . boss . . . had two places. The service and something else. Nobody knew what the other one was. Rumor was it was so hush-hush because it was into big-time illegal stuff." She poked her fingers into her ears. "And when it comes to that kind of stuff, I don't want to hear it. I can spend a weekend in the clink, but no way can I do years."

So Brandi worked for Hollis, too. That was how she and Mom got connected. But how connected were they? Connected enough for Brandi to know about Mom's baby? Connected enough to know how on earth Bill Hollis ended up with that baby? And where in the world did Dru fit into all of this?

My brain ached from all the information. It was so blasted my colors even felt broken. I didn't understand any of this.

But I felt like I was getting closer.

"I've got to go," I said. "Thanks for the information."

Ruby followed me to the door, her face etched with

worry. "I'm sorry I couldn't be more help. If I think of anything else, I'll let you know."

"I think you've been more help than I ever expected," I said. Understatement of the century.

I opened the door, and Ruby took it from me, leaning out as I lunged into the hallway and down the stairs. The air in this place felt too close, too stagnant. As if it were a member of the Hollis family itself, trying to strangle me from the inside out.

"Nikki, if I were you, I would stop asking questions," Ruby called. But I was too far down the stairs to respond.

The farther down I went, the faster I got. All I could think about was getting to my car and getting out of here. Going home. Where I could process all the lies and half-truths and questions. But just as I bounded onto the landing, the door I'd originally knocked on opened up. The eye appeared again.

"Hey," a voice said from the other side of the door. I stopped, despite myself. "Hey," she said again.

Reluctantly, out of breath, I went to the door. She opened it a little wider—just enough for me to see a pair of full pink lips. "What?"

"I have something for you."

23

I SAW RAINBOW," the girl said, stepping aside just barely enough for me to squeeze through the doorway. Unlike Ruby's, this girl's apartment was spotless, though filled with so many charms and runes and bowls of herbs and celestial everything it carried the illusion of being cluttered. "Luna. I saw her about a week ago. She was getting into a car with another girl outside a club downtown."

"Are you a witch?" I asked, taking in the decor, more than a little uneasy.

She shook her head. "I just like to collect things. I'm Blue, by the way." She pointed apologetically to her blue hair, which was the color of sapphires or cupcake icing, or, in my world, strength. "Actually, I'm Celia, but you know how it works. No real names. Prism." She said the last with a twist of her mouth that hinted at holding back a laugh.

I felt myself flush, as I always did when I thought about that terrible time I'd posed as an escort for Hollywood Dreams and ended up with my knife at Stefan-the-disgusto's throat. I'd been Prism for that one night. A color name. Of course.

Ruby. Blue. Peyton, leading me along her rainbow.

I trailed my finger along a table filled with little cones of incense, wanting to change the subject. "Does everyone here work for Hollywood Dreams?"

"Not anymore," she said. "But yeah. They own this place. They let some of us live here for free. Some of their favorites. Well, *his* favorites, anyway." She moved over to a window seat that looked out onto the squat front yard, and sat. Two bicycles were abandoned there.

I picked up a dragon tear and rolled it between my fingers. "So what will you do now that they're gone?"

She placed a hand flat on the window, pressing her palm into it, as if she wanted someone on the other side to reach through and grab her. "They're never gone," she said softly.

"Well, right now they are. Dubai. No extradition. They're not stupid."

She leveled her gaze at me. "And if you believe they're still in Dubai, you're the stupid one."

"What does that mean?"

"It's not like a Hollis to stay hidden. They don't do ano-nymity very well." She spread her fingers out by her face, jazz hands. "Never let the limelight die. I would guess they showed up right around the time that Luna got sprung. Which would also be right around the time that you got arrested, am I right? Pretty convenient, huh? Almost like someone was pulling some puppet strings behind the scenes." She mimed doing just that. "Anyway. Like I said, I have something for you." She turned so that her legs hung off the window seat, and then she bent to open a drawer beneath it. From inside she pulled out a box. She held it out for me.

"What is it?" I said, still staying rooted by the table of tears and scents. Something about Blue made me afraid to trust her. Or maybe what made me so uneasy was that she was the first one to sound like she was telling the truth.

She shook the box. "It's for you. I've been holding on to it." I still made no move for it, so she shook it again. "It's from Peyton."

Crimson. So deep and red I felt like I was wading through it. The color I always thought of now when I thought of my sister. Even *sister* had turned into a crimson word from me, while before it had been butter yellow. That was how much Peyton had infiltrated my life.

My legs shook as I crossed the room. I didn't even hear the dragon tear leave my fingers and rattle to the wood floor.

I felt beamed in by Blue's eyes, which I had just noticed were so light green they almost looked otherworldly. They were mesmerizing. I fell onto the seat next to her.

"Take it," she said, shaking the box at me one more time. "It's not a bomb."

I was afraid to touch the box. Afraid that the moment my fingers landed on it, a bomb actually would burst—a crimson bomb.

"Now you're supposed to open it," Blue said, and giggled. She hooked her feet together and swung her legs, and not for the first time I was reminded what a couple of pigs Bill and Vanessa Hollis were for using girls like this to make money.

"Peyton gave this to you," I repeated. "For me."

She nodded. "For the one and only Nikki Kill." She nudged me with her shoulder. "Nobody else."

"And why are you just giving it to me now? Why didn't you bring it to me when she was in the hospital? Or when she died? Or . . . I don't know . . . like a thousand times between then and now."

"She said if she did everything right, you would come for it. And that I should just wait. So I just waited. And here you are. So wait no more. It's yours. Open it." She nudged me a second time.

I licked my lips, which had suddenly gone very dry, and pulled the lid off the box. Inside was a wad of cotton. Under that was a key on a nondescript ring. I picked it up and let it dangle from my fingers.

Blue tapped it with her fingertip, and it swung gently back and forth. "She said if she was right about you, and if you understood everything she left behind for you, you would know what to do with it."

"What's it to?" I asked. I turned it, studying it for any hint or clue, but there was none.

Blue shrugged. "That, she didn't tell me. She didn't want me to get mixed up in anything just in case her parents should get wind that you were snooping around. Which they obviously did."

I shook my head, dropped the key back in the box, held it out for Blue to take.

She leaned away. "No can do, chickie. I had orders to give it to you. I'm giving it to you. It's yours now."

"But I don't have the first clue what to do with it," I said. "Peyton was wrong. She . . . overestimated me."

Blue tipped her head to one side. Her choppy bangs fell over one eye, and in that moment I could see why someone would want to be with her. She was mysterious and beautiful . . . and vulnerable. All things I was not. "According to Rainbow, you have all the clues. You just have to put them together."

"Why did Peyton give this to you? Why did she trust you?"

"We were friends." She shrugged, staring down at her feet. "I think she felt bad, like her parents were using me or something. But they kind of saved me from the streets. I'd rather be Blue, high-end escort, than the alternative, you know?"

"Well, neither one is exactly ideal," I said.

"Yeah, well, neither was my home life. This was a step up." She gave me a *whatcha gonna do* smile. "Anyway, she came over to check on me sometimes, hang out, and I read her fortune, did tea leaves, pulled cards, whatever. Between you and me, I don't know how to tell fortunes at all. I was making it up as I went along. But she was Peyton Hollis, you know? I mean, who gets lucky enough to have her for a friend, right?"

Only half the free world, I thought. Or at least half the free world hung on to her like she was their friend. Which, now that I thought about it, was not friendship at all. It was kind of the opposite of friendship. Not for the first time, I felt a pang of sorrow for Peyton.

"So she gave you a key."

"She figured I was the last person anyone would go to if she was in trouble. Anyone except you, that is. She knew you'd come. And she was right."

I ran my finger over the key's surface. "Yeah, I guess."

She brightened, jumped off the window seat, looking so much more like a sixteen-year-old kid than a worldly

Hollywood Dreams escort. "You want me to tell your fortune?" she asked. "I mean, I'm getting better."

"Better at making it up?" I asked. We both snickered.

"Totally," she said. "I'll show you."

"Maybe some other time. I'll come back." I closed the box, glad to see the key gone, and held it in my lap. "I've got to go. You said you saw Luna. Recently."

"Yeah, she was getting into a car with some dark-haired chick. I would have followed them, but I was kind of, you know, with a guy. Working. Pretty sure the dark-haired chick plays in a band or something, because she was hanging out with some real rockers. Or maybe she's just a groupie. All I know is she was making out with a guy with a green Mohawk in the parking lot before she got in the car and picked up Luna. I think he was a guitar player for some punk band."

Viral Fanfare. She'd seen Gib Talley from Viral Fanfare. He was making out with a dark-haired girl who knew Luna.

Shelby Gray.

Shelby knew exactly where Luna was. And she was hanging out with her.

I fucking knew it.

I FIGURED YOU were too quiet this morning not to be into something," Detective Martinez said the next morning, standing in my driveway, leaning against my car. This time he had only one coffee in hand. He must have gotten tired of buying me coffees to throw away.

I glanced around, my face burning. "What are you doing here?"

"I haven't heard from you since you left my place, so I thought I'd stop by on my way home from breakfast"—he held up his cup, cheers-style—"and talk you out of whatever it is you're planning to do today."

"What makes you think I'm going to do something?"

But even I wasn't buying it. The inside of my sunglasses turned liar gray.

"Because you're you."

"Maybe I'm going to meet a friend," I said. "To go shopping."

He stifled a grin. "Right. You, with a friend."

I put my hands on my hips. "What's that supposed to mean?"

"Cut the crap, Nikki. You aren't going shopping with a friend."

I pushed past him, letting my shoulder catch his full-on. He jumped back to avoid a splash of coffee that popped through the lid. He was too slow. I smiled to myself and unlocked my car, but when I went to pull open the door, it wouldn't open. I looked up; he was holding his hand against it, above my head.

"Move."

"I'll move when you talk."

I sighed, exasperated. "I'm going to get a doughnut."

"No, you're not."

"I don't have to tell you where I'm going. I don't let people in, remember?"

He pursed his lips and nodded thoughtfully. "True. But I'll just follow you."

I grunted and knocked my head against the car door a

few times. "You suck, do you know that?"

"I've been told."

The truth was—and I hated to admit it, even to myself—he was right. I did have plans. Plans that had come to me out of the blue in the shower that morning. Plans that made so much total sense, I couldn't believe I hadn't thought of them before. Plans that seemed urgent.

Plans that he would definitely not approve of.

"You're burning daylight." He leaned forward and whispered, "All the good bargains will be gone."

"Fine," I said. "If you must know, I'm going to Gold Goose Studios."

His brow creased while it sank in, and then his eyes bugged so hard I could see them through his sunglasses. "The production studio?" I nodded. "As in Bill Hollis's studio?" I nodded again. "Are you crazy? I think you might be. You are officially clinically insane."

"This is why I didn't want to tell you," I said, taking advantage of his surprised state to pull the car door open. The paint had a yellow handprint on it.

"I'm not going to let you."

I barked out a laugh. "You sure as shit can't stop me."

"You're just going to walk in? And what?"

"It's Saturday. Nobody will be there." I hoped that was true, anyway. If I ran into any die-hard super-employees who just couldn't stay away on a Saturday, I was going to have to do some fast talking. "I just . . . want to look around a little, is all." I felt the key that Blue had given me poke my leg through my jeans pocket. I had no idea what it might open, but Bill Hollis's office was just as good as any other place to start looking. "You can get in your car, drive away, and pretend you don't know." I turned the key and my car roared into life. "You're blocking me." He didn't move. I put the car into reverse. "Fine, I'll push you out of my driveway."

"Son of a bitch," he muttered. He tossed his coffee into the yard on the way to his car.

IT WAS NO surprise that Gold Goose Studios was lavish. Every bit as lavish as Hollis Mansion. Bill Hollis liked his luxuries, there was no doubt about it. And he could afford them.

Unsurprisingly, the building was surrounded by a locked gate with a key card scanner.

If I had learned anything, it was that people didn't suspect you of things if you just acted like you were supposed to be there. I pulled right up to the scanner and pushed the help button. After a second, the speaker clicked on.

"Help you?" said a bored voice on the other end.

"I lost my key card," I shouted into the speaker. "Can you buzz me in?"

"I'm afraid I can't let anyone in without a card, ma'am," the voice said.

"I'm cleaning crew. You can't make an exception?"

"Sorry."

"Mr. Hollis will fire me if I miss another Saturday." There was silence, so I added, sounding as tearful as possible, "Please? I won't tell anyone. I'm just here to dust stuff, I swear. I'll be in and out. Please don't make me lose my job. I have kids."

There was more silence, and I had my finger out to poke the button again, when the gate slid open.

"Thank you," I said to myself as I pulled through. I could see Martinez's car idling at the curb, too upstanding-citizen-yellow to follow me in. The gate closed slowly behind me, officially leaving me on my own. Just the way I wanted it.

Getting into Gold Goose Studios from the parking lot was nothing. I pressed the help button at the door and got the same bored voice. This time I didn't have to explain anything before the door clicked open.

I was in.

The administrative office was on the tenth floor, and I took the elevator up. My every move was probably being recorded by some sort of state-of-the-art security-camera system, and the thought of a Hollis watching me roam through their offices sent a chill down my spine. I shook off the fear and pressed on.

All the lights were out, the place lit only by the glow of computer monitors. It was a cubicle farm, but it was a posh one. Every desk was home to a big-screen monitor and a cushy leather chair. I wondered who had been running the place while Bill Hollis was in Dubai. I wondered if the police had been here after Dru's death. Probably not. Why would they? What would they be looking for?

Hell, what was I looking for?

"I don't know, but I'll know it when I see it," I whispered, moving quickly through the cubicles to a bank of offices on the far wall, trying the key in every single door. It didn't work. All of the offices were gorgeous, but one was more than gorgeous. One was something you'd see in a magazine. It had to be Bill Hollis's office.

The door was open, but I tried the key anyway. It didn't turn. I strolled in like I owned the place, trying to be unimpressed by this gross show of wealth, but even I couldn't help marveling at the floor-to-ceiling windows that looked out over Los Angeles. I walked over to them and spread my hands out, leaning my forehead against the glass to gaze down at the street below. My phone immediately lit up.

"What are you doing? Get away from the window," Detective Martinez snapped when I answered it. I hung up without responding. I could see him on the sidewalk, staring up at me, his phone to his ear. I flipped him off.

"Fine, fine," I said. "I've got shit to do anyway."

I started with the bookcases, which were just as big and impressive as the windows. And stuffed with books—books about acting, books about directing, books about the history of movies, actor autobiographies. I pulled a few out at random—they were all signed. He had a fortune on one bookshelf alone, and it was all I could do to keep from lifting a few. After all, a man like him deserved the karmic retribution of being robbed blind, right?

But I could only imagine what Detective Martinez would do if I showed up outside with an armful of Hollywood loot. He would probably take it all away and turn it in, and have me locked up for the night just for pissing him off.

I pawed through the bookshelf for a long time, then pushed along the walls surrounding them, half expecting a secret door to open up. A part of me indulged in a fantasy that it would happen, and inside said secret room would be Arrigo Basile, cooking boxed macaroni and cheese on a hot plate, the cane—coated with Peyton's DNA and Rigo's fingerprints—in a locked closet that my key would magically fit, and my nightmare would be over.

But of course that didn't happen, because on the other side of that wall was another office. No secret doors.

Another wall was dwarfed by a huge glass case, the shelves lined with movie memorabilia. It reminded me of the trophy case at school. These must have been Bill Hollis's version of trophies. There was a lock on the case, but the key didn't even fit in it, much less turn. I pawed all over the items on an unlocked shelf nearby instead.

The shelves scoured, I turned to a closet. But all that was inside was a beige raincoat and an umbrella. So totally normal, you'd never think this was the closet of a complete psychopath. I examined the doorknob—no lock.

I turned to his desk, a polished antique monster that was home to more movie souvenirs—a pair of glasses nestled in a box with a note that proclaimed them to be Gregory Peck's Atticus Finch glasses, a Batman figurine, a *Return of the Jedi* metal lunch box covered with scribbled autographs, a baseball from *A League of Their Own*. And then there were memorabilia from Bill Hollis's own productions—a chewed cigar, a doll head, a cowboy hat, a horseshoe in a glass dome. All items anyone would recognize. All items anyone would want to have. Even me, before I knew the man behind the movies.

There wasn't really anything else on top of his desk, except for an in-box with two office memos—one about paid time off and the other about open insurance enrollment— and a desk calendar with nothing written on it. I pulled open drawers. Nothing, nothing, nothing. One drawer had a lock, but it was left open. I tried the key just to be thorough. No luck.

I plopped down in his chair, feeling completely defeated. Detective Martinez would be full of I-told-you-so's when I came out empty-handed. It would be such a grand oppor- tunity for him to remind me that going into situations with no plan was stupid, and a big old waste of my time, and, in this case, all kinds of illegal. I swiveled the chair so it was facing the window, using my foot to idly turn a giant globe that was sitting on a nearby stand. It didn't help that I knew he was down there on the sidewalk right now, just waiting for me to—

I stopped the globe with my toe, then sat forward and gazed at it. There was something off about it.

It was the word *Kenya*—orangey with brown spots. It was split by the equator. Only it was *split* split, the *Ke* above the line and the *ya* below, off-kilter a little, the *n* completely missing. Since when did globes have an equator line lie over the name of the country? Since when did the country boundary lines have jags that didn't match up? I ran my finger over the equator.

Since it wasn't a line.

Since it was a crack. An opening.

I stood, the continents all going mint green, surrounded by spearmint oceans, and felt along the line. Sure enough, it went all the way around the globe. I unscrewed the top of the stand and turned it to one side, leaving the globe free to take out.

Or free to open.

I stuck my fingernails into the crack and wiggled them until they had a hold. Then I pulled, the top of the globe coming off effortlessly. The world exploded with a ruby fountain.

Inside the globe were papers. Phone numbers written on scraps and napkins, business cards with women's names on them, and Polaroid photos of half-nude girls, their names and numbers written across the bottom. I recognized Blue. And Brigitte, who had worked in the front office of Hollywood Dreams. Each of the photos and papers and cards had stars scrawled across them, under the phone numbers. Gross. He rated his conquests. Just like movies. It was almost as if he kept these things as memorabilia of his success, just like the things in the glass case and on top of his desk. Trophies.

I dug through—it was all disgusting, but nothing earth-shattering. We already knew about Hollis's little hobby. What was earth-shattering was how many there were. And how far back they went—some of the girls in the photos wearing seventies-style clothing, some of the papers yellowing with age.

One of the papers said *Carrie*, with five stars. I dropped it, wiping my palms on the seat of my pants. God, what if that was my mother? No, not what if. Probably. My stomach turned, my hands suddenly done searching.

But as I dropped the *Carrie* paper back into the globe, I noticed something. A pop of official-looking navy. Business forms. I dug down to them. Under the scraps of paper were what looked like invoices. They seemed out of place here. Why not keep invoices in his file cabinet? Or in accounting?

I studied one. It was from a Dr. Slovenka, the scrub-blue words *surgical, elective* the only notation under services rendered. Five hundred dollars. I leafed through. They were all from Dr. Slovenka, all ranging in price from three hundred to a thousand dollars, all listed as *surgical, elective.* Who was Dr. Slovenka and why were his bills stored in here?

I stuffed the papers back into the globe and shut it, screwing the base top back on, then went out into the cubicles.

I lowered myself into a cushy chair and pulled up Google on my phone. One search got me a hit.

Anton Slovenka, MD

Femalternatives Health Clinic

It was a clinic in Pomona that specialized in women's health.

They specialized in birth control, pregnancy verification, ultrasound, and . . .

"Abortions," I read aloud.

I sagged in the chair, disappointed. The globe had seemed like such a huge find. The only find, really, at Gold Goose. But we already knew that Bill Hollis was a regular john. It wasn't a huge leap to believe that he had gotten a few girls pregnant. Especially since I already knew he had gotten my mom pregnant.

But nothing in the globe, in the office, in anything got

me any closer to Rigo, and I was going to have to face Detective Martinez downstairs and admit he was right. This, too, was a dead end.

But as I made my way back down to my car, I couldn't get those invoices out of my head. All those elective surgeries by Dr. Slovenka were abortions. And Bill Hollis had a collection of them. He was paying for Dr. Slovenka's services and had been for years. The question was, how many of those surgeries were actually elective, and how many did Bill Hollis just make happen?

And why did that seem like an important distinction to make?

25

DETECTIVE MARTINEZ HAD been unexpectedly—and unusually—gracious about me finding nothing at Gold Goose, probably because he could see on my face how frustrated I was. He had driven off with promises that even though it looked hopeless, we'd come up with something. This wasn't the end. We would prove my innocence, one way or another. *You can't give up when it looks like you're out of ideas, Nikki,* he'd said.

I'd been driving around ever since, the key to nothing rattling in the cup holder in the center console. I wasn't ready to go home yet. Detective Martinez called three times, but I ignored my phone. I wasn't in the mood to talk. There were too many things to think about. The things Blue and Ruby had told me, about Bill Hollis, about my mom, about the mysterious other business they owned, and about Peyton. About how all these things fit together. What was Peyton trying to tell me? To what answers was she leading me?

And there was the cane. *Rigo's* cane, which had probably— if they'd done what I would have done—already been destroyed. My biggest hope of exoneration had undoubtedly been fed to a wood chipper or a fire pit or was floating in the Pacific by now.

I found myself driving past Tesori Antico, slowly, one way and then the other, time after time. At one point, I thought I saw a light, probably originating in that back room. I got out of my car and cupped my hands against the window and peered inside. Nothing. A feeling that there was movement, but not movement that I could actually see.

I got back in my car and decided to hang out in front of the store for a while. Maybe the next plan didn't need to be any more complicated than this. Maybe the SUV would round the corner and I could bust into the store behind them and wrestle the cane away and be done with it.

And then what? Having the cane was not the same as having Rigo.

Still, I waited. I watched. I moved only to get food and go to the bathroom and then came right back. The sun went down. I'd been there for hours and literally nothing had happened. The entire family was gone. *Or hiding.*

I called Martinez back.

He picked up on the first ring. "Martinez." Low, serious.

"Hope I didn't interrupt anything important?"

"Where were you?"

"Chill, Detective, I've been driving around. Thinking."

I heard a leathery squeaking sound and knew immediately that he was on his couch. Leaning forward, probably. Elbows propped on his knees while he talked to me. A serious crease in his forehead. Feet bare, probably watching something romantic with Blake. Barf. "Listen, I'm sort of in the middle of something."

"Well, you were the one obsessively calling me, not the other way around. Did you call just to make sure I hadn't run away with the circus, or did you actually have something to say?"

"I've been going through that paperwork," he said.

I drew a blank.

"The paperwork from the evidence box."

I vaguely remembered him flipping through bills and statements. "And?"

"I'll bring it to you tomorrow," he said. "I think I might have seen something important in there, but I'll need you to confirm."

I chuckled. "So serious, Detective. So . . . policey." I lowered my voice into my best impression of him. "I'll need an affirmative on that ASAP please."

"Uh-huh, it's all pretty by the book," he said, still in his professional voice. He wasn't going to play at all tonight. A straw-brown thought that I pushed away quickly. Why would I be disappointed that he wanted to keep it professional?

"Okay, got it," I said. "I'll see you tomorrow and we'll go over it."

"Sounds good," he said. "See you then." He hung up abruptly.

I stared at my screen, which confirmed that the phone call had disconnected. "Well, good-bye to you, too," I said, even though I knew he couldn't hear me. "Jeez."

I decided to call Dad next.

"Hey, Nik, how are things at the homestead?" I could hear a mouse clicking in the background. He was working, as always. Even on the road, he was editing photos.

"Fine. Quiet. When are you coming home?" Right now I wasn't sure what to trust with Dad, but I knew for sure that I could trust him more than Luna. And I wasn't too thrilled with being alone for much longer.

"Maybe tomorrow night, if we work fast and get out of here in the morning." He paused, the clicking stopped. "Everything okay?"

"Yeah," I lied. "Of course. I'm safe, Dad, you don't have to keep worrying about me." Another lie. Or two. "I just miss you, is all."

"Well, I'll be back soon, and then I don't have another

trip for at least a few weeks. We can spend some quality time together. Maybe go to the beach a little? Work on our tans."

I laughed. Dad was epically white. He didn't tan. He burned, peeled, and freckled, and then went right back to white. But he was always trying, as if forty-plus years of effort were just a warm-up and he had yet to perfect the formula for being brown-skinned.

"What? What's so funny?" he asked, which only made me laugh harder. I could hear the laughter straining in his voice too, and suddenly I was hit with an intense blanket of gross brown sadness. Even if he was kind of lame and hands-off, Dad could always at least make me laugh. And it sucked to think that this man who'd had me giggling for all these years had been somehow involved with Hollywood Dreams and had never said anything.

"Keep it up. Keep laughing. You'll see when I'm so sun-kissed you won't even recognize me. You'll walk right past me, thinking, 'Who is this god of tans?'"

The laughter trailed off. Little did he know, I already didn't recognize him. "Whatever," I said. "You keep trying, old man. I'll show you how it's done."

"Great. It's a date, then. I'll call you tomorrow on my way home, okay?"

"Sure." Then, before he could hang up, and before I could let myself think about it, "Hey, Dad?"

"Yeah?"

"I was just wondering. Did you and Mom have friends?"

"Did we have friends?"

"Yeah, you know. People you hung out with. Any movie people or anything like that?" I held my breath, bracing for an answer. This was his chance to tell the truth. If he did, I would know it was all just a mistake and that we were still good. If he didn't . . .

"Ah. You want to know if we ever had any brushes with fame. Nope. Believe it or not, our whole lives in Hollywood, and not a one. Although your mother swore she saw Judge Reinhold at Fatburger once."

"Who?"

"That's what I thought. No. The short answer is no. Mom and I were pretty much stay-at-home types. Especially once we had you. Your mom was always about being the best mother she could possibly be, and she hated to leave you. Too bad we didn't have any more kids. We would have liked to. Though I suppose that turned out for the best. I had my hands full with you."

"I try," I said, deadpan. "But you didn't have any friends? Nobody that I would know or anything?"

"Why are you asking?"

"I don't know. I was just curious, I guess. Been thinking about Mom a lot lately. Ever since . . . you know . . . since what happened last fall. It just reminded me of when she died, and I was wanting to know more about your life together. It's no big deal."

"Well, sorry I couldn't give you more exciting news. Would it help if I lied and told you Sylvester Stallone was our dog sitter or something?"

"Ha-ha, you've never had a dog," I said, but the words wanted to get closed in my throat by hearing him say, *if I lied*.

"Tell you what. We'll talk more about the good old days when we go to the beach, okay? I'll try to think up some stories about Mom that you don't already know."

You mean the one where she ran away to give birth to another baby? I wanted to ask. *Or the one where the two of you hobnobbed with the Hollises and gave them my sister?* Instead, "Sure. That sounds great. Have a fun last day."

"Good night, Nik."

"Good night, Dad."

I hung up. He would come up with stories about Mom between now and when I next saw him. How was I supposed to read that? Was he going to make up stories? How deep did the lying go?

I drove home, thinking about the box under his desk again, and mulling over possible lock combinations. I didn't have anything going on tonight—I would spend some time under the desk trying to crack the code.

I went in through the garage, but the second I was

inside, I could sense something was off. I smelled fresh air. Or maybe the house just didn't feel as sealed as it should.

I had only half a second to notice broken glass on the floor, glittering in the moonlight by the kitchen table, a breeze pushing in the curtains where the window used to be. "Hello?" I said, hunching back into a ready stance, my fists clenching, my heart immediately jumping into overdrive. "Luna? I know somebody's in he—"

But I didn't get to finish my sentence before I was hit from behind.

26

THE WIND WAS knocked out of me as my midsection rammed into the kitchen counter. The scream that I'd just been ready to let loose instead came out as a grunty *oof*, followed by a lot of coughing and gagging and gasping for breath that wouldn't come.

Whoever or whatever had hit me from behind was most definitely not Luna. She was tiny—smaller than me—and this force felt massive. And male. There was no way I could beat it from this position.

Yes, you can, Gunner said in my head. *Calm down. Never say never.*

I writhed, still coughing and gasping, trying to find a

weak spot, a way out. Instead, the body pressed against me harder.

"Stop moving, bitch."

"Let me—let me up." I continued coughing, but the air was coming a little easier to me now. A dull ache panged through my ribs where they'd hit the counter. The wind had been knocked out, that was all. *You can handle that, Nikki. You've experienced worse. Way worse.* I pushed my head up, hoping to use the leverage to break free.

Instead, a hand covered the back of my head and slammed it into the counter. I saw white as my nose made contact. Blood instantly began gushing, tears rushing to my eyes. I let out a scream and the hand pushed my face forward again. This time I was able to turn my head just enough so that it was my cheek that took the blow. Still painful, but less so. Instinctively, my head moved back again, and again he slammed it forward. My teeth smacked against my lip and now I felt blood in my mouth too. This time, I kept my head down, just turned my face to the side.

"What do you want?" I cried out. "If this is about Luna, I just want her to leave me alone. I'm not planning to do anything to her." Perhaps a lie, but I needed to do something to make him stop before he bashed my brains out right here on the kitchen counter.

"Who is Luna?" he grunted, tightening up against me.

My hips creaked against the countertop. I could feel my skin scraping painfully against the edge. "I want to know why you're following us. What are you after? What do you want?"

Us? Us who? My mind raced, trying to push away the thick asphalt fear long enough to form a thought. "I don't know who you're talking about," I gasped, accidentally raising my head.

"You lying bitch!" He slammed my head forward again and, unprepared, my nose took another blow. Pain renewed. My face slid on warm blood, which was pooling on the countertop.

Pooling blood. Mom's outstretched arm. *Nikki . . . go . . .* All that crimson. Crimson waiting to swallow me up.

Screw that.

I remembered my last spar with Detective Martinez, how he'd used my own momentum against me. How he'd worked to knock me off balance so he could move in for the kill. Gunner's voice was inside my head again: *Use his hand against him, Nikki.*

Suddenly, the bumpy gray and black cleared long enough for me to think. I reached back and clamped my hand down over his, pushing it into the back of my head. Before he could react, I drove my foot backward in a rear kick, cracking him on the kneecap, hard.

Instantly, he let go of me, crying out, dropping back. I slithered out from under his arm, lunged for the other side of the kitchen, and grabbed a knife out of the knife block. The handle was slippery in my palms. I hadn't held a knife like this since that night at Hollis Mansion. The thought made me shake, and I tried to slow my breathing to keep myself from panicking. *You did this once, Nikki,* I reminded myself. *You can do it again if you have to.*

But I didn't want to have to.

I just wanted this to be over.

"You bitch!" the man was screaming, bent over and rubbing his knee, which I'd at the very least hyperextended. I still didn't know who he was. He was in all black, including a black ski mask—a look that was so Nighttime Intruder it was terrifying. He was here to kill me. I wouldn't get out of this without beating him to the punch. "You've been following us for days!" he bellowed. "Coming to the store. Coming to the auction."

Oh, God. The store. The auction. *Us* were the Basiles.

"Watching from your car," a voice said from the other side of the room. A deep voice. A growl, almost.

Shit, there were two of them?!

Two Basiles. Basiles, who had been to prison. Who had run gambling rings and been in the drug business and who killed Peyton. Standing here. In my house.

"I don't know what you're after," said the man I had kicked. "But you're going to stop right now. You're done coming to the store, you're done following us around, and you are never going to so much as think about our family again. And the guy you're always with. Same goes for him. You tell whoever's sending you after us they're sending you on a death mission. You got that? Because if I see you around my family again, I will kill you myself." He straightened and came toward me. I held the knife out in front of me in both hands, to try to stop the shaking.

"I'm not— Nobody is—" I stammered.

"I'm not playing with you, bitch. Back off."

Panicked, I swiped the knife toward him. The man was quicker than I expected him to be, even with the hurt leg. He reached out and grabbed the knife handle, pushing it against my thumb until it popped free. I struggled, and he swept the knife up, slicing into my collarbone on the way. Now he held it, although, behind the mask, his eyes looked surprised to see that he'd cut me. The other man, dressed exactly as he was, rushed toward us.

"Fuck," he said. "Let her go, Antony. You scared her. That's enough." There was something familiar beneath the growl in the other guy's voice. I'd heard it before. But the adrenaline was rushing so hard through my ears I couldn't make sense of where. Had I heard Rigo talk? When?

But "Antony" didn't move, didn't take the knife away from my chest. "She knows something. She's after something. I can tell she's lying."

The other guy moved toward him. "She isn't worth it. Let's just go."

"Antony" stared me down for a few long seconds, during which I tried to remain as calm and steady as humanly possible, even though on the inside I was a trembling storm of colors and everything in me cried out in pain and fear.

At last, he dropped the knife onto the floor, then kicked it away with his boot. "If we see you again, we will come back, and I can promise you will regret it," he said, pointing into my face.

"Come on, man," the other guy said urgently. He was already halfway out of the kitchen.

I waited until I heard the front door slam before I moved from my spot. My whole body was shaking so hard I thought I might fall down. Instead, I hurried to the broken window and peered out. I could see their two silhouettes running through our backyard. In no time, they disappeared between the two houses behind us.

"Shit," I said, studying the broken window. Dad was going to have a field day with this. So was Martinez. My feet crunched over the glass pieces as I moved to the cabinet where we kept all our extra plates and cookbooks and stuff. Mom had fallen in love with the cabinet at a flea market and had insisted Dad buy it for her. It was huge, heavy, and way too big for our kitchen, but Dad had bought it anyway, and had declared, after spending more than half a day trying to move it in, that it was going to stay in that spot forever, even if we moved away. And it had. Until now.

I went to the side farthest away from the window and pushed. The cabinet barely budged. I leveraged my feet against the doorjamb behind me and pushed again.

It took half an hour to get the cabinet in front of the broken window. But at least I could breathe again.

I slid down the side of the cabinet and curled up in the corner, once again gripping the knife.

I fell asleep there.

27

I WAS AWAKENED in the morning by the rattle of my phone against the floor. I hadn't realized in the scuffle that I'd dropped it. Or maybe it had fallen out of my pocket when the guy rushed me from behind. I didn't know. All I knew was that I felt like I'd been hit by a truck. My face and collarbone throbbed. My hand hurt from being curled around a knife handle all night, and my neck hurt from sleeping sitting up.

Not that I slept soundly, of course. Every few minutes I would jerk awake, certain that I'd heard footsteps above my head or a car outside my door. Certain that it was Luna or Rigo or now Rigo's guys, or whoever else might decide that today was the perfect day for me to die.

I pulled myself off the floor, grimacing as the slice through my collarbone pinched. I put my hand over it; it came away covered with flakes of crusted blood. At least it had stopped bleeding. It couldn't have been too deep if it stopped bleeding on its own, right?

My legs were asleep from being bent all night, and I staggered over the broken glass, my shoes landing heavily on the tiny pieces. I would need to sweep that before Dad came home. I would need to come up with an explanation for what had happened, or Dad would never let me be alone again. Worse, I wasn't sure anymore if I wanted to be.

Either way, I hoped that it wasn't him on the other end of the phone, telling me that—good news!—they'd gotten an early start and he was nearly home right now. I needed time to figure out how I was going to explain everything.

I wanted everyone to leave me alone.

I wanted to sink into myself and be washed away by colorful dreams.

I just wanted everything to stop for one day and let me pretend that my life was normal.

It wasn't Dad; it was Detective Martinez. I'd completely forgotten about getting together with him today. I grimaced, holding my side where it had made contact with the counter, and sent the call to voice mail. Then I pulled up my messaging and texted him. Every part of me knew I should tell him what happened. Every cell in my body screamed that he would freak out if he discovered it on his own—and oh, he would discover it on his own. He would set up camp in my backyard. He would put a tail on me 24/7. He would sit over me like a worried nanny and treat me like a precious, fragile piece of glass.

Which was exactly why I couldn't tell him.

Sick. Going back to bed.

And that was exactly what I did.

I WOKE TWO hours later, my stomach rumbling and my sweaty hair sticking to my neck. I was getting super tired of feeling so shitty every time I woke up.

I decided a bath was needed. I soaked so long, all the bubbles died and the water began to turn cold, so I got out and dried off, and sat for a long time wondering what to do with myself. I was feeling a little better, but I needed a day off. Just one day off from the crazy. I settled on getting into a clean pair of pajamas, grabbing a frozen pizza, and watching TV.

I had just the television entertainment in mind.

While the pizza baked, I shuffled into Dad's office. He'd said we would watch Mom's videos together soon, but it hadn't happened. And if I hadn't even known about them for eighteen years, I didn't have any reason to believe he was in a big hurry to show them to me now. I hadn't thought anything of it before. But now that I knew Dad was hiding things from me, I wondered if the videos were hiding things, too.

I felt a prickle of nerves, reminding me of chalkboards and slippery rocks, then tried to shake myself out of it. This was stupid. It was my dad's office. It had been here since before I was born. There was nothing scary here. Some curious things that had me wondering, but nothing terribly out of the ordinary. To prove it to myself, I sat at his desk and pulled open the bottom drawer. I would thumb through the photos again and see if maybe I'd seen things wrong. If maybe I saw something different this time. Maybe the words had been something else and my synesthesia was confused and saw glittery lilac where it shouldn't have been. The Hollises were on my mind every day, so it was totally possible.

But when I opened the drawer, I found it empty. Completely cleaned out. I reached all the way until my fingers bumped the wooden drawer back, and still came up with nothing. The photos. All of them were gone.

Who had taken them?

Dad, of course. He had to have done it. Other than the two guys last night, he and I were the only two who could have possibly been in here. What use would they have for them? He'd taken them away. The only question now was why? Had he hidden them in the locked box under the desk? How could I possibly know, when I had no idea what could be in there at all?

I got down on my hands and knees and stared at it, part of me expecting it, too, to be missing. Or to have never been there at all—for this whole thing with Peyton to have officially driven me crazy. But it was still there.

I army-crawled toward it, pulled it out, and sat with it on my lap. I turned the dial. I tried my birthday. My dad's birthday. Mom's birthday. Our house number. Random numbers. Nothing worked.

The front of the box rippled with color in the back of my brain. Cheater blue to the deep indigo I associated with betrayal. Mint-green suspicion that sent dots of candy up into my mind, then morphed into that ugly, horrible lime green of mistrust.

Quickly, I stood and opened the top cabinet, my heart in my throat. I almost expected the white box that had contained all of Mom's videos to be gone too, but fortunately, it was still there. I didn't realize I'd been holding my breath until I let it out with a whoosh, sending a new round of pain into my side. I hesitated, my hands hovering near the box. Did I really want to do this? What if I found something worse than what I'd found in those pictures?

Don't be stupid, Nikki. If there was something worse in this box, he would've taken it right along with the pictures. Sadly, I settled on this as the truth and grabbed the box.

It was heavier than I remembered it being, and my sore muscles didn't help any. I gave it a heave. Something fell from the top of it and landed on Dad's desk. I froze, staring at it.

It was my mom's teardrop aquamarine earring. The one that had gone missing on graduation day. It had a little piece of paper wrapped around the clasp. I straightened the paper. In tiny block letters, it read: *BOO!*

I dropped the earring back on the desk and spun so I was facing the door, my entire body shaking. Who had been in here? Who had stolen Mom's earring from my room and brought it down here? I had been looking at this very box only days ago—it had to have been after that. The Basiles had been in the house last night—I knew that much—but how would they have had the earring in the first place? And how would they have known to put it here? No. Whoever had been in my house had been someone who knew me. Who knew how to get to me.

BOO!

The backyard of Hollis Mansion. The pool gurgling in the moonlight. The trash can I was hiding behind, full of empty bottles. *Boo! Found you!*

Luna.

IT TOOK ME a few minutes to calm myself. I checked every lock on every door and every window. Of course, the broken one wasn't locked, so I left the cabinet in front of it.

Jones called while I was at it, sounding tight and

tentative. "How are you, gorgeous?"

Distracted. Terrified. Busy. "Okay."

"You sure? You sound kind of funny. You want to hang out? Go do something?"

"Not today. Sick."

"Really?" He sounded skeptical. "Want me to come take care of you?"

Jesus. No. That would be the last thing I would need right now—Jones in my face, asking how I felt and if I needed a ginger ale every five seconds. "We'll talk tomorrow, Jones."

"Sure, we will." That skeptical tone again.

Only after I had checked every closet and bathroom and under every bed did I feel comfortable enough to go back to Dad's office, back to the box of videos.

I pulled it down and set it on Dad's desk. I opened the top. Inside were rows and rows of VHS tapes. Old-school. I ran my fingers down their edges. None of them were labeled.

I carried the box into Dad's room. His TV was the only one left with a VCR attached. I used to make fun of him mercilessly about keeping the old thing, but now maybe it made sense. If he got rid of his VCR, he wouldn't be able to watch Mom's movies again. Not unless he converted them into disks, and as I touched each tape, I thought I understood why he wouldn't want to do that. Mom's hands had touched these. These movies were probably the only thing distinctly Mom left in this house. I pulled one out of the middle and smelled it. It smelled like plastic, but I told myself it smelled like overripe peaches, trying to convince my colors to come along for the ride. But that wasn't the way my synesthesia worked. It didn't come and go on command. It was always there, except when it wasn't, and that was just the way it was.

I ran back downstairs and grabbed my pizza and a couple of sodas, took them up to Dad's room, popped in the first movie, and leaned back against his pillows to watch, trying to push everything that had happened out of my mind.

God, she was beautiful. She could have been a model. Or an actress. *Or a high-end escort?* I batted the thought away. She popped in and out of the camera's view, fussing with someone's costume or instructing their movement or just calling for a break. Every time she realized she was on camera, she smiled, her entire face lighting up, and would wave like an awkward girl rather than an aspiring film director.

People used to tell me I looked like her. *You have her smile*, they used to say to me, and I really did. At the time, I did. But something happened on that day I came home from Wendy's house and dropped the Tootsie Rolls in Mom's blood. My smile changed. It came out as rarely as the sun on a cloudy day, and even when it did, it was tentative, stopping at my cheeks. Nothing lit up my face. Nothing made me beautiful in the same way Mom was beautiful.

I paused the frame with her in it and studied her face; looked for myself in it.

Chalk that up to the many things her murderer stole from me—her smile. My smile. Whatever.

I watched until my pizza and both sodas were gone. I watched as the sun baked overhead and started to fall again. I watched until my eyes felt sandy and the back of my head felt numb against the pillow. I watched with the intention of watching every movie in that box.

I felt like I was watching an old friend. Like I was watching my past. A past I didn't know I had.

A short film about a man and woman who were in love but separated by a brick wall—experimental, weird, and my favorite so far—ended and the tape went to fuzz. I got up and used the bathroom, then came back and ejected it. I reached back into the box—only a couple left now—and grabbed another tape. I popped it in and sat leaning forward on the edge of Dad's bed.

The first person in the frame was Dad. He was waving, acting goofy, a beer in his hand. There was noise—a lot of people talking over one another and dishes clinking, that kind of thing—and suddenly music started. A party. Dad began to dance, and then held out his hand and Mom joined him, her head tipped back and laughing as he bit at her throat.

God, they were so in love.

Soon another couple joined in the dancing, their bodies half cut off by the camera, and some more people, and soon there was a lot of hooting and hollering and cheering and raising glasses.

"The man of the hour! Cheers!" Dad called, holding his beer up high. Several others joined him, including Mom, although her smile had withered a little.

"To Bill Hollis," another woman cried, and they all drank.

"Speech, speech, speech!" people began chanting, and the next thing I knew, an impossibly young Bill Hollis was coming into the frame, hair dark and slick, body trim and hard. He looked rich and powerful—and dangerous—even then. My throat dried up seeing him there.

"No speeches," he said. "Save it for the Oscars." Everyone laughed, and Dad let go of Mom and slung his arm around Bill Hollis's neck jovially. I felt tears come to my eyes. My palms had started to sweat and nausea had set in. It was like my brain couldn't make sense of what it was seeing. Couldn't make sense of my dad standing there, buddy-buddy with the man who'd tried to kill me.

You know the Hollises?

Not really. I did a shoot with Bill Hollis once.

"Liar," I said to the TV. It was official. I hadn't imagined anything. Dad was involved with Bill Hollis, too. But I didn't know how, and I didn't know why he would keep it from me.

"Turn that thing off," Dad said to Mom in the video. "I

want to kiss you. A lot." They laughed and kissed, and Mom started toward the camera, but just before her arm blocked the entire view of the lens, something caught my eye.

Or maybe it was someone.

I backed up the tape and paused it. In the back of the room, so fuzzy it was maybe my imagination, a big poof of platinum hair above a whole lot of cleavage. Hanging on to the arm of a very tan white-haired man. Vanessa Hollis? And where had I seen that man before?

The camera blipped off and went to snow, but just as I was about to get up to pull the tape out of the machine, it flipped back on again.

Change of scenery. This time the camera was pointing out over a lake, the sun low in the sky, bouncing sparkles off the water. It looked like a professional shot.

Mom's voice, off camera. "Go stand by that rock, will you?"

Another woman's voice. "I don't want to be in one of your weird movies. You'll probably have me eaten by a lion or something."

Mom's tinkle of a laugh. "I will not. I'm just setting up the shot. It would help to have a body standing there so I'll know what it looks like. Just do it . . . please, B?"

B.

GONE 2 SOON. B.

Pink. Primary blue.

I could hear the woman sigh, and then she stepped into

the frame. She was short, blond, with an almost comical 1980s tease-out, and very, very pregnant. She stood in front of the camera uncomfortably. "This good?"

"Ladies and gentlemen, the Honorable Reverend Carter," Mom intoned in a low announcer's voice. My eyes bugged out of my head. Was this her? Right in front of my face? Not Brandi Courteur; Brandi Carter. Mom's friend, the escort slash mystery woman. The woman Peyton knew. The woman who started this whole crazy thing. The woman I'd been looking for . . . and not looking for . . . all this time.

Mom laughed at her own joke and Brandi protested, waving her hands at the camera. She started to walk away. "No, no. I'm just kidding. I need you there. Just stay for a minute. Pastor." Mom laughed again, and the woman waved her hands again, but her irritated face turned into one of humor as well.

"Stop it, Carrie, it's not funny. I'm serious about this," she said.

"I know, I know. I'm sorry." Mom's voice got somber, but I could tell it was difficult for her to do. "It's just that you're a little weirdly serious."

"Christ's love is serious," Brandi countered. "There's nothing weird about it."

"But it sounds like you're having church in a seaside shack," Mom said. Aqua blew up in my mind.

I paused the screen and studied Brandi's short stature,

her blond hair. She looked so much smaller than I expected her to be. Somehow she'd grown into this huge force in my mind, but here she was, just an ordinary woman. An ordinary woman with an ordinary name: Carter. Someone who was leaving the escort business to find Christ.

I went to my room, forgetting all about the video, and pulled up my laptop. I tapped my fingers impatiently on the desk while I waited for it to load. As soon as it did, I entered *Brandi Carter*.

About a zillion results came up. Of course, with a name like that.

I tried *Brandi Carter* and *church*. Still too many.

Brandi Carter and *Brentwood* and *church*. Nothing.

Brandi Carter and *church* and *California*. Back to too many. I would never get this.

I tried all those searches again, with different spelling variations: *Brandie, Brandy, Brandee* . . .

Nothing.

Aqua nagged me. Mom had said it sounded like Brandi was going off to worship in a seaside shack. I paired her name with every sea- and ocean-related word I could come up with. Same story—either too many results, or zero results.

Sea. Ocean. Boat. Ship. Shore. Sand. Buoy. Fish. Shell. Net.

Lighthouse.

I got a hit.

There was a Brandi Carter at a church called Lighthouse Dimensions Chapel. I clicked.

A website came up. I scanned it until I found an address. Oildale, California. What had Ruby said? That she'd heard a rumor that Mom had gone to a town with the word "oil" in it? *Oil Well, Oil Slick*, she'd thought.

Oildale.

I pulled up Google Maps and plugged in Oildale. Where the hell was Oildale?

The screen zoomed in, lining in red a small area inside Bakersfield.

Bubble blue, muted gray, spongy tawny.

Salinas, Modesto . . . Bakersfield.

Dad could remove the photo, but I didn't need it anymore, anyway. Bakersfield had been one of the stops on the monitor behind Mom at the bus station.

I tabbed back over to the church home page and clicked on *Meet Our Staff.* I scrolled past a lead pastor and a children's pastor and more Sunday school teachers than I could count. And then, at the bottom, a head shot. Still blond, still with the crazy eighties tease-out. But the face hadn't changed. Not much, anyway. She was smiling at the camera.

Secretary, Brandi Carter.

I placed my forefinger over her face and pressed, as if that would make her more real.

"Found you."

I N A PERFECT world, I would have jumped in my car and rushed right to Bakersfield. I would have found Lighthouse Dimensions Chapel and walked in and confronted Brandi Carter and gotten the entire story, including why she'd approached Peyton in the first place—and, to that end, why she hadn't come to me the way she did Peyton, since it was my mom we were talking about.

But Bakersfield was a good three hours away, and Dad was coming home, and there was this stupid broken window that I was going to have to explain. Not to mention, I wasn't sure I wanted the answers to those questions. I still wasn't sure I really wanted to find Brandi Carter at all. Finding her wouldn't make Peyton any less dead, and it wouldn't make me any less the suspect, and it wouldn't make Rigo and Luna any less out there.

Dad had texted while I was watching Mom's movies. He was on his way. I'd spent so much time reading up on Lighthouse Dimensions, he was almost home before I even saw his text. I went back to his room, packed away the movies, and took the box back to his office. Dad and I had a lot of secrets between us, and I didn't exactly know if I could trust his word anymore, but I still didn't want him to know I'd watched the movies without him. Even if he'd kept things from me, maybe he'd had a good reason for it. He was still all I had in this world.

Not true. You have Detective Martinez. I stopped in my tracks. Where had that thought come from? I didn't care—I shooed it away. I had more important things to think about. Like the earring, which was still on Dad's desk, the BOO taunting me.

With shaky hands, I palmed it and took it to my room.

I HAD PUT on makeup to cover the bruises that the Basiles had left on me, pushed the cabinet back in its original place, and was sweeping glass into a dustpan when Dad walked in. The bruises felt like neon signs on my face. My fat lip felt a thousand times bigger than it was. My chest ached where my shirt was brushing up against the knife wound. I'd fitted a bandage over it and put on a dark T-shirt, so Dad wouldn't see and start asking questions. As it was, I had enough questions to concoct answers for.

"Hey, what happened here?" he asked, dropping his camera bag and duffel right inside the door. "Are you okay? You didn't call. I thought we had an agreement that you'd call if anything went wrong. Was it Luna? Oh God, Nikki, if she—"

I stood and held my hand out. "Stop. I haven't swept there yet. And nothing went wrong. Everything was fine." The lie rolled off my tongue so easily. Maybe I had no right to be mad at Dad at all. Like father, like daughter?

He took the dustpan from my hand and walked it to the trash. "Well, obviously not everything was fine. How did the window get broken?"

I rolled my eyes. "Stupid middle schoolers. They were jackassing around and a ball came right through. Scared the crap out of me."

He stared, first at me, and then at the window, his face scrunched up all mint green like he didn't believe me. "What kids? What middle schoolers? We don't have middle schoolers on this street, do we? And what were they doing playing ball in our backyard, anyway?"

Shit. "I don't know who they were. I think they were coming through from another neighborhood or something."

"What neighborhood? They should be held responsible for this. You could have gotten hurt."

I touched his elbow. "Dad. I'm fine. It was just an accident. I'm glad you're home." I hugged him. He held the dustpan awkwardly at the small of my back.

When I pulled away, the mint green on his face had intensified, a mask of disbelief. "You're lying," he said. "Tell me what really happened."

I felt all my blood rush to my cheeks. My forehead felt so slate gray I wondered if Dad could actually see it, even though he didn't have synesthesia. I shook my head helplessly, trying to hang on to the lie, because it was all I had. I couldn't let him know what was really going on. I was way too far in at this point to even consider it. If I didn't get myself out of this mess, he would find out soon enough when they came to haul my ass to jail for good. "It was the kids," I said. "I swear."

He scrunched his lips together. "Mm-hmm," he said. "There were no middle school kids, Nikki."

"Yes," I said. "There were." But even I didn't sound convincing to myself. An inky finger of outrage threatened to poke through my chest. If he was going to call out my lies, would I be able to stop myself from calling him out on his? Even if I wasn't quite sure what they were yet? My jaw clenched.

He took the broom out of my hand and bent to sweep more glass into the dustpan. "So how big was the party?" he asked to the floor.

Party? Oh my God, I was so stupid. Why didn't I think of that? *Way to go, Nikki. Making things a thousand times harder for yourself, as usual.*

"I didn't have a party," I said, just to keep things convincing, but I tried to let it show on my face that he had caught me.

"You don't think I was ever eighteen? You think your grandparents never went out of town and left me alone?" He straightened, his face red from having been bent over, but the mint green was gone. "Granted, I never destroyed the house while they were gone. Must have been a hell of a night."

This was much more familiar turf that I was in now. Dad being the unattached friend, trying to look like a dad, but failing. We both knew better. He wouldn't yell. He wouldn't even get mad. I supposed because of how suddenly Mom had been taken from him, he figured if he ever yelled or got mad at me, and I ended up dead the next minute, he would have all kinds of regrets. He had no idea how close I seemed to come to death on a semiregular basis. And he had no idea that I no longer trusted him enough to let him in.

"I'm sorry," I said, trying to look hangdog without overdoing it. "I'll pay for it."

He took the dustpan back over to the trash, his back to me. "Does that mean you got a job?" he asked. "Or are you still carefully plotting what comes next?"

And that was it. Window discussion over. Just as I knew it would be. And back to the tired Get on with Your Adult Life, Nikki conversation, right on schedule. "No, but when I get a job, you'll be the first to know, trust me. And I'll pay for the window. I promise. Somehow. I'll figure it out."

He tucked the broom and dustpan in the pantry and waved his hand at me. "It's just a window. Not the end of the world. So what else did I miss while I was gone?"

I shrugged. *Dear God, so, so much.* "Pretty quiet, I guess. Boring." *Not by a long shot.*

He picked up his bags and headed toward his office with them. "Well, I would much prefer quiet and boring over the alternative," he said. "Have you eaten?"

"Frozen pizza," I said. "But if you want me to make you something . . ."

He came out of the office. He kicked off his shoes and slumped into his recliner. Had he known that Jones and I had made out in that recliner, would that have finally gotten a rise out of him? Probably not. Knowing Dad, he'd be happy I was busy with something normal for a change. If you could call what Jones and I had normal.

"Nah, I ate a sandwich in the car. All I want to do is drink a beer, watch some baseball, and go to bed." He glanced up at me. "You weren't the only one who had a late night last night."

"Oh, really? And her name was?"

"Don't get your hopes up. It wasn't that kind of night. You're looking a little tired. Your eyes are puffy."

It wasn't why my eyes were puffy, but I was tired. Not up-too-late-partying tired. Not think-I'll-nap-today tired. The kind of bone-deep tired that comes with months of being surrounded by crimson and asphalt and blood-pumping fireworks that make you want to squint and scream at everyone to watch out, even though you're the only one who can see them.

"Yeah. Maybe a little," I said.

"You're still in your robe, so I'm guessing you haven't been up for long."

"Not really."

"Lucky." He yawned. "Listen, you can go ahead. I'll figure out something about that window."

"I'm just going upstairs," I said. I bent and kissed him on the cheek. "It's good to have you home." Truthfully, it was. I felt a little safer with Dad there, whether I could trust him anymore or not. He was still my dad, which meant hopefully he wouldn't let me get hurt if he could help it.

Dad smiled. "Good to be missed," he said.

When I got back to my room, my phone screen was still lit up from a recent call. I sighed, going to it. Come on, Jones, was it so damn hard to just let somebody have a whole day to themselves? I picked it up and studied the screen.

Martinez.

Of course. He'd called six times. I knew him. He would call another six. Or sixty, if that was what it took. The man was relentless. *Almost as relentless as I am,* I thought. Truth.

The phone buzzed again while I was holding it and a text came through. Martinez again. **Since you won't answer your phone, I'm coming by. I have something to show you.**

Crap. I pressed the call button. He answered on the first ring.

"It's about time," he said.

"Sorry. I didn't realize I was at your beck and call today. I told you I was sick."

"Yeah, but you were lying."

How was it that everyone just seemed to know when I was lying all of a sudden? "How would you know?" I spat into the phone. "You're not here. I've spent the whole morning puking my guts up. Would you like me to take a picture next time and send it to you, Detective, so you can put the case to rest?"

"I'll pass," he said. "But, regardless, you don't have time for a sick day. I looked through Blake's files this morning, and they are moving faster than I thought they might."

"You were snooping in your girlfriend's work files? God, that's kind of smarmy, don't you think?"

"Do you want to go to prison?" he asked. I said nothing.

"I didn't think so. And it isn't smarmy. It would be smarmy if that was the only reason I was with her."

"Is it?" I knew I was poking him and he would blow up at me soon if I kept it up, but I couldn't help myself. There was something about his little love affair with the honorable Blake Willis that irritated me to no end. And it wasn't just about how she was involved in the case against me. If she was being honest, she was doing what she could to help me out, so in reality I should have really liked her. Or at least kind of liked her. It was just . . . of all women, why *her*?

"I'm not going to dignify that," he said, and then, "Actually, you know what? I am going to dignify it. I'm with her because she's beautiful and smart and funny, and to be honest, she's erotic as hell. Killer body, and she knows how to use it. Feel better?"

No. I actually felt like I might be sick after all. "So much better," I said bitterly.

"Good. So let's move on then. I'm going to come by. I have something to show you in those bank records we took from the Hollis evidence."

"What? No. You can't come here." I thought about Dad, probably by now dozing in his recliner downstairs. Maybe on the phone trying to get someone out to do an emergency fix on the window. I imagined Detective Martinez showing up at our doorstep—a cop. Dad's least favorite kind of person. He would definitely want to know why I was hanging out with him. And there would be no good answer. No reason that would seem good enough to him. "I'll come there."

"I thought you were sick."

"Do you want me to come or not?"

"I'm at the station."

"Okay, give me fifteen minutes."

"Bring a barf bag," he said.

"Jackass," I muttered as I ended the call.

Dad was already asleep, an old Nikon box duct-taped over the broken window. Cardboard and tape wouldn't keep bad guys out, but it was better than nothing, I supposed.

I scribbled a note on a napkin and left it on the table next to Dad's recliner, where he would see it when he woke up, and snuck out.

I DIDN'T THINK I would ever be comfortable walking into the police station. Maybe even less so now that I knew beautiful, funny, smart, erotic Blake with the killer body was gunning for me extra fast. Like I would walk in a free woman, and end up not being let out forever. It was irrational, but it was what it was.

Fortunately, Detective Martinez was waiting for me right inside. He gave me a long stare and I could feel myself tense. I hadn't thought to check how I looked before I left. Would he be able to tell that I had been beaten up last night?

"You actually look like you're sick," he mused. He pointed

to the top part of his cheek. "Your eye almost looks bruised."

"I fell asleep with my head on the toilet and slid off and hit my face on the edge of the bathtub."

He stared, as if he maybe didn't believe me. "You must have been feeling pretty awful. Now I feel a little bad for doubting you."

I went with it. "I told you. Hope I don't heave on your shoes."

"We'll make this quick."

He placed his hand between my shoulders and guided me past the front desk and through the station. I felt like I was being escorted as a prisoner and all eyes were on me. Foreshadowing of my not-too-distant future.

"Here," he said, directing me into a tiny hole of an office. It was packed with stacks of papers, files, and books. Everything was sleek and dusted, as I would expect his office to be, but there were zero decorations. It was all work, also as I would expect his office to be. An ancient desktop computer took up most of a nicked-up desk. The only chair in the room was the one behind it.

"I'm guessing you don't get a lot of visitors in here," I said. "You didn't exactly knock yourself out on interior design."

"You can sit there," he said, ignoring me. He gestured toward the chair. I worked my way behind the desk and sat.

"So am I special? Because this doesn't feel special. It

feels depressing. A little color wouldn't kill you. Maybe a plant or something."

"You done assessing my work space now?" he asked. He half sat on the edge of the desk, facing me, a little too close. "And want to tell me the truth about your face? Because we both know the sick story is bullshit."

"It's your space," I said. "And not really, no." He crossed his arms and stared me down. I sighed. "Okay. Fine. But you're going to freak out." He raised his eyebrows expectantly. "The Basiles broke into my house last night. And there was . . . an altercation."

He came up off the desk so fast I thought he might launch through the ceiling. "What? When? And they did this to you? How do you know it was them?"

"Whoa. Stop. See, I knew you'd freak out. It's no big deal. They caught me by surprise, but I turned it around. Got a tiny bit stabbed, but you should've seen the other guy." The joke fell flat.

"I'm making a report," he said, heading for the door.

"No, don't!"

He turned, impatient, and like he was having to explain astrophysics to a kindergartner. "They broke into your house and beat you up. That's a crime. Actually, it's multiple crimes. You have to report it."

"They said they'd come back if I so much as thought about them again. They've seen us both. If we go after them, they'll know you're a cop, and Rigo will disappear completely. We'll never find him."

"Nikki . . ."

"Please?" I said. "If they come back, you can write a hundred reports or shoot them or whatever it is you want to do, okay? But I handled it. It's okay. Just let it go, so we can do what we need to do."

His fists on his hips, he shook his head at his shoes, like he couldn't believe he was getting ready to do what he was getting ready to do. "You have to promise to stop lying to me. If they come back, you call me immediately."

I held up my pinkie. "Pinkie swear."

"I don't like it—"

Someone knocked twice on his door frame and kept walking down the hall. "Shit," he said. "I'll be right back. Been waiting to hear back on a case all morning. Just give me a minute."

"Whatever," I said, swiveling in the chair. "I'll just sit here and be a good girl." But as soon as he left, I jiggled the mouse to wake up his computer. I didn't do good girl. Never had. "Let's see what you're working on these days, Detective," I said to myself. "Other than me, that is. And sexy Blake."

He had three tabs open. None of the pages looked familiar to me. They looked like internal network police pages. I could probably get into a shit-ton of trouble for looking at them. I scanned the information and saw the same name on all three.

"Heriberto Abana," I read aloud. "You naughty boy, Heriberto, what have you done to get the po-po after you?"

I couldn't make sense of the pages Detective Martinez had open, but I knew how to work Google. I opened Chrome and started to type in Heriberto Abana's name. To my surprise, it was the first thing to pop up as soon as I typed the H. Martinez had searched for this guy before, that was for sure. I went over to his search history.

Holy crap. He had obsessively searched the shit out of old Heriberto. Whatever the guy had done, it must have been serious.

He had also searched a bunch of addresses in South Central L.A. Looking for Heriberto's house, maybe? I plugged an address into Google Maps.

"Better look out, Herbie," I said. "The fuzz is coming for you."

"Go ahead and make yourself at home," Detective Martinez said as he came back through the door. He was holding a fistful of papers, which he promptly stacked on top of a billion other papers on a file cabinet.

"How will you ever find that again when you need it?" I asked.

"Well, in theory, it's my job to find stuff," he said. "And I think I'm pretty good at what I do, so don't worry about it."

"Looks like you haven't found Heriberto Abana. What did he do? You've been looking for him pretty hard. And for quite a while." I scrolled down through the search history again to prove my point.

He reached across me and pushed the button to turn off the monitor. "Don't worry about that, either," he said. But he'd lost the playfulness in his voice.

"Why not? You afraid I'll beat you to finding him? You know, like I did the Hollises a few months ago? Let me see what I can figure out. It'll be my little freebie to you. As a thank-you for all your help finding Rigo. If, of course, we actually find Rigo." I reached to turn the monitor back on, but he grabbed my hand.

"That's not why you're here." Sharp. And I got the same weird vibe I'd gotten off him before, when I asked about the bullet holes in his car. He'd been so cagey about it. So touchy. Was Herbie the reason those holes were there? Was that why the detective was so focused on him? Did it have nothing to do with work at all? Was Heriberto the personal case he had mentioned?

I yanked my hand out of his. "Whoa. Okay. Whatever. What is your problem?" *I see gray all over you*, I wanted to say, but then remembered that a sentence like that wouldn't make any sense to him.

"It's personal, okay? Just . . . let's get to what you're here for," he said.

"Yes, sir." I swiveled so I was facing the desk, on which he'd laid out several papers. I recognized them right away. They were Dru's bank papers that we'd taken from evidence. "So what am I looking for?"

"Tell me if anything jumps out at you," he said. He came around behind me and rested his palms on the desk, leaning over me so I could smell his cologne. Something spicy and luxurious. He was in a suit today, too. The jacket was draped over the chair I was sitting in. Must have been a special day.

"Um, not really," I said, staring. But then something did. Almost literally jumped out at me. Scarlet. Avocado. Maroon. Scarlet-avocado-maroon. Scarletavocadomaroon. I'd seen that combination before. D-O-M. "Dom Distribution," I said, pointing to a line on the sheet. "The van at the auction."

"Yep," he said. "Remember when that happened, I told you the name of the company sounded familiar? That's because I'd seen it here. Over and over." He ran his finger down the sheet and to the next one, and, sure enough, there it was. *Dom Distribution. Dom Distribution. Dom Distribution.*

"So Dru was paying Dom Distribution a whole hell of a lot of money. For what?"

Detective Martinez shook his head and pointed to the money column. "He was *receiving* a lot of money from Dom Distribution."

I scanned the column. Dru had received thousands

upon thousands of dollars from them over the course of a couple of months. "I don't get it. Why would they be paying him? Did he work there?" It seemed impossible that a guy like Dru would have worked for an ordinary distribution company.

Detective Martinez flattened his hand against the papers and leaned forward so he was facing me. "I don't know. I'm still trying to run down all the paperwork. I'm not sure who the technical owner is of Dom Distribution, but I'd be willing to bet the real owner is a Hollis. Maybe Dru himself."

"Or Luna. Since the van clearly wanted us dead," I said.

He shrugged. "I suppose that's possible, but less likely with her being so young." I turned in my chair, pushing myself back a few inches to get some thinking space. Detective Martinez was not good at personal bubbles.

"So you're thinking, what? That Dom Distribution is paying off the Hollises for something? Like hush money?"

He turned and sat on the corner of his desk, scrunching the papers beneath him. He rubbed his chin while he thought. "Perhaps. Or perhaps they're only giving the Hollises back their own money."

"I don't get it."

"Where do the Hollises get most of their money?"

I shrugged. "I don't know. Movies?"

"Not likely. Bill Hollis hasn't produced a movie in almost ten years."

I blinked. I hadn't realized that. But, yeah. Martinez was right. Bill Hollis was one of those quasi-famous names that had just sort of dropped out of existence over the past decade until his daughter ended up dead. So where else would the Hollises get a bunch of money? "From the escort service," I said. "It went through Dom so the feds couldn't track them down."

"Right."

We both sat there for a few minutes in silence, thinking. There was a Hollis connection with Dom Distribution, which meant that there was a Luna connection to Dom Distribution. Made total sense; otherwise, why would they have wanted to run us over? And Ruby had said that the Hollises owned another business. Nobody seemed to know what the other business was. Could it have been a distribution company? And then the big question—how did the Basiles, and Tesori Antico, fit into all of this? Was it just coincidence that the van was at the auction, coming at us just as they were getting away?

Maybe. Maybe Luna, and the van, were already there because they had followed us there.

I turned on the computer monitor. Detective Martinez started to reach for the button, but I swatted his hand away.

"Don't worry. I won't mess with your Abana case," I said. "I just want to look up something."

I pulled up the internet and searched for Dom

Distribution. Bingo. Immediate hit. I clicked the link. Before I could even read the words, I saw the connection, in a dusty grayish blue that made me want to sneeze.

"Restoration products," Detective Martinez read over my shoulder.

"Antique restoration products," I added, pointing to the sneezy word *antique*.

"So Bill Hollis's distribution company just happens to sell antique restoratives."

I nodded. "And the Basiles' business just happens to be antiques."

"We've got a connection," Martinez said.

"I say we go to Tesori Antico," I said.

Detective Martinez rubbed his jaw a couple more times—I could hear the *scritch scritch* of his palm against his whiskers. "Why? What are you thinking?"

"I don't know. It's a gut feeling mostly. But I'm thinking if we go to Tesori, Dom Distribution will follow. And when they show up, we can bust them. Figure out who is behind the wheel and why they want to kill us. Or figure out that it's Luna and have her put away again. Or that it's Rigo, trying to finish the job that Dru screwed up. Either way, we win."

He tick-tocked his head from side to side, as if mulling over what I'd said. "Unless they actually succeed in killing us. Then they win."

A sarcastic laugh jumped out of me. "As if."

He narrowed his eyes. For a second it felt like he could see the roiling fire oranges and yellows that were now swirling around me, and I felt naked, connected in a weird way that was so much more intimate than Jones had ever succeeded in connecting with me. The oranges and yellows twisted into pine as I twisted into embarrassment. "Another gut feeling," he said.

"What about it?"

He scraped his top teeth over his bottom lip a few times, never losing eye contact. I'd begun to burn so hard with pine I felt like I was in a forest. I half expected to see a carpet of needles under my feet.

"What?" I snapped, a little too harsh, but I needed to get the heat off me somehow. The rainbow was threatening— I could feel it.

"You sure do have a lot of them."

"So? I'm intuitive. I'm sure you have a few hunches here and there, too, Detective."

He stood up and reached toward me. I stared at his hand, and then reluctantly took it and let him pull me out of the chair. "Exactly," he said. He didn't move, so that I was standing only inches away from him, a mirror of the way he blocked me with his body at the hospital the very first time that I'd met him. He was totally not good at personal space. "Have you ever thought about becoming a cop, Nikki?"

I laughed out loud. Long, hard guffaws that would have

doubled me over if I'd had room. Imagine me, a cop. Joining the forces of people who'd only continuously let me down for most of my life.

Except for him, my brain interrupted. *Martinez hasn't let you down. He wouldn't.*

Bullshit, I countered. *He just hasn't yet. In the end, everyone lets each other down. The only person I can definitely count on to fight for me is myself.*

The thought sobered me quickly.

"I didn't realize I'd told a joke," he said, turning and moving toward the door.

"Well, that's exactly what it is," I said, following him. "A complete and total joke. No way would I ever become a cop."

He turned again and I almost ran full frontal into him. "It's not like you have a lot of other big plans, right?"

I pretended to think it over. "Hmm, well, there is this possible job opportunity I have working in a prison for the rest of my life. Which will turn from possible to probable if we don't get to the bottom of this case and find Rigo Basile. Can we go now?"

He smiled with only one half of his mouth, as if he were privy to a joke that I couldn't hear. "Yes, ma'am," he said. "Let's go find us a van."

W E WAITED FOREVER, parked around the corner from the front door of Tesori Antico in a car
borrowed from one of Martinez's buddies. I was so sick of
waiting and watching and watching and waiting and coming
on dead end after dead end. I just wanted this to be over.

"Maybe we should stand outside or something. Bait
them a little," I suggested.

"I thought we were trying to keep from being recognized. Standing outside is not very subtle, is it?"

"Neither is trying to run over two people in a parking lot.
Or shooting your brother in your backyard. I would hardly
call Luna subtle."

"And if it's not Luna?"

I shook my head. "It's her. I know it's her. Who else could it be?"

"I'm afraid to start counting possibilities," he said.

"Well, as you can see, subtlety is not really my specialty. Which is part of what makes your earlier suggestion so ridiculous."

He shifted on the seat and it let out a vinyl groan. "What earlier suggestion?"

"That I should be a cop."

"Ah." He did a quick visual sweep of the area. "You could get a handle on your subtlety. You'd be good at it."

"What, are you an expert on the Inner Workings of Nikki Kill now? What makes you so sure you know what I would do or how good I would be?"

He reached forward and flicked on the radio, fiddling with buttons until he landed on some R & B. He turned it down so low it felt almost imaginary. "I used to be just like you."

"Excuse me? Back in your gangbanging days, you were like me? I don't think so."

"First of all, I wasn't a gangbanger."

"Oh, right," I said. "You were just banging a gangbanger's sister. You're right. Not so subtle." I grinned.

He tilted his head sideways and gave me a *Really?* look. I rolled my hands, gesturing for him to continue. I wasn't much for listening to stories about people's glory days, but anything had to be more interesting than watching nothing.

"I was passionate. Like you. And I had a huge chip on my shoulder." He poked my shoulder with his forefinger. "Like you. And I was angry."

"Gosh, you're making me sound like such a charmer," I said. Sarcastic, but on the inside I felt uneasy, because I knew what he was saying was the truth. Even if I didn't like to hear it.

"And," he said, "I watched someone get hurt. Really hurt. And my first instinct was to hurt back, but I knew I couldn't do it. Our family had been through enough. I couldn't get rid of the feeling that it was somehow my fault or that I should have stopped it or settled the score or . . . just something. I felt like I did nothing, and I couldn't stand that feeling. I had to do something. To at least feel like I tried."

I swallowed. The air in the car had gotten kind of heavy. He was talking about himself, but he was also talking about me. Problem was, I wasn't sure if he was talking about the me who felt helpless to stop my mom's murder, or if he was talking about the me who needed to do something about Peyton's. And how sick and fucked up was it that I had a menu of murders in my life to choose from?

He shifted again, traced the stitching on the steering wheel with his forefinger. "So I became a cop. And I worked my ass off. And I put everything I had into it. And now . . . now I feel like I can do something. You know what I mean?"

I nodded, feeling dangerously close to tears, and unsure why.

"I don't suppose you're going to tell me who got hurt," I said.

"I will. Someday. Today's not that day."

The song ended and a new one started and he turned up the volume just the tiniest bit, bouncing his thumb to the beat, making little plastic tapping sounds with each bounce.

"Fair enough," I said. And I didn't know what compelled me to say the next thing. Maybe it was because he had shared something, or maybe it was because I was tired of hiding it, or maybe it was because I was scared he was really overestimating my detective abilities and if I didn't come clean, he would push me into becoming something I would be really bad at. "So these hunches," I said.

He turned and raised his eyebrows, which shot squiggles of fear through me. "The infamous Nikki Kill hunches," he said in a radio commentator voice.

"They're not, like, from out of nowhere."

He gave me a curious look.

Suddenly, I wasn't sure how to go on. How did I tell him about myself without sounding like a crazy person? "Peyton and I had something in common. It was about . . . God, this sounds so crazy . . ." I took a breath. "We see things differently. I mean, we see them the same as each other, but different from everyone else. And also kind of different from each other."

"Wait. You see things the same but you see them differently?"

"Yes. No. That's not at all what I meant. We have this thing. I don't even know what you call it. A disorder or a condition or a . . . a skill. I'm not sure. All I know is—"

A car came out of nowhere and settled into the space behind us. I could make out the shadow of a person in the rearview mirror—dark hair, perma-frown. It was the man who'd been at the auction. The one who'd bought Rigo's cane.

A Basile. *The* Basile? The one who'd told me he would kill me if he saw me again? Could be. I wouldn't know for sure until he came back to finish the job. Which he was definitely going to do if he saw me here.

He parked and got out of the car. He was going to walk right past us.

"Shit," I said.

"What?"

I frantically looked around for somewhere to hide. My first inclination was to duck, but if Perma-Frown Basile looked in the window and saw me hunched on the floorboard, he would for sure get curious. Not to mention that the man who had attacked me knew what Detective Martinez looked like, which meant that even if Perma-Frown hadn't been that guy, there was a pretty good chance he knew, too. Where was Martinez going to go? Under the steering wheel?

The man got closer—so close I could hear his shoes on the pavement.

"Just go with this," I said, grabbing Detective Martinez's biceps with my hands.

He didn't say anything. I didn't give him time.

I twisted my body and leaned in, pressing myself hard against him, and kissed him. Deep, slow, melty, letting my hair fall like a curtain in front of our faces. At first he just sat there, tense, breath held, but then I felt his hands clutch the small of my back, soft, warm, and then move up to the sides of my face. Our lips parted and we kissed again, more delicate and purposeful, and he pulled me toward him. When we parted again, I could feel his breath mingle with mine, our noses touching. I peeked past him and saw that the man had gone by and was pulling open the door of Tesori Antico.

My hands dropped away from Detective Martinez's shoulders and I slumped backward, reeling over the rainbow that had burst under me. Violet screamed at me, but it didn't come alone. And, just like last time, it terrified me. I had no idea what it meant.

"What was—"

"A Basile," I interrupted. "Don't get all excited. I didn't want to do it any more than you did."

"Was he the one who threatened you?"

I shrugged. "Could be. I didn't exactly make eye contact with him. I had to do something quick. Kissing you was the only thing I could think of. Sorry."

"No, it's okay. Next time you might give me a little heads-up, though."

Violet. Violet, violet. The whole damn car was violet. Grapes and passion fruit and neon signs and every purple thing that was ever purple paled in comparison.

I leaned toward him, closing the distance between us further. "There will be no next time," I said. I stared straight ahead. We sat in awkward silence. I felt like an ass for saying that. And I felt like an ass for kissing him. I basically just felt like an ass.

"We should probably go," he said, reaching for the ignition.

I nodded. Please, God, please, get me out of this car. "Maybe next time we'll find a van."

He pulled away from the curb, steering us toward the highway. "So you were saying? About your condition or skill or whatever it was?"

Every color imaginable was popping in my head. Confusing me. Overwhelming me. The moment was definitely over. I couldn't believe I'd let it get so close. I definitely wouldn't let that happen again.

"You going to finish?" he prompted, glancing at me.

I aimed my face toward the window, watching the trees and cars and buildings whiz by. "Today's not that day."

I WAS RESTLESS when I got home. Too much stimulation. Too many new details. Too many roads leading out of the same damn family. And, of course, that kiss. It had been spur-of-the-moment. It had been practical. But it had also been that swooping color wave. Not just violet. And I didn't know what that meant.

Dad was awake from his nap and eating a bowl of cereal at the kitchen table.

"There you are," he said. "Home for the night, or is that wishful thinking?"

I pulled out a chair and sat next to him. "It's only eight o'clock."

"So it is wishful thinking," he said. He took another bite. "Oh, to be eighteen again."

"Yeah, it's bliss," I said, but I didn't feel jokey.

He paused, milk dripping from his spoon back into the bowl. "That boy stopped by. He didn't look so blissful, either."

Boy? The only boy who might stop by would be Jones. "Jones was here?" I asked. I waved my hands over my biceps. "Big muscles? Dimpled chin?" *Damn it, I told him I was sick and to stay away.*

Dad dropped his spoon back in his bowl and clasped his hands beneath his chin. "And, oh so dreamy!" When I grunted, he scooped another spoonful of cereal. "Sorry, sorry. Yes, that's the one. I'm guessing there's trouble in paradise."

I remembered Jones storming out of the *dojang*, his fists clenched by his sides, and how tense it had been between us since. How would I have talked my way out of it if he'd seen that kiss? "Something like that. I'll call him." But what would I say? *Sorry I missed you, Jones. I was busy making out with Detective Martinez in the front seat of his car.* Something told me he wouldn't take that very well.

Dad gave me a suspicious glance. "Something else going on? Is there something you need to tell me?"

Is there something you *need to tell* me? I wanted to counter. *Something you've been hiding for about eighteen years, maybe?*

What I knew about Dad and Hollis made me so uncomfortable, I could barely stand to be in the same room with him. I had to know for sure. "Hey, Dad? Do you remember when Dru Hollis was taken to jail and we were watching it on this TV? You said that family was trouble. That they thought they were above everyone else. Remember?"

"I suppose," he said, his cheek full of cereal. "Not really. That was a while ago. And a lot of stuff has happened with that family since."

"But you remember seeing it on TV, right?"

"Sure, I guess."

"But you didn't know them before that? The Hollises?"

He set his spoon in the bowl and regarded me, his brow creased. "No."

"You'd worked with Bill Hollis on a shoot, though, right?"

His eyes flicked up and to the left. "I don't remember that, no."

"You said you did."

"Okay, I must have, then, but I don't remember it. We wouldn't have had much of anything to do with each other, even if I did."

"And Mom never worked with him? Like on a film project or something?"

The crease in his brow deepened. "No, Nikki, why?" And there it was. Cheater blue. Right there in the bowl of cereal, on the table, on the walls. I let out a defeated sigh.

Because you're lying to me.

I WAS COMPLETELY on edge from our failed stakeout and my run-in with Dad. Detective Martinez might have been able to just go on about his night knowing that someone was trying to run us over with a van, but I couldn't. Especially not since I knew for certain that Luna was out there and her family was connected with the business. These things were not coincidental. It was so obvious it was laughable. It was just a matter of flushing her out.

The hard part was finding her.

All I needed to do was find out where Viral Fanfare was playing, and I could get to that someone. But someone knew how. At least according to Blue.

My laptop wouldn't pull up. Just a blank black screen, no matter what I did, what buttons I pushed, or how much I cussed at it. Talk about the shittiest timing of all shitty timing.

I slammed it shut and ran downstairs with it tucked under my arm.

"Hey, can I use your computer?"

"Something wrong with yours?" Dad asked.

I held it out for him to see. "It's dead."

"That's weird. Was it having problems?"

No. And in the grand scheme of my life, a dead computer was the least weird thing I'd encountered. A pain-in-the-ass thing. A thing that would slow me down. But normal nonetheless. "Hard drive probably fried itself," I said. "It's old, anyway."

Dad took it from me. "We'll get you a new one, I guess."

"In the meantime . . . ?"

He waved his hand at me. "Yeah, sure. Use mine. Just don't mess with any of the photo files."

It only took about three minutes of trolling Facebook to figure out where Viral Fanfare was playing that night. Lowery's Body Craft, an auto body shop in Culver City. Not surprising—auto body shops and basements and fields and abandoned churches were just the type of places Viral Fanfare made their name playing. When they weren't playing at Hollis Mansion, of course. Which they wouldn't be doing ever again. A sobering thought.

Most likely, somebody's stepdad or uncle or brother's friend owned Lowery's Body Craft, and said stepdad or uncle or brother's friend was stupid enough to go out of town and leave his keys behind. A perfect situation for Viral Fanfare to swoop in and organize a "private" party.

I called Jones as soon as I pulled out of my driveway.

"Hey," he said, when he answered. Flat.

"You stopped by?" I asked.

"So glad you're feeling better, by the way." Bitter.

I merged onto the highway. "I'm going to hang up if you're going to act like that."

A breath thundered into the phone. "Okay. You're right. I'm sorry." But he didn't sound sorry. He just sounded mad. "I stopped by because I missed you. That's all. Where were you?"

"I was just out," I said.

"With him?" I didn't know what to say. "That's what I thought."

"Jones," I said. "Come on."

"No, Nikki, you come on. The least you could do is be honest with me. If you're with someone else, tell me and I won't keep wasting my time."

"I'm not with anyone," I said, realizing that I was kind of yelling now. "I keep telling you that. Besides, what happened to all that crap about you not caring if I was?"

There was a long pause. I tried to just concentrate on the road and ignore that I felt a catch in my breathing. I refused to be upset about a boy. Refused.

"You're right. Can I come over now?" he asked. "So we can talk this out?"

I hated having to say this. "I can't."

"I figured," he said. "Maybe next time."

"Yeah." I felt about as small as my voice sounded. There was no way to convince Jones that nothing was going on between Martinez and me. Especially after that kiss.

"I should let you go, then," he said.

"Sure," I said. "And Jones?"

"Huh?"

I swallowed. I didn't want to do this—I knew I was hurting him—but I really felt like I had to. It was the best for both of us. "You should probably stop wasting your time."

I was met with the click of the line disconnecting.

I HADN'T BEEN to Culver City in a long time. Mom used to take me out there to climb to the top of the Baldwin Hills Scenic Overlook. We would climb the long staircase and find a place at the top where we could sit and look down over the Los Angeles basin. From the top of the overlook, the Hollywood sign looked so small and far away, a proud, white necklace on Mount Lee. In my mind now, though, the sign was rusty peach, the memory so sweet it was almost painful.

I was glad for the darkness, and the oppressive summer heat, even in the nighttime, to distract me. I was afraid if I looked around too much, I would see everything in crimson. Probably not, but these days I never really knew when crimson would show up, it seemed.

Or violet, I thought. Because that seemed out of control these days, too. I wondered if it was possible for your synesthesia to go on the fritz as you got older. *Wishful thinking, Nikki.*

Lowery's Body Craft wasn't yet hopping. I checked the clock on my dash. The band wouldn't get up and running for at least another hour, probably. People would likely begin streaming in at the very last minute, nobody wanting to be hanging around an empty and silent auto body shop.

Nobody but me, that was.

Shelby had answers that I needed, and I intended to get them.

I parked directly in front of the shop but walked around back to get in. I didn't need to try the front door to know that it wouldn't be open. What was the point of having a private party, starring a popular underground band, if anybody could walk in off the street and listen?

I could hear chatter as soon as I opened the door, but Seth—the drummer—was the first person I saw. He was coming out of the bathroom, tugging on his zipper.

"What the hell are you doing here?" he asked, instant belligerence. Seth and Gibson were not exactly my biggest fans. With good reason, probably. No doubt Gibson still sported a scar where I'd once beaned him with a rock.

"I need to talk to Shelby," I said, breezing past him. I wasn't their biggest fan, either.

"About what?" he called, following me. I didn't answer; just pressed on into the spacious lobby, where a door led to a basement. Lights were on. He grabbed my shoulder from behind. "About what?" he repeated.

I shrugged off his shoulder and whirled around. "About my business," I said. "Is she downstairs?"

"Any business of the band is my business too," he said, squaring himself up tall.

I had to force myself not to laugh. "*Any business of the band,*" I repeated in a voice meant to mock his. "Whatever, dude. Just move. I don't have time for you."

He didn't move, so I pushed around him, my shoulder bumping into his. He didn't make an effort to stop me, but he followed me close as I went down the dusty wooden stairs.

"Why don't you just go?" he said to my back. "You're not wanted here. Don't you get that? Why are you always around?"

"I just can't quit you, Seth," I said in a droll voice, not even pausing to give him a second of my attention. Seth was nothing to me. A speed bump on the highway to answers.

Shelby was testing a mic when I walked in. She stopped, her face going ashen, and then quickly recovered with her usual dead-eyed smirk. Vee, busy plugging cords into an amp, also looked up.

"Hey, Nikki," Vee said uncertainly. "I didn't know you were coming."

"Neither did I," I said. "But I need to talk to her." I pointed at Shelby, never letting my eyes leave hers. In some ways it felt like I was staring down something dangerous and deadly, like a wolf, and the moment I looked away, I would be mauled.

"So talk," Shelby said into the microphone. The sound felt like it came from everywhere. It was unsettling, and suddenly I had the creeping sensation of slate. Just because Vee talked to me sometimes now did not mean we were friends. Would she stop Shelby from doing anything stupid? Would she stop Seth and Gib? Probably not. I was definitely outnumbered here.

I didn't respond.

"What's going on?" Vee asked, but still Shelby and I were staring. I felt like I was being sucked into those black-hole eyes, and like there would be nothing but hell on the other side of them. "Hello? What's the deal?"

Finally, Shelby peeled herself away from the microphone and came to me, her gait steady and confident and maybe even a little bit cocky. I wanted to rush her, to choke her, for being so sure of herself. She was wearing a pair of very high-heeled brown boots—totally out of season, and she had to be roasting in them—and they clacked along the floor as she made her way to me. When she was just a foot or so away, she stopped.

"Talk," she repeated, raising her eyebrows.

"Have you been helping Luna frame me?"

She rolled her eyes. "You really do think the whole world revolves around you, don't you? Why would I want to frame you?"

"I don't know. Maybe because your best friend will get off the hook if she can convince everyone that I killed Peyton. Were you the tipster?"

She adopted her typical Shelby arrogant, flirty personality. "I've told you. I haven't talked to Luna since she got out. I have no idea where she is."

I sighed like I was bored, even though I was almost in full-on yellow-orange fire at that point. So fiery I felt my feet begin to sweat. "Come on, Shelby. We both know you gave her a ride the other day. Luna is out of jail and suddenly my things end up in Peyton's car. At the same time, a mysterious eyewitness tells the cops that Peyton and I were fighting. You were that eyewitness, weren't you?"

She laughed, which meant finally she looked away, but somehow that was even more unsettling. "What-the-fuck-ever, Nikki. Why don't you get out? I don't have to talk to you."

I widened my stance, crossing my arms over my chest, my hands squeezing into fists under my forearms. "Tell them you lied. Tell the prosecution the truth. Just do the right thing and I'll go."

"No, I think you'll go now," she said. She reached out one palm, placed it against my shoulder, and pushed. I didn't move much, but stutter-stepped backward, a bright spot of pain reopening on my cut where she'd just pushed me.

"I wouldn't do that again if I were you," I said.

She laughed a second time, only now it was totally mirthless, like listening to a demon laugh. "Or what? You'll be mad at me?" She stuck out her bottom lip in a pout. "If I knew where Luna was, I wouldn't tell you. If I was the tipster, I wouldn't take it back, either. Because you're a bitch and Luna is my friend and how do I know you didn't do it?" A smug look crossed her face as she reached out and shoved me again.

This time I was ready. I sprang forward, placing both of my hands on her chest and shoving her backward so hard she crashed into Seth's drum cases, landing hard on the floor.

Everyone raced toward us, including Gibson Talley, who appeared out of a back room somewhere.

"Hey-hey-hey," Vee was saying, stretching her arms out as if to hold us apart, even though we were several feet away from each other.

"Get her the hell out of here," Seth was yelling, pointing at me.

Gibson Talley was saying nothing, just helping Shelby up from the floor.

Shelby was grinning again. "Testy," she said when Gib had righted her. He stood between us protectively, glaring at me.

"Vee," I said. Breathing hard, trying to convey the gravity of everything with my eyes. "This is important. For Peyton. I know you care. She was your friend."

Vee let her arms drop to her sides. She seemed to think it over, and then looked at Shelby. "Just tell her what she wants to know. Did someone set her up? Was it you?" Shelby crossed her arms and gave Vee a standoff look. Vee took two steps toward her. "I'm serious, Shelby. Peyton *was* this band, and if you know something about what happened to her, you need to say so. Or you need to find another band to sing in. That simple."

"Fine, but I swear I don't know anything," Shelby said. She was clinging to Gib's shoulder from behind, but not in a protect-me sort of way. More of an I-own-you sort of way. "I picked her up and we drove around for a little bit, and then she had me drive her to this gross building downtown. I did, and she got into a van outside it and took off. It was the first time I saw her since she got arrested, and I haven't heard from her since. I'm not your tipster. Sorry."

"That's it?" Vee asked. "That's everything?"

"I told you I didn't know anything," Shelby said. "That's what I know."

"She told you. Now go," Seth said, grabbing for my arm.

I shook it off violently. "If you want to keep that hand, you won't touch me with it again," I said.

"Come on, Nikki," Vee said, but much more softly than Gibson had. "We need to warm up."

I ignored her. "What did Luna tell you when you were driving around?"

Shelby leaned forward, hitching up onto her tiptoes to jut her head over Gib's shoulder. "Nothing."

"Bullshit."

"Fine. We talked about you. It wasn't very nice. I wouldn't want to hurt your feelings."

My ears perked up. "What about me?"

Shelby rolled her eyes. "Oh my God, that you're a total bitch, okay? And that she wishes she'd killed you, because at least her brother was good for some money when she needed a bailout. And that's it. We talked about school and stuff after. And she told me about that place she was in. Juvie or whatever. And she told me that she was super worried about getting tossed back in."

"You're done here," Seth said, but at least he didn't touch me this time.

"Yeah, Nikki, take your drama somewhere else so we can get set up," Shelby said. She turned to Gibson. "Gibby, make her leave." *Gibby.* Barf.

Gibson ran a hand through his Mohawk—surprisingly not flattening it at all—and took a step toward me. "Time to go," he said. "You got what you wanted."

I held my hands up, surrender-style. "I'll go, I'll go. Thanks for nothing." But just as I was getting ready to turn for the stairs, it hit me. "Wait a minute. You said you dropped her off and she got into a white van?"

She snapped her fingers. "Snaps for Nikki for getting the good listener award. Please leave."

I went, but as I made my way back upstairs and around the building, my mind was swirling. A white van outside a building downtown.

Scarlet avocado maroon.

D-O-M.

Of course. Dom Distribution wasn't just a Hollis business. It was a Hollis-Basile business.

Rigo was connected to the van. And I'd seen it somewhere before. Somewhere other than at the auction. Had I seen it at Tesori Antico? Maybe, but that still didn't feel like the right place.

If I could just remember where the right place was—where I'd seen that scarlet-avocado-maroon—maybe I could finally find Arrigo Basile.

30

I HAD RUN into a dead end with Ruby before, but I needed to try again. Ruby knew things about the Hollises she wasn't telling me. Maybe she knew where the building downtown was. Maybe she knew what the connection was with the white van. Maybe if I told her everything—even about the key that Blue had given me—she would feel a little more comfortable talking to me.

The first thing I noticed when I parked across the street was how dark Ruby's building looked. Like nobody was moving inside. I checked the clock—maybe I had been in Culver City longer than I thought—but it was still early. Or at least early enough for someone to be awake.

Unless, of course, they were all out working. But even

then wouldn't someone be around?

I locked my car and instantly the air lit up mint green, the street turning feathery sage under my feet. Something was off. I didn't know what, but I could feel it.

My phone lit up. Jones.

Shit. Always at the worst possible time.

"Hey," he said. "You got a minute to talk?"

I closed my eyes, banged my forehead gently against the top of my door frame. "No, I'm sorry, Jones. I'm sort of busy."

"When will you be home?"

"How do you know I'm not home now?"

A pause. "You're never home anymore. One of the many ways to make it hard to have a relationship with the elusive Nikki Kill." Bitterness again. Great. Just what I needed: another fight with Jones.

"Well, the good news is there is no relationship for you to have. I thought we established that already."

"Ouch," he said. "You're right. We did. I guess it's just hard to let go."

"Well, please do, Jones," I snapped. "For both of us." There was another pause. "Listen, I need to go."

"Yeah," he said. "Of course you do. And, Nikki?"

I sighed, making no effort to conceal it. This game with Jones had gotten beyond old. "What?"

"I'm sorry, okay?"

"Sorry for what?" It came out nasty, and I hated that,

because he actually sounded like he meant it.

He hesitated again, and I could hear the old Jones in that hesitation. The Jones who wasn't eaten up by jealousy. The Jones who'd swept me off my feet at the beach. The Jones who would go to college in a couple of months and make some girl very, very happy. I was almost envious of that girl, because she would be able to appreciate what I couldn't. Her life would be full of magenta and she would love every minute of it. "Just . . . for everything."

I took a breath. *Oh, Jones, someday you'll see it—you're too good for me.* "You don't need to be sorry. People break up. And it's not all your fault. I know it's not easy to be in my life." *Not for anyone,* I wanted to add. But I also wanted to forget that about myself, because being difficult really didn't ever get me anything but frustration and heartbreak, and there was a part of me—maybe even a big part—that wished I was easier to get along with. If I'd been friendlier, would Peyton have been in my life before the accident? I didn't like to think about the possibility. "We can still talk, Jones. Later, though, okay? Like, maybe when you come home for Christmas or something. We just need a break, I think. By Christmas, everything should be settled down." *Or I will be in jail and it won't matter anymore.*

"Yeah. Probably not, but okay," he said. "I'll let you go." He hung up before I could say good-bye.

Sometimes I thought maybe I wasn't the only difficult one.

There was a gang of kids standing on the corner. They turned and watched as I crossed the street. They seemed to be leaning in close, whispering. It was a sound that made the sage deepen.

I jogged across the street and pushed into the vestibule. Everything seemed normal. The sickly fluorescent light in the hallway buzzed, and . . .

Wait. That wasn't normal. You didn't normally hear the buzzing of a lightbulb in an apartment building. Normally you heard the muffled sounds of TVs and radios, of dogs barking, of people talking and laughing. I had definitely not noticed a buzz last time I was here.

I heard nothing but the buzz.

The thought that I should have brought Detective Martinez with me edged in, and I batted it away. It was too late now, so why did it matter? I'd faced a lot of things without him. I'd battled Luna in her backyard. I'd gotten away from the Basiles in my own kitchen. I could face many more. When had I gotten so dependent on him? On a *cop*, of all things?

I swallowed my misgivings and climbed the stairs, taking them two at a time to prove to myself that I wasn't scared of what I would find at the top.

Before I knocked on Ruby's door, I pressed my ear to it. Maybe she was asleep. Or working with someone who wanted to keep things quiet. Only one way to find out. I knocked, spearmint clouds puffing into the air each time my knuckles made contact. There was no answer. I knocked again, harder. Nothing. I pounded. Still nothing.

I stepped back and leaned over the stair rail to see if maybe Blue was peeking out at me again. But her door, too, remained firmly closed.

"Ruby?" I called. "Everything okay?" I listened. Nothing. "It's Nikki Kill. I just wanted to talk to you." There was still no response, and once again I was stuck with the dilemma of following my green, green, deepening green hunch and going inside, or just turning around and leaving well enough alone.

But still. There was something wrong. I could feel it. The door swirled with all the colors of green that told me so. But the floor underneath my feet began to tell me something else. Yellows, oranges. Boiling. Bubbling like lava.

I was going to go in, whatever was on the other side of that door.

Which meant I had yet another lock to pick. Great. This hadn't gone all that well before, not to mention that Blake Willis currently had my penknife in a plastic evidence bag, anyway.

I bent to assess how secure the dead bolt seemed. Looked pretty tight. Only the best for Bill Hollis secrecy, of course.

But the doorknob was about as beat up as the door itself, the gold color dulled into rusty brown, the keyhole scratched within an inch of its life. I decided to jiggle it to see how sturdy it was.

And was shocked that it turned in my hand. I stood in the hallway, my hand still outstretched as if I were reaching for that knob, though the door had squeaked open into a dark apartment.

"Hello?" I called. "Ruby?"

But I could tell by the way my voice came back to me, before even reaching in to turn on the light, that the room was empty. I swallowed, my throat tasting like gravel. The fire colors had receded a bit, but they were still there. I took a breath to fan the flames a little, to talk myself into stepping through that doorway.

I pushed the door open all the way and fumbled along the walls on either side until I found a switch. I flicked it.

Nothing.

Not a stick of furniture. Not a single ashtray or discarded bra or even so much as a staple poking into the wall. I walked from room to room, pushing open doors and turning on lights, the whole time bracing myself for a punch or a bullet or God knew what else might be waiting for me. Every room, empty. Not just empty, but the kind of empty that looked like it had never been anything but. Like Ruby had never existed at all.

"Ruby?" I called one last time, though I knew it was fruitless. There was literally nowhere that she could be hiding.

And why would she be, anyway?

I left the lights on and the doors open and jogged down the stairs to Blue's apartment. I only knocked once this time. When it wasn't answered, I tried her door. It, too, pushed open easily. Her apartment was bare. Not even a single dragon tear left behind. I realized only distantly that her floor wasn't actually red, but that ragemonster red that had begun to creep through me like a sea of angry ants, trying to drive back the black and gray. My fists clenched and unclenched. My jaw tightened.

They were gone.

I had talked to them, and now they were gone.

Just as Luna had made Peyton disappear and Dru disappear. Problems had a way of disappearing around the Hollises. Even problems that had heartbeats.

I burst back out into the hallway and raced through it, throwing open the doors to all the apartments. Each and every one was the same. Deserted, hollow, echoey. An abandoned building, just like the one where Peyton had been beaten.

I finally stopped in the foyer. Sweat ran down the back of my neck. My entire body felt rigid, tense. I was taking in long, steady breaths through flared nostrils. I was supposed to be scared. But I was tired of being scared.

"I'm not scared!" I yelled to the ceiling. "Do you hear me, Luna? I know you want to scare me, but I'm not scared!"

But the gray that tinged the very tops of the walls told me otherwise. I might have been the tiniest bit scared—I was just covering it up with other, bolder colors. I'd done this before, so many times in my life, especially after Mom died. I lied to myself. I shielded my colors with other, more distracting ones. And I told myself those distracting colors were the truth.

Because being afraid and being alone in that fear would tear you up inside if you let it.

I shoved my way angrily through the front door, turning around to stare at the building, as if it had answers written across the front. The group of teens was still hanging out at the corner, so I made a beeline for them.

"You guys know who lives in there?" I called while I was still several steps away. They looked startled, cupping the weed in their hands protectively, the smoke drifting up between their fingers. Nobody answered. "You know Ruby and Blue?" One of them shook his head, so quickly it almost looked like a shiver. "I don't suppose you know what happened to them, then, huh?" Again, they all looked at me with slack mouths and slumped shoulders. "Of course not," I said. "Why would you?"

I turned and walked to my car.

The back tire was flat. Of course.

Damn kids.

WHEN I WOKE up the next morning, my mind was bursting with had-to's. I had to find that white van. I had to find Rigo Basile. I had to talk to Brandi Carter. I had to go to Oildale. I had to find out how close they were to arresting me. How much time was left.

I quickly showered and dressed, guzzled two cups of coffee, speed-smoked a cigarette in my window, then went downstairs and pulled up Dad's computer. I wrote down the address for Lighthouse Dimensions Chapel and crammed it into my pocket. I also printed out a photo of Brandi Carter, and then cleared my search history. Dad didn't need to know what I would be doing today. He wouldn't like it. He would get in the way.

My stomach was growling, but there was nothing in the house. I would have to stop and grab something on the way to Bakersfield.

I poked my head into Dad's bedroom. He was stretched out on his bed, head and shoulders propped up on the headboard, his glasses halfway down his nose as he read a book. "Hey, I'm leaving."

He popped up, surprised, and checked his watch. "It's early. For you."

"I'm going to the beach," I said. "Morning sun is the good sun."

"Got it." He went back to the book. "God forbid I should stand in the way of a good tan. Have fun."

Fun. Did I even know what that was anymore? I wasn't going to have fun. But with any luck, I would finally have answers.

"Will do."

I was ready to go. Except for one thing.

One more had-to. I had to let Detective Martinez in on my plans to find Brandi Carter. Even if I didn't exactly want to.

I turned on my phone and sent him a text.

You got a few hours? I need you.

Only a few seconds later, he replied.

Not really. Urgent?

Isn't it always? I texted. And then, NVM I'll do it myself. If you don't hear back from me by tonight, go to Bakersfield. I knew that would get him moving.

I'll clear my day.

Yep, I was right.

Be here in an hour.

I HOPED AN hour would be long enough to do what I needed to do. I pointed my car toward the city, my palms sweating around the steering wheel. Butterflies gnawed at my stomach lining and I tried my hardest not to think about where I was going. There was bold, and there was stupid. Sometimes I wasn't sure which one I was. I would never ask Detective Martinez which one I was. I doubted I would like his answer.

I had never been inside the big brick-and-glass district attorney building before, but somehow I knew where it was anyway. I was probably courting all kinds of personal headaches just by thinking about going inside, but when did that ever stop me, right?

I sat in my car until the heat drove me out, my shirt

sticking to my back. I wiped my palms on my jeans a few times, coaching myself through the conversation I was about to have, and then got moving.

Outside, the building was institutional as hell. Inside, it was almost worse. Ugly, graying tile led the way to an office filled with even grayer walls, which colored over with baby-vomit yellow as I walked by. This had to be the most depressing place I'd ever walked into. Or maybe I was just projecting that.

A receptionist sat at a squat metal desk right up front. She looked up when I came in.

"Help you?" she said in a bored voice. Her lips changed to the same sickly yellow when the words slipped through them.

"I'm here to see Blake Willis?" I said. It came out as a question, and I dug my fingers into my palms to remind me to stop being such a baby and do this with confidence.

The receptionist consulted her computer screen, clicked a few things, then looked back at me. "And you have an appointment with her?"

"Uh, no. I don't," I said. "I only need to talk to her for a minute."

She rolled her eyes, and I could practically feel her hating her job from all the way across the desk. "She doesn't see people without appointments. Nobody here does. For obvious reasons. We don't do surprise visitors here." I wondered if the receptionist also kept a handgun in the top drawer of her desk and 9-1-1 on speed dial, for the same obvious reasons. I probably couldn't blame her if she did.

"Can you just tell her Nikki Kill is here, please?" My voice had gone from whiny to impatient. Not any better than whiny. Impatient always made things harder on me. Impatient made me have to kick people and break things. This was the last place on earth I needed to be kicking people and breaking things. "If she doesn't want to see me, I'll leave. Promise."

But the receptionist's eyes lit up like I'd said something that changed the game completely. Of course I had. I'd told her my name. There was no way anyone in this office would have not heard of me. For some crazy reason, I felt a tangerine pride that wet my mouth with citrus. *That's right, I'm Nikki Kill, bitches.* Of course, the pride was swept away when I saw the wry grin pulling up one half of her face. A grin that said, *We're going to get you, Nikki Kill.* Pride zapped.

She picked up her phone and mumbled into it, then waved toward a bank of empty metal folding chairs on the other side of the room. I had barely lowered myself onto one when Blake Willis came around the corner. She looked alarmed.

"Nikki?" she said.

I stood. "Hey. Um, can we talk?"

She squinted at me, and then looked uncomfortably

around the room. "Okay, yeah. Come on back." She gestured toward the hallway she'd just come out of. I followed her, noting how easily and confidently she glided along in her skirt and heels. It was no wonder that Detective Martinez would be attracted to a woman like her. She was polished and mature. And she had a plan for her life. Or at least she looked like someone who would have a plan for her life. Walking behind her, I realized that I couldn't blame my lack of life plan on what had happened with Peyton. I would never be someone like Blake Willis, even if Peyton had never existed. I would never own a hallway the way she did. I would never walk with her poise. I would never be able to get out of my prism long enough to even try. Some people just weren't life-plan kind of people, and I was one of them. Hell, I was their queen.

She disappeared through a doorway without looking back. She waited by the door for me, and then quickly shut it when I'd followed her through. I sat in a beat-up leather-upholstered chair, my hands tightening around the armrests. I took a breath and loosened my grip.

She didn't sit behind her desk but rather rolled her chair around to one side of it, so that we were closer. If her intention was to intimidate, it was working. She sat, crossed her legs, pushed a curtain of red hair over one shoulder. "I definitely didn't expect to see you here today."

"Me either," I said. I rubbed one of the brass upholstery

brads on the chair arm with one finger.

"And you came because . . . ?" She sat so rigidly, like she was being graded on posture. My colors picked up nothing about her, though. She wasn't putting off a bitchy vibe. Or even an aloof one. Not a particularly friendly vibe, either. She seemed to be pretty much a . . . void. It was weird.

I licked my lips, pressed on the brad harder. "I was wondering . . . I mean . . . How close are you?"

She furrowed her eyebrows and tilted her head to one side. "How close? To what?"

"To putting me away," I said. "To proving that I was Peyton's murderer. How close are you? Is there a case? Do I still have time?"

She shifted, uncrossing her legs, and then crossing the other one, which she held in place by clasping both hands over her knee. "I guess I'm not following. Time for what?"

Finally, a glimmer of suspicion, coming at me like spearmint gum.

"Time to get the evidence I need to prove that I didn't do it," I said. "I'm almost there. So close. All I need is a few days—I can feel it. Can you slow things down? Just, you know, as a favor? Since you have . . . theories. And since, you know, you've been helping Detective Martinez a little?"

She thought it over for a minute, that crease between her eyebrows deepening. She chewed on the inside of her cheek. Finally, she uncrossed her legs and leaned forward, her elbows on her knees, her hands together with fingers tented. "Nikki," she said softly. "You know I can't discuss this with you, right?"

"I don't want discussion," I said. "I just want . . ." God, I didn't know what I wanted. I wanted the train to stop moving and let me off. I wanted the world to slow down. I wanted to go back seven months and not answer my phone when the hospital called. I wanted out. "The witness. The one who told you guys I'd been fighting with Peyton. Did she have black hair? Kind of spiky? Was she Luna's friend? It was Shelby Gray, wasn't it?"

"I can't . . ." Blake trailed off, pressed her lips together.

"Right. You can't." I didn't know why I'd thought I might be able to get answers, or help, or a break at all, much less be able to get any of those things from Blake Willis. "This was stupid," I said. "I should go." I stood. Blake reached out and grasped my wrist lightly.

"Listen," she said. "We have reason to be looking closely at you. That's really all I can tell you, and you already knew that. I can't give you any specifics about where we are with it or what we're doing. But I can tell you that if you can clear your name, you should do it. I would love to hear what kind of evidence you have to prove someone else did it."

I pulled my hand away from hers, my heart beating quickly. "Martinez wouldn't like me being here by myself at all," I said. "I shouldn't have come."

She gave a wan smile, nodding her head a little. "Yeah," she said. "He probably wouldn't, especially if it could come back on you somehow. Because he's smart and you should listen to him. And I probably shouldn't know about his involvement, either." She gazed up at me, and the world turned icy white. "Whatever it is."

"He's helping me," I practically whispered, feeling small and stupid and wishing more than anything that I'd just U-turned past this place and gone back home; just concentrated on getting to Bakersfield.

"He's very helpful," she agreed. "A little too."

"It's not like that."

She patted her knees contemplatively, two, three times. Then stood, this time crossing her arms over her chest. We were only inches apart now. I could smell her perfume, which was sweet and flowery like an island in summer. "I know what it's like," she said. "It's like he just can't help himself when it comes to saving people. He can't get out of his own past. The big mystery that he keeps locked up tight inside himself."

I didn't know why, but I had for some reason imagined them sharing every little detail of their lives. Legs wrapped together on his couch or her bed, fingers entwined, whispering secrets, understanding each other. But if I was hearing her right, he hadn't told her about his past. He hadn't even told her the things he'd told me.

"All I know is he won't ever get over whatever it was as long as he's so focused on being everyone's savior."

"He's not everyone's—"

"You're right," she said. She huffed a chuckle of air through her nose, shaking her head at the ground before leveling her eyes at me. They didn't look threatening or even hard. They looked . . . hurt. Worried. "He's only focused on being *your* savior."

"I don't need a savior," I said. I edged my way toward the door and opened it a few inches. A man in a suit walked briskly past, not even so much as looking in my direction, but seeing him gave me a jolt anyway. I was not in a place that would be friendly to me. I was stupid for coming here. "I didn't ask him to save me."

Not entirely true. I did ask him, in the Hollis backyard, when I'd been hiding from Luna behind a trash can outside the pool house. I'd called him and begged him to come. And he'd done so. And we'd somehow been entwined in this mess ever since. I was the one owning his mysteries. I was the one on his couch.

"That's the thing," she said, following me to the door. "You didn't need to ask him."

It wasn't worry I was seeing in her eyes. I could see a magenta creep into the baby blue, and turn it to turquoise. The colors swirled around her pupils, a sherbet of jealousy. She was in love with him. And she felt threatened.

I didn't know what to say. I was too entranced by the swirl, which had leaked out of her eyes and pooled over her face.

She sighed. "Listen, Nikki. This isn't someplace you should be hanging around. Do yourself a favor and stay off our radar for as long as you can." She pushed the door just enough to close the gap. "Lie low," she whispered. "Let us get distracted by other cases."

"Cases more important than the murder of a Hollis?" I whispered back. "What does that even look like?"

She eased her hand away from the door and let it fall to her side. "Tell Chris I said hi," she said.

She moved to her desk, sat behind it, and opened a huge book, then began writing down something into a legal pad as if I wasn't even there.

Dismissed.

I started through the door.

"Oh, and Nikki?"

I turned. She laid her pencil down on the pad and shook her head, rolling her eyes at herself, as if she couldn't believe she was even talking to me.

"It wasn't a girl with spiky hair," she said. "The witness? Was a guy."

32

BEFORE ANYTHING ELSE, I need food," I said, as soon as I got into Detective Martinez's car. I'd made a promise to myself not to mention my little meeting with Blake Willis. She was right—I would be wise to stay off their radar, and the last thing I needed was a lecture from him telling me the same thing. It had been foolish to go there. I didn't need another reminder. Besides, there was that whole awkward swirl going on. I didn't want to have to tell him what she said . . . and what she didn't say. And I didn't even know where to begin with the revelation that my so-called witness was a guy. Who could it have possibly been? Surely not Rigo himself. Maybe one of his brothers, though? Who could the Hollises have paid off to sink me? "I don't care where, just hit a drive-through somewhere."

He gave me a look over the top of his glasses.

"I've got money," I said.

Again with the disapproving look.

"What? I haven't eaten today."

"You don't think you should maybe tell me what this is all about? Out of the blue, you need to go to Bakersfield. And for some reason you need me to go with you. And now I'm supposed to just grab a burger and drive three hours out of town like this is some high school road trip, no questions asked. I need more than that. Are we going to do something illegal?"

I clasped my hand to my chest. "Why would you assume I would do something illegal?"

He didn't respond. Just gave me The Stare. "Okay. Fine. But only if you drive while I talk." I didn't want Dad getting curious and seeing me taking off. Granted, Detective Martinez's car wasn't a cruiser with lights on top, but it still screamed police. "It's not illegal," I added. "Jeez."

Slowly, reluctantly, he pulled away from the curb.

"And I don't want a burger. What about tacos?"

"Not in my car. You want to eat in my car, you get a burger. No ketchup."

"Wow, Captain Clean. Control issues much? You should add OCD to your list of things you need to mention to your therapist."

"Talk or I stop again." He let up on the gas to show me he was serious.

"Okay, okay. Remember the letter from Peyton? She talked about a woman in it."

He nodded. "Brandi. Courteur or something like that."

"Good memory. Yes, but her name is actually Brandi Carter. And she was friends with my mother."

"How do you know?"

I sank down in my seat, trying to look nonchalant, but knowing that I was going to hear it no matter what. "I've been sort of investigating on my own."

"Why am I not surprised?" he muttered, shaking his head. His jaw worked angrily as he stared out the windshield. I felt the car speed up. Finally, he looked over at me. Not being able to see his eyes under his glasses was driving me crazy. I wished he would just take them off. "Do you know how dangerous that is?"

"Do you know how dangerous I am?" I countered.

He brushed just under my collarbone with his forefinger. "Dangerous enough to get attacked in your own home?"

"Come on, that's not fair. They took me by surprise. Plus, I held them off, right?"

"You're not invincible, Nikki. I know you think you are, but you're not. Am I going to have to have you tailed? Is that what you want?"

I made *yak-yak-yak* motions with my hands. "You sound

so official. Have me tailed. Whatever. You know if you could have me tailed, you wouldn't be the one following me around everywhere I go."

"Not true," he said, but then the air in the car got awkward and we both just sat there in the feathery fern feeling.

"So this woman—Brandi—has answers, I think. About Peyton. About my mom too, maybe. I'm not sure. All I know is I need to talk to her so I can get to the bottom of things. Maybe she'll be able to give us something that will prove the Hollises were behind Peyton's attack. Or lead us to Rigo. You never know. I can't rest if there's a stone unturned."

He guided his car into a parking lot where a taco truck was parked. Such a pushover. "But you don't think you should be a cop."

"Oh God, don't start that again. No. You will never convince me, so stop trying. N-O. No. Got it?"

He parked, and I practically bolted out the door before he'd even come to a full stop. "Got it," he said to my back. "Let's get tacos and talk to Brandi Carter."

LIGHTHOUSE DIMENSIONS CHAPEL, aside from being all kinds of aqua in my mind, was a modest brick building set on a large, tree-lined plot of land. A couple of cows grazed in a field behind it, kept out by a simple white slat fence. It was all very Norman Rockwell. If Norman Rockwell housed secrets of hookers and mystery children.

Detective Martinez parked the car and we both stared at the front of the church. "You're sure she's here?"

"There's one way to find out," I said. I licked my lips, suddenly nervous. I wished I hadn't ordered such a large drink, or so many tacos; my stomach sloshed around disagreeably.

"The office is over there," he said. "There's a sign."

"Okay." But still I didn't move.

"Hello?" He leaned toward me, waved his hand in front of my face. "You change your mind?"

"No way," I said. "I just realized I have no idea what I'm going to say. I'm trying to formulate a plan."

"We've been driving for three hours and that wasn't enough time for you to formulate a plan?"

"I was listening to your riveting talk radio."

"I like to be informed," he said. "And I like the company. It's a habit. You could have interrupted. Three hours and you spent most of it eating tacos and browsing the internet on your phone."

"It seemed shorter than that. I don't know. I just didn't think about what I would say, okay?"

"How about we go in there and just start talking?"

"Well, barging into places asking questions hasn't exactly worked out real well for me lately," I said. "And I can't even believe that you, of all people, are suggesting it."

He held up a finger. "Correction, barging into places *by yourself* and asking questions hasn't worked out for you. But you have me this time."

"Because you're so good at getting answers? Need I remind you who got to Hollis Mansion first?"

"Need I remind you who had to go to Hollis Mansion to help you out?"

The air felt weird. Charged and angry—rusty gold fireworks that died in tiny puffs of smoke as they trailed into my lap. I didn't like being reminded of that night. "Let's just go," I said.

We pulled open the door and found ourselves inside a musty-smelling office, staring at a blond woman who was sitting behind a desk, holding a phone. The blood drained from her face when she saw us. Even if I had never seen a photo of Brandi Carter, I would have known it was her by her reaction. "I'll need to call you back," she said, and hung up. "Can I help you?" Her voice wavered. She knew damn well who we were. I could see it on her.

Brandi Carter definitely looked older than she had in the video, and of course she wasn't pregnant, but the face was the same. Kind, soft, full of wonder. And, right now, also full of fear.

She knew my mom. This woman had been *friends* with my mom. A piece of my mother that hadn't died. Part of me wanted to hug her, to let her hug me and see if any tiny leftover piece of my mom rubbed off between us.

"Actually, I imagine you'll be a lot of help to us," Detective Martinez said.

She looked over her shoulder to a cheap wooden door with a plastic sign glued to it, the letters yellowing. PASTOR. Undulating cloud white. As always. "Can we do this later?" she whispered.

"I don't think so. We drove all the way from Brentwood to talk to you," I said. "About Peyton? About the things you told her?"

She threw another glance over her shoulder and then pushed a couple of buttons on her phone and turned off her computer. She got up and ducked her head into the office, spoke for a moment, and then came back, grabbing a purse from under her desk on the way. "Not here, though," she said. "My house. I just live down the hill there." She pulled keys out of her purse and headed for the door.

When she said she lived down the hill, she literally meant she lived down the hill, a few hundred yards from the church. In a rusted-out trailer with holes poked in the window screens, pressed up against a corner of land where two tree lines met. It was surrounded by overgrown weeds. Her house number jumped out at me—melon, melon, brown, 771—but mostly I was overwhelmed by the spongy brownness of the place. So depressing.

Also, so isolated. Other than the church and the cows,

Brandi Carter's trailer seemed to be the only thing out here.

"You might as well come in," she said when we reached the trailer.

Inside, the trailer was dark and smoky, but clean, and dominated by a trio of mewling cats. They wrapped themselves around Brandi's legs, sweet-talking her, until Detective Martinez came through the door; then they ran away. I could smell the morning's breakfast—bacon—stale on the air.

She dropped her purse on a tiny cigarette-pocked kitchen table and then reached over to turn on a living room lamp. The effect didn't so much brighten the place as highlight its flaws. Half-filled ashtrays sat on every table. Bowls with cat food spilling out of them dotted the kitchen floor. A dented olive-green refrigerator hummed from a corner of the kitchen, which was really just an open space off the living room that contained a sink, an oven, and a fridge. The brown inside my mind deepened, pushed on me so hard I almost felt like I needed an ice pack for my head.

"You can sit," she said. She went to another lamp and switched it on, shooed a cat out of a chair, and sat in it.

I sat on the couch opposite her, the smell of smoke wafting out of the cushions making me want a cigarette, bad. Detective Martinez stood behind the couch. I could feel him gazing around the room, cataloguing any potential evidence. I suddenly kind of regretted bringing him here. This wasn't just about Rigo Basile or Luna or Dom Distribution or me going to prison. This was a piece of my personal life, my history, my family. He wasn't part of that. As much as it sometimes felt like he was.

"Nikki Kill," Brandi said, wonder filling her voice. Her features softened into what might have been fondness. "I guess I never thought I'd see you right here in my own home."

"I guess I never thought I'd be in your home," I countered. "Especially since I didn't even know you existed until last fall."

She ducked her head, trapped her hands between her knees, palms pressed together as if she were praying.

"I guess I want to know . . . who are you?" I asked. "I mean, I know you're Brandi Carter and I know you knew my mom, and I know you told Peyton some things that messed up her life. Ended it, really. So who are you? And why did you find Peyton in the first place?"

"I was curious, I guess," she said. "It's not a good reason. I feel such remorse over what happened to her. I should've known Bill would never let her be a threat. It's just . . ." She gazed off into nothingness and then went back to studying her hands. "I needed to get it off my chest. I needed her to know who I was. I think I intended for all of you to know. Maybe I would have found the courage to tell all of you at some point. And now you're the only one left, and I'm afraid to tell you anything. Because of what happened to her."

"The only one what?" Detective Martinez said from behind me. He'd been silent until that moment, and I think we'd both kind of forgotten that he was there.

"You really shouldn't be here," Brandi said, ignoring his question. "It's not safe."

I narrowed my eyes. "How so?"

She didn't answer, only chewed her bottom lip and continued staring at those folded hands.

"Come on," I said, exasperated, throwing my hands up into the air and flopping back on the couch. "Give us something. I can't take all this secrecy anymore. This isn't some soap opera story. This is my life. And my life keeps getting shittier and scarier every single day. And soon I will be in prison because everyone was too afraid to talk."

Detective Martinez came around the couch and sat next to me so he was closest to her. He leaned forward, his body language almost mirroring hers.

"Who are we not safe from here, Brandi?"

She chewed her lip, contemplated, and then let out a sigh, and for a minute I could see a shadow of the young woman in the video admonishing my mom not to make fun of her new church. *Christ's love is serious.*

"You already know who," she said.

"Hollis," Martinez replied, and she nodded. "Why?"

Because they're dangerous and unhinged, I wanted to say. *Is there any better reason?*

Detective Martinez stretched his neck and then tried again. "Let me put it this way. How are you involved with the Hollises?"

"She used to work for them," I said. "With my mom, right? You were both escorts. I know that much."

"For a time, yes," she said. "But I'd prefer if that didn't become public knowledge. Pastor Paul knows I have a history, and he is very forgiving, as is the Lord, but I would like it if he didn't know the full extent of that history. And he wouldn't be happy if the congregation found out about any of it. Neither would I. I've changed. Completely. I changed a long time ago. Your mom knew it. That's why she came to me."

"Came to you? For what?" Detective Martinez asked.

I put my hand on his arm to stop him. "My mom was pregnant," I said, before Brandi could answer. I raised my eyebrows. "Right? She came to you because she was pregnant and needed help." Suddenly all the pieces, which had been floating around in my head, teasing me, confusing me, were falling into place. It was as if I was watching a movie. One my mom might have made, only starring herself. Pregnant, terrified, nowhere to turn. Except her friend, who'd recently given up her life for the Lord. Her friend who would help her.

She nodded.

"And the baby wasn't my dad's."

Her face began to crumple in on itself. I could almost feel her dumping more and more brown into the room, spoonfuls, bucketfuls, truckfuls of dirt. It almost hummed, it was so thick. I was getting close to not being able to handle it anymore. She shook her head. "Let the past go. Please."

"It was Peyton," I said to Martinez. "Her dad was Bill Hollis. My mom got pregnant by hooking."

Brandi held out her hands. "No. Not exactly. You have to understand. He was so powerful and charming and he was on TV all the time, and we knew this secret about him—that he was a regular at our service. We felt like we were in a special club."

"No way," I said. "No way could my mom have fallen for that crap. She loved my dad."

Brandi Carter nodded vehemently. "She was madly in love with Milo, yes. And she tried to stay away from Hollywood Dreams. She'd quit years before, right after she met Milo. But something happened."

"What something?" Detective Martinez asked.

She shrugged. "I don't know. She didn't like to talk about it. There were some money problems or something. Some . . . rift. Milo was taking it hard. And they had you to take care of." She gestured toward me. "You were just a baby yourself. And Bill . . . must have charmed her. Somehow. He had lots of ways."

"And she fell for that shit?" I asked, my voice getting

shrill. To think of my mom—of the woman who scorned the men who stared at and objectified her at the beach—as someone who would fall for schmoozy lines just because he was the Rich and Famous Bill Hollis angered me.

"You have to understand," Brandi said. "He had a way of making things true just by saying them. That's how he got so successful."

"Well, running a couple of illegal businesses might have played into his success just a little bit," Detective Martinez said.

I couldn't take it anymore—the energy of ragemonster red stirring through me, zapping itself into inky pops. I stood up. Brandi flinched as if I were going to hit her. "How? How on earth does a smart person like my mom get pregnant by a guy like that? How was she so stupid?"

"We both did," Brandi said sheepishly. "And maybe others. Probably others. He didn't like to use condoms. He said he wanted things to feel more intimate than that—and he made us believe that we were special because he wanted that intimacy. We believed everything would be okay. Because he told us so. He said he could fix any mistakes. We were stupid. We were taken in by it all."

I flashed back to the video, and Brandi's very pregnant belly. "You had Hollis's baby too," I said. "Of course you did. God, I can't even imagine how many people did." My mind whirled, trying to sort out what relation Brandi's baby might have been to me; what relation any of Bill Hollis's children might be to me. I thought none—there was no blood shared between us—but everything was so confusing, it felt like I was related to half the world.

She nodded. "When I found out I was pregnant, I left town. Bounced around a little." She glanced between Detective Martinez, who was still sitting patiently on the couch, and me, and then started talking fast, words spilling over one another. "I was really lost, and I was afraid of having his baby. I knew he wouldn't want me to."

I remembered the invoices from Dr. Slovenka I'd found in Hollis's office. "Elective" surgeries going back years. Of course. That was why he'd kept those invoices. They were trophies of his conquests. His power over people in black and white. "He'd made others get rid of theirs."

She nodded. "I was scared to death. Always looking over my shoulder. And then I found the Lighthouse and got settled. I figured he would never find me here. He'd never even be looking for me here."

"But Mom knew where you were. She knew about your baby."

"And when she found herself in the same position, she panicked. She didn't want Milo to find out she'd gone back to Hollywood Dreams, so she came to me. She knew I would protect her. And she knew I would protect the baby."

I sank back onto the sofa. It all made sense now. Mom's

belly was showing in those pictures. She might have been willing to pretend the baby was Dad's, but she knew Bill Hollis would never believe it. He had been sleeping with her, too, and wouldn't take the chance that the baby might be his. She knew he would force her to abort Peyton, on the off chance that she might have been his. She must have made up a story about a project and come to Brandi to wait out the pregnancy in safety.

Keeping everyone in the dark. It was the only way to keep Peyton safe.

"God, my dad didn't know at all." This, which should have been a relief, only served to mystify me even more. He was clearly lying about something to do with the Hollises. What was Dad hiding, if it wasn't Mom's secret? What was in that black box?

Brandi leaned forward and reached for my knee, but came up short and ended up tucking her hands between her knees again, hanging off the edge of her chair as if to bolt. "Your mom cared about Peyton a great deal, Nikki," she said. "It killed her to give her up. But she couldn't keep her, for the same reasons I couldn't keep my baby around Brentwood. And she couldn't leave Milo. Or you. She just . . . had no choice. She left Peyton with me and went back to Milo like nothing had ever happened."

Mom had given up Peyton for me. She had chosen me over my sister. I thought of Peyton, covered in crimson, lying in that hospital bed, the urge to cry stronger than it had ever been. Peyton had been given up for me, yet she still reached out to me when she needed family.

I wished I would have known the real Peyton Hollis when she was alive.

Detective Martinez cleared his throat. "So if Nikki's mom had her baby here, how did Peyton end up being raised by Bill and Vanessa?"

"It took them a couple years, but they found us. And they took her. They took both of them," Brandi said, her face clouding over with anger. "They took your mom's little girl and my little boy."

"Both?" Detective Martinez echoed at the same time that I said, "Oh my God. Dru. Your baby was Dru."

Now tears did flow. She nodded, her chest hitching with held-in sobs. "He found out about me. Somehow word got out where we were and Bill found me. He couldn't stand the idea of Hollis blood living in 'a trashy trailer.'" She made air quotes with her fingers. "So he and his hideous wife took them. Ripped them right out of my arms, crying their little eyes out. They were still such babies then. He told me if I tried to follow them, or if I ever surfaced at all, he would have me killed. He had a guy who could make it look like an accident, he said. Someone who would do anything without questions." She leveled her wet face at us. "I believed him."

Detective Martinez glanced at me.

"Rigo?" I said, and he nodded.

"I always watched them," she said. "When they didn't know it. I followed them in the papers, and I hid in places where I could see them. Outside school and so forth. And they seemed happy. The Hollises were definitely able to give them more than I ever could have. They were too young when he took them. They didn't remember me at all. They weren't sad about me."

"But then Peyton stopped looking happy," I said.

She didn't need to answer. We all knew where the story went from there. Brandi reached out to unhappy Peyton, told her the truth, and Peyton ended up dead.

We sat in silence, absorbing everything Brandi had just told us. Peyton was reaching out to me when she knew she was likely going to be killed by her own father. She knew I would help her the same way my mom knew Brandi would help her.

But I could feel the mood in the room change. That familiar gray was creeping in on me again, only this time it wasn't coming off Detective Martinez.

"There's more," I said.

Brandi didn't move. She looked between us again, seemingly weighing her options.

"There's something more," I repeated. Detective Martinez turned to me, a quizzical look on his face. "Hunch," I whispered. He seemed to accept that. I leaned toward her;

she edged back in her chair, quivering. "What is it? Please. You have to tell me." She still didn't move, but the gray rolled in thicker, like smog. "I'm in a lot of danger. If you cared about my mom at all, you will help me out. I'm begging."

She rocked back and forth a few times, and then nodded. "Okay." She got up and went into another room. I could hear what sounded like a drawer opening and closing. She came out holding a DVD. "There's this."

Detective Martinez got up and took it from her before I could get there. "And this is . . . ?"

"It's Peyton," she said. "It's for you, Nikki."

B RANDI CARTER DIDN'T have a DVD player or a
computer. The only computer she ever needed was the
one at the church. We said our quick good-byes, Brandi and
I standing awkwardly in front of each other, unsure what a
good-bye should entail between the two of us. I knew we
weren't related, but everything between us was so personal,
it somehow seemed that we were. Would Mom have wanted
us to be friends? It was hard to say what Mom wanted anymore. Mom was the stranger now.

"Would you be willing to come up to Brentwood and tell
the police what you just told us?" Detective Martinez asked.

She blanched. "I don't think I can."

"They're in Dubai," I said. Blue had said I was stupid

for believing that, but surely they wouldn't come back. Not while knowing they were wanted for so many crimes. "They can't hurt you from there. Just steer clear of Luna—she's the real danger right now."

"Nikki," she said. "There's one thing you need to keep in mind. They can hurt anyone from anywhere."

We left the trailer dejected that Brandi wouldn't testify, and so full of emotion I couldn't concentrate on my own name, but at least we had the DVD. Another clue left by Peyton. Or maybe just a good-bye.

We drove around for another thirty minutes, looking for a library. We finally found one and asked the librarian to let us use a computer in one of the soundproof study rooms.

The door clicked shut behind us, and it was so quiet I swore I could hear both of our hearts beating.

"You ready for this?" he asked, holding the DVD.

I nodded. "Not really, but . . ." I tipped my head toward the computer.

He booted it up, slid the DVD into it, and we waited. There was only one file. He clicked it.

Peyton's face blinked onto the screen. It wasn't the old Peyton—the one I'd known to be a snotty, uppity bitch ruling the hallways at school. It was the Peyton I'd sat beside in the hospital. Her hair was short and chunky and dyed brown. She had a tattoo on her neck.

A rainbow.

Live in color.

I blinked away the crimson that wanted to push in. The crimson that always wanted to bring my mom with it. The crimson that was exhausting me.

Peyton adjusted the camera and then sat back. She smiled, and I only realized then what her smile looked like up close. Engaging. Warm. Trusting. I'd never noticed it at school. I was too busy in my own little world, avoiding that crowd as much as humanly possible.

She waved. "Hey, Nikki." She seemed to get lost after just that much, her eyes darting to the side, but then she relaxed, letting her shoulders slide down. "Hopefully I'm just being dramatic, right? And like, six months from now I'll be asking everybody for my stuff back." She chuckled, pushed her hair out of her eyes. "That'll be embarrassing." She sobered, thought some more, and looked into the camera again. "But I don't think I am being dramatic. God, I'm so stupid. Of course I'm not, if you're watching this. You wouldn't be watching it if I was alive. Right? I mean, that's the point of this whole trail I've been leaving. So. Yeah. Dramatic. Not so much." She rolled her eyes and chewed her nail thoughtfully, then squared up at the camera again.

"Okay, so here's the deal. I found out some really bad shit about my parents. And since Brandi gave this to you, I'm guessing you know about it all too. All about Daddy Dearest and the step-monster's little side businesses? Selling drugs, selling girls, whatever. And all the while Vanessa try-ing to get her own stepson into bed, which . . . don't even get me started. Joke's on me. I really thought I was going to be an actress. Maybe in one of my dad's movies. I was convinced I was going to be famous one day." She chuckled darkly. "Yeah. That's not happening. Unless I'm famous now. I guess that's possible. In the news and everything. Just shows you should be careful what you wish for, huh?" She paused again. "Oh, and then, of course, there's the matter of a little baby stealing. Stealing! Can you believe it? Who steals a baby, right? Someone who is as power hungry as my father. He gets what he wants. And the rest of us have to live with the consequences. Speaking of which . . ." She waved her fingers in the air on each side of her face and singsonged, "Sisters." And then in a regular voice, "We're sisters. As you know. Anyway. I found out all this shit about my family and now I'm pretty sure they're going to kill me. Well, have me killed. Same difference."

She glanced down and then back. "You know, there've been so many times I've said I would rather die than be in this stupid family anymore. But now that it's coming true . . . I don't know. I wish I'd had the chance to see what we could have been like."

She shrugged, glanced down again. Then took a breath and blurted out the rest. "Okay. So here's the thing. My fam-ily has this place. It's like a secret hideout or something. Only that's not what they would call it. But that's exactly what it is. A place where they put things they don't want found. I've been there, but I don't actually remember where exactly it is, because I wasn't driving the one time I went there, and some gross client had made me do Molly with him before and I was seriously out of it. And I don't think I have time to figure out where it is now. Dru might know, but I'm not entirely sure I can still trust him. Which is sad. He's a pretty good guy. He's just all wrapped up in our shitty family. He doesn't even know yet about who his real mother is. I've tried to tell him, but he's in some serious denial. Do me a favor? Be there for him when this all goes down? He'll need you." Another pause, during which I felt miserable. Peyton saw what was coming to her, but she never expected Dru to get caught in the crossfire. "But anyway, the hideout. I know this much for sure. You know where it is. You've seen it. Hopefully you have the key by now. You'll put it together. And I'm not saying any more than that, just in case Daddy Dearest or the step-monster somehow got ahold of this. If you're watching, Vanessa, I have a message for you." She raised both hands and flipped off the camera, the same way I had done with those girls on the beach. I smiled. I couldn't help myself. She was my sister, all right. "Anyway, Nikki, I'm hoping you'll find evidence there. Not a what, but a who, if you know what I mean. Well, and also some whats." She smiled, a pair of perfect dimples appearing in her cheeks. "I've been watching you. Not in a creepy way. Just . . . I don't know . . . learning. You seem cool. Sorry I didn't notice that before now. I kind of think I bought into the Hollis elite thing for so long, I forgot that I was just a girl like everyone else, and I kind of wish we could have had the chance to get to know each other. I think it would be safe to say that we'd be a great combination." She thought for a few seconds. "We probably have all kinds of strange things in common. Like, the last two digits of your locker number and the digits of my birthday month both add up to eleven or something. That kind of stuff that only sisters care about." She laughed, pushed her hair behind her ear again. "Who knows? Maybe I'm making a huge deal out of nothing and we still can be sisters. If this all goes the way I want it to, I'll be living in like, some cornfield in Iowa or something, and when the coast is clear I'll have you out for a picnic or a hoedown or whatever it is they do in Iowa. Let's hope, right?" She held up a pair of crossed fingers and wrinkled her nose, and then reached forward and the picture blinked out.

Detective Martinez clicked to start the video over. "Let's listen again and then we can turn it over to Blake."

But I didn't need to listen again.

Everything my sister had said made perfect sense.

A *place where they put things they don't want found*. . . . *You know where it is*. . . . *You have the key* . . . *Not a what, but a who* . . . *Well, and also some whats*.

Scarlet. Avocado. Maroon.

A white van.

A purple haze. One of the few phrases that looked exactly like what it said it was.

You have the key.

You have the key.

"Holy shit," I said, clutching at Detective Martinez's arm. "It's been right under my nose this whole time."

He stopped, mid-click. "What?"

"I know where Arrigo Basile is."

I HAD DETECTIVE Martinez drop me off at home so I could find a few things. Because Dad was home, I made him leave, with the promise that I would join him at his apartment in an hour.

"Hey, Nikki," Dad called when I came in. I was already halfway up the stairs, but I stopped and came back down. I found him in the den, reading, wearing the T-shirt and shorts he used for pajamas.

"Hey," I said.

"Did you eat something?" he asked without looking up from his book. "I made a salad. It's in the fridge if you're hungry."

"I ate," I said. Detective Martinez had picked us up some

sandwiches at a gas station in Bakersfield on our way home. We ate them, partly because we were hungry, but mostly because we didn't want to have to talk about what Brandi had said more than absolutely necessary. It was a lot to take in, and I think even Detective Martinez knew I needed time to digest it. "I'm actually only here for a few minutes. To change clothes. I'm heading back out."

Dad carefully folded the book closed, using his finger to keep his place. He rubbed his eyes patiently, one by one. "Who is he?"

"Huh?"

He tipped his head to the side. "Well, you're not out all day by yourself. And I ran into Jones this afternoon, so I know you haven't been with him. So who have you been with?"

I let out a breathy laugh, trying to stall. I supposed I should've been grateful to Jones for not volunteering the information. Jones could get mad at you, but he'd still never betray you. That was just the way he was. "Honestly, it's my business."

"The last time I left you to your business, you were almost killed."

"Dad—"

He held out his hand. "No. Nikki." He took a steadying breath, but I could see a film of sweat on his temples. I didn't see Dad get angry very often. I didn't see Dad show emotion very often, period. "Now I know I haven't been the best father in the world. I can't be a mother and a father, and knowing that I had to be both made it very difficult for me to figure out what to do most of the time. But I've always kept you safe. Always. Until a few months ago."

"Dad, you can't hold yourself responsible for that—"

"But I do. I wasn't able to keep your mom safe. I should be able to at least keep you safe. If for nothing else, for your mother. And if you had died that night . . ." He shook his head, and I thought maybe I saw some sweat break out on his upper lip as well. "But part of why I couldn't keep you safe was because you were lying to me. About everything. Keeping me totally in the dark. It's unacceptable, and I'm not going to let it happen again. You have no right to lie to me."

Starbursts the color of Arizona dirt surrounded me, my breath coming out in indigo butterfly wings. I was swept up in it before I even knew what was going on. The anger had pounced over me like an azure lion, drenching me in fury.

"I have no right to lie to you?" I said, my teeth clenched. "Are you kidding me with this right now? I have no right to lie to you. Well, what about your lies, Dad? Huh? Since we're being so goddamned honest around here now, why don't you fess up about the things you've been hiding?"

"I have no idea what you're even tal—"

"Right! You have no idea. You pretend you are so worried about not being there to protect me from the Hollises, and the whole time you're telling me you've never had any-thing to do with that family."

"I haven't."

"I've seen it, Dad! I've seen the pictures and the video. You knew Bill Hollis very well, and so did Mom. But some-thing happened and Mom ended up dead and you pretend Bill Hollis is a complete stranger, and I can't . . ." I scrunched up my forehead and held it in my hand. "I can't for the life of me get rid of the feeling that those things had something to do with each other. Am I wrong? Tell me I'm wrong." I was breathing heavily, my chest rising and falling, my fore-head still in my hand, and it wasn't until I'd said the words out loud that I realized that was exactly what I'd been thinking—that Dad might have had something to do with Mom's death. The realization brought tears to my eyes. I blinked and they ran down my cheeks. "Tell me I'm wrong," I repeated.

Dad had gone stony. "You're wrong," he said.

"So correct me. What's right?"

"I don't know what you're talking about," he said. Robotic. Party line. So fucking frustrating.

"Of course you don't. And I don't have anything to hide, either."

We stared each other down for a long, silent moment.

"Did you and Jones break up?" he asked, still using that robot voice.

I wiped my cheeks. "Unbelievable. Yes, okay? We broke up."

"And you're not going to tell me who you're spending all your time with now?"

"Why would I? It's not like we're open and honest with each other, is it?"

He tapped the book on his leg a few times. "I think you owe me a name at least."

I rolled my eyes. "His name is Chris, okay? But you're never going to meet him, because it's not like that." A flash of rainbow made me flush. He didn't say anything. "I'm an adult now. I can take care of myself. You're just going to have to trust me."

"It's not you I don't trust."

"The Hollises are gone," I said. "So what is there to worry about? I guess you would know better than I do, though, huh? I'll be home in a couple hours."

Truth, I didn't know exactly how long this was going to take. Or if I'd come home at all. But I just needed to get away from him.

"I don't like it."

I stood and headed for the stairs again. "Noted."

"Nikki?"

I leaned over the railing, but couldn't see him from where I was.

"Promise me you'll be safe?"

"I can take care of myself just fine."

Now I couldn't see him because of the gray.

"TOOK YOU LONG enough," Detective Martinez said when he opened the front door. Again he ushered me in, and again he swept a look along the sidewalk behind me.

"I had to run interference with my dad."

"And?"

"And he doesn't believe a word I tell him, and I can't blame him." I pushed my way through the door and into Detective Martinez's hallway. "Unlike some people, I'm not great at hiding things." I shot him a *you know what I'm talking about* look, but he didn't seem to notice.

"Well, hopefully this'll be over real soon and you won't have to run interference anymore."

"Yeah. Hopefully."

He let us into his apartment. He'd cleaned it since I was last there, and there was a scent of pine cleaner and bleach in the air.

This time the TV was off, but the radio still played softly in the background. Some sort of R & B that might have been old-fashioned if it weren't for the sexiness of it.

"So what do you have?" he asked, sliding onto a bar stool, where a beer sat sweating on the counter.

"These." I pulled out the stack of photos I'd had printed at the pharmacy and slapped them on the counter in front of him. "I forgot all about them."

"Pictures?" he asked, leaning over them. "This is what you're so excited about?"

"I've led us to most of our answers using pictures," I said. Or more like Peyton had, but it was the same thing, really.

He swigged his beer. "You ever going to finish telling me how you do that?"

"I tried to. The answer was in a file folder in Peyton's car, which I handed to you on a silver platter. You didn't take it. You snooze, you lose."

"I could always just get the file from evidence and give it a once-over," he said.

I swiped his beer out from in front of him and took a swig of my own. "You could, but you won't."

"You're awfully confident that you know how I work."

He reached for the beer, but I refused to let it go. A long moment went by, both of us holding on to it, both of us refusing to look away, a comet trail of roiling fire expanding between us. "Oh, I definitely know how you work," I said. I opened my fingers and let him have the beer.

"Please. Do tell."

"I think it's better to keep a little bit of mystery between us, don't y—what the hell is this?" I'd spied a packet of paper laid neatly on the counter by the microwave, familiar colors screaming out at me in bold across the top. I stretched across the counter and picked it up. "Police academy application?

Are you freaking serious with this? I told you no."

"How do you know it's for you, Miss Center of the Universe? Maybe I've picked it up for someone else."

"Bullshit. But you might as well throw it away, because it's not happening. Here. I'll do it for you." I started around the counter. "Where's your trash can?"

But Detective Martinez caught me by the wrist when I walked by. "I don't think so."

"Let me go," I said, straining against him, the papers falling out of my hand and fluttering to the floor.

"You're so tough, get out of it," he said, tightening his grip.

"Not a problem." I twisted my arm to the side, putting pressure against his thumb so that he had no choice but to let go. "Challenge me next time."

"Fine, you win. I'm not really in the mood for challenges right now."

I stacked the papers back where I'd found them on the counter, and then, unsure what else to do, sat on a bar stool, pulled out a cigarette, and lit it.

"Somebody kick your white horse in the shins?"

"Very funny."

"No, I'm serious. What's the deal?"

He pulled the cigarette out of my hand and dropped it into the beer bottle. "If you must know, Blake and I broke up a few minutes before you got here, okay?"

"Oh." A flutter, like flags in the wind, all colors, snapping at me. I flicked them away. "I hope it wasn't because of me?" I remembered what Blake had said when I was in her office. That he needed to let go of his past, and there was no way he could do that when his present was so wrapped up in saving people. Particularly in saving me.

"In a way, yes. But in a bigger way, no. It's stupid for a cop to try to date a DA. And she was way too mature for me, I guess. Or I was too immature for her. Stuck in my past. Wanting to save the world. Whatever." He laid his hands flat on the counter. "I'd rather be trying to save the world than trying to put away an innocent person. And that is probably why it never would have worked for us in the first place."

If I were a decent person, I would have gone back to Blake's office and told her that he wasn't out to save me. That he was so not stuck in his past, I could hardly ever get him to talk about it. I would tell her that she had nothing to worry about with me—that I didn't fall in love, ever, and that I wasn't going to be getting involved with anyone, given my current status and my uncertain future. And even if I was going to get involved with someone, it wouldn't be a cop, for God's sake.

And if I were a decent person, I would have told him not to let her go so easily, because despite the fact that she was a DA, she seemed to be pretty honest. And she seemed to be in love with him. And someone honest with a future and a heart full of love for him was definitely not worth throwing away to save my sorry ass.

But I didn't do it.

Either I wasn't a decent person, or I didn't believe those things were true.

So why was it easier for me to accept that I just wasn't a decent person?

Because of that weird pulsing rainbow, Nikki. That shit freaks your ass out and you know it.

So instead of going there, I silently fired up a second cigarette.

"Put that out," he said, taking it out of my hand and dropping it into the bottle with the other one.

"Hey! Do you know how expensive cigarettes are? That's seriously uncool, dude."

"Not as expensive as cancer." He scooted the bottle to the other side of the counter. "You need to quit anyway."

"Okay, thanks, Dad. Should I eat my veggies too?"

"Let's just get to work," he said, picking up the stack of photos again. "So what are we looking at here?"

Conversation over. I stood and leaned over his shoulder.

I tapped the picture. "That building," I said.

"Okay?"

I flipped through the rest of the photos—Jimi Hendrix, synesthete, staring out at us from different angles in each one—until I got to the last one. Half of Jimi's face was blocked. I waited for him to see it.

"You recognize something?"

"The van," he said.

I'd wondered where I'd seen that van before. It wasn't until after I'd seen Peyton's video and I'd gone through the photos again. There it was, nearly drowned out by the purple of Jimi, the scarlet-avocado-maroon I knew so well now. "Notice anything familiar about it?" I asked.

"It's a Dom Distribution van."

"Exactly."

He shrugged, dropping the photos back on the counter. "I don't get it. You've got a van outside a building. Why is that so important?"

"It's important because Peyton left these pictures. She left them for me. Dru took the camera card out of her car and I found it in that evidence box. I almost got it at his apartment, but he took it away from me. I thought it was gone forever. He didn't want anyone finding these pictures. Why not? They're just pictures of Peyton and some old building. I mean, what's so incriminating about that?"

He looked at me blankly. "Connect the dots here, Nikki. What makes you think these pictures mean anything at all? Maybe she accidentally snapped them."

I slid back onto my stool and leaned over the counter sideways so I was in his line of vision. "She left me a key, too." I pulled the key out of my pocket and dropped it on the counter. My heart sank a little seeing the key, knowing that Blue was missing and I was probably the only person in this world who cared. Maybe the only person in this world, other than the Hollises, who even knew. He opened his mouth. "Don't worry about where I got it. She left me a key. Now think about the video we watched. She said that I knew where the building was and that I had the key." He still didn't seem to be comprehending. I grunted with frustration, jabbing my finger at the top photo repeatedly. "Right there. That building is the Hollis hideout."

He finally sat up straight, turned to me, his eyes blazing. "And that's where Arrigo Basile is staying."

I nodded. "Exactly. We just have to figure out where this building is."

He sprang up from his stool and strode over to the coffee table, where his gun was sitting. "I know exactly where that building is," he said, pushing the gun into a leg holster. "It's in my old neighborhood."

DETECTIVE MARTINEZ WAS grim and quiet as he drove, confidently and quickly, into L.A.

"Do we have a plan, Detective Martinez?" I asked when I couldn't take any more of the silent treatment.

His face was a straight line, his hands gripping the steering wheel so tight I thought he might break it. Once again I was aware of the cologne smell in his car. I was starting to think it wasn't cologne, but his natural scent. He'd changed into a pair of black jeans and a tight black Henley, the buttons undone, showing off a bit of brown chest.

"When are you going to stop calling me that?" he asked.

"What? Detective Martinez? It's your name, isn't it?"

"So is Chris."

"I don't know. That seems so . . . casual. We're not really that close, do you think?"

He smirked. "I think at this point, Nikki, we're close enough. Remember the stakeout?"

I felt my cheeks get hot. Damn it, I would not blush over this guy.

"That was strategy, and I'm not talking about it. What I am talking about is how this is going to go down. So what's the plan, *Detective Martinez*?" I repeated, emphasizing his name in an obnoxious voice.

"I guess we go to the building in the photo and then we figure it out when we get there."

I gaped at him. "That's it? That's your grand plan?"

He nodded. "Pretty much."

"After all the crap you gave me for doing the same thing in Bakersfield?"

"I'm a professional. You're not."

"Oh, okay, that makes sense. So it's all right for you to go in without a plan because you solve all your cases that way, but it's bad for me to do it because I'm not an actual cop? Is that why I keep beating you to the solution?"

"Very funny. I solve plenty of cases. It's a gut thing. I would think you, of anyone, would be able to appreciate that."

I pushed myself farther back into the seat. "Yeah, I suppose I do."

He wound his way off the highway and into a neighborhood. I was immediately lost, the dark not helping at all. Numbers and street signs and graffiti and building signs jumped out at me—blues and reds and vibrant pinks and yellows. A black Monte Carlo parked at a curb—glossy, red racing stripes, the words *Monte Carlo* flashing out in silver. A baby-blue VW Bug, the old style, rusted out around the wheels over here, a statue of the Virgin Mary over there. We drove through neighborhoods filled with suspicious-looking teenagers and porches full of alcohol-swilling men, but the farther we drove, the fewer streetlamps blazed overhead, the fewer people hanging around, and the more boarded-up windows we saw. There was a sense of being watched, though, even if we couldn't see who was doing the watching. It was the most alive abandoned area I'd ever encountered.

"You grew up here?" I asked.

"Not too far," he said. "I told you it was a rough neighborhood."

I gazed at a truck, parked in front of a fire hydrant, all of its windows bashed out. I tried to imagine Detective Martinez as a little boy, holes in the knees of his jeans, playing in the dirt patch that was supposed to be his front yard. I tried to imagine him hiding in his room, hoping nobody shot through his window at night. I tried to imagine him as a teenager, stepping out onto this very street, jaw set, determined to get revenge on the man who killed his sister. "It's definitely not Brentwood. Do you really think a Hollis would ever come out here? Even to hide?"

He turned another corner, and warehouses-turned-loft-apartments squatted around us. "It's a pretty good spot for them to disappear, don't you think? Nobody would ever expect to see someone like Bill Hollis in this neighborhood. Plus, it's just a hideout for their thugs. Doesn't have to be nice." I thought about Ruby and Blue's apartment building. It had seemed slummy to me—impossible to believe it was part of the Hollis empire. But this was worse. Way worse.

Finally, he slowed, edging up to a curb. "There it is," he said. "Jimi Hendrix."

"Purple Haze," I said, seeing the purple jump off the wall.

A dim light glowed through one of the high windows— one of the only lights in the whole area.

"And it looks like somebody's home."

"So what're we going to do, now that we're here?" I asked.

"We go inside."

"And . . . ?"

"And we take it from there. How can I say when I don't know what to expect in there?"

Suddenly I had a feeling of chalkboards and rocks again. Nerves. *At least it's not fear*, I thought. *Not yet.*

"Maybe we should, like, call the cops or something," I said. "Maybe it's a bad idea for us to go in there alone." He didn't respond. "You said yourself you don't know what to expect in there. We have one gun between the two of us, and—" Truth was, I didn't want him putting his job on the line for me. Again. He'd worked hard for what he had, and he didn't deserve to keep losing things because I was in his life. And, most of all, he didn't deserve to lose his life over me, the way Dru had.

"We know that Rigo is dangerous, right? What if he's waiting with ten grenades or a machine gun or something?"

"Grenades? Are you serious? His signature is a cane, remember?"

"Against seventeen-year-old girls, maybe. But against you . . ."

He reached over and clasped my shaky hand in his. "Nikki, we're not going to call the police. We don't have a search warrant. We don't even have a good reason to get one. I'm not a cop right now." I pulled my hand away and turned back toward the building. "Look," he said, "if you're that worried about it, you can stay here. I'll go in alone." Well, that was new. Usually I was the one going in alone.

"Never," I said, pulling the door handle.

He turned off the car and we both skittered across the street, our footsteps sounding exceedingly loud to me, and the asphalt under our feet feeling even bumpier and darker than usual. No doubt about it, I was scared. But in the back of my mind, I sensed undulating fire.

We pressed our backs against the building, taking a few minutes to make sure nobody had seen us.

He assessed the side of the building that we were on. There was a rusted metal door. Adhered to the door was a small sign—one that couldn't be seen in the photos Peyton had taken. Scarlet-avocado-maroon. Dom Distribution.

So this was it. This was the Hollises' other business. This was where the van came from.

He pulled the key out of his pocket and handed it to me. With his other hand, he pulled out his gun and aimed it at the door. "Go ahead."

"Just like that?"

"Just like that."

"And if he's waiting for us on the other side?"

"We'll take care of it. Go."

My hands were almost too shaky to hold the key, much less slip it into the doorknob quietly. I was very aware of the gun pointed at my back, and the chance that I could get caught in a hail of crossfire bullets.

But I had to do this. My life, literally, depended on it. I had fought for my mother. I had fought for Peyton. I had fought for truth.

Now it was time to fight for myself.

The key sank home and I glanced back at Detective Martinez. He nodded, one time.

I turned the key. The door unlocked. But I had barely

opened it half an inch before Detective Martinez's boot slammed into it, knocking it with a solid metallic boom against the wall.

"Police! Freeze!" he shouted, moving in.

I had no choice but to follow.

"WHAT—WHAT—WHAT—" SHOUTED A man who was running toward me, completely ignoring the gun Detective Martinez had trained on him. I dropped back into a fighting stance and tried to take in my surroundings in the dark. I was standing in what looked like a showroom. There were shelves all around me, filled with various antique preservation chemicals, books on how to restore old things, and a few moving aids like dollies and straps and quilts. All around me were smartly restored pieces of furniture—very expensive-looking. But behind the man, there was an open door, which revealed living quarters. A couch and TV, a table, a hot plate, a mini-fridge. And, stacked against one wall, bags and bags of the colorful Molly I'd seen in Luna's hand in a photo that I'd stolen from Peyton's apartment not so long ago. So much Molly it was hard to wrap my head around it. In the farthest corner of that room, barely visible from where I was standing, was a large safe. If they left their drugs out in plain sight like that, God only knew what they hid in the safe.

"Stop!" Detective Martinez shouted beside me. "Get on the ground! Get on the ground!" I'd never heard him really yell before. Raise his voice, yes, plenty of times. But not bellow like this. I turned in his direction.

Mistake.

"I wouldn't do that if I were you," I heard from my other side, right at the same time I felt cold metal press against my temple. I froze. I knew that voice.

Jones.

P UT IT DOWN, cop," Luna said, stepping out from
behind Jones. "Rigo, get his gun."

As the man came closer, I began to be able to make out
his features. Short, balding, small gut. The same man I'd
seen in the surveillance video. The man we'd been looking
for all this time. We'd found him, but I was too stunned to
really care. I'd built him up in my head to be a monster, but
he looked like a sad, saggy middle-aged guy. Not even very
big. He scurried forward and took the gun out of Detective
Martinez's hand. Martinez didn't fight him.

"Jones?" I breathed, my brain swimming, literally unable
to make sense of seeing him here. And with a gun to my
head. "What the hell? What's going on?"

"Don't talk, Nikki," he said. "You had your chance to talk. Now I do the talking." I could feel the barrel vibrate against my skin—he was shaking. His voice cracked on the word *talking*.

"I don't understand," I said. "What are you doing here?" But it was starting to sink in. I'd recognized the voice behind the mask on the second guy in my house. I'd been unable to place it at the time, because he'd lowered it to a growl and, besides, why would I ever, in a billion years, think it might be Jones? But it was. I could hear it again right now. It was Jones that night.

"I said don't talk!" he yelled. Behind him Luna giggled and hopped on her toes, her hands clasped under her chin like a swoony cartoon character.

"Oh my God, don't you think he's so sexy when he's mad, Nikki? I don't know why you let him go. I'm just glad you did. And you did it so epically bitchy. Made my job so easy."

"Put the gun down, Jones," Detective Martinez said. "You're going to get yourself into a whole lot of trouble. But you can back out of it now."

"Shut up!" Luna spat, then turned back to me and giggled some more. "Did you know how heartbroken he was? Totally heartbroken. But don't worry, Nikki, I convinced him you're not worth it. I convinced him of a lot of things. He's so . . . willing."

"Jones," Detective Martinez said again. "Think about your future. You don't want to do this."

Luna rolled her eyes. "Go ahead and shoot the cop, Rigo. I'm sick of being interrupted."

"No," I heard myself breathe. "Don't do it. We just—we just want to talk to you. I swear. Jones, we can work this out. We didn't even know you guys were here."

She laughed, that cold crocodile laugh. "Clearly. You wouldn't be stupid enough to come into a dark room with me a second time, would you, Nikki Kill? And with no Dru to protect you either. I wonder if Dru would have been so eager to eat a bullet for you if he knew how cozy you were about to get with your little wind-up cop over there." She sidestepped a few steps so she could see Detective Martinez. Or maybe so he could better see her. She loved to be the center of attention, after all. She took the gun from Rigo. "Go get some rope, Rigo. Lots of it. For our best friend Nikki here. I know some people who are going to be very happy to see that you and I have reconciled our differences, Nikki, and you just couldn't separate yourself from me." She laughed again, tossing her hair over her shoulder. I tried not to let the motion send me back into that night at Hollis Mansion. She turned her head and snarled, "Go, Rigo. Since you won't kill the cop, I'll do it." She aimed the gun at Detective Martinez. "Hey, cop. Did you know that boys who protect Nikki Kill have a way of ending up dead? Pow, pow." She jerked the gun with each *pow* and giggled again. "Two for flinching. This is fun." She moved back over to Jones and patted his cheek with her free hand. "I don't know what you see in that pig over there, Nikki Kill. This one's so good-looking. Check out these muscles." She ran her fingers over Jones's biceps. I saw him recoil, just slightly. "And he's smart. He knows whose side to be on. Although you did make it pretty easy for him. I had no trouble at all getting him into your house, your car. Your pants. Kind of gross, if you ask me, but hey, he was pretty pissed at you. That's what you get for fooling around. I hope Officer Friendly was worth it." She turned and aimed the gun at Detective Martinez.

It was my only chance.

I tapped my toe against Detective Martinez's shoe, hoping that he understood what I was communicating. *Be ready.* I sensed, rather than saw, his head twitch down in the tiniest of a nod. I tapped his shoe again. *Go time.*

I rushed her, striking her hands with both of my palms. At the same time, Martinez took three big steps forward, head down, and shoved Jones. The gun almost flew out of Luna's hand, but the trigger guard got caught on her finger and it simply spun and swung. I turned, jamming my elbow into her gut and trapping her arm under my armpit, frantically fumbling to knock the gun from her hand. Finally, it fell to the floor—once again I braced myself for the bang— and I kicked it away. It spun out of my reach.

Luna yanked free, but before I could get set, she came at me, grabbing a handful of my hair and pummeling my face. They weren't hard hits, but they were scrappy ones. Luna liked to fight dirty. I was going to have to get dirty too, if I wanted to survive.

I put my hands up to cover my face from the blows and low kicked her to the side of the knee, but my kick was weak. I leaned in to elbow strike her to the face, but her hands, my hands, and my hair were all in my line of vision and I missed. My elbow ended up striking her temple instead. Which was just enough to make her let go.

I could hear Detective Martinez and Jones fighting somewhere near me, a lot of meaty smacks and grunts and sounds of tussling. Every so often, Martinez would tell Jones to just stop, give himself a chance to turn this around. But from the sound of things, Jones wasn't going to give in anytime soon. Which still made no sense to me. Luna had gotten to Jones? How? He'd been on her side this whole time? How had I been fooled by him?

I shoved Luna hard with my shoulder, and she fell back a few steps, taking a handful of hair with her and crashing into a stack of cleaning supplies. Somehow she managed to keep her balance, and before I could even think what to do next, she had grabbed a broom and was coming at me again.

"Not this time, bitch," she snarled.

She swung the broom handle at me, and I turned just

enough to absorb the blow on my side. My ribs were still sore from my encounter with the Basiles in my kitchen—correction, a Basile and Jones in my kitchen—and I cried out. She cocked her arm back to swing again.

Distance was usually my advantage. I could kick an opponent in the face before they knew what was coming. But Luna had evened that advantage with the stupid stick. I had to go inside. I was lousy inside. I tried to remember how Detective Martinez had gotten the advantage on me from up close. He was quick, and he never stopped coming at his opponent. I blocked her swing with one hand—pain ringing up my arm—and punched her as hard as I could in the neck. Instantly, she dropped the broom and doubled over, grasping her neck and coughing.

I pushed away from her, dropped back into a ready stance, then front snap kicked her, the top of my foot groaning as it made contact with her face. I felt a dull, crunching thud and Luna nearly flew backward, her head cracking hard on the concrete.

She was still.

I was breathing hard, my hand and ribs and head aching. Detective Martinez, distracted by the sudden silence, paused, giving Jones just enough chance to rear back and smack him a good one. Martinez's head jerked from the motion and he stumbled backward a few steps.

Jones and I locked eyes. For a second, I thought I

recognized the person behind those eyes. The Jones that I thought I knew. One who would do anything for me. One who would never think of joining Luna. One who would never dream of holding a gun at all, much less against my head. But that Jones was a lie. That Jones was gone.

Maybe Jones was just like Dru, was just like Dad, was just like Mom. Maybe he was a stranger and a liar, too. Maybe I was so easily played it wasn't even funny.

"You can stop this," I said.

But he took off before I could say any more, barreling the way Rigo had gone.

Martinez stumbled a few steps after him, but decided against it, electing instead to stay near me.

"You okay?" he asked. My muscles twitched. I wheeled around in circles, sure Rigo was poised to slam into me at any moment. "Nik? You okay?"

I nodded, gulped, tried to catch my breath. "Yeah. Fine. I don't know if she's breathing, though." When I dropped Luna, no crimson had faded into my periphery, but my mind had been a July Fourth finale at the moment, so I might not have noticed even if it did.

"We'll worry about her in a second. Get the gun."

"I don't know where it went."

"Find it."

Still gasping, I followed the general direction where I thought the gun had gone, squinting in the darkness, trying to make out shapes, jumping at every tick and click and scrape along the concrete. Finally, I saw it, a black blob nestled between two boxes. I picked it up and jammed it into the back of my waistband, absolutely hating the feel of the cold metal against my skin.

There was a noise and both of us jumped, just in time to see Rigo, hurrying along with a length of rope, as he'd been instructed. Detective Martinez lunged for him, knocking into him full force, both of them ending up on the floor, with Martinez on top. The two struggled, but it really wasn't much of a fight. Rigo wasn't young and muscular like Jones. Martinez managed to flip him to his stomach. A pair of handcuffs appeared out of nowhere, and Martinez had them tight on Rigo's wrists before I could even focus on them.

Sweat was dripping off his forehead and chin in rivers, and it was only after he'd secured Rigo that he finally let out a breath. But only for a second, because next thing I knew, he was dragging Rigo into the living area, so he could see him in the light.

"Go ahead. Arrest me," Rigo was saying, his jaw set with defiance. "I'll get out. And then I'll be looking for you, cop."

"Quiet," Detective Martinez said, shoving him back down to the ground. "You killed Peyton Hollis, didn't you? Didn't you?"

"Fuck off," he sneered. Sweat lined his forehead, too. He didn't look like someone you would think to be afraid of. He looked like someone's kindhearted uncle. Which was sort of what made him scariest of all.

For a moment, I was transported back to that abandoned parking lot. It was windy and I could hear the rattle of leaves and trash skittering around in the loading dock. This was the face Peyton had last looked at. A face she knew, and probably never thought would hurt her.

"Peyton trusted you," I said.

He made a mock crying face. "Aw, now I feel so bad." He finished with a glare.

"How could you? How could you do that to her? Someone you knew. How could Dru?"

"Pssht. That little fuck couldn't do nothing. Changed his mind at the last minute, just like the little pussy he was, trying to get in my way, beating the crap out of me and taking my cane. He turned on me without even thinking twice, and he knew as long as he had that cane he had the upper hand. I couldn't do nothing to him until I got it back from him and got rid of it. Little shit hid it from me. Everything would have been different if I'd killed him instead. Everything. I'm glad Miss Fairchild did the job for me. I put the dent in the princess's head and she put the hole in the prince. Nice to get a break."

I spit on him. It landed on his cheek and slid down. His face grew red and serious.

"That was my sister," I said.

"Work is work and family is family. Lock me up. Won't be the first time. And won't be the last. You've got nothing but circumstantial evidence. Nothing physical."

"The cane," I said. "Is it in that safe? Your family bought it at an auction."

He made a face. "And if you think it wasn't immediately destroyed, this is going to be even easier than I thought." He raised his eyebrows, all innocence. "What cane? I don't know what you're talking about. And I don't know what's in the safe, either. But it ain't the cane. I know that much."

Detective Martinez and I exchanged glances. Not having any physical evidence would pose a challenge, but it didn't make things impossible, did it? Detective Martinez was a good detective. Respected. If he told his colleagues—if he told Blake—that this was their guy, they would believe him, right?

Right?

But how many bridges had he burned to help me? That, I didn't know. I suspected there might have been many. Would Blake even listen to him anymore? Or would her broken heart get in the way?

"What's the combination?" Detective Martinez asked.

"I don't know."

"Bullshit," Detective Martinez said. "I'll give you another

try. But only one more. What's the combination?"

Rigo glared hard, his nostrils flared. "I don't know anything about that safe."

The word *safe* lit up in my mind, just like it always did, in gorgeous cottony peach. Instantly, I thought of Peyton. Her face, looking right into a camera, her cheeks pink, her eyes nervous. *Safe.* Cottony peach that made me want to curl up inside of it. *Safe.*

I think it would be safe to say that we'd be a great combination, she'd said. *We probably have all kinds of strange things in common. Like, the last two digits of your locker number and the digits of my birthday month both add up to eleven or something. That kind of stuff that only sisters care about.*

I had thought nothing of it at the time. I hadn't even bothered to do the math. She was wrong. The last two digits of my locker number—bronze, sea green—were nine and six. Added together, fifteen. And Peyton Hollis's birthday was such a big damn deal at school, everyone knew it was in October—brown, black—one plus zero. Also not eleven.

Safe to say . . . great combination.

Safe. Combination.

Peyton had so much faith in our synesthesia. Clearly hers had been much nicer and more reliable to her than mine had been to me. Still. She knew she could send me messages—so many messages—and I would be the only one to get them. She'd told me, plain as day, what the combination was.

"I know it," I said, rushing toward the safe.

I knelt in front of it, twisting the lock a few times. My hands were shaking.

"You don't know shit," Rigo was saying from the other side of the room.

I tried 9-6-15. Nothing. Okay. I took a breath. 1-0-1. Still locked. 9-10-10. God, this was going to take forever. *Think, Nikki, think.* I closed my eyes, took a deep breath, let Rigo's jeers disappear into the background. She'd said if you added the numbers, you came up with eleven.

She couldn't have made it simpler.

I rotated the knob a few times to clear it and then tried again. 15-1-11.

The safe unlocked.

"Holy shit," Rigo breathed.

I pulled the door open. Stacks of money tumbled out at me. Inside, bills were crammed to the top and then some. I pulled out a few. Hundred-dollar bills. Every single one of them.

A fortune.

A fortune of Hollis money.

The drugs, the escort service, Dru's bank statements, the fake receipt book at Tesori Antico. It was all starting to add up now. The Hollises were taking in a shitload of illegal money and funneling it all through the Basiles' businesses, which just happened to be Hollis-backed. The Basiles marked up the sales in their books, and then paid Dru for a dummy job to get the money back to the Hollises, keeping a portion for themselves. In return for a hefty paycheck, the Basiles did the Hollises' bidding, including using Rigo for their dirtiest deeds. Rigo was as cold-blooded as someone could get, and he was really fucking good at hiding. Bonus, Rigo was friends with Dru. Or had been until Dru had double-crossed him.

I sat back on my heels, wiping my hands on my jeans. They felt dirty from just touching the money.

"Get a picture of it, Nikki," Detective Martinez said, and I numbly went through the motions of pulling out my phone and snapping several photos of the safe and its contents.

"Guess who's going to prison, Rigo?" Detective Martinez said. "Here's a hint. It's not me. And it's not Nikki."

Rigo grinned. "I don't know why you think it's me. You bent a lot of rules to find me, Detective. I'm golden. You bring me in, and you got a heap of shit to explain."

"I'm willing to take my chances," Martinez said. He dug into his pocket and pulled out a set of keys, which he tossed at me. "Nikki, go get the car and pull up to the door."

I caught the keys but didn't move.

He gave me a reassuring nod. "I'll stay with our friend here. We'll talk about our next move in the car."

"Is he right, though? Is it pointless to bring him in?"

"Just honk when you get to the door. Okay?" I still didn't

answer. I was swimming in so many what-ifs, not the least of which was what if I just hadn't answered the phone that night? What if Peyton had been forced to reach out to someone else?

What if I'd gone with my first instinct and not trusted this cop to save me in the first place?

I didn't want to go. I wasn't done getting answers for myself. There was so much more I wanted to know—what had it been like for Peyton in those last few minutes? Had she suffered? What had Dru done to stop Rigo? What other setups did Luna have waiting for me?

But I guessed the answers to any, or even all, of those questions wouldn't change a thing. Peyton would still be dead. Dru would still be involved. And I would still be set up.

And I would still be royally screwed. Detective Martinez was right. We had to take Rigo with us before he slipped away again.

"Nikki. Go." He looked very serious.

So I went.

Which meant I had to walk past Luna. Luna who might or might not be breathing. And if she wasn't, how much shit would I be in this time? And would Detective Martinez be in trouble too? No. I would make him leave. I would take the blame for all of it. After all, it really was all my fault. Without me, he wouldn't even be here at all.

But halfway across the showroom floor, I realized that

Luna was gone. All that was left behind were a few drops of blood where she had been. My throat squeezed shut.

My first instinct was to go back to Detective Martinez. But I never got that far. As soon as I turned to go back to the living area, I was blocked by Jones, who had stepped out from behind a stack of boxes, holding the broom in his hand.

"Sorry, sweetheart," he said. He swung the broom over his head and everything went black.

37

AFTER I CAME to, it took me a few minutes to figure out where I was. The floor underneath me was hard and cold, like metal, with grooves under my back, my head, my feet. It was vibrating, and as I blinked away the fuzz, I realized everything was vibrating because I was moving.

Slowly, I sat up and looked around. I was inside the back of an empty van. We were heading down the highway. The person driving the van was familiar.

Jones.

I crawled up behind his seat and scanned my surroundings, searching for something I could use to defend myself when we stopped driving. I had no way of knowing where that might be. Once, I'd thought I knew Jones. Now it was clear that everything I knew was a lie. A lie that made me feel broken in half on the inside.

"Where are you taking me?" My voice felt thick, hard to get out.

He let out a breath and glanced back at me. I thought I saw relief in his face. "Jesus," he said, and then, "You're awake."

"Where are we going? Stop the van," I said. As my head got clearer, panic set in deeper and deeper. Where was Detective Martinez? Did he know I was gone? Would he be able to find me before Jones and, God knows, Luna did whatever they planned to do to me?

"You know, I didn't mean for it to be this way," he said. "I was just so pissed. So. Fucking. Pissed." He pounded the steering wheel with the palm of his hand with each word. "I thought I could make you love me. How stupid was I? You can't love anyone but yourself." He glanced back again, hoping, I was sure, to see me react. But the thing was . . . he was right, and we both knew it. He wasn't telling me anything I hadn't already told myself a thousand times. I was selfish. I was an asshole. I had done him a favor by not loving him.

"Jones. Stop the van. You can still get out of this."

"Somebody really should warn him, you know? That guy. That cop. Someone should tell him he's wasting his time with you."

"I told you not to," I said. "I used those exact words."

He glanced back again, holding my gaze for so long I started to jolt toward the steering wheel, afraid he would crash and kill us both.

He turned back and shook his head at the windshield. "It was too late by then. Way too late. I had given up a long time before that." He shook his finger in the air. "She told me. Said you would ruin my life. And guess what? She was right."

"She wasn't right, Jones. I don't want anything to do with your life. You can stop the van and let me go and just . . . get out of town or something. Go to college. I won't say a word about you being involved at all. I swear."

He laughed, high and shrill. "You really think I can just move on now, after everything that's happened?" He was silent for a minute, and I thought maybe I heard his throat click like he was holding back a cry. "I don't want you anymore, Nikki."

"That doesn't mean you have to hate me."

"I don't hate you. If I hated you, I would've run you down in that parking lot. Instead, I pretended I hit a pothole. If I hated you, I would have let Antony stick that knife in your gut. But I didn't. I talked him out of killing you. I got him to leave your house. But I'm locked in now. I can't get out."

"What does she have on you?" I asked, finally realizing exactly what was going on. Jones wasn't afraid that I'd ruined his life; he was afraid that he had ruined it.

"Nothing!" he shouted. He banged his fist on the steering wheel again. "At first, nothing. She was just so . . . seductive. Sexy. And she hated you as much as I did. And I thought what we were doing was just to freak you out a little, you know? Moving stuff around your house, lifting your cigarettes and jacket, that kind of thing. I wanted you to be scared, so you would come running to me and for once—for once!—I could be the one to turn my back on you. But then it got bigger. Stealing things out of your pockets and drawers while you were asleep. Killing your computer and slashing your tires. And talking to the DA. Pretending I was a witness. It was so easy. Your dad wouldn't notice if an army walked through your house. I was caught up in it. I didn't know how to say no to her. And, sometimes, I didn't want to. And that was your fault, Nikki. That was all you."

"Dear God," I said. "You were the one framing me this whole time?"

He shook his head. "Not just me. Not at first. There was this other guy. He was helping her. He kept some journal about you, and he planted the Molly in your car. She made me find you at the party to be sure you stayed there until they called the cops about seeing you deal drugs from your car. I kept you busy and the other guy called it in."

"What other guy? You mean Rigo?"

"No, I don't fucking mean Rigo. If I meant Rigo, I would

have said Rigo. Some dude with white hair. Always wore this huge belt buckle."

Candy cane and mustard flashed in my mind. Candy cane and mustard on a belt buckle. Where had I seen it?

"The photo," I said. "I saw a guy like that in a photo. Did his belt buckle have letters on it?"

He shrugged. "Why would I even care?"

Candy cane and mustard. V-P. At the time, I'd wondered what he might be the VP of.

Who was he? And why did I feel like I'd seen him somewhere else too? Like I should know exactly who he was.

"I don't get it, Jones. If Luna has nothing on you, why can't you just split?"

"It's not Luna I'm afraid of. It's Hollis."

The spot on my head where he'd hit me with the broom suddenly lit up with pain. I pressed my fingers to it; they came away bloody. Again. Damn, I was tired of bleeding.

"Bill Hollis is in Dubai," I said.

Jones shook his head. "No, he's not. He was just at the warehouse yesterday. He brought all that Molly you saw."

I sensed sulfur on summer air before I saw the fireworks this time. They bloomed across the floor of the van, lighting my panic. Blue had told me. Brandi had tried to tell me. I was too stupid to hear it, even though everyone had insisted that it was no coincidence that Luna was out right when evidence started to pile up against me. Crimson edged its way into my vision. The Hollises and death were forever combined in my synesthesia. I swallowed, suddenly struck with a sobering thought. "You're taking me to him, aren't you?"

He ran his hand down the length of his face. "I don't have a choice anymore. I've seen what they can do. I've seen what they do to people who talk. Bill Hollis doesn't like loose ends." Again I thought of Ruby and Blue. Now I knew for sure that Bill Hollis had made them disappear. "I don't want to kill you, Nikki." This time there were real tears in his voice. "But it's you or me. And it's not going to be me."

38

TESORI ANTICO WAS closed, the front lights extinguished and the interior lights dimmed. The door, however, was left unlocked, and we walked inside. The same frizzy-haired woman I'd talked to before was sitting at the glass case again. She looked up when we came in. There was no sign of Detective Martinez anywhere. God, had Rigo killed him back at the warehouse?

The woman immediately disappeared through the beaded door, leaving Jones and me alone among the antiques. He shoved my shoulders from behind, inching me along toward the back of the store. I resisted, planting my feet, trying to buy as much time as possible. Trying to think of a plan.

I swept my hand over my pockets. My phone was missing. If Detective Martinez was out there, I was cut off from him. I sent him mental notes, even though that had never worked before. *I'm still here. Come and help me.*

But I couldn't guarantee he would. I couldn't even guarantee that he was still alive. I was in this on my own. I had to think fast. I had to take my chance.

"Hello?" Jones called. The woman didn't come back. "We're here," he said. "Luna?" He raised up onto his tiptoes and craned to see where the woman had gone.

It was my one chance. I lifted my foot and stomped as hard as I could backward. I'd hoped to feel the crunch of Jones's arch giving way, but doing it blind, I was off center. I managed to catch the side. It was enough, though. I turned and barreled into him like a linebacker and just kept going. Silently, I raced down the aisle and rounded the corner, sliding on my knees under a crowded shelf and disappearing under the antiques. An angel with a missing nose stared me in the face. I gulped in air as quietly as I could, my heart hammering away.

"Hey! Damn it!" I heard Jones say, but he didn't exactly yell it.

I pulled my knees close to my chest and waited for his footsteps to go by, trying not to look at the bloody depiction of World War II on the canvas to my left. Crimson. Even on the paintings, crimson.

"Nikki! Where are you?"

I held my breath. Tucked in tight. I could hear his footsteps getting closer. *Please don't find me, please don't find me.*

"Damn it, Nikki, don't do this," he said. There was a clang as something nearby got knocked over. A bang as he lifted and dropped something else.

I made sure I wasn't touching anything, pulling myself into a tight ball. Behind me was a cinder-block wall. If Jones peeked down, there would be nowhere for me to go. I swore my heart was beating so hard, you could hear it outside my chest.

Finally, I could see his shoes. Scuffed white boat shoes. Sand caught in the creases. My stomach soured at the memory of our night on the beach. That entire night had been a setup.

I pressed myself harder against the wall. The shoes stopped. A pillow dropped right in front of the shelf, enclosing me in total darkness. Shit. Now I couldn't see anything. I turned my head. The empty-eyed angel stared back at me. I could still see that. I wished I couldn't.

Finally, I heard his shoes move, his footsteps begin to echo away. I waited until I couldn't hear them anymore, then leaned forward and moved the pillow just half an inch or so. He wasn't in the aisle anymore but was close.

I would have to be fast.

I could be fast.

Trying to make as little noise as humanly possible, I bolted, scrambling up onto my knees and then onto my feet, running one way, and then, when met with a dead end, running another. The aisles seemed to fuse together in my panic. Everywhere I looked, there seemed to be the same trinkets and statues and chairs. I felt like I was running in circles, my path obscured by the gray and black that closed in on me, the starbursts of metal that blinded me. The snarling face of a tiger statue, the pursed mouth of a chipped doll face. A mannequin, torso only, draped in a black lace shawl. An unsettling painting of a nude woman wearing a wedding veil and wrapped around the hips of a skeleton. A jack-in-the-box. Finally, I made myself pause and take two breaths, squeezing my eyes shut. I could hear Jones coming toward me, but I refused to bolt again without knowing where I was going first.

A peacock feather. I'd seen it coming in. It was poking out of a vase with a monogram painted on it in gold. Letters that meant nothing to me. But letters that would stand out in color when I saw them again. I knew if I passed the vase and turned left at the end of this aisle, I would be able to make a break for the front door.

Tensing every muscle in my body, I bounded toward the feather, my legs pumping, my hands outstretched to punch the door open.

But I never got the chance. The door flung outward

when I was still three feet away from it, and in raced a dark blur. It was too late for me to slow down. I ran chest-first into it and skidded back on my butt into a giant plastic clown head.

39

IMMEDIATELY, I SPRANG to my feet. The person I'd run into was coming toward me. I threw a front snap to keep him back. He paused to dodge it, then advanced on me anyway. I started to throw another kick, but then it came into focus who it was.

"It's me," he breathed. "You're okay."

Detective Martinez wrapped me up in his arms, and I clung to him just to prove to myself that he was real. Just as quickly, we both pulled away. He grabbed my hand.

"Come on, let's get you out of here."

"Rigo?"

He shook his head. "I had to follow you."

"He got away?"

"How cozy," I heard. A familiar, and chilling, voice that made both of us stop and turn. "The cop and the snitch together."

I saw Jones first, as he inched around the corner, through the stack and jumble of art, his hands up surrender-style, the shadow of a figure that I knew well pressed up behind him. The shadow held a gun to Jones's head. It was only then that I realized whose voice it was that had sounded so familiar.

"Bill Hollis," I breathed, the air sucked out of me as if I'd been punched in the gut.

"And delivered to me with Nikki Kill," he said jovially. "Is it my birthday? Jones, you shouldn't have."

Next to me, Detective Martinez had taken out his gun and was pointing it forward.

"I hate it when I have to mix business with pleasure. But I guess I'm going to have to, because we have unfinished business, don't we, Nikki Kill?"

Gold fireworks burst in my vision, refusing to let the asphalt black niggle its way in fully.

I had been warned. I had been told. I understood that Bill Hollis was no longer in Dubai. But seeing him some-how made it more real, more dangerous. But something had changed. Shifted inside of me. The terror that once gripped me from hearing his voice in the dark of Hollis Mansion was still there . . . but it was underneath. Muted. Buried by the certainty that I just needed this to be over. I didn't want to face him again. I'd been avoiding even thinking about it.

But I would face him.

I would.

It was time to be done being afraid. If this was where it all had to end, then so be it.

"I let you get away once," I said. "I won't do it again." My voice sounded much more cold and confident than I felt on the inside.

"That's tough talk for someone who's completely outnumbered."

I felt rather than heard the door open behind us, the air sucking wisps of my hair backward. I didn't need to turn around to have a pretty good idea of who was standing there.

"Go ahead and drop your weapon, Detective."

I caught movement out of the corner of my eye and flicked a glance backward. Sure enough, Vanessa Hollis stood just inside the doorway.

Behind her, bloody and unsteady, but smiling smugly, stood Luna Fairchild. "Boo," she said, and then lunged at me and wrapped me in a choke hold from behind.

"I would be more than happy to let Luna strangle her," Vanessa said, leaning close to Detective Martinez's ear. "Is that what you want? I wouldn't blame you. She is a bit of a deadweight. Put the gun down." She licked his earlobe.

"I'm not the only one," I gasped, my back groaning as I

strained to keep my footing. Luna was shorter than me by a lot, and her grip was wicked. "I'm not the only one who can tell."

"Empty threat," Luna said, and her arm tightened around my neck. "And nobody asked you to talk." Gray spots danced in front of my eyes, only this time it wasn't my synesthesia doing the choreography; it was lack of oxygen.

"Oh, you mean the trailer whore," Bill Hollis called. "Or should I say the dead trailer whore. Things would have worked out for her a lot differently if you hadn't gone down there. I warned her not to talk. She didn't listen. You just can't teach some people."

"Although it does make sense. She was dumb trailer trash if I ever saw it," Vanessa added. "Luna, honey, you're letting up." The grip around my neck, which had loosened enough for me to get my hands between her arm and my throat, tightened again.

"In case you haven't had the chance to watch the news lately," Bill continued, "and you have been pretty busy, it seems the trailer of a certain ex-whore has burned down. And she must have been in a drugged stupor—you know how hookers and drugs go together—because she never even attempted to get out of bed. Weird, huh? Your only witness. Poof! Up in smoke."

My mind reeled. Brandi was gone? We had just talked to her. Just gotten to know her. She had told us that talking to her put her in danger. And the Hollises had burned her up. And it had been my fault. If I'd let her stay hidden . . .

"Well, not the only one," Vanessa added. "We also got rid of those two apartment rats. They were a money pit anyway. What's two more dead nobodies, though?"

"We're about to find out," Luna said, her breath tickling my ear.

Oh God, Ruby and Blue. Tears filled my eyes, and I wasn't sure if they were from my inability to breathe or from something else. I began to well up with putrid brown ink, the color of raw sewage. I couldn't. I couldn't succumb to my colors now. I closed my eyes and breathed, pushing them away.

"This is getting boring, Mother," Luna said. I could tell by her voice that she was talking through gritted teeth. I could also tell that she was getting tired. Her grip had loosened. I could hear Gunner in my head. *Wait for your chance, Nikki. You can get out of this. She's hurt, remember?*

"Yes, let's get a move on this, Bill," Vanessa said. "We have a flight to catch."

"Last chance, Martinez. Drop it now," Bill Hollis called.

"You won't shoot anyone," Detective Martinez called back.

"Oh, really?"

Bill shoved Jones, who stumbled three steps forward, bumping up against a floor vase, which tipped, spilling a clutch of walking sticks onto the ground. They clattered and rolled. I could see the old Jones in his face. The Jones who got in too deep and regretted it. The Jones who didn't mean to hurt anyone. The Jones who just wanted to go off to college and start a life free of the Nikki Kill drama.

"Go, Jones!" I cried, but then, just as Jones tensed as if to run, Bill Hollis fired two shots into his back.

Crimson bang. Jones's face morphed into Dru's and back into his own as he gasped out his last breaths. Bumpy gray and black pulsed over me, crimson splashes. Mom, Peyton, Dru, Jones, Mom, Peyton, Dru, Jo . . .

The frizzy-haired woman, who was standing in the beaded doorway, screamed and pressed her hands over her ears. Her eyes were huge as she watched Jones fall to the floor. She began shouting gibberish, distracting Bill Hollis. Luna had jumped at the report of the gun.

I twisted to my right, wrenching my head out of Luna's grasp. Detective Martinez dove in the other direction, behind a table, grabbing my wrist and pulling me with him as he went, before I could get ahold of Luna again. He shot three times, each report pounding colors into my head. I wrapped myself up into a ball, covering my head and wincing with every bang.

Luna scrambled away, while Vanessa calmly walked toward the frizzy-haired woman, who now had her face buried in the hem of her sweater.

Luna's movement broke me free. I lunged out from behind the table, ramming into Vanessa's side with my shoulder. She let loose a *gawp*, and we landed in a tumble on the floor, skidding into a cabinet full of carnival glass. Several cups tipped over the edges of the shelves and crashed around us.

Neither of us said a word. There were more shots and the sound of things breaking. The frizzy-haired woman screamed repeatedly. Vanessa and I furiously untangled our bodies from each other. She reached out and clawed at me, her fingers raking painfully down my ear and neck. I grabbed her arm and twisted, and then axe-kicked her shin once, twice, three times. She cried out each time, even though my leverage was shit and I was still trying to catch my breath and I was exhausted from fighting with Luna earlier. Vanessa was pampered, and used to Rigo doing her dirty work for her. She wasn't good at fighting. But she wasn't afraid to get nasty, either.

She flipped over so she was straddling me and started pummeling me in a flurry of untargeted blows. I covered, but she didn't stop.

I had no choice. I was going to have to get street about it.

Blindly, I reached up and grabbed a fistful of hair, yanking until I felt the individual strands tear, ripping a scream out of Vanessa. My hand came loose, still holding an alarming amount of hair, and I grabbed for it again, pulling with everything I had, until she stopped hitting me. The third time I went for it, I got an earring instead, something I didn't realize until I held it, and a bloody chunk of ear with it, in my palm. Vanessa's shrieks intermingled with the sound of gunfire and the cries of the frizzy-haired woman. Finally, Vanessa managed to yank herself loose and crawl away. I grabbed for her leg, but she was too fast. She got to her feet and raced across the store toward Bill.

Oh, hell no.

I got up and followed her, staggering and holding on to my side. Everything hurt. There was blood everywhere, including on me. Was it mine or someone else's? Was it Detective Martinez's? Was he even alive?

"Nikki!" he shouted, as if he could hear my thoughts. "Watch ou—"

I had been so busy racing after Vanessa, I'd forgotten all about Bill. Which seemed impossible, given that he was firing a gun over and over again. At some point, he had moved, disorienting me. I tripped over something and fell hard on my knees, my palms slapping into something wet on the floor. I only realized when I raised them to my face that the wetness was blood. The something I'd tripped over was Jones.

Nikki . . . go . . . Mom's wristwatch flashing crimson, crimson, crimson, as the life beat out of her. My shoes slipping in the blood.

"Oh God," I whimpered, hurrying to right myself, staring at my hands, feeling an old, familiar panic well up inside of me.

"Nikki!" Detective Martinez shouted again, but his voice sounded distant, faint. As if he were yelling at me from far away. I couldn't respond. I could only stare at the blood. The crimson. It was on me.

The Tootsie Rolls weren't the only thing that had fallen into my mom's blood that day. So had I. Dropped to the floor, pulled at her clothes, pounded on her arms, her chest, screamed at her, *Don't die, Mom. Just don't die.* I had forgotten. I had forgotten the blood soaking my jeans and the tops of my shoes, smearing my forearms, coating my hands. And everything after that moment was a blank. Everything between me frantically shaking her and my dad taking me to my grandparents' house while he sorted things out, gone.

There was more shouting, pulling at me, prying my attention away from the blood on my hands. I looked up, feeling like I was coming out of a fog.

And that was when I finally saw Bill Hollis. He'd been crouched behind the cash register, but now he was standing upright and coming at me, the barrel of his gun large and smoking and aimed right at my face.

I pulled myself up and sprinted with everything I had, ignoring Jones's blood and my ringing ears and the smell of burnt things on the air. I raced toward Hollis, not knowing what I would do when I got to him; only knowing that I had to do something. I had to stop him.

Just as I broke into the open space in front of the register, a bang ripped through the air. I felt a bullet whiz past me and glanced back just in time to see Detective Martinez come around the corner, raise his gun, and fire. Bill's eyes opened, wide and surprised, as a hole appeared in the center of his forehead, and then he dropped.

I didn't wait to see what happened next. I flew through the beaded curtain and toward a back service door that had been flung open. I saw a blur of blond in the doorway, running away. Luna.

Everything on me hurt, and my lungs felt like they were going to burst. I could taste gunpowder in the air. I thought I could even smell blood, though it might have been my imagination.

But I couldn't let Luna Fairchild get away. Not again. She wouldn't be satisfied until I was the one in the ground. This had to be over.

I gave it everything I had and reached the door just in time to see her dive into the passenger seat of a silver truck, the license plate candy cane and mustard—VP—followed by a repeated number. The truck turned in a U, a very tan, white-haired man behind the wheel. They screeched out of the parking lot.

Luna was gone again.

"Damn it!" I raged, pounding the door frame with my fist. "Son of a bitch!" I kicked a short metal shelf filled with cleaners and wood restorers. It overturned, sending cans flying everywhere. I didn't care. "Shit!" I was breathing hard and rough, pacing in that tight space.

"Such filthy words for such a squeaky-clean girl," I heard.

I whipped around.

Vanessa stood between me and the beaded curtain, a butcher knife in her hand.

"Where did you get that?" I asked, backing away.

"I brought it just for you. Since you're so fond of knives," she said. "Or have you forgotten what happened last time? Looks like Luna got away. Guess we'll all get away and you will be dead. Just like my weak, lovesick stepson and his pathetic sister."

"Those were your children."

"Correction. Those were my husband's children. Children that he didn't want in the first place. They were nothing to him. And less than nothing to me."

"Then why? Why did you take them? Why not leave them with Brandi?"

She looked at me like I was a complete idiot. "Because they were Hollises. And Hollises don't live trash lives."

"I disagree," I said. "Just very rich trash lives."

She gave me a condescending smile—one that I'd seen on the lips of so many kids in my school. "But at least we still have our lives. Unlike you and that cop."

"And your husband," I said coldly, getting the slightest satisfaction out of the look of shock that passed over her face.

"Bullshit."

"Listen. No more shooting," I said. Indeed, all we could hear was the continued warbling cry of the frizzy-haired woman.

"All that means is he shot your new little bed buddy. I have to admit, Nikki. Banging a cop is a pretty brilliant move. You can pretty much do whatever you want now, can't you?"

"What I want is to be left alone," I said. "But your family makes that impossible."

She started toward me in a slow, easy step. "Well, we can solve that whole problem right now, can't we?" She held up the knife. "We'll just put you and your boyfriend out of your misery. And Rigo too. Why not? He was a danger anyway, letting that spineless, pampered brat, Dru, get the better of him." She took another step. "You're not going to fight your way out of this one, Nikki Kill. Unlike Luna, I won't leave you alive. I can promise you that."

Out of habit, I began to assess what tools I had in my immediate area. How could I disarm her? How could I take her down? There was nothing. All I had was an overturned cabinet, a bunch of wood polish, and a trash can.

And then I realized . . . there was cold metal still pressing against the skin under my shirt.

I hated guns.

But I hated Vanessa Hollis more.

"What makes you think I'm going to fight you?" I asked, pulling the gun out and pointing it at her.

She stopped and laughed. "Really? You think I'm scared of you with a gun?" Her face went serious. "You had more than enough chance to shoot my daughter in the backyard, Nikki. You would have saved Dru if you'd done it. But you didn't. You're scared of guns." She laughed again, straightening the knife and absently touching her bloody earlobe. My hands shook around the gun handle. Was she right? Was it that I was actually scared of guns?

Or was I scared of death? Of killing? Of being the person who did to Vanessa what someone had done to my mom?

She started toward me again, this time walking faster, a crease drawing between her eyebrows. "You're wasting both of our time, Nikki," she said. "We both know you aren't going to shoot me, so you might as well pu—"

She dropped before I even registered that I'd pulled the trigger.

Blood puddled under her at an alarmingly fast rate. She didn't move, not even when it formed a little lake under her cheek. She still clutched the knife, but in a slack hand.

My hands spread open and the gun fell out, landing in her blood.

I started to back away, toward the back door, when I felt someone's arms around me from behind. I shrieked and started to fight, but the arms loosened, and when I turned, my face was buried in Detective Martinez's chest.

"You had to do it," he said. "You had to do it."

40

WE STAGGERED ONTO the sidewalk, the frizzy-haired woman sobbing as she walked behind us. Our shoes left bloody prints on the pavement. Vanessa's blood. Bill's blood. Jones's. So much blood.

"You okay?" Detective Martinez asked, pressing his palm against the side of my face. My cheek felt sticky, and I imagined a red streak staining it like war paint. There was a dark stain on his shirtsleeve. It looked extraordinarily wet.

I nodded, still breathing hard, still shaking, still trying to push away the colors. "Yeah. I'm fine. Did you get hit?" I reached for the sleeve, but he ducked away.

"I'm fine. It's done. I've got some first aid in my car."

"But Luna . . ."

"I've called it in," he said. "We'll find her." Indeed, I could hear police sirens—lots of them—in the distance.

Detective Martinez started toward his car, but got only about four steps before an old-fashioned but glossy black car with red racing stripes squealed around the corner. The words *Monte Carlo* blinked out at me—darting silver.

I'd seen this car before. It had been parked on a street that we'd passed in Detective Martinez's old neighborhood.

My gut went orange, a blast so bold I reeled.

"Chris!" I yelled. "Watch—"

He turned toward the sound of the squealing tires and began to duck back to where the woman and I stood, but he didn't even get a full step in before the car sped up and veered right toward him. He only had time to brace himself as it hit him full-on.

Instinctively, I covered my head and crouched, pushing myself back against the building. I opened my eyes only in time to see Detective Martinez's body flip through the air and then hit the sidewalk, every part of him looking broken.

The car roared away, the tires shrieking as they took another corner.

"Chris!" I screamed. "Chris!" I raced to his side. His eyes

were open, but staring at the sky blankly. I pressed my hands against his chest, his arms, his face, looking for wounds, and yelled to the frizzy-haired woman, the tears in my eyes making it almost impossible to see.

"Call 9-1-1! Call an ambulance!"

THEY WOULDN'T LET me follow him into surgery. Of course they wouldn't. But I fought them. I screamed and kicked and grabbed for his gurney and raised hell in the ER hallway until security came and ushered me outside, where I finally collapsed into a pool of crimson tears.

How many people would die trying to protect me?

How could I allow another one?

THEY LET ME into his room, even though he was still in critical condition. The cop securing it said he knew how Chris felt about me. I wondered what that meant, maroon building inside of me. Maroon that, for some reason, I wasn't quite able to push away. "He'd kill me if I didn't let you in," he said.

I'd come to hate that term *kill me*. It was easily done. So quickly and carelessly.

He hadn't woken up yet, giving me a hell of a déjà vu feeling when I walked in. Tubes and machines and wires everywhere, wrapping him up just like Peyton had been. Crimson, crimson, crimson tugging at me from every direction. It was what I'd been reeling from when I met him for the first time. I'd have never guessed we would, only seven months later, end up here.

I set down the flowers I'd brought. Why would I bring flowers, anyway? He would have laughed at me for that. *I'd never have taken you for a flower girl*, I could hear him saying. *Going soft on me, Kill?*

"Yeah," I said, reaching down and tracing his eyebrow, down his temple and cheek with my finger. "I think I am. Damn you."

I pulled a chair next to his bed, just as Dru had done, day after day, with Peyton. And now I understood why. The guilt he must have felt, knowing that he could have stopped her death and didn't. Knowing that he'd watched her suffer and then watched Rigo beat her until she seemed all but dead. Until she truly was all but dead.

"So, good news," I said. "Rigo talked. They got him on Highway 15, all the way down in San Diego. But they brought him back and he confessed everything. I think that means Blake offered him a plea deal, but I guess that's better than getting nothing out of him, right? I gave her the photos I took of the safe, and the address of Dom Distribution. Has she been here yet?" I smoothed a crease out of his sheet. "Probably, huh? She's the kind of girl who would come see you even though you broke her heart, you playah." I nudged his shoulder very lightly and tried to laugh, but it came out flat.

His eyelids were so purple. Why were they so purple? I wanted to find his sunglasses and put them on him.

"Oh, hey. I almost forgot." I pulled out a manila envelope and waved it above him. "I bet you don't know what this is. Yep, it's that police academy application. Well, not the exact application, because that's in your apartment and I'm kind of done with breaking and entering for a while. But I got a new one."

I picked at his blanket for a minute, remembering him griping at me to put my cigarette out and taking his beer away from me. I hated the way the memory made me feel— peach and magenta all at once, like an open flower with a dazzling center.

"I'm not saying I'm going to apply, so don't start hassling me about it all the time. But I'm not saying I won't apply, either. My dad is going to be so happy about that. Not." I chuckled. "He is going to *hate* the idea. But I think you're right and it might be the path for me. Oh my God, I can't believe I just told you you're right. Don't get a big head about it, Martinez. Even a stopped clock is right twice a day, as my dad says." I watched the monitors for some sort of hint that he'd heard me. Nothing. I swallowed. "You know those hunches you keep pestering me about? It's this thing called synesthesia. I see colors with letters and numbers and words. And emotions. Not, like, with my eyes. It's in my mind. You, by the way, are yellow as hell. And that's a good thing.

Anyway, Peyton had it, too, and that's how we've been sort of talking. She left me clues that would stand out only to me. It's not magic. But I'll admit, it was kind of fun letting you think it was. So there you go. I guess today was the day. Hopefully now you'll tell me the rest of your story. It's only fair, right? So you have to wake up to hold up your end of the deal." I felt much better having finally told him the truth about me, even if he might not have heard it. I didn't want him to die not knowing. I didn't want him to die, period. But if he was going to, I wanted him to be the one person who knew the true me. "I think I might make an okay cop. I think I'd like to try, anyway. But I need you to help keep me out of trouble. Because trouble has a way of finding me. As if you didn't know." I thought about that black hole in my memory. The mystery of Mom. I knew so much more about her now, but I still didn't know who killed her. I still didn't know what my dad was hiding from me, or what was in that box under his desk. "And maybe you can help me study a little bit. When I catch up with Luna again—and I will—I want it to be by the book, as they say. Do they say that? Or is that just on TV?"

He didn't answer, of course. Just showered me with his crimson, his face pale and slack. I felt a tear slip down my cheek as I wrapped both of my hands around his one. It was warm. When I held it, the crimson faded just the tiniest bit.

"You have to beat this, Chris. You're stronger than this.

I should know—you've kicked my ass more times than I can count. I will never admit that to you when you're awake, by the way, so hopefully you're listening now, because it's the only time you'll hear it. You snooze, you lose." I stared at his face, willed it to twitch or move or do . . . something.

"Who were those guys, Chris? Who hit you? Do they have something to do with those bullet holes? Do they have something to do with that guy you were searching for online? Heriberto Abana?" I leaned in close. Even here, I thought I could catch a faint whiff of cologne. It was just him, just the way he smelled. "I'm going to find him, Chris. I'm going to find whoever wants you dead. And I'm going to find my mother's murderer too. Because it's time to finish this. But I need your help." I rested my forehead against his. "I need you."

I unwound my hands from his and got up. I ran my finger down the side of his face again. "Come back to me, okay?"

I leaned down and kissed him softly.

And maybe I was crazy, but a tiny bit of the crimson parted.

A crack of maroon peeked through.

And a sunburst of yellow.

But was the yellow his . . . or was it mine?

ACKNOWLEDGMENTS

As always, I want to thank my agent, Cori Deyoe, for illuminating my path, for holding my hand, and for pointing out my timeline flaws.

Thank you to Melissa Miller for leading me through the twists and turns of Nikki's life, and for always being there to answer questions when I get stuck. Thank you also to Katherine Tegen, Claudia Gabel, Kelsey Horton, Valerie Shea, and Kathryn Silsand for believing in Nikki Kill and for working hard to find her a place on bookshelves.

Thank you to Joel Tippie for the beautiful cover design.

Thank you to Scott Brown for once again choreographing some pretty badass fight scenes.

And thank you to my friends and family—especially Scott, Paige, Weston, and Rand, for angsting when I angst and cheering when I celebrate. You are the pot of gold at the end of my rainbow, and I love you all.

And, finally, thank you, Readers, for following Nikki Kill into some pretty dark places, and rooting for her to fight her way out. You mean the world to me.

Don't miss these books by Jennifer Brown